W9-AHZ-399

Further praise for Charity...

"Poet Callen's first novel, set at the turn of the century, tells of the love and friendship between two women—a story that, for all its up-to-date politics, is really an old-fashioned celebration of its title virtue . . . an unusually satisfying tale."

—*Kirkus Reviews*

"Lyrical."

—*Library Journal*

"With great beauty and style, the prose of Paulette Callen flows across the page. Don't miss this rare treat—a debut novel that is every bit as good as the books turned out by seasoned writers. If this first novel is any indication, Callen is an author who is sure to bring us years of fine writing."

—*Out*

"An ambitious start for a writer with a talent for stylish storytelling."

—*Los Angeles Advocate*

"Enjoyable . . . well written, well paced, and more than entertaining."

—*Lambda Book Report*

CHARITY

A NOVEL

Paulette Callen

Paulette Callen (signature)

B
BERKLEY BOOKS, NEW YORK

CHARITY

A Berkley Book / published by arrangement with
Simon and Schuster, Inc.

PRINTING HISTORY
Simon and Schuster edition published 1997
Berkley edition / December 1998

The Penguin Putnam Inc. World Wide Web site address is
http://www.penguinputnam.com

ISBN: 0-425-16516-7

BERKLEY®
Berkley Books are published by The Berkley Publishing Group,
a member of Penguin Putnam Inc.,
375 Hudson Street, New York, New York 10014.
BERKLEY and the "B" logo
are trademarks belonging to Berkley Publishing Corporation.

PRINTED IN THE UNITED STATES OF AMERICA

10 9 8 7 6 5 4 3 2 1

Acknowledgments

Writing is a solitary venture. Nevertheless, I did not write this book in a vacuum. Without the support and stern criticism of a group of wonderful writers who have dubbed themselves the "Every-other-Monday-night Brilliant Writers Workshop," *Charity* would not have been written. No writer ever had a better Bloomsbury than I in these talented people.

I must give a special thank-you to Gary Reed and Greg Carstens, who kept my boat afloat in some choppy waters, and to Laura Caroccia, who kept me paddling.

This book is dedicated
to the memory of my grandfather
William F. Magnus.

The names for the months (moons) varied among the different branches of the Siouan family. I have chosen, somewhat arbitrarily, the Dakotah winter count used by the Santee Sioux, as translated into English by Paul War-Cloud.*

January	Moon of the terrible
February	Moon of the raccoon
March	Moon when eyes are sore from the bright snow
April	Moon when geese return in scattered formations
May	Moon to plant
June	Moon when berries are good and ripe
July	Moon when chokeberries are red
August	Moon when all things ripen
September	Moon when wild rice is stored for winter use
October	Moon when quilling and beading is done
November	Moon when horns are broken off
December	Twelfth Moon

*_Dakotah Sioux Indian Dictionary,_ by Paul WarCloud, published in 1989 by Tekawitha Fine Arts Center, P.O. Box 208, Sisseton, SD 57262.

She nursed him until he was old enough to ask for it, then they told her she must stop—that it was not decent. But she continued in secret, long after they forbade it. "You'll always be my baby," she whispered.

She nursed him long after they had forbidden it, and even after her milk finally dried up, she held the boy in her arms and gave him her breast. It was a comfort to them both. "You'll always be my baby, won't you?" she crooned.

When he became too big for sitting on her lap, they lay on her bed together. She undid her buttons and he found the comfort he remembered. At times, there would be just the nipple budding in his mouth. At other times, the nectar would flow.

"You'll always be my baby, won't you, dear?" she whispered.

"Yes, Mama. Yes."

Sometimes he felt a loathing for the bud and its nectar, but then he would find her crying in pain and he would try to remember the old sweetness, for her sake, undo her buttons, and lie down beside her. "I'm here, Mama. Don't cry, your baby's here."

PROLOGUE

She has lived many years. Close to the earth. Her home, her safety, her life's burden on her back, she makes her ponderous way forward on stubby, powerful legs.

To the young watcher, it is an agony of time before she pulls herself up the slope of the gully and continues across another stretch of prairie toward blue water.

"Coming back to the lake," the old woman mutters. "Comes back every year."

The young woman asks, "Grandmother, how do you know it's the same one?"

The old woman pulls her blanket closer around herself against the sharp spring winds. "I know. Before I came to this place, she was here."

"Where does she come from?"

The old woman points with her chin toward the south. "The slough."

"Why does she travel so far?"

The old woman shrugs and the blanket brushes her ear-lobes. "It is her way."

As the turtle comes closer, the two women stand back so she can progress in her timeless plodding in a straight line toward the lake. She passes close enough for the young woman to observe her leathery face, her slow-blinking eyes. The young woman smiles, ever so slightly, for she is reminded of the ancient face of the old woman at her side.

"Why does she come?"

"She lays her eggs in the sand. It's warm there."

"She still has such a long way."

As the young one, on light moccasinned feet, steps up behind the turtle, the old woman shrugs again and warns, "She's a snapper."

"I'll be careful." She places her hands firmly around the shell toward the hind feet. The turtle withdraws her head and feet and tail. The turtle is heavy, but the young woman is strong and carries her easily down to the lakeshore and gently places her on an open stretch of sand. She steps back quickly.

The old woman, still standing on the rise, wrapped in her blanket, smiles and says, "*Wasté! Wasté!** She will have many children!"

"Mm," the young woman replies drolly. "I'll have to watch my toes."

The old one laughs and claps her hands. "Maybe. Maybe not. The Mother will protect you."

The women watch the old snapping turtle inch along the shore searching for the right patch of sand to dig her womb hole.

*"Good! Good!"

Moon When Berries Are Good and Ripe

Alvinia Torgerson's youngest child had the whooping cough. Cradling little Kirstin in her arms, Alvinia walked the floor all through the cool June night, from room to room, window to window, humming "What a Friend We Have in Jesus" to comfort her suffering infant.

It was she who reported seeing Will Kaiser staggering out of Pa Kaiser's barn before the sun was up and just before the old man was found lying comatose on the dusty threads of old straw, looking peaceful except for the bright spot of blood emblazoned on his left temple.

Will was picked up while he was still drunk and left to sleep it off in the county jail. This was nothing new. However, when Will woke up, Sheriff Sully did not unlock the door and let him go with the usual "Yup, Will, better get home to that pretty wife of yours."

When Will heard his pa was dead—murdered—he buried his face in his hands and cried. When told that he was the only suspect, he stopped crying and sat, hands dangling between his knees, staring at the floor. A man of great appetites, that morning Will Kaiser ignored his breakfast.

Dennis Sully rode over to Will's house to break the news to Lena. He stood outside, peering through the screen door, savoring the warm yeasty fragrance of fresh baking and the sight, dim in the darkened shanty, of a small woman with reddish hair and a pink complexion. *Guilty or not,* Sheriff Sully thought, *Will Kaiser is the biggest damn fool in the county.*

Lena did not bother to open the door and invite him in. The sheriff or his deputy often stopped by to tell her that her husband was in jail and as soon as he woke up they would send him home. She seldom responded with more than "I expected as much." What could she say? She had swallowed so much unleavened humiliation over the years, she was full up to her throat.

This morning Dennis Sully looked like a man who needed sleep. He crushed his hat in one hand and scratched the overnight growth of beard with the other while he told her, in few words, how they had found her father-in-law, not dead when they found him, but dead now, and that they'd arrested Will.

Lena Kaiser was not given to faints. "Thank you for coming yourself, Dennis," was all she said.

"Can I do anything for you? Get your sisters? I could send Fritz over to Wheat Lake."

"No, they've got a plateful as it is. I'll be all right."

Lena closed the inside door against the beauty of an early spring morning which had nothing anymore to do with her. Through the tiny shanty, past the pegs where Will's jacket hung next to her sweater (beneath them, rubber boots—his and hers) she went, her mind spinning, into her kitchen. She had baked bread and cookies that morning. On the nights Will did not come home she slept poorly, if at all, and was up long before dawn. The sun was just now sifting into the corners of her kitchen. Four loaves cooled in a row on the counter. Their rounded crusts, lightly brushed with butter, gleamed like polished oak. Lena was struck by how much they resembled coffins. She draped a dish towel over them. That was worse. She pulled it off. One thing she knew for sure: Will, faulted through and through though he was, could never kill anybody. Never. The man didn't even swat flies.

There was nothing more to be done with the bread. The cookies were cool. With a thin spatula, and in spite of her shaking hands, she slipped them one by one off their baking tins onto her best china plate. When that was piled high, she filled the cans she had already lined with paper.

She might have known something like this would happen. This was the third thing. It had started on Monday when workmen, digging for a new road north of town, found some little bones and the remnants of a child's laced shoe. Doc Moody determined that the remains were of four children—probably the children of some early immigrants. They had been buried in shallow graves in a sand pit by a lake where immigrants were known to have camped. The thought of those children dying had saddened Lena, but the little laced shoe spoke rivers of sorrow; it broke her heart. Then, on Tuesday, her cousin Alma had told her about Clifford Czmosky's horse. Clifford was Alma's closest neighbor. He heard horrible screaming coming from his barn and went out there to find that someone had cut the tongue out of his horse. Clifford went crazy seeing the animal screaming, her eyes white and blood gushing out of her mouth. Howling bloody murder he ran to his house, got his gun, and shot her in the head—dropped her right there in her stall with one clean shot. Then he went looking for the devil who'd done it. That and the vision of the little shoe kept Lena crying all Tuesday. She'd had a bad feeling. Things like this always came in threes. It was Wednesday, and this was the third thing.

Lena had cried for the children and for the horse. She bit her lips now and vowed she would shed no more tears for Will Kaiser. She sat down to think some more, with one hand in her lap still holding the dish towel, the other at her mouth where she absently sucked on the tips of her thumb and forefinger.

The first thing she should do, of course, was bring him a change of clothes. She hung up her towel and her apron, then went into the bedroom and pulled out the drawers in the chiffonnier where Will's clothes were folded, clean and carefully pressed. She took out underwear, pants, shirt, and suspenders, and put them all into a clean pillowcase. On her way through the kitchen she dropped in a can of cookies and knotted the end of the case. She tucked her pocketbook under one arm, pulled her sweater off the peg in the entry, and stepped outside.

Charity, South Dakota, like the other prairie towns in which Lena had worked since she was twelve years old, was a stagnant pond. Gossip grew like scum on a slough. Rumors, opinions, and judgments spawned and flew about, greedy for blood and spreading their venom with each bite. This morning, Lena knew the blood they'd be thirsty for was hers and Will's, so she avoided Main Street, walking three blocks east on the dirt road that passed by her house to another that ran north the length of town, just inside the city limits. On her left a few houses looked across the road at the plowed fields and marshes on her right. Lena walked briskly, wrapped tightly in herself, carrying her bundle high, pressed hard against her chest. Last week this road had been muddy and impossible to walk. It had since dried, so that with each step little clouds of fine dust billowed around her ankles. Only Main Street was topped with gravel. The town elders were planning such refinements for Charity as befitted a county seat and growing town reaping the benefits from prospering farmers with burgeoning families buoyed by turn-of-the-century optimism. Everyone's well-being, however, hung precariously on the weather: tear-freezing winters, mud-drenched springs, hot summers, and autumns either too dry or too wet. They could stand anything as long as nothing went on too long.

Lena was a true sodbuster's daughter, with a sharp eye for the skies, but she did not think about the weather now. She kept her eyes straight ahead and marched, resolute and joyless. After twelve blocks she turned left, back into town, till she came to the plain wood building that was both city hall and county jail.

Dennis Sully sat behind his desk sipping coffee. He looked

up, surprised to see her, and offered her the straight-backed wooden chair next to his desk. "Coffee?" He nodded toward the coffeepot that perched uneasily on the stove in the middle of the room.

Lena shook her head and sat rigidly on the edge of the chair, facing him, her lumpy pillowcase in her lap. As many times as Will had been here, she had never before set foot inside this place. The sheriff's office was a small room, devoid of decoration: rough wood floors (she thought they could have used a good scrubbing), a second desk and chair that she supposed were for Fritz the deputy, some cabinets against the back wall, and hanging on the wall above them, a document of some sort in a black frame.

Dennis Sully waited for her to speak.

Lena began with a question she had forgotten to ask earlier. "How was Pa killed? Was he shot? You know Will doesn't own a gun."

"Nope. Wasn't shot. He was cracked a good one upside the head with a pipe wrench or rock or something. We couldn't find anything. We're still looking."

"Well, you probably won't find it. Whatever it is, it's probably at the bottom of the slough or somebody's toilet."

The sheriff nodded. What she said was likely true. He waited again for Lena to have the next word.

Finally, looking at him directly, stabbing her finger on the desk top with each statement, she said, "He's a drinking man. He's a fighting man. It's no secret. The whole town knows it. And I know it, too. But he's not a killing man." A final stab of her finger on the desk settled the matter.

"Will's a mean drunk, Missus Kaiser," Dennis said, not looking at her.

The stillness curled itself around Lena. She often thought Will had killed her love for him. But even now, when she heard a word like this against him, though it was true, and not said to be unkind—she felt a twist of pain. And shame. No, even now, she was not beyond humiliation. Her eyes tracked the seams in the wood floor. "I know that," she said. "But I know there's a line he wouldn't cross." She drew a line with her finger on the desk between them and tapped the place softly. "No matter how drunk he was. I know it, because if he got that drunk, he would be too drunk to stand up, let alone throw a punch—let alone kill somebody." She threw her hand up and let it fall into her lap beside her bundle. "Dennis, you know it, too."

The sheriff nodded his head and rubbed his face with a meaty hand, as if he could rub away his tiredness and responsibility. "But I got to keep him in here. Everything points at Will. I got to keep him till the hearing. Then it's up to the judge."

Lena rubbed the space between her eyebrows. "When will that be?"

"Circuit judge is due here some time next month. Will'll just have to sit it out."

She nodded, still memorizing the floor, and rubbing her forehead. "He's sober now."

"Yup. In rough shape though." The sheriff slid his chair back from the desk. "You want to see him?"

She didn't, but she stood, placed the pillowcase on the corner of Dennis's desk, and followed him the short distance to the back of the office. He opened the door for her. "Back there. He's the only one we got."

Lena felt a pressure square against her chest, like something trying to keep her from crossing the threshold. She had never wanted to come here. By not coming here, she could pretend that this place didn't exist, that Will hadn't been here, that things weren't so bad. But now it was too real. Will had forced her to this, and she was suddenly very angry. She stepped into the dimly lit hallway—so furious she did not wince at the sight of the bars along either side of her, or at the barren yellow light bulb suspended from a cord in the middle of the narrow swath of ceiling that ran between the bars to the end of the hall, or at the rank smell. She could see a small north window in the far wall, the glass dulled by a dirty, oily film. There was no light, nor any windows, in the four small cells, two on each side. The smell was concentrated in the second cell to her right, where she saw her husband, caged. He sat on the edge of a narrow cot with his head in his hands. He had not looked up when Dennis opened and closed the office door. She knew as she stood looking at his soiled, stained, and damp clothing that it wasn't only the chamber pot, brimming with excrement and vomit, but the man himself who stank. Lena clenched her teeth until he looked up. When he did, she did not give him a chance to speak first.

"Will Kaiser, you have shamed me for the last time!"

"Oh, Duchy." He put his head in his hands again and rocked once back and forward. "I'm sorry."

"Sorry doesn't change what you've done."

"I haven't done anything." His voice cracked. She suspected the puffiness in his face was as much from crying all morning as from the whiskey the night before.

"Oh, I don't mean you've killed anybody, you fool, but if you weren't a drunkard you wouldn't be in this mess. Now, I'll stick by you till you're clear of this thing, and then I'm through with you. Do you hear me?"

"Don't leave me, Duchy."

"Don't you 'Duchy' me!" She thrust her purse at him, emphasizing every word. "I won't leave you till you're free and clear. You're a lying, drunken, dirty man. But you're not a killer. I'll do what I can for you."

She left him there, water streaming from the living blue of his one good eye and from the dead white of the other, his powerful hands wiping the tears from his face.

On her way out, she stopped at the corner of the sheriff's desk. Her gaze fixed out the window, she said, "See if you can get him a bath. There's his clean clothes." She pointed to the pillowcase still lumped where she had left it. "There's fresh-baked cookies in there." Suddenly, Lena was embarrassed. Her father-in-law was dead, her husband was in jail for murder, and she had brought cookies. But it was all she had, so she continued, straightening her back. "You and Fritz help yourselves. He can't eat them all."

Outside the office, Lena stood on the street and wondered what to do. She had to keep moving. Keep busy. Think. Most of all she needed someone sensible to talk to. It was a long walk out to Gustie's, but Lena did her best thinking on her feet.

Lena walked east, across the road she had come uptown on, and continued due east on an even narrower dirt road that led straight out into the country. Not much thinking was required to know where to look first for Pa's killer. You didn't have to strain your eyes looking beyond his own family. A nasty bunch, the whole lot of them. Always fighting one another—like badgers in a sack. She sighed. They'd had a reputation, the Kaiser boys. Will chased her around three counties before she consented to marry him. It was because he had chased her, and because . . . well, never mind he was the tallest, best-looking man in those three counties—he was, in spite of his family, a kind, gentle man, and full of fun. At least he was before the drink took him. But blood tells, and it had spoken loudly in him eventually. They'd had ten good years. He had taken to booze and throwing his fists around after he'd lost the sight in one eye and the hearing in one ear the same year. The blinding had been an accident; he caught a tiny piece of metal shaving in his eye at a drill sight. The ear was lost when Oscar took a shot at him. The shot was so close it had destroyed his eardrum.

Anyway, she reflected, Will never did any fighting when he was sober, and he was sober more than half the time. That was still the difference between her man and his brothers. Stone-cold sober, Walter had shot Oscar's arm off when they were kids in some quarrel nobody could remember anymore. Even with one arm, Oscar remained a violent man with his wife and his horses, and he seldom drank. He'd been sober when he fired at Will, too. These boys were mean whether they were drunk or not. *They're mean when they're asleep,* she thought. Frederick, the youngest brother, was not a brawler or a drinker, but Lena had never completely trusted him in spite of the fact that he had always been pleasant to her and was the only member of the Kaiser family to make a habit of wearing clean clothes. (Will had not had clean clothes every day till she married him.) Lena thought Frederick was lazy and some kind of a conniver. He did no visible work, and yet he always had money to spend. Then there was Ma Kaiser. She could have killed the old man. She was strong enough. Gertrude Kaiser had the size and strength of a bull, if not the sweet disposition.

Her thoughts went back to Oscar, the oldest, the one who was most like his mother. Silent and brooding; one never knew what Oscar was thinking. Maybe he didn't think at all. He walked with a stoop that made him look much older than his years. Lena imagined he had developed this hunched-over posture to make his missing arm less noticeable. Hank Ackerman had remarked once that because they up and sawed his arm off—never mind that it was to save his life—Oscar had got cranky. Lena always chuckled at that. "Cranky" did not describe Oscar by half. They said that as a boy of about twelve he killed a dog his dad had brought home for him because he got tired of it always following him around. Walter, now, was much better-natured than Oscar. Strutting around like a banty rooster, that cigar always cocked up between his teeth, he did not seem a likely killer. With him, it would have been some fool accident. He got scared and ran off . . . and yet, when he shot Oscar it had been no accident. Frederick. Hard to think of Frederick as a killer. It was hard to think of Frederick at all. The youngest brother was sort of invisible. One didn't think of him in his absence. He left little or no impression. Lena only thought of him now as she was ticking off the members of the Kaiser family, one by one. Frederick was handsome and noted for a certain gracefulness. He did not have the heavily muscled frame of his brothers because he hadn't worked from dawn till dusk with well equipment and horses. As far as Lena knew, he seldom even mucked out the barn. He drove his aunt and his mother around, and since they never could go anywhere together, that could be a full day's work. *It wouldn't hurt either of them to walk.* She was back to the two old sisters. They had tasted plenty of gall on account of that old man over the years. Still . . . Lena's mind went round and round.

Any of them could have done it, but which one *would* have? In Lena's estimation, they were all crazy and wouldn't have required much of a reason. One thing she was sure of: all of them, guilty and innocent alike, would sit by and let the blame fall on Will.

Lena had been walking and thinking for half an hour. The air warmed. Flies buzzed around her head. She waved them away. Why Gustie wanted to live way out here was a mystery to Lena. The house was nice enough, but this far out of Charity she wasn't going to get electricity or indoor plumbing any time soon.

The sight of Gustie's small white house sitting there on unclaimed acreage made Lena feel lonely. She didn't know how her friend stood it with no family, no neighbors. Lena had offered to help her find a place in town. She'd even invited Gustie to stay with her and Will till she found something suitable of her own. But Gustie had refused. "I like it out here," she'd said, somewhat wistfully Lena thought. "I like it very well."

"Well, you'll find out," Lena prophesied with a finger beating the air. "In the winter it won't be so easy. You'll be cooped up here all by yourself. You're always welcome to stay with Will and me. Anytime it gets too much for you. Just make sure

you have enough food put by. For yourself and the horse—
now, both of you, I'm talking about. I'm going to check your
pantry and barn myself come November and make sure. You
folks who just come out here don't know how bad or long a
winter can be. Snow gets so deep you can't open your door, let
alone go someplace. And you get yourself a couple ropes and tie
them to the house. Run one to the barn and one to your outhouse. Tie them good and tight. I'm not foolin'! Alfred Ficks-
dahl, Alvinia's uncle, that old bachelor lived up north of the
Paulson place—they found him in the spring with his drawers
still down froze solid because he was a stubborn old fool and
didn't listen to his neighbors and string a rope to his toilet. January came along and they all said, Alfred, where's your ropes?
And he said if the weather hadn't come by January, it wouldn't
be comin'. Well, it came all right. It came and he went."

Gustie got her ropes, Lena made sure her house and barn
were provisioned for the worst that first winter, and her friend
appeared to weather it just fine. No, there was nothing stiff-
necked about Gustie. She took the advice given her and made
the best of it. Lena worried about her out here all the same.

Lena walked the slender wagon path that wound from the
road up to Gustie's doorstep. A field mouse skittered across the
path in front of her and disappeared into the low grass, which
Orville Ackerman, one of Gustie's pupils, kept scythed down
neatly. Gustie earned little money—less than some teachers in
the Dakotas, Lena knew. The school year was divided into two
terms of about two and a half months each, in the fall and
spring. She was paid twenty dollars each term. Between terms
Gustie tutored a few youngsters whose parents cared enough
to provide them with extra help. She'd been given this house to
live in until such time as a homesteader, willing to prove up the
land it sat on, appeared to claim it. On their mother's baking
days, the children brought her bread and cakes and pies. Milk,
eggs, and butter were discreetly dropped off by farmers who

claimed they had too much that week. Gustie's needs were few. So far she had managed. But Lena wondered for how long.

Lena peeked around the side of the house. No horse, no wagon. She opened the front door and called in, "Gustie? You home?" Lena stood for a moment and took a deep breath, bitterly disappointed. "Phooey! Well, I'm going in to sit down a little." Once inside she decided to fortify herself for the long walk back home. She was in no hurry. She put the coffee on, then sat at Gustie's table to wait for it to perk into something drinkable. On Lena's first visit out here, almost two years ago, Gustie had served her a cup of freshly brewed coffee. Lena took a mouthful. It was the strongest, bitterest coffee she had ever had and it would not go down. She had to run outside and spit it into the weeds. She came back into the house, demurely patting her mouth with her handkerchief, saying, "That's not Lutheran coffee!" Gustie had laughed so hard the tears came to her eyes, and Lena laughed with her. They both still laughed whenever they thought of it.

Now Lena's eyes wandered around Gustie's small, sparsely furnished living room. Her tabletops and chests were bare of the crocheted and embroidered frills that women made for themselves and for each other and passed down to daughters and granddaughters. Still, Lena was comfortable here. Other things bespoke the life her friend lived within these walls.

The main adornments in Gustie's home were her books: a shelf full of them, richly bound and wearing the patina of affectionate use. Lena had never seen so many fine books, not even at Doc Moody's or in Pastor Erickson's study. She ran her hand across the bindings, reading some of the names: Shakespeare, Dickens, Sand, Austin, Bronte, Emerson, Thoreau, Hawthorne. Once, with Gustie's permission, Lena had pulled some off the shelves and tried to read a bit. She quietly put them back; they were beyond her understanding. One needed more than a fourth-grade education and being able to read from the Bible to make much of books like these. On the wall hung two paintings Lena suspected were something special, since Gustie had carted them all the way across country. But Lena was not interested in paintings or pictures, unless they were of people she knew or scenes from the Bible. These were neither. One depicted sea waves breaking on large rocks against a stormy sky, and the other a tranquil sea with circling white birds.

Glancing into the bedroom, Lena saw on the bedside table the leather photo album which had appeared last year. Gustie had never offered to show Lena the pictures inside. She was tempted to look at them now, just for something to do. *No. I'll wait till I'm invited.* Lena noted the white nightgown hanging on the closet door. Lena thought there was something peculiar about it, but at the moment she couldn't think what.

Lena heard the coffee perking up a commotion, removed it from the heat, and poured herself a cup. When she had drunk it, she washed the cup and carefully returned it to the shelf where she'd found it. Then she decided she might as well do the few dishes Gustie had left too: a plate, knife and fork, and the frying pan.

Lena's virtually sleepless night was finally taking its toll. She lay down on Gustie's bed for a nap. She could rest a few minutes, get up, drink the rest of the coffee, and go home. Maybe Gustie would be back by that time. As she drifted off to sleep, she realized what was odd about the nightgown: It was too small. It could never fit Gustie.

The coffee was stone cold. *Oh, for heaven sakes.* Lena looked outside. The sky was dimming. She felt addle-headed. *Well, how could I sleep all day?* She could not now make it home before dark. Lena wasn't afraid of the dark, but she didn't feel like walking home in it either. Anyway, at the moment she had nothing to go home to. Nothing at all. She went back to bed.

This time she undressed and crawled under the covers. It felt good to sleep. To forget.

After leaving a scribbled note stuck in Gustie's screen door, Lena walked back to Charity early the next morning. The sky was a clear, light blue, lacking substance. A few wisps of white cloud floated higher and higher, till they dissipated altogether. For a bird to get enough purchase with feather and wing in such a thin sky to be able to fly seemed impossible. And perhaps it was, as all the birds around her were hopping from brush to branch, or perched on stalks of grass, chirping at one another and preening themselves, passing the time, waiting for the sky to thicken up a bit.

Ma Kaiser's house squatted at the edge of town—huge, dark, musty, and unkempt, like Ma herself. Lena never liked going inside. Today, more than ever, she didn't want to go in or even talk to Ma. But she was sure nobody would come to her, and she had to start somewhere to try to find out what was going on.

The gate screeched as she pushed it open, then swung askew since the latch was rusted out. The wooden porch steps squeaked under her weight.

Lena stopped to listen for voices. She heard nothing but the buzz of flies and the *woo*ing of a mourning dove. She opened the tattered screen door. "Ma?" Lena listened. "Is anybody home? Ma?" Only a steady creaking answered from the bowels of the house. Lena followed the sound through the sour-smelling kitchen, the dining room which was lorded over by a mahogany china cabinet crammed with God knew what, and into the living room, the darkest room in a dark house, full of more heavy pieces of furniture that loomed about her, shapeless and colorless. On every one lay a dingy antimacassar.

As Lena's eyes adjusted, the source of the monotonous creaking issuing from the farthest reaches of the gloom took form: Gertrude Kaiser, her great bulk shrouded in black taffeta and squeezed into a wooden rocker, rocking back and forth, back and forth. The few timid rays of light that trespassed through the sagging draperies were drawn to the one bright spot in the room. Her thick white hair glowed with reflected light like a patch of snow in a dark gully catching a moonbeam at midnight. *Such beautiful hair,* Lena thought, *on such an ugly woman.* Ma's hands gripped the armrests of the chair; her eyes stared at nothing Lena could see.

"Ma?" She stepped closer, but the old woman did not acknowledge her. "Ma!" Short on patience, Lena took two strides to the side of the rocker and shook her mother-in-law by the shoulder. "Ma! Where are the boys? Where's Mary and Nyla? I thought they'd be here."

"They're at Molvik's seeing to Pa," her mother-in-law wheezed. "Seeing to things."

Molvik was the undertaker. Lena had almost forgotten there was a body to be prepared for burial. She ventured in a more civil voice, "You know they think that Will did it." Maybe Ma didn't know that. Maybe they hadn't told her. Maybe they thought the death of a husband was enough news for the time being.

"Of all the boys," the old woman wheezed, "I never thought it would be Will."

"He didn't do it! But I mean to find out who did, believe you me. Now what do you know about this mess?"

Ma Kaiser turned her small eyes upon Lena. "I don't know anything," she mewled.

"Well, when did you last see Pa?" Lena resisted the urge to smack her. "What was he doing in the barn? There's nothing in that barn."

"I don't know." The old woman's voice slipped into a higher register and she started to rock again. "I don't keep track of what-all that man does."

Neither Ma Kaiser nor her house ever smelled good, but today the smell of a woman who casually believed all her sons capable of murder and took for granted the guilt of her favorite was too much. Lena felt herself beginning to gag. She left as fast as she could, and once she had passed the gate, took a deep breath.

Lena found herself going next door to Julia's.

Julia's house was modest in size. A fresh coat of white paint brightened both the outside walls and the length of fence running in front of it. The fence, wrought iron with some scrollwork about the gate, did not go around the house; it kept nothing in and nothing out, but made a very pretty picture when viewed straight on. Two peony bushes on either side of the front door were in bud.

Julia met her at the door, a limp handkerchief in one hand and her cat in the other held close to her breast. She wore a gray linen dress, trimmed at the neck and sleeves with thin strips of white lace. She was dressed for company. The cat was gray with white paws and throat. Even in her agitation, Lena was amused at the resemblance between them. As she held the door open, Julia said, "Oh, Lena, he's gone. Pa's gone." Tears rose in her eyes.

"Yes," was all Lena could say. She stepped into Julia's kitchen and sat down at her small table. "Julia, they think Will did it."

"I know. It's a pity." Julia, with one hand—her other still cradled the cat to bosom—set a cup in front of Lena, then she filled it with weak coffee. As she did so, Lena saw that the ring on her right hand, an opal in a gold setting that Julia always wore, was, on the palm side, wrapped in string. Lena commented on it and Julia explained, "Oh, yes. These old hands are getting thin, especially when they're cold. I didn't want the ring slipping off, you know. It was Mother's."

"Yes, that happened to my mother." Lena nodded. "She lost

her wedding ring in the bread dough. Didn't know where she'd lost it till Will bit into it in a piece of toast. Nearly broke his tooth!" Julia smiled at the story, returned the pot to the stove, and sat down. When she moved, her fine white hair, held softly in a loose bun at the nape of her neck, waved gently, cloudlike about her head. With that puffball of white fine hair, she reminded Lena sometimes of a dandelion gone to seed.

Lena didn't know where to put her hands. They went from her lap to playing about her mouth and chin, to touching the tabletop, and back to her lap again. Finally, with one hand and a toss of her head she indicated Gertrude's house a few yards away. "*She's* no help. His own mother, sitting over there like a fat spider, thinking he might have done it. '*Of all the boys,*'" Lena mimicked Ma Kaiser's wheezy voice, "'*I never thought it would be Will.*' Oof! She makes me tired. How you've stood her all these years, I don't know." Lena thumped her fingers on the tabletop, then took a quick sip of coffee.

Julia did not answer or remove her loving gaze from the cat in her lap, who, with perfect attention, licked the inside of a curled paw. "Is Feather getting clean? Kitty Feather . . . ," she crooned as she stroked his back with her thin blue-veined hand. "Cats are so clean, aren't they?"

The kitchen warmed with light cascading through Julia's white lace curtains. Julia's house, like Julia herself, always smelled faintly of lavender. For a moment, Lena almost relaxed a little. Then she blurted out, "Who do you think did it? You know it wasn't Will, don't you?"

"Of course, we all know it couldn't have been Will," Julia answered. "Not Will." Julia continued to stroke her cat.

"No. That's right." Lena's hands began their nervous search once more. "Well, who do you think, Julia?"

Julia just shook her head and her eyes filled with tears once more.

"Well, I don't know either," said Lena kindly. She felt sorry for Julia. Pa Kaiser had been good to her, in his way. She had taken in sewing over the years, but he had helped her out financially from time to time and paid her a little for doing some bookkeeping while he was still in the well business. Pa had been generous that way.

Julia was dabbing her eyes. "We'll all miss him, that's for sure."

"Yes, that's for sure," said Lena. She suddenly saw Pa as he had been the day of her wedding. He was smiling. It was so unusual that she'd mentioned it to Will at the time. "Your dad seems happy," she'd said. Will had grinned and nodded. "Yeah, he thinks I did pretty good marrying you." "Well, he's right. You did," she had retorted. Later, as Pa was leaving the reception, he had slipped a few bills into her hand and murmured awkwardly, "Get yourself something nice now."

It was hard to believe he was gone.

Lena finished the cup of coffee, kissed Julia on the cheek, and left her to the comfort of her cat.

As she walked slowly home, Lena wondered over Julia and Gertrude. No two sisters could be more unalike. All the qualities that usually got mixed up in people, the good and the bad, the light and the dark, had been separated: all that was heavy and dark had fallen on Gertrude, and all that was delicate and light had gone into Julia. There was something of the fragile aristocrat about Julia, even though she'd grown plump around the middle over the years, and nothing, Lena thought with distaste, but the thick peasant about Gertrude. The relation between them was apparent only in the squareness of their faces and the color of their eyes, a rare cloudy shade of hazel. But there the resemblance ended. The expression in Gertrude's eyes alternated between the dullness of a fish and a bovine fierceness, like that of a placid cow roused to defend her calf. In Julia's eyes there flickered a girlishness that was at times becoming, even charming, and at other times disconcerting, emanating as it did from a face creased with the myriad fine lines of old age. Lena wondered at those times where had she been, this old lady, while her body aged, not to have matured at the same rate on the inside. But these were fleeting impressions and Lena did not dwell on them, except to attribute Julia's manner to her spinsterhood and her never having had children of her own.

Lena shuddered. She was not a spinster, but she was thirty-four and still childless. There was no point to a life without children. Now that she was getting older, she felt it more painfully than ever. Anyway, Lena would never be girlish again. She already felt old as the hills.

Lena entered her own house gratefully. It wasn't much, this house, but she had taken pains to make it comfortable and pretty, sewing curtains for every window and covers for the old furniture. She kept the wood floors shining the way her mother had taught her: cold water and vinegar. Nothing else. Scrub them with that every week—the wood bleached out pale and glowing. She never had to wax them. She couldn't afford wax anyway.

Lena lit her stove, put on the coffeepot, then went down to the cellar for a jar of her sweet rhubarb sauce, which, besides the bread and cookies, was all she had left in the house to eat. There was still plenty of coffee and sugar, thank the Lord. But she did not know what she would do a few days from now. There was no money. Without Will working, there would be no money.

She took down a bowl, then unscrewed the cap on the jar of sauce. The jar slipped out of her hands and fell to the floor. Half the contents spilled out. She grabbed a rag, sopped it in the bucket of water in the sink, wrung it out, and got down on her hands and knees to wipe up the pink, sweet mess. She was on her hands and knees again, on all the floors she had cleaned and scrubbed since she was old enough to tote a bucket of water, first for her mother and grandmother, then for all the people she'd been hired out to for pennies a week and a place to stay—up to her elbows in water, scalding hot or freezing cold, depending on the job to be done and the whim of the lady of the house. Lena's hands were ugly from work. But this, at least, was *her* floor.

She began to cry. This floor was the reason she put up with Will Kaiser—this floor and the lace curtains in the bedroom, the cotton curtains in her kitchen. The wood cabinet that held her dishes and baking things and still supported the neat row of loaves was *her* cabinet, made simply, beautifully, and without a nail by Will's own hands, when he was still more in love with her than with whiskey. This little house, the garden outside, the clotheslines that stretched across the yard—these things were hers, and without Will she would lose them and have to go back to working for other people, living in other people's houses, caring for other people's children, having nothing of her own. She couldn't go back to washing other people's dirty clothes, cooking their moist cakes and puddings that needed hours of steaming and molding just so, while neither she nor anyone she cared a snap about ever got to eat them.

No, Will was not perfect. But life was infinitely better with him than without him. And no one could take the first ten years of their marriage from her. Unlike some drinking men, he never raised a hand to her. And him sitting in jail was no justice: not for him, who'd done no killing, whose only crime was in having been too drunk to prevent one; and not for her. For without Will, she could keep nothing she loved and had nothing to look forward to. Without him, there would never be a child.

She sobbed into the rhubarb-soaked rag. She was sobbing loudly, with abandon, when a shadow fell across the kitchen. Lena looked up. Framed in the doorway was a tall, slender woman wearing a threadbare black skirt and equally worn white blouse. The high color in her face graced wide-set gray eyes that shone very dark behind her wire-rimmed spectacles.

Lena choked and sobbed harder into the rag she held in her fist. "Oh, Gustie!"

The ladies of the Ruth and Esther Circle met every other Sunday, taking turns offering their homes as meeting place. Lena enjoyed the circle, especially when she could play hostess, except for one Sunday afternoon when the Bible reading was done, the planning completed for next Sunday's luncheon after the baptismal service for Marvin and Kate Gullickson's first baby, and the conversation over coffee and sugar cookies had turned to gossip about Augusta Roemer. A few clicked their tongues and shook their heads and said it was *such* a shame. Gustie really needed a man to take care of her. And why, for heaven's sake, didn't she pay any attention to Nemil Glasrud? Sure, Nemil wasn't going to win any beauty prizes, but then neither was Augusta, and he was a good worker and had had his eye, however shyly, upon her ever since she came to Charity—now what was it—two or three years ago? And never once had she even given him the time of day. A woman in Gustie's predicament, and not getting any younger after all, they clucked, could not afford to treat a man like an old shirt.

Lena, who on principle might have agreed, having made similar observations herself about other women, bristled when such sentiments were tossed about over Gustie. With a glare at her sister-in-law Nyla that said unmistakably *You better not say anything or I will tell a few things I know about you, too,* she countered, "And what does Gustie need a man for? So she can have twice as many clothes to wash, and clothes that are twice as dirty to boot? So she has three times the cooking, and somebody she has to pick up after all the time? And wait up for? She's happy the way she is, and maybe all of you aren't so blissful in your married nests as you'd have us believe either, and are just jealous of her freedom. It's none of anybody's business whether she has a man or not. The idea!" Lena was hell-bent. "And, as for Nemil Glasrud, he's as homely as a fence and smells like his barn, and I didn't see any of *you*"—she cast her fury upon the younger, newly married women in the room— "taking up with him, and you were all given the eye by him at one time or another."

Lena's back was up, but not everyone took the warning to quietly finish their coffee and go home. Harriet Kranhold, always in need of the last word, tilted her head so that her double chins trebled as they flopped over her collar. Stirring another spoon of sugar into her already syrupy brew, she began with a grunt: "Hmph. She goes off—somebody said she goes to Argus for books, supplies, whatnot—but she's gone two, three days, sometimes longer. Where can *she* afford to stay in Argus? And on a Sunday? There's no books or supplies to be bought on a Sunday. She just trots off as she pleases to nobody knows where. It doesn't look right. Not at all, I don't think." After a significant pause, she looked up and continued in a more confidential tone, but still audible to all present, "And Axel told me that Harold Schenecker said he saw her, a couple of times, in her wagon going east—*east,* mind you. Argus is *west*." She paused for effect. "She'd have a long trip going to Argus that way." A light giggle rippled around the room. Harriet nodded and smiled, stirred and stirred.

Lena often wondered where Gustie went to but had not felt it her business to ask.

Mathilda Langager opened her mouth, but before she could speak Lena snapped, "What do you care where she goes? She's always in that cold, cramped schoolhouse come a Monday morning of a schoolday, isn't she? And if it weren't for her, that boy of yours, Mathilda"—Lena pointed her finger at Mathilda—"wouldn't even be able to scrawl his name, let alone read a book or add two bags of feed in a wagon to two on the ground and know he had a pile of four." This was true, of course, and everybody knew it. Arthur Langager was sixteen years old before he could write his name. Gustie had worked with the boy and he could now even read a few lines from the Bible and do simple sums. Mathilda blushed and her mouth puckered into an unattractive pout.

Now Lena's back was more than up; she was ready to throw the whole pesky lot of them out of her house. So they finished their coffee, hastily nibbled the last crumb of the last cookie, and, sucking sugar crystals off their fingers, at three o'clock, went their separate ways, almost all offering variations of the smug excuse that they had to "be getting home to the family to start supper." There were those who knew very well that after twelve years of marriage, her childlessness was as big a wound as Will's drinking. But Lena kept her back straight and her chin out and willed a gleam to her eye that defied anyone to ever say a direct word to her face about any of it. No one ever did.

And now that Will was in jail, maybe for keeps this time, people did not know quite what to do. In the past, Lena had refused comfort or criticism, and now that she might need some of the former, even the most well-meaning in Charity were hesitant to offer it.

Gustie, confronted by the white paper crumpled in her door, read Lena's message, jumped back into her wagon, turned Biddie around, and headed for the south of town to Lena's house.

She found Lena on the floor surrounded by a pink sticky mess and choking with sobs. Gustie lifted her gently by the shoulders, seated her at the table, and cleaned the floor. When she had poured the coffee, she sat across the table from her friend, who was still snuffling, making little moaning sounds, and blowing her nose. Gustie had not failed to notice as she was cleaning things up that the cupboards were all but bare.

"What's happened?" Gustie coaxed when Lena had exhausted her sniffling.

"You don't know?"

"Your note just said 'come see me.' Then I find you on the floor making a big fuss over some rhubarb sauce."

Lena laughed and choked into her dish towel. "Oh, Gustie, you always make me laugh." She wiped her eyes, blew her nose again, and said, "It's Will."

It usually is, Gustie thought dourly. But even Gustie was surprised when Lena poured out a story far more serious than his usual drunken episodes.

"Dennis says he's got to hold Will for the circuit judge. I told him, I says, 'You know Will could never do anything as bad as this,' and he says it makes no difference. Will is the only suspect and he's got to hold him." Lena blew her nose fiercely into the dish towel. As her anger got the better of her grief and fear, she pummeled the air with the wadded-up towel. "And then I went to see Ma Kaiser. She's just sitting there in that house rocking and staring off. She's worthless. And thinks Will done it. And Julia . . ."

"Yes, what does Julia think?"

"Julia doesn't think Will did it, I don't believe, but she's pretty tore up over Pa, so she wasn't saying too much. Pa did a lot for her, you know, one way and another. I don't know. I don't know what to do. I've been sitting here so all alone and I didn't know what to do. Where were you?" Lena began to cry again.

Gustie reached across the table and took Lena's hand. "I'm sorry, Lena. I'm here now."

"Oh, fiddlesticks. You can be anywhere you want. I'm not like some other people around here who have to know everybody's business. I just . . . no one else around here is any good."

Lena was looking out the window in some embarrassment and didn't notice Gustie's smile.

"Well, we'll think of something." There was a short silence between them as Gustie took up the vigil out of the window and Lena searched for inspiration in her coffee cup.

Gustie asked, "When is the judge due?"

Lena shrugged. "Two weeks, I guess. Maybe more."

"We have a little time. Let's rest, and we can think clearly in the morning. We'll come up with something."

"Oh, Gustie, I'm so glad you're back." Lena took in her friend through watery eyes. "You're a brick, Gus."

Gustie, often mystified by Lena's expressions, assumed *brick* was good.

"Let's get some food into you. I'll bet you've had nothing but coffee all day." Gustie dished up what little was left of the rhubarb sauce, and sliced two healthy portions of bread. Nobody baked like Lena. Since there was no butter or sour cream they dipped their bread in their coffee. Lena sprinkled hers with sugar.

"Now," said Gustie, rising and taking her cup and saucer to the sink, "you'll come back with me. We'll pick up a few things at O'Grady's and this evening have ourselves a good supper. I'm hungry myself. Bring your sweater, it's going to get cold." Lena did not move. "Let's get out of here. You can't sit here by yourself another day."

"I want to finish my coffee first," Lena whimpered.

"All right." Gustie rinsed her cup and bowl and set them to dry on the sideboard. "Has anybody notified Ella and Ragna?"

Lena told her of her decision not to.

"How about Tori?"

"No. He usually comes in Saturday nights and stays over. I don't really expect him before that." Lena still had not moved from the table. She suddenly brightened. "But you never know. He might come. I should be here if he does."

"Do you want to go to O'Grady's with me?" Gustie was getting exasperated.

Lena still did not move from her chair. She took a sip from a coffee cup that Gustie knew was empty. "I don't feel like it, really. I don't feel like going there just now."

Gustie rested the tip of her finger on her lower lip and considered. "Perhaps you're right," she said. "You wouldn't want to miss Tori if he came by. I need some things. I've been gone a long time." Gustie took herself briskly to the door. "How about . . . if I just go and get what I need, and then I'll come back for you. If Tori isn't here by then, we'll leave him a note."

"Well, that sounds all right."

Gustie thought Lena was going to cry again. She left quickly, so this time Lena could finish her crying in private.

The man stepping down from the 4:30 train out of Saint Paul was obviously not a homesteader. Nor was he a traveling salesman, teacher, or preacher. His gray suit was too finely tailored, his matching hat and gloves too expensive, his skin too pale, his hands too soft. He was thin, of medium height, with sparse sandy hair, and the mien of one who, having been accustomed to taking orders, and having chafed under the taking, now gloats in the giving. The stranger checked into the Koenig Hotel and, after inspecting his room and locking his luggage securely therein, asked for directions to the sheriff's office.

Dennis Sully was alone, fingering a tin cup of tepid coffee and pondering the fact that he had nothing further to offer the circuit judge in the way of evidence for or against Will Kaiser in the murder of Frederick Kaiser, Sr.

Dennis had never expected to do much as sheriff. He had no inflated ideas about his position as a lawman. He simply wanted a quiet, steady life. In Charity he got it. Mostly, he broke up occasional brawls between the heavy-drinking Germans and Poles, and between Indians and whites—again, only the drinkers of either community ever fought—and picked up Will Kaiser three or four times a year and locked him up for a few hours or hauled him home, depending on his condition. Dennis suspected that the city council had hired him more to keep up appearances in Charity as the county seat than because they had any real need for a sheriff. Dennis was not pleased, therefore, to be investigating a murder. Not that he was squeamish; as a young cowboy in Missouri and Nebraska he had seen a few gunfights. He had fired his own pistol a time or two, though he had never killed anybody and never meant to. Dennis was a crack shot if he had to be. In his younger days he could, on a galloping horse, bring down a deer with one bullet. He never left a duck or goose flapping and gasping for bloody breath. If he couldn't kill with the first shot, he didn't fire. And he had seen some heated skirmishes with Indians in their last efforts to save their place on the land. Now the cattle were fenced in and the cowboys mostly out to pasture, the game was thin, the Indians had lost, and Dennis's pistol lay in his desk drawer.

Dennis Sully was forty-two years old and going to fat, but underneath the expanding paunch he still had plenty of grit and gristle. He had never married. He liked his quiet life, and the people who surrounded him.

While he had not had more than a few years of country schooling, Dennis did have common sense, an easy way with people, and a scalp that itched when he heard a lie. If he had had any hair left on the top of his head it would have stood up as soon as the man who walked through the door that afternoon introduced himself with "Good afternoon, Sheriff. My name is Steven Springer."

Not his real name. Hell, thought Dennis, *I reckon I don't have to do much for a man who's just lied to me.*

Both the front and back doors to the sheriff's office were left open to encourage a breeze. Will Kaiser, with nothing else to do, was happy to be able to listen to conversations in Dennis's office. Most talk was about the weather, stock prices, the skyward progress of wheat and corn. Will's interest was piqued when he heard a strange voice.

"I am looking for a young woman who I believe may have taken up residence in or near Charity."

Not from around here, Will thought.

The stranger removed his hat, gray felt that perfectly matched the shade of his suit. He held it with both hands in front of him like a shield to his midsection.

"What's her name?" asked Dennis.

"Her name is Clarice Madigan."

Dennis took a moment after each of the stranger's answers before asking his next question. "Why you looking for her?"

"She has taken something that doesn't belong to her." Springer had a petulant quality threaded through an apparent arrogance that annoyed the sheriff.

"Whereabouts you from?"

"Pennsylvania."

"All the way from Pennsylvania." Dennis considered that, rubbing his chin. "What do you do back there?"

"Family business."

Dennis waited, and Steven Springer added, "Dry goods. We're an old established firm." He turned the hat a few degrees clockwise.

"Must be a pretty important 'something' for you to come all this way from Pennsylvania yourself."

"What do you mean?"

"Why didn't you hire somebody? You look like you could afford it."

"It did not occur to me."

That, Dennis decided, was the truth. "Well, I haven't heard the name. What's she look like? How old is she?"

"Oh," Steven Springer said. "Yes. I suppose she might not be using her real name." He said this with such an air of genuine revelation that Dennis laughed. Springer looked puzzled and offended. After some hesitation, however, he offered, "I have a photograph."

Dennis nodded sagely. "Well, that would sure be a help," and noted the slight reluctance with which the stranger brought out a flat leather wallet from the inside pocket of his suit coat and carefully removed a photograph.

While the man held the photograph with what Dennis would have described as tenderness, his lips pursed, as if Steven Springer suddenly had a mouthful of bitterness and nowhere to spit.

Dennis took the picture when it was finally given to him and beheld the likeness of a young woman. Unruly hair billowed about her small face. Though she was not smiling, she did not look grim; merely composed. A small nose and delicate mouth. A Slavic cast to her eyes reminded Dennis of many of the fair-faced young women in the Polish settlement of Rennville two townships to the southwest. Dennis considered the face. Interesting. Intelligent. When animated, probably pretty. He handed the photo back to Steven Springer. "Never seen her before, but if I do I'll give you a holler. You stayin' at Koenig's?"

Springer nodded and carefully returned the picture to its place in the wallet, which he slid back into his pocket.

"How long you stayin'?"

"Till I find her, Sheriff."

Dennis took a sip of his cold coffee, grimaced, and thought, *That could be a mighty long time—this is a big country.*

"Miss Madigan was traveling with a companion. Her name is Augusta Roemer. Tall, unattractive woman. Wears spectacles. Brown hair." He said the word "brown" as if he held the color itself in disdain.

In his jail cell Will, hearing the name of his wife's best friend, cupped his hand behind his good ear and strained even harder to hear.

Dennis remained completely slack-faced. "Augusta. I don't

know. Don't ring any bells." He took another sip of his coffee. Dennis Sully had liked Gustie the first time she pulled her mare and wagon up in front of his office and announced, "I'm the new teacher. Can you tell me where I might stay until I find a place of my own?" She appeared competent enough—after all, she had got there with all her worldly goods from wherever it was she came from, apparently alone. And yet she had a shy, dazed look, not of a woman who had been sheltered, but more of one who wanted to shelter herself. She wore an expression of resignation that had made Dennis unaccountably sad. He pointed her to the only hotel in town, Koenig's, and to the livery next door, and said he would get in touch with the head of the school committee to call on her later.

Steven Springer squirmed inside a suit that was too warm for the weather. Dennis assessed him as a man who never went around in his shirtsleeves.

"I reckon it's money she took? This Clarice Madigan?" questioned Dennis.

"My money, the firm's money. I—we want it back. Sheriff . . ."

"Sully," Dennis cued him.

"Sully. I didn't come here to be interrogated. I require your assistance as the local representative of the law." He looked like he might have added "and civilization."

Dennis put his coffee cup down carefully and said with an almost friendly grin, "I'll keep my ears open and my eyes peeled."

Though the stranger's face betrayed some doubt about Dennis Sully's good intentions, he had no choice but to take the sheriff at his word. "In the meantime, you won't mind if I make a few inquiries on my own?"

"Suit yourself." Dennis gestured broadly. "It's a free country."

As soon as Springer was gone, Dennis got up, took a small sip of the cold coffee, made a face, ran a hand over the top of his head, and ambled back to the cells.

As usual, Will was sitting on the side of his cot. He looked up at Dennis. "Sure didn't like the sound of that guy."

"Didn't look any better."

"Gustie better stay out at her place for a while and not come to town."

"Mm-hm. She probably better."

"Don't you worry—whatever it is, she wouldn't have taken anything that wasn't hers. That's not Gustie. I don't know who Clarice is. Never heard her talk about any Clarice. I'll ask Lena. Don't know what she done, but whatever it was, it's nothing to do with Gustie."

"It wouldn't be right—my warning Gustie about this fella. Might be obstructing justice. You never know what this could be about." Dennis leaned casually against the bars, his arms folded across his chest and one leg crossed over the other at the ankle. One hand worried the stubble on his chin. "You know what I mean?"

"Yeah, I know what you mean," Will replied just as casually. "I'm in no position to obstruct anything much, am I?" He grinned up at Dennis amiably.

"Nope."

"I'll just talk to Lena. Maybe it'll come up."

"Maybe. What do you want me to bring you back from Olna's for supper? The fried chicken should be good tonight."

"Throw on some biscuits. That would go good."

While the gossip about each other flourished among the people in Charity, when it came to strangers—outsiders in fancy suits—folks became grim-faced and tight-lipped. Gustie had been an outsider. Now, by virtue of the two years they had baked her pies, churned her butter, and entrusted their children to her care, she was magically, unobtrusively, one of them. That evening Steven Springer asked everyone in Olna's Kitchen, where he ate his supper (and where he was disappointed to find there was no wine), and could find no one who knew a blessed thing about anybody called Augusta Roemer.

"You want to be alone with him." Gustie opened the door for Lena, who carried another pillowcase full of clean clothes for Will.

"Oh, heck. I don't want to be alone with him. Come in with me, Gustie."

In the sheriff's office, they found Fritz Mulkey at his desk and Dennis pouring thick black stuff that Gustie presumed was coffee into his cup.

"Got some things for Will," Lena announced. "You want to check it?"

Dennis didn't smile. "No, Missus, you go right in. Morning, Miss Augusta."

"Good morning, Sheriff. Morning, Fritz."

"Morning, ma'am." Fritz grinned broadly, unabashed by his mouthful of brown, snaggy teeth.

Will lay on his back, his legs crossed and his arms folded under his head, staring at the ceiling. He scrambled to his feet when he saw Lena and Gustie.

"Here you go, Will. Some fresh clothes. Put your dirty things in the pillowcase and I'll pick them up tomorrow." Lena couldn't fit the bag through the bars of the cell. She began handing each item—pants, shirt, underwear—through one by one. Then she folded up the pillowcase and handed that through last. Gustie could feel Lena's shame and wondered why she wanted anyone to see this.

"Hello, Will."

" 'Lo, Gustie. Nice to see ya."

Lena looked lost as she stood there, her eyes fluttering in every direction but her husband's.

Will scratched his neck. "You know, Gustie, there was some fella here yesterday looking for you."

"What?" Gustie was surprised. "Who? What did he want?"

"Said his name was Steven Springer."

Something was familiar about that name, but Gustie couldn't place it. Lena twined two fingers around a bar.

"What did he look like?" Gustie asked.

"Don't know. Couldn't see him. The sheriff could tell you that." Will's hand drifted to the bar just above Lena's fingers and Gustie knew it was time to leave them alone.

"I'll ask him, then."

She left Will and Lena touching fingers through the iron barrier between them, and slipped back into Dennis Sully's office. "Someone was looking for me?"

"Yup." Dennis made a sucking noise on his teeth and turned to his deputy. "Fritz, you wanna go down to Olna's and get our dinner? I'll take the beef and gravy, Will the same. Extra biscuits for him."

Fritz said, "But it's early yet . . ."

The sheriff got official. "Don't want her to run out of biscuits. Go on now."

"Yup," Dennis repeated as Fritz closed the door behind him. "Know a Steven Springer?"

"No. Not that I can remember." Gustie sat in the same chair Lena had sat in the day before. She frowned. Something about the name nagged at her.

"What did he look like?"

"Pretty fancy duds. Suit, hat, gloves, all to match. Must have cost a penny or two. Said he was from Pennsylvania."

Gustie's spine prickled. "Did he say what he wanted?"

"Well, he wadn't exactly lookin' for you. He was looking for somebody else he said you was with. A Clarice Madigan."

The sheriff saw Gustie go white.

"You all right?"

"I'm fine." She asked again, "What did he look like?"

"Kind of pale-all-over-lookin'. Thin. Beady blue eyes."

Gustie felt herself trembling and hoped the sheriff wouldn't notice.

He did. "You sure I can't get you something? Have some coffee. It's bad, but it's wet."

"No. Yes. I'll take a little. Please."

He poured her half a cup. "Thank you," she said. She gripped the cup tightly.

"You know this guy?"

"Yes. His name isn't Springer."

"Didn't think so." The sheriff took a sip of his coffee. Gustie took a sip of hers. It made her own coffee taste like spring-water.

Dennis gave her time before he asked, "What's his name then?"

"Madigan. Peter Hawksworth Steven Madigan the Second, to be precise."

"You mean there's another one like him?"

"No, probably not anymore."

"Just a joke. Bad one. Where'd he get 'Springer' from?"

She knew now why the name Springer was familiar. "His mother's maiden name."

"You know a fair bit about him."

"What did he say, exactly?"

"He said he was looking for this Clarice Madigan. That she had taken something that belonged to him."

Gustie's blood surged in the opposite direction, flushing her throat and face, burning the roots of her hair. She growled, "He's a liar."

"I thought that, too."

Another pause.

"He her husband?"

"No." Gustie placed her cup on the desk.

"Are you in any danger from this fella, Gustie?"

"Not the kind you mean, Dennis. Nothing you can help me with."

"You sure?"

Lena came through the door, her face a picture of bewilderment. "Dennis, Will says the judge is coming tomorrow. I thought you said next month."

"I got a wire this morning. He's early. Don't know."

"What are we going to do?" Lena was ready to panic.

"Will's going to have to stand for the hearing. Then the judge will decide if there's enough evidence to hold him over for trial or not. If there is, he'll set bail, maybe. If Will pays it he is let out of jail to wait for trial, which would probably be the next time the judge comes through."

Gustie looked at her friend and knew exactly what she was thinking. There was no money for bail or anything else.

"I'll take you home," Gustie said, getting to her feet.

Lena just nodded and sucked the tip of her forefinger.

Lena went out the door and Gustie followed her, then turned back to the sheriff. "Do you know where Peter Madigan is now?"

"Well, seems like nobody was much help in town, so I reckon he's out checking around some of the farm places. Maybe going over to Argus. Funny how people around here don't seem to have any recollection of you."

Though Gustie did not feel like smiling, she was suddenly filled with a sweet affection for the whole town of Charity.

"Gustie." The sheriff ran a hand over his shiny head. "Me and Fritz, one of us is always here. Don't get yourself in a jam." Gustie nodded and was out the door.

She trotted Biddie so fast down the side streets that Lena, forced to hang on to her seat, complained, "What's your hurry?"

"I've got some things to do. I have to go out of town again.

You will be fine for the hearing. I'll be back before the trial, if there is a trial. They don't have anything but circumstantial evidence. With a good lawyer . . ."

Lena threw her hand up in despair. "Phaw! How're we going to get a lawyer?"

"Isn't there a lawyer in Charity?"

"Two of 'em. So what? I can't afford a lawyer, Gustie." Lena's eyes were swimming. In a thin voice she repeated, "I can't afford a lawyer."

Gustie had no time to offer comforting words or gestures. She turned Biddie up the winding road to Lena's house.

"Two lawyers? Who are they?"

Lena wiped her eyes. "John Anderson and Pard Batie. Pard's supposed to be the best, I hear, but it makes no difference to us."

"Whoa!" Biddie came to a stop and blew the dust out of her nose with a loud snort.

"Where you going, Gustie? Is it to do with that man looking for you?"

"Yes."

"Are you in trouble, Gus?"

"No. Lena, don't worry. You and Will— You'll be all right. Now take your groceries."

"Gustie, I'll pay you back for these things. You know I will."

"Don't be silly, Lena. All the meals you've cooked for me? I owe you more than this. Cook for yourself now, and get some sleep. You look a fright."

"Do I?"

"Yes. You do. Look nice for the judge tomorrow. It can't hurt. Judges are human."

Lena brightened and patted a wisp of her hair into place.

Gustie raised the dust driving Biddie back toward the center of town. She hitched her to the rail outside the Charity Farmers and Merchants Bank, hoping she wasn't too late to find Lester Evenson still in his office.

Cecil Helwig, the teller, told her Lester was about to leave, and could she please come back first thing in the morning?

"No, I can't come back in the morning." Her sharpness left Cecil wide-eyed and clearing his throat. She softened her manner. "Is he here? I need to see him now, please. It won't take long."

Lester, in a loosened tie, suspenders, and shirtsleeves, came out of his office, his suit coat draped over one arm. "Miss Roemer." He beamed upon seeing her. "A pleasure." Lester extended his hand and Gustie returned a firm handshake. "I haven't seen you in quite a while."

"Lester, I need to talk to you. I'll be brief." Lester checked the clock on the wall, took a split second to access his priorities, and said, "Come in, please."

Lester Evenson managed the Charity Farmers and Merchants Bank. He was the only other man in Charity besides Doc Moody to own more than two suits. He knew that in a community as small as Charity, his business would prosper only to the extent that he kept his mouth shut. Once inside his office, those who came to him with money or in need of money might just as well have been closing the door of a confessional behind them.

Half an hour later, Augusta and Lester were shaking hands again. She clutched a sheaf of papers under one arm, and a heavier purse over the other. She left Biddie where she was and walked the two blocks west across Main Street to Pard Batie's office. In another half hour, she was without the papers and tying her mare to the rail in front of O'Grady's General Store.

Gustie entered, grateful to be the only customer. She could conduct her business quickly and be gone, she hoped, before anyone came in.

"Afternoon, Miss Roemer." From behind the counter, Kenneth O'Grady greeted her pleasantly, closed the ledger book he was writing in, and stuck his pencil behind his ear. Morgan slid a box he was unpacking out of the way so Gustie could walk by. With his curly hair, rolled-up shirtsleeves, and suspenders holding up loose serge trousers, Morgan was a seventeen-year-old version of Kenneth. All he lacked to be the mirror image of his father were the broadness of maturity and the lines in his face of a good life lived for forty years.

"I need quite a lot of things today, Kenneth," Gustie began. The storekeeper took the pencil from behind his ear, tore off a small piece of brown wrapping paper and wrote as Gustie briskly gave her order: two bags of flour, a pound of salt, five pounds each of sugar and coffee; tins of dried fruit—peaches, apricots, prunes, and apples; a large bag of oatmeal, a pail of eggs, a chunk of butter, a box of tea.

She took some satisfaction in the surprise on Kenneth's face as he began to write. Not only did she usually order only a few things, measured out in ounces, but this was her second order in as many days.

Among the barrels of dry foods lined up against the back wall stood a barrel of bologna packed in salt brine, and another of the evil-smelling fish that the Norwegians loved. She ordered some of the bologna, and passed on the fish.

While Kenneth and Morgan scrambled to measure out each item, wrap or bag it, and load it onto her wagon, Gustie wandered over to the racks of ready-to-wear: pants, shirts, and overalls for men; dresses, skirts, and blouses for women. In glass cases were displayed handkerchiefs, gloves, ornamental hairpins and combs, even a fan and a parasol.

She held up the skirts and the blouses, looking for the largest size available. She found several items she thought would do. Then, under the glass she spied something that made her smile: a pair of enormous bloomers, trimmed with lace and ribbons. She pointed to them and Kenneth brought them out and wrapped them along with the other garments in brown paper. She went back to the rack where a nicely tailored split skirt had caught her eye. She bit her lip, then impulsively whipped it off the hanger, chose a high-necked yellow blouse to go with it, and added it to her other purchases.

Behind the display cases, on a corner shelf, lay stacks of paper in creamy linen finishes, matching envelopes, and notebooks, lined and thick. Since coming to Charity, Gustie had never indulged in such things. Now, with a subtle trembling joy, for herself alone, she chose a supply of paper, envelopes, notebooks, and a handful of pencils and pens, and two jars of ink—one black, one blue. She brought them to the counter to be added to her already lengthy bill. She thought Kenneth O'Grady was looking worried, knowing as he did how frugally Gustie had lived since coming to Charity. He added the sum of her purchases and, with an effort, kept his mouth closed as she counted out new bills in full payment.

"One more thing." She looked up. "That. Morgan, can you tie it in my wagon securely so it doesn't bump around? I have a long drive ahead of me."

"Yes, ma'am." Father and son stood on chairs and cut loose the bentwood rocking chair that was suspended from the ceiling. The heavy, beautifully crafted oak chair, Kenneth had despaired of selling. They lowered it carefully. Kenneth wrapped it in sacking material so it would not get scratched and Morgan tied it in the back of the wagon.

Gustie counted out more bills to cover the cost of the chair, plus a few extra. "This is for Lena Kaiser. The next time she comes in, tell her you made a mistake somewhere in her account, and she has a credit. Give her whatever she needs. And please don't tell her anything about this."

"No, ma'am. I sure won't." Kenneth shook his head earnestly.

Gustie hesitated at the counter.

"Help you with anything else, Miss Roemer?"

"Can you take a special order for something you don't have here?"

"Yes, ma'am. Most anything we can get from Saint Paul, or even Chicago, if you've got the time to wait for it."

"I want two beds. Two small beds." Gustie spread her arms to show the size she was talking about.

"Sure. I can order those from Saint Paul. You'll have them in a few weeks. Come by train."

"I will need you to deliver them. May I borrow your pencil?" She tore a piece off the roll of wrapping paper and drew a rough map. "And don't tell anybody about this either. Here's half the money. I'll give you the other half when they are delivered. Is that all right?"

"Yes, ma'am." Kenneth studied the map that Gustie had sketched. "This is out on Indian land isn't it?"

Gustie nodded.

"Well, then, we might wire the stationmaster in Wheat Lake—that's Joe Gruba—to take them off the train there. I'll tell him where they go. He'll take care of it. Rather than bring them all the way into Charity and have to haul them back."

Gustie looked uncertain.

"Oh, sure. We'll make the arrangements. They'll get there. Joe's an old buddy of mine."

"That'll be fine then." She paused a moment more. "I'll take this too." She picked up a bag of hard candies tied with a red ribbon and strode out, leaving Kenneth O'Grady a very happy merchant.

Gustie went home. She watered her horse and added the groceries she had purchased for herself the night before to her wagon load. She had not expected to be leaving her home so soon again. In these few weeks she had felt quite changed—charged with hope—and now this. She walked into her bedroom, right up to the closet door, grasped the sides of the white nightgown hanging there, and buried her face in it. She remembered the last time she had left this house, a few weeks ago, driven by a familiar terror. . . .

Clots of earth; sprays, spumes of dirt rising and falling, muddied her skin, blinded her. The dirt worked itself into her hair, through her clothing. And all the creatures that thrived in darkness squirmed and writhed in the painful light, were hacked and tossed with the earth up into the air only to fall and be crushed by earth and metal. Some of them—some parts of them—found their way into her hair, inside her clothes. And they grew. Their blind mouths, red-rimmed, cavernous, protesting their catastrophe, grew larger, sought her blindly, but surely with probing tongues and razor fangs, nipping, bearing down upon her, forcing her into deeper darkness, where rasping sounds, like chewing, or breathing . . . She woke with the usual terror, gasping and flinging her arms to ward them off. Conscious now of the gentle light illuminating the muslin curtains of her bedroom window, but still filled with the horror of that avalanche of earth burying her alive and of those gaping mouths, Gustie sat up, wiped the sweat from her face with her sleeve, and checked it, as she always did, to make sure that it was merely sweat and not mud, alive with squirming things. She remained still, waiting for the cold fear to pass, for her heart and breath to return to normal.

The nightmare plagued her almost every night, but when the terror overwhelmed her so completely, she knew the time had come to go back. See it again. Touch it. Dig her fingers into the soil again. Be with Dorcas.

The last time she had awakened shrieking and tearing at her bedclothes was in March, when the snow had lain so deep, the temperatures fallen so low, that travel was impossible. She had had to endure sleepless nights, when the nightmare woke her, or when she made herself stay awake for fear of it. She took to sleeping with her photo album, and finally she had brought the white nightgown out of Clare's cedar chest and hung it on the door of the closet, where it would be the last thing she saw at night and the first thing she saw when she opened her eyes in the morning—not as good as tasting the soil, but it helped, and gradually the nightmares receded into simple, bad aching dreams. Since then, the album had stayed on her nightstand; the gown remained hanging on the closet door.

School was out. The weather was fine. There was nothing now to delay her going.

Gustie sloshed water from a flowered ewer into the matching bowl on her dresser and stood naked on a towel while she washed herself with a chunk of hard soap. She rinsed, then dried herself with another towel. Both towels she tossed over the bedposts to dry. She dressed quickly and made up her bed, stuffing her own nightgown under the pillow. She did not fold it. She was not by nature tidy, but she had so few things it hardly mattered.

In the next room she lit the stove and put her kettle on to boil. Then she grabbed her shawl and scurried out to her privy.

The quiet of a prairie morning still captivated her. Birds and insects entered into the day with a kind of reverence, trilling softly, building slowly to their full-throated cadences as the sun rose higher. Gustie came out of the privy and gazed across the unbroken prairie that stretched for miles behind her house. Tall grasses leaned together in waves before the wind. Wild plants bloomed in rainbow colors, attracting clouds of yellow butterflies, bees, and birds with bright yellow or ruby eyes on their wings. Unseen, in the shelter of the grass, the less showy members of the population scuttled about their business: mice, gophers, rabbits, skunks, badgers, snakes. She had no fear of any of them and did not disturb them.

On just such a morning as this, the earth glorying in a candescence of morning dew, she had seen the doe. Gustie had been at the pump bringing up her day's water supply. She straightened up for a moment to rest her back and saw the animal watching her from a short distance away. Gustie had not seen her approach. The two gazed at each other, the doe with unwavering eyes that reminded her of Clare's. A door opened and for a moment Gustie felt a breath from another world, lighter, more tranquil than the one she knew . . . then, as quietly and quickly as it had opened, the door closed; the doe turned and bounded away in graceful arcs. Her four feet appeared to skim along the tops of the grasses as she disappeared into the distance. Gustie discovered tears on her cheeks and felt a sweet ache over her heart, as if she had just experienced a blessing and a loss. She went back to her pump.

Since then, Gustie had trained herself to fill her ewer and kettle before she went to bed so she did not have to struggle with the pump in the morning, but she always took time to scan the horizon.

Lena was afraid Gustie would go crazy living alone out here, seven miles from the school, three miles from Charity. But Gustie did not want to be passed around from family to family for her room and board, as was the custom with unmarried schoolteachers. This house with its one large main room and small bedroom had been well made by Elef Tollerude for himself and his bride. After Ardis Tollerude died in that bedroom, along with her child striving to be born, Elef had no heart left for homesteading. He went back to his brother's farm in Wisconsin. The house stood empty till Gustie came. She liked the house, and was relieved that she did not have to explain the nightmares to anyone, and where she took off to on a fairly regular basis, weather permitting.

On the cookstove, her kettle rumbled as the water boiled,

rocking it back and forth across its uneven bottom. She made coffee and stirred up two eggs in some pork fat left over from the night before in her skillet.

Gustie finished her breakfast, slipped into her woolen jacket, and went to the barn.

As she slid open the barn door, her mare nickered and tossed her head up and down in greeting. Before putting her in harness Gustie took a little time with the big black horse, stroking her head and caressing her wonderful, velvety nose.

The black mare had introduced Gustie to her first friend in this new land. On her third day in Charity, she had come out of O'Grady's with a bag of groceries to find a tiny woman with a lot of fine reddish hair, her purse tucked under one arm, nuzzling the black horse and making sounds, a combination of baby talk and imitation horse. The mare did not mind the attention. Gustie said nothing until the woman noticed she was being watched. Then she turned her enormous cornflower blue eyes upon her and asked, "Is this your horse?"

"Yes."

"She sure is a nice horse."

"Yes, she is." Gustie put her bag of groceries in the back of her wagon.

"I won't hold you up," the red-haired woman said. She backed away from the mare a little but continued to caress her. "She just reminded me so much of a horse I grew up with. Dolly." The woman twisted her fingers gently through the horse's mane, as if she were getting a hold upon some moment in her childhood. "Oh, not in looks. Dolly wasn't much to look at—not like this horse. Dolly was heavier, you know. She pulled my pa's plow—" the woman laughed "—when she felt like it. Oh! Pa used to get so mad!" She shook her head, all the while patting Gustie's horse and calling back that other horse of her childhood. "No, Dolly was just a workhorse, but it is something in the eyes. You can tell a horse by its hind legs and its eyes, you know."

"You can?"

The woman nodded with certainty. "I can always pick the winner in a horse race if I can just go see the back legs and look into a horse's eyes. But this one . . . What's her name?"

"Biddie. That was her name when I got her."

"Yes, she reminds me of Dolly in her eyes, you see. There's somethin' going on in there. You're the new teacher for the section school, aren't you?"

"Yes."

"Getting settled?"

Gustie nodded.

"I didn't know you were in town till yesterday. I'm Lena Kaiser. Say, do you have time for a cup of coffee?"

Gustie was still not used to such overtures of friendliness from strangers, but this woman, totally unselfconscious and genuinely friendly, was irresistible. She accepted, somewhat shyly. "Yes, I suppose so."

"Olna's Kitchen is right down the street there. Just leave Biddie here where it's nice and shady. Kenneth won't mind. Now, I recommend Olna's pie, but stay away from her cake. It's dry as toast, but never tell her I said so."

Gustie led the mare out of the barn, hitched her to the wagon, and brought her around to the front of the house. She put down a blanket in the corner of the wagon to cushion a pail of fresh eggs packed in straw. Around the pail she placed a sack of flour, a bag of coffee, and a bag of oats. Back inside her house, she lifted up the trapdoor to the small cold cellar. Six months of living in this house had passed before Gustie could bear to lower anything into that hole in the earth below her floor. The practical necessity of storing food and keeping it cool forced her to use it. She still had potatoes, turnips, and carrots. She hoisted out the three small bags of vegetables and added them to the supplies in her wagon bed. She went back in for her old train conductor's cap. She needed it to shield her eyes as she drove east, into the morning sun. Then she got up into the wagon seat and headed Biddie out toward the road.

Gustie traveled east on Dryback Grade—a road built up with tons of mule-hauled dirt through the middle of Dryback Lake, which was really a slough that sprawled out for several square miles. Some years, the old folks said, it had lain dry as dust and the old Norwegians used to cut hay out there enough for a winter. This year, between the clumps of fat marsh grass the still water shone blue with reflected sky. Ducks paddled and bobbed in purposeful circles. One made a *chip chip* sound, like a tiny spoon striking a tin plate. Muskrats quietly parted the waters with round backs, sleek as chestnuts, where last year they had waddled in mud.

A cloud of tiny insects enveloped the mare and wagon. Gustie waved one hand about her head and slapped the reins on Biddie's rump. The mare lurched forward and pulled them out of the swarming gnats. "Good girl!" said Gustie and reined her back to a comfortable pace.

Once past Dryback Lake the land on either side of her alternated between marsh, unbroken prairie, and perfect black squares of tilled soil.

Gustie allowed Biddie to go at her own pace, an easy trot, which lulled Gustie into simple enjoyment of the rhythmic motion under a warm sun, breathing cool air.

The twenty-mile journey was always a pleasure for Gustie. She loved this Dakota land, especially now, as it was waking up green and wet after eight months of cold sleep. The sweet wind lifted her hopes and ruffled her desires at the same time as it honed the edges of her sorrow.

After several hours the ground began to roll, imperceptibly

at first, then Gustie was aware of Biddie's laboring up the first hill. The farther east they traveled, the more the land undulated, becoming rockier. She passed cows grazing on a hillside. They looked at her with large sleepy eyes and switched at flies with their tails. Filled coulees glistened like oval mirrors among the green and yellow grasses.

In the early evening Gustie finally turned off the dirt road and endured the jolting of the wagon on its unforgiving wood wheels as it traversed the lumpy ground. Over the next rise she saw Crow Kills.

From her present vantage point Crow Kills looked like a small lake, but she was seeing only its western loop. Crow Kills lay like a satin sash draped around the hills. At no point could one see the whole of it; it lay long and winding, deep, cold, clear. And while the lake appeared still in the quietude of evening, Gustie knew it was never really still. There were, even on the most breathless of days, small ripples, a slosh against a rock here, the splash of a fish there, a wave rising subtly and merging silently back into its smooth surface. Crow Kills lived and breathed and freely bestowed its soothing spirit upon even those who cursed it, as Gustie had once done. The lake had absorbed her anger, and everything she had flung into it, with grace, with merely a ripple, and was as before, visibly unchanged. Crow Kills understood and forgave. Now she found balm in its nearness. Someday she would like to live here. She felt that if she could live near this water, the nightmare would leave her.

Gustie turned Biddie and the wagon bumped and clattered past the southwestern tip of the lake, past the irregular groves of cottonwoods, one of the few naturally occurring trees on a land where wheat grass was regent.

A gust of wind brought her scents of fresh water, moss, and rushes mingled with a subtle fishiness. She was close enough now to hear the whispering of the trees and to see their seeds nestled in beds of cotton floating on the breeze. She did not have to rein Biddie to the right, away from the lake and up a slight incline, because the mare knew where to go and when to stop. Gustie climbed down from the wagon and let the reins brush the ground. She was in no hurry. The light always lasted longer over the lake than anywhere else. She walked to a mound of earth at the top of an incline marked only by a tender cottonwood that Gustie had transplanted there two years ago. She had been afraid that the first winter would kill it, but the sapling had survived.

Gustie sank to the ground. Since the prairie grasses had overgrown it, the mound was hardly visible any longer as something separate from the hill.

She sat with her legs tucked under her, closed her eyes, and dug her fingers into the soil. The plants had formed a tight network of roots and fibers; getting through to black dirt was not as easy as it used to be. Gustie needed the dirt itself on her hands, and she dug through till she had it. She resisted the urge to spread it across her face as she used to do. She just sat quietly, her eyes remaining closed, and felt the release of tension that had been mounting inside her for weeks, culminating in the nightmare.

Gustie sensed a presence and looked up over her shoulder. Dorcas stood there, arms crossed over her breast, watching her patiently. The fringes of her shawl flapped in the wind. Wisps of iron gray hair flurried about her round, deeply lined face. She looked as she always did except when she smiled, which was seldom: very stern.

"Come and eat." Dorcas tipped her head slightly, turned and walked down the other side of the incline.

Gustie hiked after her, marveling that with all of the old woman's girth and age, she could still walk faster and with more ease over this lumpy prairie ground than Gustie could, and Dorcas never got winded. *Maybe it's her moccasins,* thought Gustie.

Gustie stopped. *My goodness. I forgot Biddie.* "Dorcas, wait, we can ride." She lifted her skirts, turned back at a run, and almost twisted her ankle. The mare greeted her with a snuffle of affront at being an afterthought. Gustie snatched up the reins and hauled herself onto the wagon seat. Dorcas was nowhere in sight. A gentle shake of the reins and the horse moved leisurely up and over the rise and down the other side, in an arc that took them back toward the lake, but farther east, along the southern shore.

In front of Dorcas's cabin a tripod stood over glowing sticks. The smell of beans drifted up from the black kettle hanging from its center, and coffee steamed from a pot that sat directly upon rocks placed in the fire.

Gustie pulled Biddie up behind the cabin. Dorcas's workbench—a board laid across two tree stumps—evidenced her recent fish-cleaning. Scales stuck to the wood and scattered over the ground caught the light in prismatic specks. A few yards away blackbirds fought over fish heads and entrails. Gustie unhitched the mare and led her down to the lake. While the horse drank her fill, Gustie washed her hands and splashed the cold water on her face and neck.

Even though Dorcas had told her more than once to just come in, she had never gotten used to walking into someone's home without knocking. Gustie rapped softly on the door of the cabin before carrying in her bags of flour and vegetables. When she opened the door, she was greeted by the sharp scent of herbs and roots. The spotted calfskin still hung on the wall to her left over one bed, and the red cowhide, its edges crackling with age, still covered the opposite wall. Gustie felt like she had come home.

She made a second trip out to her wagon for the eggs and

coffee. As Dorcas took them from her, she tipped her head slightly and peered at Gustie through squinty eyes.

"Not so bad this time. Hm?"

There was nothing wrong with Dorcas's vision, Gustie knew. Squinting helped her come to conclusions.

"No, just last night. No school, so I came right away."

Dorcas took two plates and spoons outside. "Good. That's good. Always good to come early and stay long."

Gustie followed her with two cups. "Not too long. I'll wear out my welcome."

Dorcas spooned beans onto each plate. "When you are not welcome, I'll drown you in the lake. Feed the fish." She pointed with her chin toward Crow Kills.

Gustie lifted up her skirt to wrap around the hot handle of the coffeepot and filled their cups. As Lena and Will would have said, it was the kind of coffee you could stand your spoon in. Gustie loved it.

They ate outside on the small porch that fronted the cabin. Dorcas settled on two wooden boxes that were stacked against the outside wall, and Gustie sat on the step and leaned against one of the poles that supported the small overhanging roof. She looked at the crates supporting the old woman and wished she could buy Dorcas a rocking chair. The beans, flavored with onion and bacon fat, had cooked down all day to a thick sauce. They ate slowly.

"Fishing good?" Gustie asked.

Dorcas nodded. "Yup. Pretty good."

"That's good."

A bird called from the willow that bent over Crow Kills. Gustie swatted at a mosquito. She had gotten used to Dorcas's long silences while she lay in bed, unable to speak, not being required to speak. The quiet that surrounded the old woman was a full and comforting one which Gustie craved, even though she lived alone, in silence much of the time.

They finished their supper and Gustie washed the dishes and the pot in the lake. Dorcas disappeared into the cottonwoods to the east.

Crow Kills was now blue-gray, flecked with silver sparkles—tiny waves, rivulets on the surface ever reaching for the shore. As the pale sky deepened in hue, the green of the farther shore darkened, dissolving the trees and bushes into silhouette. A deer stepped down to the water's edge to drink, then vanished like a ghost. A few birds warbled their evening songs, a warm-up for the night insects that would take up the concert with frogs when the darkness was complete.

Gustie needed these times when her mind emptied and she enlarged and entered into her surroundings. She felt herself blowing across the lake, felt the ripples in herself, reaching to herself the shore, and another part of herself the birds singing, and again herself answering in the ratching sound of the crickets. She was the grass. She was the cottonwoods and the sound they made rustling softly in herself the breeze. This was losing the painful part of herself, her memories, her fears, her frustrations and limitations, and finding the best, that which existed in everything. This feeling lasted only a moment and then it passed. Try as she might, she couldn't recapture it or make it last. It came; it went; a visitation over which she had no control.

A lone waterbird floated on the lake in the thickening dusk. She watched it until its form disappeared into the night. Gustie rose, stepped down off the porch, and walked up the path out of the trees to where she stood in the open. On three sides there was nothing but rolling land, and behind her, Crow Kills with its cottonwood sentinels. Gustie looked up at the night sky. The stars! She could almost hear them, singing a siren song, a multitude of beautiful melodies, far as infinity, close as her heart, seducing her. She knew she could never again live without the open sky, just like this, anytime she needed it. Even when she could not get to Crow Kills, even in the dead of winter, she could walk a few steps out away from her own little house and get this sky, fill herself with it, feel herself soar up into it. She drank it like nectar, like black sparkling wine.

The scattered clouds hung low and heavy. The nearest cloud was dark at its belly, where it appeared to touch the earth, and lightened to piles of frothy white at its top.

The birds twittered in contentment, but perhaps it was her own contentment Gustie heard. No doubt birds had squabbles and problems of their own.

A small golden brown animal appeared from around a cluster of purple blossoms and disappeared again.

The air was a delicious caress of warm and cool—the breath of the prairie poised between spring and summer. The sun drew out her scent and the wind tossed it back into her nostrils: her hair, fresh and rushy-smelling from her morning bath in the lake, her skin smelling of the strong soap she always used.

Gustie noticed how much cleaner she felt out here in the Middle West than she used to feel back east, and how much cleaner still she felt here at the lake where most of the living was done outside. Air was cleansing, like water.

The breeze fluttered around her bare legs, under her arms, through and beneath the loose fabric of her ankle-length shift. The rest of her clothing was drying on the branches of the willow. She longed to take even the shift off and run naked across the prairie.

The rough grass under her bare feet made her feel real and grounded. Her hair was loose and blew around in the breeze. Gustie held her glasses folded up in her hand so nothing would obstruct the wind from her face. For a moment she forgot everything but her sense of freedom. She stood, her head thrown back, face to the sun, and let the wind blow through her.

She could feel the wind blowing from as far back as the early 1800s, maybe even before—before this earth had been stuck by the plow, before Dorcas's people had known the scourge of the white man, his diseases, his wrath, his greed. A purer, sweeter wind blew now, she thought, than would ever blow again. She felt it blowing straight into the future and she wondered what, if anything, of herself would be on that wind, except the scent of rushes from her hair. Tiny seeds borne in tufts of white cotton filled the air around her as the cottonwoods let loose upon the wind their own hope of the future. Gustie raised her arms, closed her eyes, and began to turn. She could feel the wind billowing her shift, lifting her hair, buffeting her gently from all sides as she turned around and around. She felt light as a seed pod, transparent as a snail's egg.

Gustie stopped turning and opened her eyes. She was lightheaded, and the sun was suddenly so brilliant she thought she was seeing an apparition: the dark figure veiled in a steamy radiance astride a pale horse, poised like a flame on the grass. Gustie covered her eyes with her hand, took a moment to clear her head, then put on her glasses, and shielding her vision from the direct rays of the sun, looked again. The figure was still there. An Indian woman. The horse, not of fire but very real horseflesh after all, was cream-color, almost white. Her long mane blew about and looked like sea froth. The woman rode without a saddle.

Gustie remembered her manners. "Can I help you? Dorcas isn't here."

As she moved in closer to the side of the horse and looked up into the woman's face, she was met with large black eyes that held her in a studied gaze. The eyes looked out from a face that might have been carved by a consummate, bold hand in love with stone. Sharp cheekbones, high and wide, balanced a strong wide chin and a full, sharply chiseled mouth. Her large nose sloped straight down in line with her wide, sloping forehead. Her black hair was cropped short just above her ears. The woman was young, younger than Gustie, to be sure.

When Gustie tore her eyes away from the face and looked down she found herself level with a dark, sleek expanse of thigh where the woman's skirt was hiked up and tucked under her, allowing her freedom to ride. Her leg was well muscled, relaxed, but ready to meld into the sides of her horse. Gustie barely restrained herself from touching it, the way she might have touched a piece of fine sculpture. The young woman said nothing. Just continued to study her.

"Would you like something to drink? Some water? There's coffee, I think."

The woman unfastened a bag that hung around her waist. Something moved inside it. She handed it down with a strong large hand and Gustie took it from her. Whatever was inside struggled harder. The bag was not heavy.

The woman said, "I'll be back."

The horse, responding to a command that Gustie could not discern, side-stepped away from her, turned, and trotted off. Gustie stood with the wiggling bag in one hand, her other hand once again shielding her eyes so she could watch the re-treating figure. *She sure knows how to sit a horse,* thought Gustie. *Remarkable eyes. Remarkable face. Could have been struck out of stone, it was so perfect, so defined.* Then Gustie looked down and recalled how she was dressed—or, rather, undressed—bare feet, and her hair a mess down her back. She took a deep breath. *Well, it can't be helped.*

She opened the bag a crack and saw brown and white feathers. She opened it all the way and released two chickens, who were delighted to run around in circles in the light and scrabble for tidbits on the ground. Gustie took a handful of cracked corn from a sack by the door and sprinkled it on the ground for them. The chickens pecked eagerly.

Gustie retrieved her dry clothes from the tree limbs and put them on. Then she sat on the porch and combed the tangles out of her hair and pinned it up again. She missed the feeling of lightness and freshness she had without her clothes on. *But I can't run around here half naked all the time,* she thought, and her mind went back to that chiseled brown face, the vision that had come on a shaft of sunlight and blown off on the wind; except visions did not leave behind live chickens.

The low cloud no longer touched the horizon, but hung suspended just above it with a thin patch of light between.

Gustie watched a pelican float on the lake. He did not seem to move at all, and yet he made rapid progress back and forth. His mate appeared from around the bend and they floated together for a while.

The only thing real is the Moon against my flesh. She gallops and I rock with her. There is only coming and going and the pauses between are only waiting for the next going. It is no way to live but it is all there is for me. Moon is a good horse. She is my horse. I fought for her and I won her. Still, I am hers much more than she is mine. When I named her, some of the people laughed, "Jordis on her moon." But it is her name. It suits her.

Grandmother needs the chickens so I take them to her and find the white woman dressed in cotton that when the sun and wind play with it I can see through it the body I know so well, that is still thin like a child's though she is not young. She is not old either. She reminds me of the inside of a shell. That shining has its own light kind of smoothness. So delicate that a wave lifting and dropping it will shatter it. Her eyes are gray and there are lines around them, as around the eyes of all white people except the very young, and a red scarring on the cheeks by the sun. Grandmother told me she comes back when the dreams take her. Strange. A white woman comes to an old Indian for comfort when her mind is full of storms. Usually they go to their churches and their preachers. But this is no woman to go to a church or a preacher. I can see that. Perhaps the old woman is right. The spirits of the land have not all been driven off. Fly, Moon.

• • •

To the west, the two pelicans slipped out of sight around a bend in Crow Kills. The afternoon was softening into evening and Dorcas still was not back. Gustie had spent most of the afternoon sitting on the porch, watching the lake. She felt more relaxed and at ease than she could remember.

Certain that Dorcas would return before dark, Gustie went inside, lit the stove, and started the coffee. From a jar on a shelf above the sink, she spooned lard into Dorcas's deep iron pot.

Dorcas had taught her how to mix up dough for fry bread. For supper they would have fry bread and fish. Early this morning, Dorcas had cleaned the fish and left them headless, tailless, and gutless in a pail of cold water waiting for the hot fat.

The dough was almost ready, springy and not too sticky. She had just formed it into a smooth oval and set it to rest in a bowl when she heard heavy footsteps on the porch. Dorcas swept through the door, the freshness of the prairie whirled in about her. Her bag, made from old blanket material, was full of plants, their leafy tops ruffled out from the drawstring opening. While Dorcas hung up her scarf and shawl, Gustie poured her a cup of coffee and placed it on the table alongside the can of sugar. "You had a visitor."

Dorcas sat down heavily. She took her time stirring spoonful after spoonful of sugar into her coffee, then sipped it with satisfaction for a few moments before she asked, "Who?"

"She didn't say. She left a couple chickens."

"She ride a white horse?"

"Yes. Quite a beautiful horse."

"Jordis."

Gustie observed the old woman squinting hard at her from behind her coffee cup and said, "What?"

"Nothing." Dorcas took another sip of the sugared coffee and wiped her mouth with her hand. Then added, "Missionaries name her."

The fat had melted down golden and hot. Gustie tore off pieces of the dough, flattened each one a little between her palms, and slipped them into the fat. The hot grease sizzled on contact and the dough puffed out and browned. Just when the outsides were crisp and the insides fluffy and steaming, Gustie lifted them out with a pair of iron tongs and piled them onto a tin platter. Then she rolled the fish in flour left from the bread making and dropped them into the fat. More sizzling and popping and the aroma of frying fish filled the cabin. The fish cooked quickly and Gustie piled them onto the platter next to the fry bread.

Dorcas nodded her approval. She flourished an unusually happy mood all of a sudden. "You cook like a good Indian. Next I teach you how to do it over the fire." Dorcas cocked her chin in the direction of the tripod outside. "Tastes better that way."

The first time Gustie had tried to make fry bread she had burned herself on spattering fat; some of the pieces had cooked to little brown bricks, and the rest remained doughy and sticky inside. She had to throw the whole batch out, feeling utterly miserable as she wasted Dorcas's precious flour. Dorcas received her small share of annuities. Like everyone else on the reservation, when it ran out she had to buy what she needed until the next allotment, and money was very scarce on the Red Sand.

The evening settled upon them gently. Gustie realized they were sitting in near-darkness. She took down the lamp from its hook on a ceiling beam and lit it. There were quick steps on the porch stairs and the cabin door was pushed open. Gustie started and nearly burned herself on the match before she could shake it out. Jordis entered. She wore the same clothes she had on that afternoon—a full skirt in a dark blue-gray fabric, and a long-sleeved blue shirt rolled up to just below her elbows, clothes very similar to those worn by Dorcas. Gustie wondered if these clothes, too, were government issue. Jordis greeted Gustie with an almost imperceptible nod. Then she murmured a greeting to the old woman, who reached up with both hands and patted the younger woman's cheeks tenderly.

"Granddaughter, you have been away a long time."

"Little Bull keeps me busy."

"It is good. You stay out of trouble that way. Thanks for the chickens."

Gustie felt invisible watching this exchange between the two women.

Before she could offer her own chair, Jordis pulled up the wooden crate that rested against the inside wall by the door and sat down at the table. She tore apart a piece of fry bread and laid a fish on each half. The food disappeared quickly. Gustie poured her a cup of coffee and sat down.

She could not take her eyes off Jordis, who proceeded to devour the remaining fish and fry bread. The young Indian woman's hands were strong and large, with long tapering fingers. Everything about her was strong, rock solid. Her every movement had a wholeness about it. Though it was only her hand that moved to grasp her coffee cup, or her arm that reached out for another piece of bread, her whole body was involved in each motion, not tensely, for she was perfectly relaxed, but with total awareness of what each part of itself was doing. Gustie had never seen a human body so *collected*. She had only observed that in horses and barn cats. And still the woman had not spoken one word to her since walking through the door. Clearly she had no meaningless pleasantries in her, no chitchat. Gustie had been around Dorcas long enough to not take offense at the lack of spoken words. Besides, something inside herself felt keenly spoken to. She felt like she was encountering a new language. Gustie was patient, and determined to learn it.

The tin platter was empty. "Would you like some more?" Gustie asked. "I could fry some eggs for you, too."

Jordis looked at her squarely and said, "Thank you. I am not hungry now." Jordis had no trace of the accent that colored Dorcas's speech—the *r*'s that sprawled across the back of her tongue, the soft thickening of the *th* sounds, the way she had of speaking through her teeth in a level pitch, like the steady lapping of Crow Kills against the shore.

Dorcas said, "Tell Little Bull it is a long time since he comes to visit me."

"He will come. The chickens are from him. We have been working on the new building. It is almost finished."

"My granddaughter is helping Little Bull with a new school building. But she is a stubborn child to me." The old woman shook her head and assumed a look of grief that was, Gustie felt, a little exaggerated. "She should not be making buildings. She should be teaching children."

A tightness took over Jordis's mouth, and her body became quite still. She responded in a low voice, "Little Bull knows I won't do that. He's stopped asking. I agreed to help him with his building so he would stop pestering me."

Gustie was interested. "Are you a teacher?"

"No. They want me to be a teacher. I am not a teacher."

"I teach at the section school between Charity and Wheat Lake," Gustie offered lamely.

"I know."

"Oh?"

"Grandmother speaks of you. She thinks you must be a very good teacher."

Gustie was pleased. She asked Dorcas, "Why do you think that?"

"Because you are a good learner."

Gustie felt childishly happy at this praise. "I didn't start out to become a teacher. But I do the best I can. Why don't you want to teach?" Gustie blushed. "I'm sorry. I shouldn't ask."

Dorcas spoke quickly. "No. It is good to ask. Granddaughter, tell Augusta Roemer why you do not teach Dakotah children."

If Jordis were a cat, thought Gustie, *her tail would be twitching dangerously right now.* Gustie regretted her question and was mystified by Dorcas's taunting manner.

"I just came back to visit with you. It's late. I am tired. I'll speak with you in the morning."

Gustie was alarmed. There were only two sleeping places in the little cabin, each nothing more than a straw mattress laid upon wood crates, and she was using one of them. "Please, let me sleep in my wagon tonight. I am taking up the place that should be yours."

"No, thank you. I don't sleep in here. I sleep outside, except in the dead of winter."

"But . . ."

"It is true," chimed in Dorcas, her eyes twinkling up a storm. "Even if you were not here, she would sleep outside in her little tent. She likes to play at being Indian."

Gustie thought that Jordis might have slammed the door but for very deeply inbred good manners. The door closed quietly behind her.

"She is stubborn." Dorcas smiled widely, showing perfect white teeth. "Just like me." Then she laughed heartily. The scene Gustie had just witnessed had been tense, full of anger, and yet here Dorcas was being quite merry. An infinite number of things had puzzled Gustie about this old Indian woman. This was just one more.

Gustie took out the pail of water that she had used to clean the supper things and dumped it in the grass. The white horse grazed by the sleeping tent Jordis had already put up. Gustie looked around for Biddie. She never tethered her out here. Sometimes she wondered if she should. What if something startled the mare, or what if she just got a horsey notion to take off? It had never happened. Biddie was right where Gustie expected her to be, standing over the pail of oats that sat in the wagon bed, quietly munching. She went to the mare and stroked her long neck. Biddie interrupted her snack to nuzzle nose to nose with the woman. "Goodnight, sweet lady." Out of the corner of her eye, Gustie saw a figure watching her from the edge of the stand of trees. But when she looked up, there was nothing.

Gustie took the empty pail down to the lake to rinse it out and bring back fresh water for the morning. When she returned to the cabin, Dorcas was already lying on her bed, facing the wall. Gustie undressed quietly, blew out the lamp, and crawled into bed. She removed her glasses last, folded them, and lay them on the window sill above her head.

The light from the lantern burned with a steady yellow glow. Gustie, blinking through sleepy, myopic eyes, thought, *I'm sure I blew that out.* Then she saw Jordis straddling a chair. A blanket, tucked under her arms, covered the front of her body. Her head was down. Dorcas stood behind her, rubbing something into her back which she dipped out of a small pot on the table. A pungent, spicy smell overpowered the redolence of fish in the cabin. Jordis lifted her head a moment and Gustie thought she beheld a look of pain and relief. Then Jordis put an arm across the top of the chair back and rested her forehead upon it. The blanket fell on that side, exposing one full breast as she relaxed into the chair. The light revealed a look on Dorcas's face Gustie could only have described as terrible, and it frightened her. She watched this scene until she drifted back into sleep and forgot the night vision.

Gustie woke to the sounds of gentle clucking beneath her and the aroma of fresh coffee. The clucking came from the chickens who pecked about in the crawl space under the cabin. She could hear them through the floorboards.

The coffee, she discovered when she poured out a cup for herself, was already half drunk. She dressed, tucked her blanket neatly around the straw mattress, and carried her cup outside.

The plants Dorcas had collected the day before were laid out on the porch.

Most had been taken roots and all. Some had tiny blossoms. At first glance they all looked alike to Gustie, but on closer examination she discovered differences in leaf shape, variations in color from light green to bluish gray, and leaf and stem textures that ranged from waxy to fuzzy and spiny. Still, it would take a keen eye to spot all these nuances in the field. Gustie was only beginning to appreciate the extent of Dorcas's knowledge of plants. The old woman had made her drink thin teas that stung, then numbed the back of her tongue; thicker brews that felt slick going down; others that tasted simply grassy. She had drunk them without question. She had recovered.

When the plants were arranged to Dorcas's satisfaction she took each one and deftly tied a string around the end of it. In the same order as they had been laid out, she hung them from nails that protruded along the inside of the porch overhang. When she finished, the porch roof had a fringe of green swaying prettily in the breeze, infusing the air currents with its fragrance.

From the bottom of her bag, Dorcas withdrew two stones, each a little smaller than her fist. Each had one rounded half, and the other half sharp-edged, as if it had been struck from a larger stone. Dorcas placed them side by side in her lap and considered them meditatively.

"What are they?" Gustie asked from her usual place on the step, where she sat reclined against the pole, sipping her coffee. Jordis was standing, leaning against the other support pole, her hands clasped behind her, eyes closed, her face windward. Gustie was distracted by her profile.

"Stones. Sacred," Dorcas said. "From the sacred rock."

"What sacred rock?" Gustie's attention flew back from Jordis to Dorcas.

"The sacred rock of my people. I go there. Maybe sometime I take you. Maybe. These were on the ground. They were broken off the top of the rock. They are a gift to me. Very sacred thing."

"What rock is this? Where is it?"

"It's over by the western tip of Shoonkatoh Lake." Jordis answered the question, opening her eyes and sitting down on the step across from Gustie. "The rock is huge and just sits out there in the middle of some pretty flat land all by itself. It has always been a sacred site."

Dorcas continued. "First the Black Robes, then the missionaries say it's bad to go to the sacred rock. Say there is no power in the sacred rock. No power in rocks." Dorcas paused to contemplate the stones again. "They should be hit by one sometime. Then they feel the power of rocks." She burst into laughter. Gustie laughed, and for the first time in Gustie's sight, Jordis smiled. Gustie felt the weather change.

Dorcas went on. "They think the only power places are churches they build. How can power be in a thing you build? Now, Big Sacred Rock. It is there. No Indian put it there. No white man put it there. But it is there. Put by Something. The power is there. It is very old. Very sacred place." She shook her head. "The white man is real smart about some things and real stupid about some things. Trouble is, you never know ahead of time, which."

Gustie laughed again. She had never seen Dorcas in such a merry mood. Jordis no longer smiled. Gustie wondered at the old woman's traveling regularly on foot the considerable distance between Crow Kills and Shoonkatoh.

A stone in each hand, Dorcas got up and went inside. A moment later she came out again, with the bundle that hung just inside the door. She squatted on the wood slats of the porch floor, carefully untied the leather thongs that bound each end of the bundle, then unrolled it slowly. It was a remnant of a blanket decorated with floral designs applied mostly in red paint. The piece was worn and faded now but its beauty was still apparent. As Dorcas began the unrolling, Jordis moved up to the porch and knelt opposite her to view the contents. Dorcas's face softened and lost a few of its years as the items appeared on the open blanket: a small piece of decorated leather roughly in the shape of a lizard, a stone spear point that looked old and very sharp still, a tiny cloth pouch gathered and tied at the top with sinew and feathers, a turtle shell, a bundle of porcupine quills, a piece of bone, a long narrow object that could have been a bone or a polished stick.

Dorcas picked up the shell and held it. "This is the shell of the turtle." It filled her open hand. "Turtle is strong medicine for me." She placed it down on the blanket and fingered the piece of decorated leather. "This is the cradle guardian of my first daughter." She laid it gently beside the turtle shell, her fingers lingering on the leather a moment before reaching for the next thing. "My grandfather's spear point." She contemplated it in a moment of silence, then laid it back down. She picked up the tiny cloth bundle with the feathers. "Tobacco bundle. Medicine man make for me. Oh, long time ago." She put it down and reached for the next thing. "Quills. Old things. Never did anything with 'em. Never throw away. Hm." Dorcas recited the contents of this bundle like a litany. Gustie was mesmerized.

Dorcas picked up the bone. "Buffalo bone." She pronounced it *buff-lo*. "All I have left of the buffalo. Pretty old."

"Tell me about the buffalo," asked Gustie softly. "I've never seen one except in a picture."

"Big shaggy walkers. Wouldn't think they could run so fast,

but they run very fast, against the wind." Dorcas put her head down and her hand went up in front of her, palm out, and she pantomimed pushing into a strong wind. "Always into the wind. Into a blizzard even. The calves are born red. Then they turn brown. Black tongues. Not pink like horses or dogs. Black. They run with their tongues out and their tails go *slap slap* up and down. Wouldn't think they could run so fast." Dorcas shook her head.

She laid the buffalo bone down and picked up the long narrow stick. She held it out for Gustie to see, but gave no invitation to touch. "Sacred whistle. Eagle bone. Was my uncle's. Stands By Himself. Carried it on his first sun dance."

"The sun dance?" Gustie questioned eagerly.

"Gone, with the buffalo. The Black Robes, then the missionaries, then gov'ment say we can't dance to the sun, our Father. It was a good thing, the dance. It made the people strong. When I was a small child I saw my uncle Stands By Himself in the sun dance. He danced a long long time in a brave and sacred manner. After, I followed him to the hills above our camp. We were up north then. I found him crying from the pain of his wounds. I gave him some water and some pemmican I brought with me, and some willow bark. He would not take them from anybody else, but he would not insult a child. So he took them and ate and drank. He was a brave man. Killed by the Rhee in battle. My uncle. Stands By Himself."

"Is this a medicine bundle?" Gustie asked. She had heard of such things being of great value to the Sioux.

"No, not real medicine bundle. Not real sacred bundle like some have. But good things to me. Good memories. A memory bundle. Sometimes good memories is good medicine." Dorcas laughed again. "A good place for sacred stones."

She laid the stones alongside the other things, rolled up the blanket, and tied it securely. Then she hung it back on its nail and seemed to forget about it.

• • •

Not since her illness had Gustie spent so much time at Crow Kills. During these long, warm, and easy days she felt a deepening peace come upon her that she had never known. And, there was Jordis.

Jordis taught her to fish. She taught her to recognize wild turnips and onions. Together they ranged over the prairie looking for these edible roots, which they scrubbed in Crow Kills and added to Dorcas's ever-simmering stews. Once they found a patch of dark leaves with telltale spots of red. Jordis reached beneath the leaves and plucked out a large red berry. "Look," she said. "Heart berries."

"That's a strawberry," said Gustie. "I've never seen them this early."

"Why do you call them strawberries? They look like hearts. Don't they? We call them heart berries."

"Yes, they do. They look just like hearts."

Jordis nipped off the end of the berry and swallowed it. She held the other half to Gustie's lips. "Very good for the blood," advised Jordis seriously.

Gustie snapped it up. "Really?"

"I have no idea," replied Jordis. They both laughed.

Not many of the berries were ripe. They left them for picking later.

With Jordis, Gustie experienced a curious sensation of timelessness that she could not explain, until one day she realized that Jordis never spoke of anything in her past. Nor did Gustie. Gustie was accustomed to not talking about herself, even with Lena. The people she knew in Charity went on and on about where they came from, the things they had done, never noticing that Gustie did not do the same. Now she had found a woman like herself, who never spoke of anything but the moment at hand. It gave her a sense, not unpleasant, of fluttering on an edge.

Jordis, who loved to take off on Moon and ride for hours all around the hills between Crow Kills and Shoonkatoh, was amazed that Gustie did not ride. When she offered to teach her that, too, Gustie shook her head. "I'll just break my neck and annoy my horse." So Jordis alternated riding Moon one day and Biddie the next, and both horses were kept in good condition. Biddie took to Jordis as if she had always known her.

One afternoon Gustie and Jordis were lakeside with their fishing poles and Gustie got a bite. By the feel of it she had caught something big. Her squeal brought Dorcas running down the bank with a bucket. The old woman tucked the hem of her skirt into her waistband and rolled up her sleeves before wading out into the water, ready to scoop Gustie's catch into the bucket as soon as she brought it in close enough. As Dorcas rolled up her sleeves, Gustie had a flash of recognition and almost dropped her pole and lost their supper. The mysterious lightning that she had seen repeatedly in her dreams when she was ill—it was there: white zigzag scars along the insides of Dorcas's arms. Of course. When Dorcas had cared for her, bathed her, her arms would have been exposed. Gustie would have seen those scars. In her delirium they had registered as lightning, for that is what they most resembled, zigzag gashes of lightning.

Dorcas happily bagged the fish and took it up to her workbench behind the cabin to clean it.

Gustie turned to Jordis. "What are those scars on her arms?"

"Very old." Jordis poured all her attention on her fishing line.

Gustie pressed her. "Did something happen to her as a child?"

"She was young, but not a child. She did it herself."

"Hurt herself like that? To leave scars like that?" Gustie was shocked.

"My ancestors thought that scars on the outside healed faster than those left to fester on the inside."

"What happened?"

"Her first husband and children all died. Smallpox. Her grieving was to cut herself. To feel the pain. To bleed. To make a flesh sacrifice. Many ways to look at it. As the wounds healed outside, they also healed inside. That was one of the theories, anyway. The spear point in her bundle—she did it with that."

"Do your people still do that? Self-inflict wounds like that?"

"Some, maybe. Not so many since the white man's religion has taken over. If they do it, they do it in secret, so I don't know. They've taken away the old ways. Many don't even remember them. I only know things that she has told me. She remembers a great deal."

"She doesn't talk much, except recently, since you've been here. Is she always like this with you?"

"No. I've noticed it, too. She is very—" Jordis was interrupted in midsentence by a tug on her pole. She pulled in another good-sized walleye—all they needed for their supper. They drew in their lines and went up to the cabin.

Twilight hovered over the lake a long time before giving way to darkness. The verdancy of trees and grasses slowly faded into shades of gray, indigo, and black. A lone cricket began tentatively its scratchy evening song.

Dorcas had been gone all day, perhaps gathering plants, perhaps visiting her sacred place.

Gustie had awakened from a late-afternoon nap to an empty cabin in which darkness was already gathering in the corners. She was wondering where Jordis was when a sound down by the lake, like the snapping of a branch, had called her outside. Barefoot, Gustie picked her way over the rocks and tufts of weeds down to the water's edge. Jordis was standing hip deep in the water, her back to the shore. She pulled off her shirt and draped it on an overhanging branch with the rest of her clothing; Gustie saw the shadows of the leaves playing on her broad bare back. Rushes, quickened by breeze and the stirrings of the water, swayed like an echo against the curves of Jordis's body.

Still making no sound, Gustie walked into the water, fascinated by the pattern that seemed to move on Jordis's back as she waded farther out into the darkening water. Strange—those leaf shadows dancing across Jordis's flesh. She was too far out from the trees now, and Gustie realized there was not enough light to cast a shadow on her dark skin. Something was there. The night she had seen Dorcas rubbing something on Jordis's back in the lamplight suddenly came back to her.

Jordis turned and saw Gustie staring at her. "If you are coming for a swim, you'd better take your clothes off."

Gustie looked down at the water already above her ankles and soaking rapidly up the fabric of her skirt. She unbuttoned the skirt, pulled it over her head, and tossed it on the branch next to Jordis's things. She did the same with her blouse and her shift. She tried stepping out of her bloomers without getting them wet and still maintaining some modesty, but was unsuccessful. She almost lost her balance on the slippery stones and got them soaked anyway. She thought she caught a look of amusement on Jordis's face. Gustie took a step forward, and another. Crow Kills was thrillingly cold as it rose up to her knees, her thighs, and when it reached her belly she sucked in her breath, panted a little, and continued to wade out. Her feet tingled as they pressed into the mossy lake bed. She kept wading till she was on a level with Jordis in waist-high water.

Gustie and Jordis were the same height, though built quite differently: Gustie, slender, with long arms and legs, small wrists, delicate bones; Jordis, broad, muscular, her hips and breasts full. Gustie thought there was a shining about Jordis—her skin, her hair, her eyes. Always a shining. Gustie often felt pale and drab next to her, and old. But she was not now conscious of herself at all. She put her left hand lightly on Jordis's left shoulder and gently turned her around so she could look at her back. She felt Jordis stiffen, but not resist.

Gustie shuddered and whispered, "Oh, my Christ."

Ridges of white flesh like twisted ropes formed a web of scar tissue that crisscrossed, biting into the smooth brown skin. What had looked like a shadow of dancing leaves was a hideous caricature of the leaf itself.

Gustie cupped her right hand, dipped into Crow Kills, and poured water slowly over Jordis's back. Jordis arched slightly, then relaxed.

"Does it hurt?"

"Sometimes. It gets tight, and pulls. Sometimes it itches. Sometimes it has no feeling at all. Water and Grandmother's ointment help. She says it's not as bad as it used to be. It was not treated properly . . . at first."

Gustie's left hand remained on Jordis's shoulder. With baptismal motions she continued to bathe Jordis's back.

"How did you get this?"

Jordis took a deep breath. The moon rose over Crow Kills and let fall a trembling beam across the water.

"I was nine years old and my brother George was twelve before we ever went to school.

"Our mother kept us hidden, but she couldn't hide us forever. The Indian agency got wind of us and we were picked up and hauled off to an Indian school run by a minister and his wife. A few other teachers. I didn't even mind going. I looked at it as an adventure. I had no idea of what was to happen except they told me I was going to learn to read books and I would come back to my mother when it was over.

"My brother was wild with fear. He was older—maybe knew more of what we were in for. I don't know. He turned sullen and wouldn't speak at all. A little kindness might have helped him get over it, but at the school, they saw his long hair and before they even spoke to us, or fed us, or let us rest, they had to have it off. His beautiful long hair. 'Here, little boys don't have long hair,' they said. 'Only little girls have long hair. You don't want to be like a little girl, do you?'

"They humiliated him. Then, in front of all of us, they cut off his hair." Jordis paused and Gustie continued pouring water over her shoulders, across the top of her back and the back of her neck. Jordis relaxed and put her head down as Gustie massaged the lake water into the ridged flesh. She kept her head down, her forehead lightly brushing Gustie's bare left shoulder, and went on softly, "That night, in the middle of the night, I got out of bed and found the kitchen. I took a knife, and I cut my hair off, too. When the matron saw me in the morning she started howling and pulled me in to see Everude. He was the preacher. I'll never forget him. An ugly red-faced man always in a black suit.

"It wasn't that they cared about my hair. Some of the girls had their hair cut when they came to the school. I guess they had lice. I had no lice! They didn't care about my hair—what made them mad was that I defied them. I did something on my own. An Indian! A girl. Those teachers and preachers . . . you know, they loved Indians all right as long as we were docile, like dogs, and showed we wanted to be like them. If we showed any resistance, they were no better than the soldiers who poured lead and whiskey into our fathers and grandfathers.

"I decided . . . I was only nine, but I decided, if they made my brother, a Dakotah, cut his hair, then I, his sister, a Dakotah, would cut mine too. They didn't understand it." Jordis's eyes had been nearly closed. Now they opened and followed the track of the moon across the water. "My brother is dead. He wasn't made for changes. It's easier for the women. The changes. The men couldn't do it. The whiskey. Always the whiskey."

"It's not only your people who have trouble with whiskey," Gustie said as she kept the water flowing on Jordis's back.

"Maybe not, but like everything else, it falls harder on us. I have kept my hair short. For my brother. I will always keep it short. For my brother's hair will never grow. So my hair will never grow long."

Gustie continued to bathe the outraged flesh of Jordis's back. Jordis's head rested a little heavier on Gustie's shoulder.

"They starved me all that day. The next day I started classes. I think I enraged Everude even more by being good at my studies. I learned English. We had to. They hit us if they heard us speaking Dakotah. I learned to read and I read everything and made a game of passing their tests. And every time my hair grew out a little, I hacked it off. After I'd been there about a year, Everude had had enough. He said I would be 'severely punished' if I ever did it again. Cut my hair. My hair had become the most important thing in his life, and in mine! He was a mean man, and I had no doubt that I would get a beating. Beatings were common there. Usually a few straps in the horse shed with a belt. I knew I could take it. The next morning I showed up at breakfast with my hair hacked off down to the roots. I was some sight!" Jordis chuckled and leaned into Gustie, balancing herself by resting her hand in the curve of Gustie's left arm.

Gustie continued to massage the cool water into her back.

"I didn't even get all the way through my bowl of oatmeal and piece of dry bread before he yanked me from the table and dragged me to the shed. He made me take my dress off and lie facedown on the floor. Then he beat me with a horsewhip, or some kind of whip."

Jordis's hand tightened on Gustie's arm. Gustie stopped her massage and held her in the lightest embrace. Jordis spoke her next words slowly, between her teeth. "I did not give him the satisfaction of making a sound." She paused and then went on. "He whipped me until I fainted and left me on the floor of the shed. Later, one of the teachers and the cook carried me to my bed and dressed the wound. He wouldn't let them call for a doctor. It didn't heal, and I got very sick. They thought I was dying and somehow the cook got word out to Grandmother. Why they were so afraid *I* would die, I don't know. The grave-yard out behind the school was full of dead Indian children. Grandmother came at night to see to me. The students and the teachers kept quiet about it. Only Everude didn't know she was with me almost every night. Obed Everude. He collapsed one day. They called in a doctor for him. Didn't do any good. Something wrong with his heart. I never saw him again after the beating."

"You must hate him."

"Not for what he did to me. What he did to my brother. George was a good boy. Would have been a good man. They broke him. Taught him just enough so he could read the label on a whiskey bottle. After two years he ran away from the school, started drinking, and got into a knife fight in Wheat Lake. He was killed. He was only fifteen.

"I guess I knew what was going to happen to him as soon as I saw his face on that day they cut his hair. That's why I fought so hard. I thought if I fought, if I resisted, it would carry us both through somehow. I studied too. I knew that to really fight them I'd have to know what they knew."

Jordis lifted her head up from Gustie's bare shoulder and said abruptly, "Let's swim," then ducked under the water. Her movement was so fast that Gustie was left standing in an em-brace with the darkness. She looked around for Jordis and grew alarmed when she did not surface immediately. Finally, Jordis's head emerged. She was treading water far out in Crow Kills.

"You're still there!" Jordis laughed and flashed a wide smile that caught a moonbeam, making her dazzle, as she had that first day on her pale horse in the sun.

"I don't swim."

"I'll have to teach you this, too. If you're going to live by a lake, you must swim."

Am I going to live by a lake? Gustie's head was swimming, even if she wasn't.

Gustie floated and splashed about, feeling childish, since she couldn't go any deeper, but she did not care. Every now and then she paused to watch Jordis swimming in deep water. Then Jordis disappeared, only to bob up again at her side, pushing back her black hair that streamed water over her face.

Gustie looked with dismay at her still-wet clothing hanging limply from the tree limbs above them. Jordis saw the look and touched her lightly on the arm. "Stay here."

Gustie stood obediently and watched Jordis stride out of the water and slip up the bank into the cabin. She returned with a blanket wrapped about her under her arms, and another she held open for Gustie.

She comes to me in the water. Walking slowly into the water she comes to me. Like a frightened, brave white bird she comes to me. She touches me and I give her my story. She could have anything of me. All my stories. The ones told, those still only dreamed. Ahh. All the dreamed stories are hers.

Gustie lifted her head from the nightgown. She hesitated and then, with a feeling of protective tenderness, removed the gown from its hanger and folded it carefully. She opened the trunk that rested at the foot of her bed. She did not often look into this trunk. It was full of smallish dresses in light pretty colors, some books of poetry, one of which lay open. Gustie turned it over and read from the last lines of the poem on the open page: *She has a lovely face; God in his mercy lend her grace.* She did not finish it but turned the book over, still open, and facedown again upon the clothing. Then she laid the folded gown over the book and closed the trunk.

She was afraid to wait any longer. It was only a matter of time before he found her little house. She left and did what she had never before felt she had to do out here in this Dakota land: she locked her door.

Lena stood before the mirror. The blue dress she wore had been hanging clean and pressed in her closet. She had ironed it again this morning. Four years ago she had made this dress from the best piece of cloth she could afford. Why spend all that time working on something if it wasn't good to start with? So she bought the best, and took two weeks to sew it, borrowing her mother-in-law's sewing machine for the long seams and doing the rest by hand, in tiny, even stitches. The bodice was softly gathered at the waist. She had inset a narrow lace collar not called for in the pattern. She never followed a pattern except in the basic form of a garment. All the finishing touches were her own—a few more gathers for softness, an added bit of lace at the neck or sleeve, a sash or a belt to dress a thing up or down. One dress would last her for years and never look exactly the same twice.

This morning she had tied a small fabric rose at the neck, but it was too much. "This is no party I'm going to," she muttered, and threw the rose on the bed. Nevertheless, she was determined not to look somber, either, as if she had anything to be ashamed of, or anything to fear. She was a respectable woman and was going to look respectable, and that was that. She settled on the dress, plain, with no flowers, a simple belt in matching fabric. The blue dress brought out the cornflower in her eyes and highlighted the natural rose of her cheeks. *I still have my complexion,* she thought. *Staying out of the sun does it. Not like Ma Kaiser, nasty old brown thing.*

She held her handkerchief in one hand and her pocketbook in the other, then laid them down to run a comb through her hair, even though it was already perfect, lying in auburn waves about her head. She picked up the handkerchief, a plain white linen square around which she had crocheted a scalloped edge, tucked the purse once more under her arm, and approved her reflection. She went into the kitchen to pour a cup of coffee. It was seven-thirty. The hearing was not until ten o'clock.

She pulled her dress smoothly about her before she sat. Her Bible lay on the kitchen table and she opened it to the Beatitudes.

Blessed are the poor in spirit: for theirs is the kingdom of heaven. Blessed are they that mourn: for they shall be comforted. Blessed are the meek: for they shall inherit the earth . . .

She read the eleven verses in the book of Matthew, and read them again, trying in vain to dull the edges of her anxiety. Then she turned to her favorite Psalm, which never failed to bring comfort:

I will lift up mine eyes unto the hills, from whence cometh my help. My help cometh from the Lord, which made heaven and earth. He will not suffer thy foot to be moved: he that keepeth thee will not slumber. Behold, he that keepeth Israel shall neither slumber nor sleep. The Lord is thy keeper: the Lord is thy shade upon thy right hand. The sun shall not smite thee by day, nor the moon by night. The Lord shall preserve thee from all evil: he shall preserve thy soul. The Lord shall preserve thy going out and thy coming in from this time forth, and even for evermore.

Divine assurances helped but did not completely alleviate her desolation, her longing for human comfort. Where was everybody? No one from Will's family had called upon her. No one from her own. She had not personally notified her family, but news traveled like prairie fire in Stone County. Gustie was the only one she could count on, and now she had disappeared again. Where in Sam Hill did she go all the time? Lena peered through her curtains at the overcast sky. She really didn't need gloomy weather on top of everything. The Kaisers' excuse would be Pa's funeral preparations. She didn't know how she was going to get through this day. Still clutching her handkerchief, she rubbed the space between her brows. There was a light rapping at her door.

Now who in blazes? Before she could get up, the door opened and Tori walked in, in his baggy farm clothes, smelling like he hadn't scraped his shoes well enough after morning chores in Peterson's barn. She put her arms around him, crying, "Oh, Tori. I'm so glad. So glad you're here. Here, take your shoes off. Leave them on the porch. I'll clean them for you later."

"Mr. Peterson give me the day off. Come to go with you." Torvald was twenty-two, with mouse-brown hair and fair skin. He was small and looked too delicate for farm work. Lena worried about him all the time.

Except for his shoes, Tori looked clean and scrubbed. His fly-about hair was plastered to the top and sides of his head with oil. He looked like a boy playing at being a man. Torvald Halverson was what folks called simple. No one could say what was missing in Tori. He could read and write. He could follow orders. He could be left alone with farm chores; the animals would be well looked after, everything kept clean and in good repair. He was scrupulously honest and could be sent to town for supplies and return with an exact accounting of purchases and change. But without a specific task at hand, he would most likely be found just sitting and smiling to himself. Lena had often wondered if her brother was a saint or an idiot. Growing up he had endured teasing from other children and remained good-natured and pleasant. The only one who had never teased him, even among their own siblings, was his big sister Lena, and his devotion to her was canine.

Lena had found a good situation for him. Ole and Agnes Peterson gave Tori a little pocket change, a room in the back of their house, all he could eat, and Agnes washed and ironed his clothes. In return he worked hard doing everything they asked of him.

But the Petersons were not young. When they died, Tori would be on his own again. The Peterson place would go to their son-in-law, who was not likely to keep him on.

Lena tried to hold off that worry till the time came. By then she hoped Will would have enough business to take Tori on himself. Then she could look after him.

"Have some coffee. Here, sit down." She pulled out the chair and pushed him down into it.

He drank his coffee the same way Lena sometimes drank hers: pouring some in his saucer to cool, putting a spoonful of sugar in his mouth, and sipping the cooled coffee from the saucer.

Lena sat down again. "It's supposed to start at ten o'clock. But I don't know. I just can't seem to . . ." She was at a loss to describe her feelings, knowing her duty was to be by her husband, but not being able to face a courtroom and the hungry eyes of the curious.

Tori's eyes were full of sympathy. "You look nice, Lena."

"I don't . . . I don't think I can go, Tori." Her elbow rested on the table and she put her head in her hand to keep from crying.

"Well, I'll go. You don't have to. I'll go for you." He slurped the dregs from his saucer. "That's it then. I better get these shoes cleaned, huh?"

"Have you had anything to eat?"

"*Ja,* Mrs. Peterson fed me good before I left." Tori went out in the shanty and scraped his shoes, then brushed them thoroughly. When he finished, he came back for some more coffee.

"Well, I better go now." It was nine-thirty. "Don't worry, I'll tell Will you're okay, and I'll be right back to tell you everything. Don't you worry now."

He patted her back awkwardly and left her sitting at her kitchen table, unable to speak, tears rolling down her cheeks, sucking the tip of her finger.

Two hours later, Lena still hadn't moved. Her coffee was cold, the stove had gone out, pages had been turned in her Bible, but she couldn't concentrate. The door was opening again. She hadn't even noticed who came up the driveway. Probably Tori with his sympathetic eyes, which she appreciated and couldn't bear, telling her the latest bad news. She didn't look up.

"Hey, Duchy, what's for dinner?"

Will stood in the kitchen, his hat in his hand, grinning.

Lena didn't believe her eyes. She sat still.

"Well, I guess we'll have to go to Olna's to get us a bite to eat then." He slapped his thigh with his hat.

"Oh, Will!" She hurled herself at him. He lifted her off the floor and waltzed her around and around the kitchen. "They let you go?"

"Nope, but I can walk around a free man until the trial." Only then did Lena notice the two men waiting patiently in her shanty, both grinning from ear to ear. "Oh, for heaven sakes! Tori. Pard? Come in here."

"Pard spoke up good to the judge and got me off on bail. The judge said he didn't usually post bail in a case of murder but Pard said it was all . . . eh . . . circumstantial. And what with that and me being a married man, and Pa's funeral this afternoon, he set the bail."

Lena's eyes fluttered nervously from the lawyer to her husband. "How much bail?"

"Thousand dollars."

Lena felt sick. She lowered her head and stood close to Will, speaking softly, "We don't have any money."

Pard Batie stepped forward. "That's been taken care of, Mrs. Kaiser."

"What do you mean, taken care of?" Nobody said a word. "Well, for heaven sakes." Oscar, Walter, Frederick. For once in their lives they'd done the decent thing. She could hardly believe it but she was grateful. She and Will would probably spend the rest of their lives paying them back, but right now she didn't care.

Pard stuck out his hand. Will engulfed it in his own and shook it heartily. "Will, I'll be talking to you," the lawyer said. "Come to my office on Monday. You come along now too, missus."

Lena nodded.

"Bye now, Tori."

"Bye now." Tori grinned and nodded as Pard went out the door.

Lena bustled. Will had asked for dinner. Here it was twelve o'clock and nothing ready. She tied her apron on and carried her Bible into the dining room with a whispered "Thank you, oh Lord."

She came back into the kitchen, took the bacon out of the icebox, then stripped off slices and laid them in the skillet. "Oh, what am I doing?" she said aloud as the bacon lay there, silent in a cold pan. She reached for the box of matches that sat on the back rim of the cookstove: empty. "Gustie did our shopping. I forgot to tell her we needed matches." She held the empty matchbox in her hand and began to cry.

"Oh, now here." Will reached into his pants pocket and took out a couple of long stick matches and handed them to Tori. "Dennis allowed me a smoke once in a while. I still got these left." As Tori slipped around Lena to light the stove, Will pulled her to him. Her head hardly reached his chest. "See, I'm gone just a couple days and everything goes haywire," he chuckled. "No matches. No nothing."

Lena raised her head, still crying. "It would have been nothing if it hadn't been for Gustie! I had nothing here! You left me with nothing all right, so don't go talking!" She made a fist and thumped him hard on his chest.

Will took her blow and brought her in close to him again. "Sure, sure. I know. I know. There now, Duchy." She sobbed until the grease began to pop, then she pushed him away. She didn't trust Tori not to burn the bacon.

"Oh, it's all right. Go sit down now." She took her handkerchief out of her pocket and blew her nose and wiped her eyes. "Tori, take the plates, will you, and set the table. You know where things are." She waved in the general direction of the cupboards.

She made the coffee and turned the bacon. She sliced an entire loaf of the bread and put it on the table along with butter and jam. "It sure smells good." Will smiled at her. "Olna's a good cook, but not like you, Duchy."

Tori nodded in agreement. "Nope, not like you."

She broke eggs into the sizzling bacon fat and fried them the way Will liked them—crisp and brown around the edges and soft in the middle—and slid them onto a platter alongside the bacon. When the platter was full, she brought it to the table. The coffee perked furiously and she moved the pot to the cool side of the stove to finish.

"How'd you get in today, Tori?" Will asked between mouthfuls. "Ole bring you?"

"Yup. Ole brung me."

Lena realized she had forgotten to wonder how Tori had made it in to town, but now she asked, "How'd you get home here? Pard?"

"Pard's buggy," said Tori. "Sure is a nice one."

"Yup, that Pard—boy, he sure talks a good one." Will made an enthusiastic arc with his fork. "Don't he, Tori?"

"Yup, he talks a good one." Tori grinned at Lena reassuringly, his mouth full and his chin shiny with bacon grease.

Lena poured the coffee. "When is the trial?"

"In a month or so, I guess. Next time Judge Pike comes around. Pard says that's long enough to make a good case. He says nobody's much interested in prosecuting me anyway. Nobody thinks I did it."

"Well, I should say not." Lena sniffed. She was nibbling a piece of bread and sipping coffee. She had no appetite.

"Pard says he tried to get us a dismissal. Lack of evidence. But the judge wouldn't go for it. Pard says Pike just wants a trial because he never gets to have one because nothing ever happens around here. He wants something just to chew on, you know. Give everybody a go. But nothing's gonna come of it because there isn't any evidence. Me walking out of a barn ain't real evidence. That's what Pard says."

Lena listened, secure for the moment in Will's confidence, happy to see her nearest and dearest at her table. Her dark thoughts thinned to shadows.

When Will had sopped up the last of the yellow yolk on his plate with his bread and washed it down with the last mouthful of coffee, he pushed himself away from the table. "Well, we've got to see Pa buried."

Lena felt the darkness thickening around her again. She slowly untied her apron, and hung it in its place. Then she picked up her pocketbook and handkerchief and went with him. Tori followed.

They trotted the ten blocks up Main Street to Gethsemane Lutheran, a plain white church with a steeple and a brand-new bell. Inside, white walls contrasted with dark-stained pews and an altar and pulpit in middle-aged oak. Gethsemane boasted one stained glass window above the baptismal font in the back of the church.

In the tiny narthex they came face to face with the casket, closed. There were candles set around it and a vase of spring flowers, which Lena supposed were from Mary's garden.

Lena assumed this funeral would be the same as every other at Gethsemane and she led them to the pastor's office. *Good grief, they've squeezed everybody in here but Julia's cat,* she thought as she peered into the cramped room. Though all heads were bowed as Pastor Erickson intoned a prayer, Lena sensed an edginess in the room and felt that all present were very much aware of their arrival. Not one to disrupt a prayer to the Almighty, she bowed her head, shut her eyes, and folded her hands reverently. Will lowered his head and clasped his hands in front of him, but he did not close his eyes. While Lena went every Sunday without fail, and twice a week during Lent, he was not a churchgoer. The last time he'd been to church was for a funeral, he couldn't remember whose.

The prayer ended and the pastor said in his well-modulated baritone, "Now if you'll all gather in the narthex and follow the casket in during the first hymn." He made his way among the family, none of whom seemed to know what to do next in spite of his instructions. "Glad to see you here, Will . . . Lena. How are you, Tori?" He shook hands firmly with each of them. "Our prayers are with you."

Will knew the man meant well, but he found his manner embarrassing. It made him want a drink. The minister disappeared to don his pastoral robes for the service.

Frederick was the first to break from the flock of baffled Kaisers and come forward. He was the only brother tall enough to see eye to eye with Will. They shook hands. "Glad you're out. They shouldn't have arrested you in the first place. I guess Dennis didn't know what else to do." Everyone nodded more or less in agreement and the tension eased. Frederick held his arm out for Gertrude, who ignored Lena and patted Will's arm as she passed. Walter, the next to move, bleated solemnly, and Mary smiled rather furtively at Lena as she followed her husband out. Oscar grumbled his greeting in passing, then he and Nyla were out the door, leaving behind only Julia, who took Will's hand and then Lena's in turn quite warmly. "How are you, dear?"

"I'm fine now, Julia. Thank you."

Julia nodded and as she patted the top of Lena's hand, Lena felt the wad of string that held the opal ring in place.

The piano had already begun to sound. Mrs. Happy, wisps of her gray hair escaping in all directions from the roll she carefully tucked around her head every day, pounded out the opening chords of the Lutherans' battle hymn, "A Mighty Fortress Is Our God." A sound wave broke through the church as pews and bodies creaked and throats cleared; the congregation stood and began to sing.

Six men bore the casket to the front of the church. Right behind it, Frederick, the only single son, escorted Gertrude at the head of the family. Then, two by two, came Walter and Mary, Oscar and Nyla, Will and Lena. Julia and Tori brought up the rear. The family turned left into the two front pews. The pallbearers lowered the casket onto a wooden platform at the foot of the altar steps.

A decent number had turned out to pay their final respects to Frederick William Kaiser—mostly older folks who had known him a long time, people whose first wells he had sunk in the early homesteading days. Younger people, friends and acquaintances of the sons, were divided about whether to show up at the funeral. Lena suspected most of them came out of curiosity. The church was nearly full.

The service was simple and strangely empty of emotion. Will was the only one who appeared moved by his father's death. Very early in the service he covered his face with one hand and Lena wondered if he was going to break down, but he did not. He carried himself with dignity, and, for once she was proud of him.

The thoughts of the congregation rose to mingle in the rafters with the hymns, liturgy and prayers, and the scent of burning candles—surmises about who was responsible for the body of the old man lying, somewhat prematurely, in that wooden box; the belief that Will could not be guilty; the conviction that it must have been some stranger passing through, someone who had gotten off the train, found the empty barn to hide out in and rest. Maybe tried to get some money off Pa Kaiser when he, perhaps, heard a noise and went to check the barn. There was a struggle, perhaps. The whole thing could have been an accident, but the fellow—the stranger—had got scared and run, got on the next train out. Folks accepted the fact that they might never know for sure and took comfort in the conclusion that it could not be one of their number.

Will himself had come to the same conclusion. At first he had blamed himself for being so drunk he could not prevent the killing. But soon enough he realized that had he not been drunk, he would not have been in the barn in the first place, and therefore still could not have prevented it. Neither Lena nor any of his brothers knew that Will was accustomed to sleeping off his drunks in there. He always tried to get to the barn before he passed out somewhere else. It saved him a night in jail. Will was not a man for introspection, and once that last idea had formed, his feeling resolved into simple grief, unmixed with regret.

Lena maintained her composure until Magda Nilsen stood up to sing "The Old Rugged Cross," a hymn that always made Lena cry. Except today. Magda's throbbing soprano filled the church solemnly with the opening lines:

On a hill far away
Stands an Old Rugged Cross
The emblem of suffering and shame.

But as she launched into the next stanza,

How I love that old Cross
Where the dearest and best
For the sake of lost sinners was slain,

her exaggerated vibrato, supported by an overlarge bosom that heaved and rolled with religious fervor under dangerously taut gray silk, began to massage each word, as if she had been there only yesterday, at the feet of her bleeding Lord. By the time she reached the first chorus—

And I'll cling to the Old Rugged Cross
Till at last my life I lay down.
I will cherish the Old Rugged Cross
And exchange it some day for a crown.—

Magda was perspiring, her chubby hand beating emotional time in the air, and Lena had the giggles.

Lena, a devout Christian, was smothering herself in her hankie. Will, knowing very well that his wife was not choking on grief, put his arm around her and pulled her head against his chest. Somehow they both got through three verses, three choruses, and a key change into the fifth-chorus finale, after which Magda, spent, puffing, and thoroughly satisfied, sat down. Pastor Erickson, furiously polishing his glasses, stepped up to the pulpit for the benediction. He hooked the wires carefully over his ears and kept his head down for just a moment before he raised his head and his hand:

The Lord bless thee, and keep thee:

Lena wiped her eyes and controlled herself. She liked the benediction. She liked the minister's hand raised in blessing over the congregation. She bowed her head, angry with Magda and whoever it was who had asked her to sing. *Probably Nyla. She wouldn't know any better, the dumb cluck.*

The Lord make his face shine upon thee, and be gracious unto thee: The Lord lift up his countenance upon thee, and give thee peace.

On cue, Mrs. Happy, all stops pulled, hit the chords of the closing hymn. The congregation rose and began to sing, "Holy, holy, holy, Lord God Almighty." The pallbearers moved to the front and hoisted the coffin upon their shoulders. They were followed out by the pastor, then the family, in the same order as they had come in.

Beneath a lowering sky that made Lena think of dingy, uncarded wool, they slid the coffin onto the bed of a small wagon pulled by a single black horse and driven by Rudi Molvik, the undertaker.

Except for Mary and Nyla, who went back to Ma's to prepare a lunch for the mourners, the family squeezed together on the slat seats of Gertrude's wagon, Oscar driving, his mother and Walter in the front, Will, Lena, Julia, and Tori crammed onto the second seat and holding on while they bumped along behind the hearse. No one spoke. Lena wished she'd worn a hat.

The cemetery was a fenced acre of land donated to the town of Charity by the Hansmeyer family. About two-thirds of it had been consecrated for Protestant burial, and one-third for Catholic. Lena had never understood why the Catholics needed their own specially prayed-over soil. When you got right down to it, Lena thought, dirt was dirt.

The grave diggers had done their work neatly: a rectangular hole with perfectly squared corners gaped in the earth, and the pile of black dirt was discreetly covered by canvas weighted down at the corners with rocks.

Oscar pulled the wagon around so that Gertrude had her back to the open grave and would not see the coffin being lowered. Even with only one arm, he managed a team of horses skillfully. Lena had seen him, on occasion, hold the reins between his teeth when he needed his hand for something else. At those times his expression changed from his usual bad-tempered sullenness to a fierceness that was disconcerting.

When the coffin had been lowered and the ropes hauled up and laid out of sight in the undertaker's wagon, they all gathered around the grave, except for Gertrude who refused to get down. Lena heard her muttering "*Ach, Gott in Himmel.*" Gertrude always talked to herself in German.

Frederick assisted Julia down from the wagon and she remained on his arm through the brief graveside service. The sky was darkening by the minute. Pastor Erickson spoke the prayers as rapidly as he decently could. Only then did Lena notice that Julia was holding flowers in her hand. She had not seen her take them from the vase in the narthex, but she must have, since she didn't have them with her in church. During the Lord's Prayer, Lena for some reason kept her eyes on Julia, waiting for her to toss the flowers into the grave. But when the prayer was over, her arm still looped through Frederick's arm, Julia turned, with the flowers, and walked back to the wagon.

The dingy wool sky gave no sign that it was either going to release its downpour or move on. The weather seemed stuck. There was no wind. The clouds did not churn. They hung low, like the underbelly of a pregnant ewe unable to give birth.

A murmur of voices and the aroma of coffee perking in two large enamel pots on the cookstove filled the dark ambiance that met Lena and Will as they stepped across the threshold of Ma Kaiser's house. The windows, as always, were heavily curtained. Someone had lit a lamp here and there, but these little lights were not up to dispelling such gloom. Nor did the gathering of people lighten the place. In their dark clothing, sitting, standing, or milling around, the people seemed saturated with the atmosphere of this house, like a sponge full of dark water. The men's white shirts alleviated nothing. Only Lena, in her blue dress, bobbed along, surrounded but untouched. A kind of euphoria shielded her and buoyed her. For the moment, she felt pleasantly disposed toward everyone. Even for her sisters-in-law, whom she usually regarded as gnats—irksome, but inevitable on a summer's day—she managed a warm greeting, first for Nyla, who was slicing a pie and looking unhappy as always, no matter what the occasion, and then for Mary. Sweet Mary never spoke her mind, seldom went out, and when she did was never alone, and frequently consigned to the shadow formed by Walter's cigar smoke. Right now she was carrying a small porcelain pot she had just filled with coffee from one of the pots on the stove.

Lena and Will followed her into the dining room where food was laid on for a multitude. Neighbors and friends had brought a variety of cakes and pies. There were also hot meat and potato dishes, cold chicken, a ham, plenty of bread and butter. The coffee flowed in a constant stream and the cream pitcher was kept brimming from the jug in the icebox.

Lena noticed the clean tablecloth and attributed that nicety to Mary. It couldn't be Ma's, and Nyla, who was as slovenly as her mother-in-law, would not have thought of it.

For Lena not to have had a part in the preparation of such an affair was unusual. She found herself with most of the work at all family doings. This time, however, because of Will's trouble, she hadn't been involved and was grateful that no one expected anything of her.

Oscar, Walter, and Frederick, who had followed Will and Lena into the house, dispersed into the gathering. Ma took to her rocker and began accepting condolences. Julia busied herself in the kitchen, washing plates and taking over for Mary in the supervision of the coffee pots, her little cat never far from her feet and the dish of cream she had put down for him in the corner. Tori sat at the kitchen table out of the way and happily accepted a large slice of angel food cake from Mary. On her way into the dining room with a bowl of stiff cream she had just whipped, Mary stopped and dropped a spoonful on his cake. Lena helped herself to a piece of apple pie and a cup of coffee. She found a vacant chair in the corner of the dining room, from where she could see into both the kitchen and the living room. She enjoyed watching her brother, who let the cat lick some of the cream off his fingers. Tori took after their pa in that way, always indulgent toward animals. Will piled a plate with ham, chicken, and cake for his mother, then one for himself. After that Lena lost track of him.

Lena took small uninterested bites of her pie and sipped her coffee while she observed the flow of people through the house, a mass without detail, like the surge and retreat of inlet water. A person or event would individuate for a moment, like a wavelet on the surface of Lena's consciousness, then sink back and merge into the dark waters. Walter: glad-handing, puffing on his cigar, his gravelly voice cutting through the din, his square face thick behind heavy glasses and crowned by an oily stand of coarse, prematurely yellowish gray hair. Even here, at his father's funeral, he had to talk business and make jokes, though he was never funny, just goofy, Lena thought. Will was the only Kaiser with a real sense of humor. Anyway, this wasn't the place for it.

Oscar emerged, larger, more brooding than Walter, lodging first in one chair, then another, unable to get comfortable, speaking seldom and only when spoken to. About as funny as a hailstorm on a good day. Nyla appeared again, venturing out of the kitchen to exchange a newly cut pie for an empty plate on the table. Her perpetually sour expression made her look older than Lena, though she was not. Her long thin hair was twisted into a tight braid and wrapped around her head in an unbecoming style. She wore shapeless clothes over a bottom-heavy body and clumped around in the same heavy shoes winter and summer. In winter, Lena thought, she must ache with the cold, and in summer, from the heat.

Mary followed Nyla with the cream jug and filled the pitcher. No matter what, Mary looked nice. Her clothes were well made, always crisp and new. She favored floral prints. With her dark hair and eyes, creamy skin, and high color on her cheeks, Mary had something of the rose about her, Lena thought, albeit a rose without thorns.

Magda Nilsen, a larger wave than the others, washed up at the table slavering thick yellow cream over a hunk of chocolate cake.

Pastor Erickson surfaced long enough to have a cup of coffee and a final word with Gertrude. She seemed not to hear him.

Frederick darted from person to person like a tadpole, neither fish nor frog, at home in the water though, unruffled, accepting condolences with a serious and grateful face.

Lena saw the tall, lanky form of Iver Iverson enter the kitchen bringing a fresh jug of cream and a small cake. Julia took the cake from him and brought it into the dining room, where she lingered to rearrange things on the table. Mary put the cream jug in the icebox. "We're getting low on ice," she said to no one in particular. Tori jumped to his feet. "I'll get you a chunk. You bet. Don't let anyone take my cake."

Mary smiled. "Don't worry. It will be here when you get back." Feather slipped out the door with him, hoping, no doubt, for more cream.

The icehouse took shape and floated along the top of a wave, and Pa himself, because he was linked in her mind to the icehouse, and until then had been lost amidst Lena's worries and troubles, now came into focus. He had built it right after he bought this place. That was a long time ago. Pa had always taken care of it. Twice every winter he and his sons went out to Marble Lake to cut blocks of ice. The boys would cut, load, and unload the ice, but Pa personally laid the blocks into the icehouse just so. He spread fresh straw between the layers for insulation and to keep the blocks from sticking together. Most of the interior of the icehouse was underground, and it was his careful arrangement, he said, that guaranteed the ice would last all summer, to the next freeze. Even after he had passed the well business on to his sons, he continued to look after the icehouse. Now that Pa was gone, the job would fall to the boys. *They won't be as meticulous as Pa was, that's for sure,* thought Lena.

Pa Kaiser had been a quiet man. Since his retirement he always wore black suits, shabby but well brushed. Where Ma was a giant unmade bed, Pa was spare and neat. Lena had heard rumors of his mean-spirited youth, but he had always been kind to her. She began to feel the first twinge of grief for him, when Tori came back with a large chunk of ice gripped in heavy tongs. Even under his ruddy, sun-and-wind-beaten face, he looked pale. He slid the ice into the icebox, dropped the tongs, with a clank, and sat down. His breathing was labored. Lena put down her pie and coffee and went into the kitchen to see what was wrong with him. Julia came back in with empty plates and stacked them at the sink. "What's the matter?" She saw Tori trembling.

Lena said, "I suppose he's hauled a chunk of ice that was too heavy for him and he's sprained something."

Julia rallied instantly and waved Lena away. "Go sit down and take it easy. You don't need anything else to worry about. I'll take care of him." Julia leaned over Tori. "That's right, I suppose," she said. "You lifted too much? You should have had one of the boys help you." She poured him a glass of milk and sat next to him, speaking to him soothingly, until he began to recover himself a little. Frederick entered the kitchen and put a solicitous hand on Tori's shoulder. Lena, satisfied that her brother was getting the proper attention, wandered back to the dining room. She looked around for Will. She didn't see him. Ma's rocking chair was empty. Probably went to the toilet, she thought.

Lena had slipped back into her near-trance state, little concerned about what was happening around her, smiling and nodding when spoken to, and was moving vaguely toward the back of the house, when she heard Ma Kaiser roar. Then she heard a thud.

She opened the screen door to see Ma standing like a steam engine just come to a stop. Her heavy face was purple, and her arms, which because of her weight could never hang down straight at her sides, were curved even more, as if she were ready to grapple.

Walter was backed up against the side of the house as if flung there, his thick spectacles askew. He held his hand to the side of his face. "Ma," he whined. "Why'd you go and do that?"

Lena snapped out of her dreamy state and stood poised on the threshold, all eyes and ears. Ma had actually struck Walter on the day of Pa's funeral. Even for Ma, it was unbelievable.

"You dare—today." Ma was huffing and puffing with rage, and the exertion of her blow, which from the looks of Walter, himself a stocky strong man, had been powerful.

"I didn't mean nothing by it. Just a little drink." He rubbed his face.

So, Ma had caught Walter drinking.

Looking past Walter and Gertrude, Lena saw Will in the backyard looking shamefaced. Without a word, she stepped down the porch steps to offer her unspoken support: *I don't blame you for your family. Never did.* Will turned away, and she detected the faint smell of whiskey on his breath.

Lena barely registered the wail issuing from her brother-in-law: "Mary! Mary! Come on! Let's go home." Or the door slamming as Gertrude stormed back into the house. She was reeling. Ma had slapped Walter, not because he was drinking—Walter never got drunk—but because he had given Will a drink, and everyone knew Will's problem with liquor. Lena automatically thought the worst of Ma Kaiser; now she had the unfamiliar sensation of being on Ma's side of things. She felt like punching Walter herself. But she couldn't do better than her mother-in-law had just done.

Mary appeared at the door. Lena waved her hand toward Walter as if she were shooing a horse fly. "Take him home. Get him out of here. I'll help clean up."

Mary, puzzled, but accustomed to doing what she was told, took Walter by the arm and led him to their buggy.

Lena turned her back on Will and went back into the house.

In the kitchen, Tori's chair was empty, his cake still only half eaten, his glass of milk half drunk. Julia said, "He went out for a walk with Frederick. He just needed some fresh air. It is very close in here."

Lena found an apron and began to wipe the dishes that stood draining on the sideboard. That done, she headed out back to retrieve some cups she had seen left on the porch.

Oscar was leaning out over the railing. Will was still in the back yard talking to some folks who were just leaving. Since Walter had gone and Ma had returned to the matriarchal rocking chair, Lena was greeted by a peaceful scene and she sighed in relief, but too soon.

Lena saw Julia's cat sidling around the corner of the porch. Feather passed too close to her brother-in-law. Oscar kicked him savagely. The animal flew over the rail with a *yeowl* that brought Julia running. The cat landed on his side, righted himself and shook his head, then gingerly took one step to see if everything still worked. Julia saw him and shrieked, the dishes she carried smashed on the floorboards of the porch.

Will sank to one knee and picked up the cat tenderly, cradling him in big hands. "Okay, little pal," he soothed. "Okay." He carefully felt for broken bones. "Oscar, you didn't need to go and do that."

"Goddamn cat doesn't belong over here. Pissing up a stink on everything. Gets underfoot."

"Still no call to do that." Will was the only one who spoke a reproach to his brother. Except for Lena, everyone else was afraid of Oscar's rages.

"Here you go." Will handed the cat to Julia, who took her pet tearfully to her breast. "He's okay. Just roughed up."

"Little Kitty Feather. Sweet little Kitty Feather." Julia cried like a child. Her porcelain complexion reddened with emotion. She paused a moment and stared at Oscar. Lena thought she saw pure hatred rest upon Julia's face before she turned and left for the safety of her own house.

Oscar only grinned and shook his head. "She's nutty as a goddamn fruitcake. Always was."

"You're a mean man, Oscar Kaiser," Lena said to him, and went down the steps to join Will. No matter how mad she got at her husband, or how many times he disappointed her, there was at his core the kindness that she loved, and would love till the day she died.

The house was quiet except for the gentle sloshing of water and clink of dishes. Lena looked out through Gertrude's kitchen window and wondered what it had been like for her to stand there every day, all those long years, with Julia's house filling her frame of vision.

Her mother-in-law was in the dining room gathering up leftovers, scraping plates and bringing them to Lena to wash. Even though Lena had volunteered to finish the cleaning up herself, Ma had insisted: "I feel better to do something."

Julia's white house looked gray under the dark sky that was just beginning to grumble. Inside Gertrude's house, all the lamps in the kitchen and dining room were lit and turned up high, though it was only six o'clock.

The rain would come soon now, and Lena wished she were in her own tidy house, curled up next to Will. She wondered—there was an uncomfortable buzzing in her stomach—if Will had gone home. She had sent him off, saying Frederick would give her a ride home later. But she was afraid: that one drink might plunge him into a binge of drunkenness. They couldn't afford that now. Not with him having to work; not with the trial coming. Will needed to be on his best behavior. Perhaps he was safe. As far as she knew those matches were all he'd had in his pockets, and Leroy's Tavern wouldn't give him any more credit. But he could have borrowed money from someone at the open house, or he could have bottles stashed where she hadn't found them. He could still be drinking. He could be who knows where in the storm that was coming. There was nothing she could do about any of it. She shook her head, as if trying to physically shake off the fear clinging to her mind.

Mary and Walter had planned to stay with Ma for a few days, but when the old lady slugged Walter, the plan was altered. Now it was Nyla and Oscar who were going to stay. They had to go home to get some of their things, so Lena volunteered to keep Ma company till they got back. Julia remained in her own house. Frederick wasn't home yet. Ma's buggy was missing so Lena assumed he'd driven Tori back out to the Petersons. If the storm broke Frederick would have to stay there and, unless Will could come back for her, she would have to stay the night here with Ma.

In thirteen years of marriage to Will, this was the first time Lena had ever been alone with her mother-in-law for more than a few minutes. She was not looking forward to the hours ahead.

Lena realized suddenly that she had eaten nothing all day but a half slice of bread and a thin wedge of pie, and she was hungry.

"There's a little coffee left, Ma. Let's finish it up. And then I'll wash the pot." She considered the small portions of leftover chicken, ham, potatoes, and pie on the kitchen table. "Might as well eat this up. Too good to throw away. Too little to keep."

Ma sat herself down heavily in the chair opposite Lena and grunted her acceptance of a cup of coffee.

Lena set two small plates she had just washed on the table, and two clean forks. Among the remains of the chicken left uneaten was the neck. Lena reached for that first and with her teeth tore out slender strips of dark oily meat from the lattice-work of bones. It took concentration. The bones were finally clean. She noticed Gertrude hadn't touched anything.

"What do you want to do, Ma? Do you want to stay in this big house by yourself?" Once she said it, she realized that Ma was not by herself. Frederick still lived here. But he was somehow unsubstantial in Lena's mind and didn't count. Gertrude did not correct her.

"Don't have time to think yet."

Along with the buzzing stomach and the fears leapfrogging around in her head, Lena suffered the gnawings of a guilty conscience. She watched her mother-in-law sipping coffee across the table from her, sitting like a stranger in her own house. In spite of her size, she seemed, without Pa, diminished. Her face was hollowed and streaked brown with fatigue. The usually puffy flesh around her eyes was shrunken, leaving her eye sockets cavernous and dark. Lena felt sorry for the old woman, who slumped into herself and stayed braced upright from the front by the great bulwark of her breasts and stomach.

"Ma, I want to tell you this. I'm sorry for what I was thinking about you after that fracas with Walter."

"Thinking don't hurt nothing."

Gertrude, who had been born in Berlin, spoke with a thick German accent.

"Well, I thought the worst right off, you know. When I smelled liquor on Will, then I knew what was what, and I wanted to hit the both of them. The idea, giving Will a drink! Today of all days. After it was drink that got him in all this mess. It's like Walter did it on purpose. Why would he do such a fool thing?" Lena poked her fork around in the potatoes, but didn't take any, her appetite suddenly quelled.

"*Ach.* You said it."

"What—he did it on purpose, or he's a fool?"

"Walter—" Ma shook her head, placed her cup on the table with a sigh, and dropped her hands on her stomach. "Always had to knock sense into that head to get it to stick."

"Well, something should sure stick after the knock he got today." Lena chuckled and took a bite of the potato stuck to her fork.

"Will got all that was good in Pa."

Lena stopped chewing. The chunk of potato lay in her mouth, somewhere between firm potato flesh and starch paste. Gertrude's tone of voice, as much as her non sequitur, snagged Lena's attention and made her shiver, just a little.

"*Ja.* Will got all that was good in Pa, and his weakness too. For the drink. Will is a stronger man than Pa. The weakness takes a different way in him."

"I know, Ma. I know." Lena didn't want to talk about Will's drinking.

But Gertrude continued. "In Pa the weakness stay weak, you know. He drink. He get quiet. He get so nobody can talk to him. He don't talk to nobody. For days and days. Lotsa times you don't know to look at him he's drunk and gone. Useless."

Lena was forced to swallow finally and held the dish towel up to her mouth. The potato hadn't gone down well. She hadn't known Pa Kaiser was a drinking man. So much for his quietness.

Gertrude went on. "Will's a strong man, it takes him in a strong way. A bad way."

Will Kaiser was a belligerent, mean, fist-swinging, foul-mouthed drunk, a reversal of his personality when sober. That fact hung in the air between mother and wife, and gave them a connection that neither of them might have wished for.

"You don't have an easy time of it. That I know."

Lena nearly burst into tears. She dropped the dish towel and lightly brushed her hand across her face and stared at the steady little flame in the lantern on the table between them. Outside, the rumbles from heavy, awakening clouds began to swell. "Well, we have to take what the Lord gives us. Will is a good man otherwise . . ."

"Oh, *ja,* but maybe not a big enough 'otherwise.' "

The buzzing in Lena's stomach had turned to a cramp. She wanted to change the subject. "You know we'll do what we can for you, Will and I. You know that."

"*Ja.*"

"I suppose Julia will need some looking after too. A little. But all the boys will help out."

Gertrude shifted her eyes and focused on Lena for the first time since they'd sat down. Lena could not read her expression, but wondered if Gertrude still harbored strong feelings over the events of so long ago, and, if she did, why she would kill Pa and not Julia. She startled herself. Of course the thought had been there, the possibility that Gertrude could have killed the old man. After today, her belief in the old woman's strength was confirmed. But it was still shocking to be sitting there eating funeral leftovers, thinking your mother-in-law across the table from you a killer. But think it she did, and now that the idea had taken substance, she couldn't turn away from it. So Lena went fishing.

"It's too bad . . . you know, you and Julia. It would be so nice if the two of you could live together now. Keep each other company, you know. After all these years, maybe . . ."

The lamps that had been burning all afternoon were dimming one by one and going out. Only the lamp on the table between Lena and Gertrude still burned brightly.

Among the deepening shadows, Lena sensed a yawning in time, as if the veils on this life were lifted till only a few remained to separate this world from the next. She had felt this as a child when her first brother died, then again and again as she got older when more brothers and sisters died—five in all. The sensation became even stronger as a young woman when she lost her father, then her mother. In the proximity of death Lena felt near to the eternal. She felt she could almost reach out and cast aside that last veil and see clearly into the life beyond this one, a life she was sure was as bright and free of suffering as her religion promised. Always before, this feeling had given her comfort. This time the veils lifted not only to the future, but to the past as well. She felt a slippage of boundaries between past, present, and future, as if everything existed now; as if there were no time at all. Lena felt for a moment like she was falling.

Gertrude was muttering, "I don't need nobody else now to look after. Now Pa's gone, I don't need nobody else to look after."

"Well, it would be more company, like. Nobody expects you to take care of her."

"Julia needs looking after. Always did."

If Gertrude was aware of the moment spreading out in all directions, past and future, she didn't show any sign of it. Perhaps she was too much a part of it to notice. Gertrude seemed to be slipping back; her voice became less wheezy, less labored, her German accent stronger.

"Julia always needed looking out for. Even when she was little, she, *ach!,* did crazy things. She stood one time out in the road in front of a team of horses that was galloping down the road. She had a smile on her face, like she knew them horses would not hit her." Gertrude shook her head again and made little sucking noises on her teeth.

Lena was fascinated and afraid to interrupt, but Ma had stopped speaking. "What happened? Did the driver stop the team?"

"*Nein. Nein.* He couldn't. Going too fast. I run out and pull her out of the way just in time and she is laughing. Laughing. I shake her. I say, 'Why you do that?' Over and over I say 'Why you do that?' But she laughs. *Ach, ja.*" Gertrude continued speaking in a low voice, punctuating her phrases with sighs and mutterings in German. "Julia was always good at doing for herself. Her clothes was kept, and her hair, and her shoes. She found things. People give her things. But she couldn't do nothing for anyone else. She couldn't put a meal together. Or wash clothes that weren't hers. Some way she got people to do for her. Always found someone to do for her. *Ja.* It was usually me. Me and Pa. Then the boys, as they got older. Nothing they wouldn't do for their Aunt Julia. Soon as they was old enough, they was carrying her water, painting up her place, nothing they wouldn't do for Aunt Julia. She came to live here. Pa bought up this place thinking one of the boys would take the other house when he got married. But Julia moved in there and just stayed. She helped Pa with his books sometimes. She knows her figures and could write all them things out in his little books. Pa was a great one for keeping books on his wells and accounts and what went into each well. *Ja.* It's all there in those little books. Julia helped him with that. Of an evening."

As the wind blew the first big drops of rain against the kitchen windows, Ma drifted off, muttering now only in German. Lena could understand German, but her mother-in-law was speaking too softly for her to make out her words. But she heard the last ones clearly. "I wish she had died. I wish I had not pulled her out from under that team of flying horses. Sometimes, that's what I wish."

"Yoo-hoo! Anybody home! Lena, it's me, Alvinia."

Lena was cleaning her living room. At the sound of Alvinia's voice, she trotted into the kitchen, happy to have company, and particularly happy that it was Alvinia. The mother of ten usually brought a child or two with her. This morning, she had only one child in tow.

"Oh, Alvinia, sit down. I just made coffee."

"Always do with a cup." Alvinia settled her ample bottom on a kitchen chair.

"And you . . ." Lena beamed at the little boy.

Alvinia knew that no one could tell which child of hers was which. Like their mother, all the little Torgersons were blond, round-faced, and blue-eyed. "Eldon. This is Eldon."

"Come here, precious. Would you like a cookie?" The child nodded slowly, and Lena handed him a sugar cookie from the can she had filled that morning.

Eldon took it and ran back to his mother. He leaned into her with his head down and his arms across her lap. "What do you say, son?" She smoothed back his hair. He buried his face in her skirts and she leaned over and whispered in his ear. "Thank you, Mrs. Kaiser," he repeated in a tiny voice.

"You're very welcome, Eldon. And when you finish that you can have another one. Would you like a glass of milk?"

The boy nodded slowly.

"Lena, I'm sorry I couldn't come before, but I've had sick young ones, one right after the other and overlapping for over a month now. Never seen anything like it. Hope we're through with it for a while. But I just wanted to say I'm sorry. I feel like I got Will in trouble and I sure didn't mean to. When Dennis asked me . . ." Lena placed a cup of coffee and a glass of cold milk on the table for Alvinia and her son. "Thank you, Lena. I didn't know what happened, or I can tell you, I would have kept my mouth shut."

"You saw what you saw. You don't have to lie for my man. He gets into his troubles on his own account. This is . . ." Lena rubbed her forehead and tried not to cry.

"Well, this is just terrible, is what it is," Alvinia continued with great feeling. "And no one, Lena, no one in this world thinks Will could have done any such thing. And that's the truth." Alvinia patted the table between them with the flat of her hand.

"Are people talking . . . ?"

"Well, you know, tongues will waggle, but—Eldon, don't mess now. Eat it, don't play with it. Nobody thinks Will killed his pa. Nobody."

"Thank you, Alvinia. I really appreciate that. You know, you're the only one who has come to see me."

Alvinia asked with some surprise, "What about Gustie?"

"Oh, yes, Gustie came by. But now she's gone again. Something funny going on there, too, and I don't know what it is." Lena clasped her hands in her lap. "Well, I just have to keep going. Just keep going. Sure wish she would get back, though."

Alvinia took a sip of coffee, then said, "She is back."

"Oh?"

"That's another thing, Lena. I said tongues are wagging, and they are. I wanted you to hear this from me and not from somebody else." Alvinia paused a moment. "You know I've always liked Gustie."

Lena had expected to hear something about her husband, herself, or the other Kaisers. She was taken by surprise to hear Gustie's name. "I know." She felt that buzzing in her stomach that usually presaged bad news. But better to know it than wonder about it. She asked, "Hear what?"

"You know my Betty works over there at Olna's waiting tables and doing the washing up, and Severn—he thinks he would like to be a doctor, so Doc Moody lets him hang around his place doing little things for him. I think Doc is going to try to get him into school someplace. That would sure be nice. Anyhow, that's how I know what happened, because it's a funny thing that two of my chickens were there, in both places, to see it. I wanted to tell you before you heard it watered down, warmed up, and overdone from somebody like Mathilda. You know she never likes anyone that's not herself."

"Hear *what,* for heaven's sake?" Lena was all ears and impatient.

"Well. Betty was working at Olna's yesterday, and Gustie was in there having supper. Olna was out doing something or other. So it was just Christine and Eddy, Olna's girl and boy, and Betty. That Eddy is useless. Anyhow, these two squaws come to the back door. Christine is too scared to even talk to them, and Eddy is nowhere to be found, as usual. Betty hadn't worked for a couple days and didn't know what it was all about. The two squaws were asking about some friend of theirs. Well, Gustie sees them and goes out to talk to them. Apparently, they wanted to know where Doc Moody's office was. So Gustie gets into her wagon, and they get into their old rattletrap thing, and she leads the way to Doc Moody's. She didn't even pay her bill at Olna's."

"She will," Lena piped. "Gustie isn't that way. She'll be back to pay. She just forgot. Olna will know that."

"Oh, nobody is worried about *that.*"

"What are they worried about, then?"

"Now, Severn told me a couple days ago they brought in this big Indian. He'd keeled over out back of Olna's. You know, the one who brings in game and fish and whatnot for her Sunday dinners? You've seen him around." Lena nodded. Alvinia went on. "I think his name is Red Horse, Red Something Horse—I don't know, they have such peculiar names. Doc looked at him and said his appendix had to come out, and right now. The Indian was in so much pain he was in no shape to say aye, yes, or no, so Doc put him under and took out his appendix right there and then. When the Indian come to, he wanted to get back to his own folks, so Doc told the station manager and he got a note to Joe Gruba in Wheat Lake to get word out to the reservation. So that's what these two squaws were in town for, you see, to bring him home.

"Now Gustie takes them over to Doc Moody's and they look in on him, and Doc says it's getting late, and he doesn't like the idea of the fellow traveling so soon—can't they give him another night's rest? He was laid up there in the back of the clinic. Doc has a nice little setup there. Have you ever been back there? I had to leave Alice there once when she got bit by a horse. Doc sewed her up but she still has a hole in her leg." Alvinia shook her head. "Severn says that when Doc suggests they stay the night, Gustie seems all right about it . . . and then Mrs. Moody says, 'Of course, they can stay in the barn.' Well! It's like Gustie gets goosed! She says, 'In the barn?' And Mrs. Moody says, 'Why yes, there's plenty of room.' And Gustie, with a look that could wither a flax field, says, 'I'm sure there is.' And she says to the squaws, 'You'll come home with me.' And then she tells Doc they'll be back early in the morning to pick up Red . . . Something . . . whatever-his-name-is Horse, and did he know where they could find his horse, the Indian horse, the horse he was riding on—you know what I mean."

Alvinia stopped to breathe. "Now, do you suppose Gustie thought Mrs. Moody should have invited them to stay *in her house?* Mess up her nice linens and everything? Gustie being from the East and all wouldn't know how things are here. Can you imagine her saying to Edna Moody, 'I'm sure there is . . . ,' just like that, and in front of a waiting room full of people? A better, more charitable woman than Edna Moody does not exist in Stone County."

Lena nodded her agreement.

Alvinia continued, "I'm sure that Gustie didn't mean to hurt Edna's feelings or stir up a hornet's nest."

"No, I've never known her to hurt anyone's feelings. She's always a real tactful person."

"Things are probably a lot different where she comes from."

"Gustie has her own ways, that's for sure."

The two women shared a silent moment trying to fathom Gustie's strange behavior.

Alvinia suddenly thought of something else. "And another thing. Gustie's all bandaged up."

Lena had been studying her floor. Now her attention snapped back to Alvinia. "What do you mean 'all bandaged up'?"

"Well, Severn said—and Betty noticed it too—Gustie has bandages on both wrists and he thought she had some across her chest, too, because he saw bandages right around her neck, so thick she couldn't button the top two buttons on her blouse. And when Doc asked if she was all right and should he look at it for her, she said no, it was taken care of. Well, what do you make of it?"

"I have no idea. I guess if she's up and around and able to drive her wagon, she's not in too rough a shape. I don't know."

"Anyway, I wanted you to hear it from me, the way it was. My chicks just told me what they saw."

"Thanks, Alvinia. You're a brick."

"We just got some groceries. Do you need anything? I've got a wagonful out here."

"Oh, no, we're fine."

Eldon had wandered across the kitchen and was reaching up for the fresh-baked bread on the counter. "Eldon, leave that alone, you're not at home now. You'd think these chickens never got fed."

"Oh, here—he can have some bread and butter." Lena jumped up to cut off a slice. "You want a little sugar on it?" She sprinkled the buttered bread with sugar and handed it to him. "Mm—that's good, isn't it?" Eldon looked up at her with a shy smile forming around his mouthful of bread.

"His eyes are the size of saucers. My, but you'll be a heart-breaker one day, won't you? Yes, you will." Lena chucked him under the chin. The little boy giggled and ran back to his mother.

"Do you want to take some cookies with you?"

"No, thank you. No need to turn this little chicken into a pig." Alvinia took a small square of cloth out of her pocket, stuck the end of it in her mouth, and with the moistened tip wiped sugar and butter off Eldon's cheek. He pulled away and buried his head in her lap again.

"You have a beautiful family, Alvinia. Everyone says so."

Alvinia smiled. "It's time we're getting back. Alice is home alone with Vernon and Kirstin and they can be a handful. I don't like to leave them too long."

"Come again, Alvinia. You're always welcome. Bring the baby. I'll bet she's getting big."

Alvinia promised to bring her entire brood by and was gone.

As Lena washed the two cups and Eldon's glass, she wondered if maybe it wasn't better if Alvinia didn't bring the children with her, because their leaving was like a lamp being blown out. But, for once, she was lifted out of the mire of her own longings by worry about her friend. She said out loud, "What's got into Gustie?"

Gustie grabbed the pitchfork and began to try to work off the anger she still felt from last night.

As they had driven out of Charity, Gustie hated every white face she saw. She was so angry she wanted to take the horse-whip that extended like a skinny flagpole from the corner of her wagon, a whip she had never used, and whip them all till their backs ran blood and were as scar-ridden as Jordis's. She hated the whiteness of her own hands gripping the reins. Her bandaged wrists throbbed with pain.

Wasichu. What did it mean? It didn't mean "white," Jordis had said. What did it mean? More like "devil" . . . where had she heard that?

No one had said a word as they left Doc Moody's clinic, as they climbed into their wagons, or during the three miles to Gustie's house. Only the clopping of horses' hooves intruded upon the sighing of the prairie. She wondered whose horse and wagon Dorcas and Jordis had borrowed. Jordis seemed incomplete without Moon.

"Here we are," Gustie said, unnecessarily, as she stopped in front of her house.

Jordis took care of the horses. Gustie led Dorcas inside to start supper.

"Your wrists hurt," Dorcas said as she sat in the chair Gustie pulled out for her.

"Yes, a little."

"Been taking care of them the way I told you?"

Gustie felt like a three-year-old caught in a misdemeanor.

"Come here."

Gustie obeyed.

Dorcas unwrapped the bandage on Gustie's left wrist. The flesh was still shocking in its appearance; the damage done to it made it look like it had been through a war. It looked like butchered meat, not human flesh, where it had been gouged, but it no longer bled and was not infected. Dorcas examined it critically. "Not too bad." Before Gustie could reply, she added, "Not good either. Where is the salve I made for you?"

Gustie got the jar from the shelf above the sink, and a bag full of strips of cloth Dorcas had told her to prepare ahead of time so she would always have fresh bandages ready. At least she had done that much.

Dorcas reapplied salve and fresh wrappings to both of Gustie's wrists while Gustie, arms extended, stood like an obedient, chastened child.

When she finished Dorcas tapped her own chest and said, "And this?"

"I'll do it tonight before I go to bed."

"Good."

Gustie cut up potatoes and carrots into small pieces so they would cook quickly and put them on to boil. Then she unwrapped a large smoked bullhead that Will had given her. He'd gotten it from a farmer, but Lena adamantly refused to eat a fish that didn't have scales on it. She said it was in the Bible—things without scales were unclean. Gustie was glad she had it now. She set the table with bread, butter, and salt, and placed the sugar bowl in front of Dorcas.

Jordis was inside by the time everything was ready and they sat down to eat.

Dorcas looked around amiably. "Nice house."

"Thank you. It isn't mine, really. They're letting me live here until a homesteader shows up to cultivate the land."

"Sort of like a reservation." Dorcas laughed. So did Jordis.

Gustie felt uncomfortable. Finally, she said, "I'm sorry about what happened back there."

"Not your fault." Dorcas dismissed the incident and they fell into silence.

Gustie wished she could read Jordis, but she could not. Jordis's face betrayed nothing and she said nothing.

When they were finished eating, Gustie washed the dishes with more bustle than usual.

"I'll fix the beds," Gustie said. "You two can have the big

bed, and there is a trundle bed I've never had occasion to use. I'll roll that out here, and—"

Jordis interrupted her. "That's not necessary. We will sleep in the barn."

"What?" For the second time in just a few hours, Gustie was flabbergasted.

"Thank you for supper, Gustie," Jordis added as she and Dorcas rose to leave.

"If you were going to sleep in a bloody barn, why not save yourself the trip out here?"

"To have supper with you." Dorcas grinned as they walked out Gustie's door.

Gustie was dumbstruck, and furious—at her friends, at Charity, at all people everywhere whose actions were inexplicable to her. She went into her bedroom and pulled off her clothes and threw them into a corner, not changing the bandage on her chest as she had promised Dorcas she would. Sitting on the edge of her bed, in her nightgown, she hit the mattress with her fist. "Damn!" What kind of a place had she come to? In its way, it was as bad as the place she had left. Maybe she understood why her friends would not sleep in her house, but she would not accept it. Suddenly she rose and tore the bedding off her bed, wadded it into a bundle, and carried it to the barn. The lantern burned softly. Jordis was arranging her own blanket when Gustie entered. Dorcas, wrapped snugly in her blanket already, was lying with her back to them.

Without a word, Gustie found a place to complete the circle of three women and stamped around on the straw. She spread out her bedding. There were still lumpy places and she slapped them down with the flat of her hand. She pulled a blanket over herself roughly and closed her eyes. Jordis blew out the lantern. Dorcas's eyes shone in the darkness.

When Gustie awoke, it was daylight. Dorcas and Jordis had gone without waking her. She supposed it would be of no use to follow them. She put on her working clothes, tethered Biddie outside to graze, and set to work in the barn. If she was going to have to entertain out here, she thought dryly, she might as well clean it up.

"I had to find out from Alvinia that you were back." Lena stood in the barn door, her head inclined at a reproachful angle, her eyes moving to take in the scene before her.

Gustie paused to pull a wisp of straw that was caught between her cap and her hair and to wipe the dust from her face with her shirttail. "I didn't hear you come up."

"No wonder. You're making so much noise out here. What in Sam Hill are you doing?"

"Enlarging Biddie's stall."

"What for?"

"I have one horse. I don't need three little stalls." Gustie returned to tugging at her crowbar, prying loose the top slat of the second stall. "I'm tearing down these partitions so she can turn around in here."

"What if you get another horse?"

"Not likely." Gustie ripped off the board and threw it to the side with such force, Lena jumped.

"You should have asked Will. He'd do it for you."

"I felt like doing it now."

Dust motes soaked in the afternoon sun clouded the air between them and gave the inside of the barn a golden glow. Lena liked barns. There was nothing cozier than a clean barn, bright with yellow straw and smelling of new hay. Gustie kept her barn clean, that was for sure. Lena smiled at Gustie, who was attired in a man's workshirt and overalls and her old train conductor's cap. "Well, look at you!"

"I wasn't expecting company," Gustie responded curtly and went back to her work.

"Fiddlesticks! I'm not company. Where did you get those overalls?"

"They were hanging out here along with the shirt. Elef Tollerude probably left them." Gustie threw another board against the wall.

"Can't you wait till Will can help you?"

"How did you get out here?"

"Hitched a ride on Iver's cream wagon. He'll stop by and pick me up on his way back."

Gustie had one side of a board pulled free and began on the other side. The nails gave way with a screech and Gustie pulled the board away from the sideposts by hand. She tossed it to the side, dusted her hands off on her overalls, and began the next board. It did not want to give up its place as easily as the others. Lena stepped up to help. She pulled on the board while Gustie worked the crowbar.

"You'll get your dress dirty," Gustie grunted between pulls.

"It'll wash," Lena grunted back.

The nails gave and Lena almost fell backward. She grabbed Gustie's arm to right herself. Gustie winced. Lena saw the white rim of bandages just visible beneath the cuffs of Elef Tollerude's old shirt and took the opportunity to ask, "What did you do to yourself?"

Gustie pulled the cuff back down so the bandages were no longer visible. "I tripped getting out of my wagon and scraped myself on the way down."

"Doc Moody should take a look at it."

"I'm fine. Lena, you're not dressed for this kind of work. Please go over there and sit down."

"I've done plenty of barn work in my day," Lena retorted.

"I'm sure you have. But this is not your day. Not in a white dress. Anyway, I need to stop a minute. I've been at this for a while."

Gustie went to a bucket hanging on the wall. She lifted out the dipper and took a drink of water. She filled the dipper again and handed it to Lena.

"Thanks." Lena drank.

Gustie said, "I hear Will is out on bail."

"Yes, it's a blessing." Lena passed the dipper back to Gustie. "Surprised me, though."

"I'm sorry I couldn't go to the funeral."

"Well, you missed a fracas at the open house afterwards." Lena looked around for a place to sit and found a three-legged milking stool. She brought it out to the middle of the barn where she could continue her conversation with Gustie. "Those Kaisers can't behave themselves even for a little while. Not even for death and damnation can they mind their manners."

"What happened?"

Lena enjoyed telling a story, even an unpleasant one. "Ma hauled off and popped Walter one for bringing whiskey to the open house. He sure had that coming!" Gustie resumed her work and Lena had to raise her voice to be heard over the sounds of ripping boards and pounding hammer. "Then Oscar kicked Julia's cat and got her in such a tizzy crying and carrying on over that cat, she had to go home and no one has seen her since. Except Frederick, I guess. He brings her groceries and looks in on her. It's the least he can do. He's got nothing else to do."

"Why did Oscar kick the cat?"

Lena shook her head. "Who knows? Just his meanness. He thinks it's a nuisance. Though why he should care one way or the other I don't know. Pa Kaiser gave her that cat a few years ago. It was nice of him, I thought. She sits over in that house alone most of the time. A cat is good company. He was killing a litter and he saved one in his pocket and brought it home to her."

"How is the cat?"

"He's all right."

"I would have come to see you yesterday, but something came up while I was in town."

"Mm-hm. Alvinia told me."

"Told you what?"

"About taking those squaws home with you."

Gustie stopped tugging on the crowbar. "I'm not fond of that word, Lena."

"What word?"

" 'Squaw.' "

"Well, that's what they are. What should I call them?"

"Women." Gustie pulled hard against a rail. "They're *women*." It fell off at her feet.

"Hm. Well out here, we call them squaws."

Gustie hurled another board at the wall. It landed with a crash.

"What are you so mad about?"

"I'm sorry. I'm not in the mood for company, Lena."

"Well, I'm sorry, too, but I'm stuck here till Iver shows up because I sure don't feel like walking." Undaunted, Lena continued. "So, anyway, Alvinia came to see me yesterday."

"How is Alvinia?"

"She's fine. She brought Eldon. He's her third to the youngest, I think . . . I can't keep track. Such a beautiful little boy. He sure liked my sugar cookies. She said that Betty and Severn told her about what happened at Olna's and Doc Moody's."

Gustie threw Lena a sharp look.

"She didn't mean any harm in telling me. Alvinia just wanted me to know before the gossip train started running."

"What's there to talk about? I just tried to give them a decent place to stay the night."

Lena sniffed at Gustie's emphasis on the word "decent." "Now I know you were just doing a good deed—not knowing it didn't need doing."

For once, Lena was right. "I guess not. They chose to sleep in the barn out here too."

"See? That's what they're used to."

"Sleeping in barns?"

Lena bobbed her head around between a nod and a shake. "Well . . . barns . . . you know . . . their little shacks—tipis . . ."

"They're used to sleeping in white people's barns, perhaps."

Lena took umbrage. "You don't know these people. After all everybody tries to do for them, they always end up back in the same place—a tipi, or living like they're in a tipi whether or not they're actually in one. And they're all beggars! Nyla's mother had a nice quilt. It was cold and she had it with her in the wagon once on a trip to Wheat Lake, and I don't know exactly how it happened but she saw this family of Indians in town there asking for things, the way they do, and she felt sorry for the little children I guess. She didn't have anything else so she gave them the quilt. She found out later from Joe Gruba, when he had to go out there to that Indian's place for something, that he went in, and there was that quilt on the floor just like it was some old rag. They don't appreciate nice things. And then there was Mercy Krieger. Poor Mercy. She went to teachers' college in Argus and met this Indian—he was also in school— and, oh, she thought he was the best thing, and she married him. They lived for a while in a house in Wheat Lake, but it wasn't long before she had a little half-Indian baby. He wasn't working anymore, and, don't you know, they were all three of them back living with his mother in some shack on the reservation. The poor little baby died. He run off, and Mercy had to move back with her own folks. You know, now, no one else will have her. Even Nemil Glasrud won't look at her. That's what happens. It doesn't matter how far they come, they'll always end up right back in a tipi."

"You came all the way out here to tell me your Indian stories?" Gustie asked with a weariness that had nothing to do with her present labor.

"You don't know how things are here."

"I'm finding out. Actually, things are not so different here than anywhere else."

"I just don't want people to think . . ."

"I can't help what people think, Lena. What I do is nobody's business."

"Well, there's where you're wrong. Everything is everybody's business out here. Especially for a schoolteacher. I just wanted you to know what people will be saying, that's all."

Lena silently stared at her hands. Gustie ceased her battering of the old wood and leaned against the side of the stall, her head down, her back to Lena.

Lena spoke so quietly Gustie almost missed her next words.

"I think the world of you, Gustie. I don't like to see . . . I mean, I know how it feels . . ."

Gustie felt as if the ground had shifted and they were in a new country, with a new atmosphere, new ways, new latitudes for speaking. She turned. Lena looked so very small, hunched over to keep her balance on the little three-legged milking stool.

"I know what people say about Will, and his drinking. I know how they talk about us. How they talk about me. They snicker one time and feel so sorry the next. But they're always nice as pie to my face."

Lena was still looking down, speaking quietly. "People collect things about each other out here. And they don't forget a thing. People don't forget, they just die. Don't ruin your reputation, Gustie. Once your reputation is shot, there's no getting it back."

Finally, Lena returned Gustie's gaze with eyes full of terrible sadness.

"There's nothing I can do about what they say about Will

and me. We can never get back what's been lost. I don't want to see you in the same kettle of fish, that's all."

"I will try not to bring any more shame into your life, Lena," Gustie said, and Lena's eyes filled.

But the ground shifted again; Lena swallowed her tears, and they found themselves back in the more familiar landscape, as if the other place had never been. Lena said, "Say, I wanted to tell you . . . me and Will are going to the fairgrounds for the shenanigans on the Fourth of July. It's going to be lots of fun. You come with us."

"You sure you want to be seen with me?"

"Oh, now don't be like that. We'll show everybody there's nothing for them to talk about. Come with us."

Gustie nodded.

They heard a noise outside and Lena jumped up. The stool fell over and she carried it back to prop against the wall where she found it. "There's Iver. I've got to go." She smoothed her dress. "I promised I wouldn't hold him up. I'm glad you're back, Gus."

Lena waved and was gone in the rattle of wagon, cream cans, and horse tracings.

Gustie sat down on a pile of fresh hay and leaned against the remaining wall of the stall. She felt deep sadness for Lena, and anger and frustration for herself. No matter how far she traveled, she came back to the same place: reputations ruined, gossip, the weight of a community's disdain. Through the open barn door she saw white clouds tumbling toward her over the edge of the horizon. Her mind went back over her most recent stay at Crow Kills. The things they didn't know would give the good people of Charity more to talk about than they had ever dreamed . . .

Gustie found herself only half-awake, in that state where dream, memory, and real time blend into one eternally present moment, and she lived again the miracle of their first morning: waking up to a tangle of curls across her pillows, hair that glowed with light golden strands, mixed up with copper, against a field of wheat, hair that Gustie had lost herself in. She smiled at how it continually vexed Clare, it was so silky, so fine, it would not be confined by pin or bonnet. The feel of it laced through her fingers, in her mouth, as it fell across her face. Oh, God! Something was being wrenched out of her, and Gustie sat up and held her stomach. She bent forward, burying her face in the blanket, and tried to stifle a guttural cry. This was more hellish than the nightmares: the memory of that glorious hair, Clare's flesh, her scent . . . and it was gone. All of it, the touching, the loving, the being loved. Clare was dead. Somewhere in her mind a voice pleaded: *Give me back the dirt, the crawling, snapping things. I can bear them. I cannot bear this.* The death, the burial, were easier to remember than the laughter and the warm sweet nights she would never have again. She threw back her head and bellowed in anguish, her face contorted so wide it hurt. She flung away the blanket and staggered out of her bed to the sink. There was no movement from the old woman in the bed across the cabin. Gustie did not notice or care. She was the only human being left in an empty world. She drew a knife out of the rack above the sink, and threw it down, going for the bundle on the opposite wall. She jerked the leather thongs off the ends. The bundle fell open, dumping its contents on the table. Gustie found the thing she wanted and stumbled with it out the door.

I am swimming far out in the lake and I hear her screaming. I swim back, grab my clothes off the willow, and pull them on as I run up the hill. I see Gustie running and falling, and running—now crawling to the grave. She holds something in her hand. I want to run after her. Grandmother holds me back. She will not let me follow Gustie up the hill. I see now what is in her hand: the spear point from Grandmother's bundle. We see her cut herself in the old way. I've never seen it before. My grandmother just stands still, nodding her head, holding me back, while Gustie screams and cries and cuts herself. That pale flesh, gouged by stone. The blood is soaking all through her gown and onto the grass. It is horrible. She is a one-woman battle. I have never heard such screaming. Not even at the mission school. Grandmother still will not let me go to her. I bury my face in Grandmother's shoulder so I do not have to watch Gustie killing herself on the hill, on that grave.

Now she is silent and stretched out on the grave mound. She is losing a lot of blood. I have never seen so much blood. But now we both move. I cannot help it—I am still crying. I have never cried so before. We pick her up and carry her to the lake and lay her down in the water. I hold her head above the waves. Grandmother lets the lake wash away all the blood, and the cold water stanches the flow. The wounds are terrible, jagged and wide. Crow Kills has washed her clean and we lay her on the grass. Grandmother cuts off her bloodied and wet gown. She gets her ointment jar, and anoints the wounds of each arm and wraps them in clean cloth, and now the wound on her breast the same.

I carry Gustie and lay her on her bed. This is twice I have done so. It seems complete this time, as we pull the blanket up to her chin and tuck her in. I keep my hand on her forehead until Grandmother pulls me away and makes me sit down. I ask her, "Grandmother, does this mean what I think it means?"

Grandmother kneads the dough for fry bread. She asks me, "What do you think it means?"

I say, "Two-spirit woman is free now?"

Grandmother smiles. "Granddaughter," she says, "You are a pretty smart Indian."

Gustie had been here before, swaddled in a blanket, sipping Dorcas's medicine brew. There were differences. This time, instead of perched on crates, she was comfortable in the oak rocker she had brought for Dorcas. Instead of fever and delirium, she suffered weakness from loss of blood and throbbing pain in her arms and chest, which were swathed in bandages. Unlike before, there was no confusion, only astonishment at what she had done. She, who had never shed a tear in the presence of another person, who had never raised her voice in public, had gone simply mad. And yet Gustie had never felt so sane as she did now, or so at rest.

The land rolled gently upward away from the cabin and lay changeless beneath the ever-changing sky.

This was a land of ghosts. She herself sat bloodless, empty of feeling, transparent, ghostlike. *How quickly we are gone,* she thought. *How little mark we leave.* The mound of earth she could clearly see, soaked with her own blood, was all that was left of Clare, except for some clothes that lay folded in Clare's trunk, a book, and some photographs in the album on her nightstand. But Gustie also sensed that what was lacking in the physical world existed somewhere else. She had no belief in a heaven or hell, only the land and the sky; and the sky she knew had moods: placid, like today with billows of white floating high in the clear blue; dark, as on the days it shed benevolent rain; or black and roiling with clouds that shot hail, whipped lightning, and conjured up deadly twisters. The people suffered it, feared it, rejoiced in it, and died beneath it. The land remained.

And its ghosts. Gustie saw them, those who had lived and died on this land, beneath this sky: the Sioux, the first white settlers, even the horses and the buffalo. She saw them in the shimmer of a heat wave rising from the earth in the distance, or a sunspot dancing off a spiderweb glassy with dew, in a trembling curtain of rain, in the shadows that lurked among the cottonwoods at evening. She saw them out of the corner of her eye and felt them like a feather against her cheek on windless days. Gustie knew these feelings and visions were in her mind, but it was this land that gave rise to such mind-stuff. She had never had such thoughts before coming here. Perhaps they were real. Perhaps not. She knew for certain that she was seldom lonely out here. She *felt* presences whether she really saw them in the shadows and sunspots or not.

Over the farthest rise in the land appeared a tall Indian on a handsome bay. Gustie took him for a ghost until Jordis rose from the porch steps where she was seated and walked out to meet him.

Jordis was wearing the split skirt and yellow blouse Gustie had given her. She had hesitated accepting it, but finally conceded, "It'll make it easier for me to ride." "That's the idea," Gustie had said.

Dorcas, on the other hand, was ebullient over Gustie's presents. She had taken them for what they were, gifts given in friendship. As Gustie unloaded her wagon, handing parcel after parcel to Jordis to carry into the cabin, Dorcas had teased, "What'd you do, rob a bank? It's not Christmas."

Dorcas liked her new clothes, and when at last Gustie pulled out the bloomers, the old woman clapped her hands, grabbed them and pulled them on, and danced around, lifting and swinging her skirts. Then she took up residence in her new rocking chair, sucking her hard candies, and would not be moved until it was time for bed. Gustie said nothing about the origin of her new wealth, or the occasion for the giveaway.

Gustie sipped her tea. What wind there was blew high and warm, just enough to fluff the clouds and descend occasionally to ruffle her hair, which was loosely pinned at the back of her neck. Nevertheless, she felt chilled, and kept the blanket tucked around her.

As Jordis approached the rider, he dismounted and walked in, leading his mount, to the cabin. He had the vaulted chest and narrow hips characteristic of Dakotah men. He was dressed in worn blue work pants and a gray shirt. He wore a folded-up bandanna as a headband. His hair was not quite shoulder length.

Jordis introduced Gustie. "Little Bull, this is my friend, Augusta Roemer. Gustie, this is Little Bull."

He took the three porch steps in one stride and lightly reached for Gustie's extended hand, not commenting on the bandages. "Miss Roemer." He did not smile.

"Please." Gustie dismissed his formality with a smile. "Just Gustie."

Dorcas had spoken of Little Bull. "Little Bull will be our chief," she had said. "His father Good Wolf will not live another winter. Little Bull will be a good chief." Talk of him always made Jordis jumpy. So Gustie didn't know much more about him.

Little Bull stepped back and Jordis took the reins of his horse. She cooed softly into the stallion's nostrils, "*Whooo*, Swallow. Will you come with me?" The horse whickered softly. To Little Bull she said, "I'll take him. Grandmother is inside. She's been asking for you."

Jordis and the bay disappeared around the corner, leaving Gustie alone on the porch with Little Bull. He said, "My cousin likes my horse better than she likes me." He smiled enigmatically and made no move to go inside.

Gustie asked, "How are things with the school?"

"We finished the building. We should be able to do some teaching in there pretty soon. We need books." Little Bull was dark-complected, with a face not as sharply cut as Jordis's. Still, he had an expansive forehead, a large aquiline nose. Next to him Gustie felt small, pale, and plain. She snuggled deeper into her blanket. "You will teach the children yourself?"

"Yes. And my wife, Winnie. To get started, I'll have to teach. Till I can convince Jordis to help us." He looked at Gustie and she thought she saw flint striking somewhere behind his eyes. Jordis returned and the conversation about the school came to an end.

"They've invited us to dance at the Fourth of July celebration in Wheat Lake," Little Bull announced.

"Who has?" Jordis stood at the bottom of the steps looking out.

"Emil Withers. Farley Scroggins . . . a few others planning the celebration." Little Bull looked out, focused upon the same vista as Jordis. "It will be good to dance again."

Jordis responded with a little sound in the back of her throat.

"Will you join us?" he asked.

"No," Jordis said sharply, "I won't dance for the *wasichu.*"

"We haven't danced in many years. Some of the white people are interested. Besides, we can charge them ten cents a head."

"We are just a curiosity, something laughable. You want to parade around for them in your feathers and beads, go ahead. I don't. Not even for ten cents a head."

Gustie watched Little Bull's face, but she saw nothing.

"Granddaughter is stubborn." Dorcas appeared at the door.

"I figured it was useless, but I thought I'd ask. Will you come, Grandmother?"

Dorcas nodded. "It is good we dance again. Yes, I will come. Might dance. Show off my bloomers." She lifted her skirt just enough to show a bit of white lace and did a little step on the porch slats.

Little Bull grinned and the severe lines of his face lifted and softened. He asked, "Gustie, will you?"

"I don't know." Gustie didn't know how to feel after hearing Jordis's remark about dancing for the *wasichu.*

Little Bull acknowledged her dilemma with a nod. "Well, I hope to see you there." The corners of his mouth twitched. "We'll only charge *you* a nickel." Gustie smiled back. He turned to Dorcas. "Grandmother, can we use some of your things in the dance?"

She pointed with her chin. "In the box in there."

Little Bull followed Dorcas inside, ducking as he passed through the door frame. Gustie heard a scraping sound of something heavy being pulled across the floor. She felt light-headed.

"Jordis, I need to lie down. And I'd like to see what Dorcas has stowed away in there."

Jordis put an arm around Gustie's waist and helped her inside to her narrow bed. Gustie lay on her side so she could watch Little Bull sort through the contents of one of the crates that had supported Dorcas's mattress. He took out a large beaded medallion and a beaded headband. The items seemed old but in good condition; the colors were only slightly faded. He handled them reverently as he laid them on the table. Then he held up a small buckskin shirt that was covered with beads, mostly blue, with a smattering of red. Leather thongs laced up the sides. Fringes hung from the sleeves. "Ah. This should fit Leonard." He explained to Gustie, "My son. He is twelve. This is his first dance. He has been practicing. This will make him very happy."

He took out more buckskin shirts, not so finely decorated as the first, and a breastplate of slender bones sewn together and trimmed in leather fringe. The last item in the box was in excellent condition: a creamy white doeskin dress with blue beadwork across the front and along the bottom of the skirt. Long fringes flowed from the sleeves and the skirt edge. Gustie sucked in a breath, and propped herself up on an elbow. "Dorcas, that's lovely."

Little Bull displayed the leggings that went with the skirt. They were fringed up the sides and decorated in a floral beaded design as well.

"Belonged to my aunt, Pretty Star," Dorcas said. "She never got to wear them before she died. She worked a long time on them, too."

"They are so beautiful," Gustie repeated.

Dorcas eyed them. "A lot of work, a dress like that."

"My goodness, how much does it weigh?"

Jordis responded dryly, "Too much."

"About twenty pounds, I'd say." Little Bull estimated the heft as he held it up.

"Cloth is better," said Dorcas. "Skins still good for ceremonies. No one to wear it now." She addressed Little Bull. "Any of your dancers want to wear this?"

"No, the ladies all have their own things. I'd give it to Winnie but she's too big now."

"Winnie is pregnant. Very big." Dorcas put her hand out in front of her stomach to show how big. Then she said, "Little Bull, stay and eat with us."

He nodded and began to put the things he had chosen in a large pouch he had brought with him. With some regret he folded Pretty Star's dress, leggings, and moccasins and laid them back in the box. Then he slid the box back into the corner and reassembled Dorcas's bed.

While Dorcas began stirring up the fry bread, Jordis went outside to prepare the morning's catch of fish. Gustie felt useless and embarrassed by her weakness. Little Bull poured himself a cup of coffee and sat in a chair. He stretched his long legs out in front of him and turned toward Gustie. His eyes were kind and shrewd. Gustie found it a disarming combination.

"How are you feeling now?" he asked.

She was not sure if he knew of what she had done or was merely being polite, noting her obvious state of ill health.

"I'm weak, but that will pass. Maybe you heard . . . I sort of . . . ran amok yesterday."

He registered her statement, then his eyes took on a gleam that reminded Gustie of Dorcas, the way her eyes could light up and shoot sparks even when her face didn't twitch a muscle. Then he grinned. "That's what happens when you hang around Indians too long. You . . . run amok." A quiet laugh shook his chest.

While Dorcas and Jordis prepared their meal, Gustie and Little Bull chatted. She was more and more impressed that here was someone of seriousness, intelligence, and humor, aware that his people were sitting on the edge of a precipice in history, and knowing that any wrong moves and they would fall over the edge and be lost. He was committed to the welfare of the tribe, and already burdened with his impending chiefdom. And yet he did not seem to feel it a burden of doom, for a streak of optimism shone through him. Gustie found this miraculous, given what little she knew of the conditions on the Red Sand. Maybe it was not optimism but a warrior's fighting spirit she saw.

During a meal of fish, fry bread, turnip and onion stew, and dried fruit, the conversation remained light. Dorcas said, "This is good. You visit and eat with us. Someday, you will be very big man. You won't have time for us anymore."

Little Bull replied through a mouthful of fry bread, "Hm, between Winnie and Jordis, I'm not likely to get too chiefy." Everyone laughed.

After the meal, and when the last of a second pot of coffee was drained, they bid him farewell.

"Grandmother," Little Bull said, "on the Fourth we will stop here and pick you up. After, we will bring you home." To Gustie he said, "Gustie, it is good to meet you, at last." She took his hand again and said goodbye.

As the door closed behind him, Dorcas said to Jordis, "You should help him more."

Jordis abruptly left the cabin. All the good feelings of the afternoon were gone in a second.

"Why do you do that? Make her so angry?" Gustie could not fathom it at all.

There were times when Dorcas looked simply ancient, when her face looked as old and lined as a mountain that had endured the wind and rivulets of water down its face for centuries, when out of her eyes gleamed a consciousness that was old as time itself. She turned just such a face upon Gustie and said, "My Little Wounded Bird must learn to fly again. She must learn to fly."

Gustie lay back on her bed feeling sorrow for Jordis, for Dorcas, and for Little Bull, a young man with the future of his people on his heart. Before she got around to feeling sorry for herself, she dozed off.

Gustie was awakened by angry voices outside the cabin. Jordis's voice carried a strident quality that she had not heard before. The other voice, quieter but no less angry, was Little Bull's. Next she heard hoofbeats thudding away from the cabin.

Gustie wrapped herself in her blanket and went outside.

The sun had shifted, flooding the prairie with a softer light. Gustie stepped down off the porch and out away from the cabin. She still clung to her blanket, even though the day remained warm.

She felt heavy from her nap, which had been brief but sound and dreamless. She breathed deeply to clear her head. To her right a dragonfly hovered just above the spears of grass, its wings visible as a blur, its blue-green back iridescent and jewellike. Young grasshoppers jumped in all directions before her. She turned and walked around behind the cabin to where Jordis sometimes tethered Moon in the shelter of the cottonwoods. Jordis was standing with her head against Moon's forehead; her hands rested lightly on the horse's neck. Gustie did not now think it strange, as she would have a few years ago, to see a woman communing head to head with a horse. Since coming to Charity she often found herself talking to Biddie. Once after a harrowing night of dreams she had fled to the barn in the early-morning hours and sunk her forehead into Biddie's, exactly as she saw Jordis doing now.

Moon, sensing Gustie's approach, raised her head and snorted. Jordis looked around, one hand still rested on the long white neck.

Gustie said, "She is a beautiful horse."

There were moments with Jordis when Gustie did not know what to do or what to say, when Jordis seemed aloof, feral, as close to the wild as the pale horse who ran unshod, unsaddled, over the prairie, not ruled by but in partnership with the dark woman on her back. Jordis was from another world, about which Gustie knew nothing beyond her terrible time at the mission school. Jordis's arm remained around Moon's neck. Horse and woman seemed extensions of each other.

Gustie felt her heart swell: words might drown her, but she would choke for not speaking. "Did you get her as a filly?"

"No." Jordis moved to the side of Moon and began to run her hand flat along the mare's neck in long, even strokes.

She worked systematically, from the neck to the shoulders and withers, with firm pressure. Moon stood still. Here and there a muscle quivered in pleasure. Jordis had no brushes, no cloths, only her hands with which to groom the white horse.

Gustie sat down on a tree stump. Crow Kills gave off a freshness she could smell and feel even without a breeze, and the cool ground, which, in the shade of the cottonwoods, bore no underbrush, gave up its earthy fragrance mixed with the pungency of horse dung. A bird trilled in the branches above them.

"Did you get her wild?"

Jordis interrupted the rhythm of her stroking. She looked across Moon's back at Gustie and shook her head wryly. "No. I've only seen wild horses in my dreams."

With what blood she had left, Gustie blushed. Only an idiot could think that Indians were still running free across the plains after herds of wild horses. *My god, could I have said such a stupid thing?* Gustie thought she should just go back to the cabin, crawl under her blanket, and leave Jordis alone.

She was about to do just that when Jordis said, "She was left standing in the sun. The harness had rubbed places raw on her skin. She can't take the same treatment as a dark horse."

Jordis used both hands now, rubbing along Moon's flank to her hindquarters. Her whole body bent and leaned into the work. "I saw the bruises on her where the harness had rubbed her for too long, and I knew if I took off the saddle I would find sores. I saw the burning around her eyes from the sun. So I untied her and led her to a shed in the back of the building where she could stand in the shade. I gave her water. Then I went into the saloon."

"Where was this?"

"Wheat Lake. There were a few men in there, but I picked him out easily enough. I said, 'I'm not stealing your horse. She was too hot. I moved her. Gave her water. She's tied out back.' I shamed him in front of the other men. But I was just a squaw. What could he do to me there? Besides, he saw the knife in my boot. I made sure enough of it was sticking out so they couldn't miss it. No squaw is worth getting cut for. So he spent the afternoon drinking and came out all full of meanness. He went to an Indian camp over by Campbell Crossing where he thought I came from, I suppose. And he took his meanness out on them. He could have found me easily enough. I was at the agency, just around the corner from the saloon, waiting with Grandmother and everybody else on the Red Sand for our annuities. I hate that. That's why I was in Wheat Lake all day."

"What did he do? At Campbell Crossing?"

"He slashed a tipi. It fell down and a pole hit a little boy and killed him. They weren't even Dakotah. They had nothing to do with me or him or anything. They were just passing through. They took out after him and I saw them chase him back into town. So I followed. One of them spoke English and told me what happened. They chased him to the railroad depot and he jumped on the train that was just pulling out. He left her standing there in a lather and exhausted. I saw what they were going to do and I stopped them."

"What were they going to do? Jump on the train?"

Jordis moved to the other side of Moon and began again stroking her neck. "No. They were going to kill her."

"Why?" Gustie was shocked.

"Revenge."

"But the horse didn't do anything!"

"The horse was his. In a way they would have been killing him. I understand this. But I couldn't let them kill her."

"What did you do?"

"I ran in front of her. I said I would fight them. This whole thing started with me. I told them that it was what I did made him mad at Indians. Anyway, if they killed me the justice was done and they could take care of the horse. If I won, I got the horse and they still had a good fight to get rid of some of their feelings. One of them, the dead boy's older brother, I think, came after me. I kept sidestepping him, and when I pulled my knife his relatives pulled him back, and an older boy came for me."

"Could they have killed you?"

Jordis nodded. "If they had all jumped me at once. I fought a couple of them. Then they lost heart. They didn't like fighting a girl. That was part of it. So they gave up and went home to bury their dead."

"How did you do it? How did you fight them?"

Jordis paused in her stroking and shrugged her shoulders.

"How did you learn to fight?"

"I started fighting with George when we were children. He taught me and we fought—mock fights, but he was tough and he made me tough. We fought every day. Then at school I learned to fight for real. Even in the East, I fought. I never started a fight. And I never lost one." Jordis reached down and pulled a long slender knife out of her boot. "This helps." She gave Gustie a slight smile. A thin shaft of light fell through the cottonwood leaves and bounced off its blade. "I've learned not to be where they strike, and to cut them when I have to. I have hurt men who have tried to take me. Even here on the reservation. Now they all know. They leave me alone. Even when they're drunk. Grandmother says Dakotah men never used to be like that. Of course, Dakotah women always used to carry butcher knives. I'm the only one I know who does anymore." Jordis slid the knife back into her boot and resumed grooming the white horse.

"Little Bull is not like that. He is a good man."

"Yes. Little Bull is a very good man."

"You were arguing with him just now."

"He is angry with me because I won't teach. I won't teach, I won't dance. I make him very angry."

"Dorcas calls you her Little Wounded Bird."

"Grandmother has her name for everything. To her nothing is just what it is."

"Dorcas feels the way Little Bull does, about your teaching?"

"Not exactly. I don't want to discuss this with you, Gustie." The words were spoken softly, without anger, but Gustie felt her own blood sting her face as if she had been slapped.

"Why not?"

"Because it has nothing to do with you."

"I think it does."

"It doesn't."

"Yes, it does. Tell me why you won't teach."

"If I have to tell you, then you won't get it."

"Oh, for heaven's sake."

"The white man's knowledge killed my brother."

"It didn't kill you. It didn't kill Little Bull."

"It almost killed me. Little Bull was stronger. And luckier."

"Why did you go on then? Why didn't you just come home after the mission school?"

"I had no home. My mother was dead. George was dead and I didn't have anything else to do. The new head of the school, the one who replaced Everude, he said the church would pay for my education. He felt guilty, I suppose. I don't know. So I went east. I didn't care."

"You were a good student."

"Yes."

"Why?"

"Why what?"

"Why were you a good student? It must have been a lot of work. Why do it?"

"It filled the time."

"Between fights."

"Yes. Between fights."

Gustie was angry, and still she found this conversation funny. Jordis turned and saw the amusement in her eyes, and returned it.

"The fighting was easier," Jordis said.

"I'll bet it was."

"Do you ever fight?"

"No. There were times when I should have."

"I'll bet there were."

Gustie felt a lump growing in her throat. "It does have to do with me."

Jordis turned and faced Gustie.

Gustie pulled the blanket tighter around herself, raised her head, and tried to smile. "I am the *wasichu*"—Gustie looked away at a lacy patch of blue that flickered through the canopy of leaves "—for whom you will not dance." She continued to smile as Jordis heaved herself up on Moon's back and rode away.

Gustie sat still and released the lump in her throat in a little cry, heard only by the brown birds scratching in the dirt.

She got to her feet and headed back to the cabin. It was time to go back to Charity.

She thinks I do not feel her blood weeping. She thinks I do not know her strength or believe the heat of her. She thinks I do not see her blood singing. She thinks I do not hear her blood dancing.

She thinks she is part of my wounding.

The Moon cannot outrun my tears.

Gustie got up and brushed the hay off her overalls. She was no longer in the mood for demolition. She had to clear away the boards and make sure that nothing was left in here that Biddie might hurt herself on. Her wrists throbbed wildly.

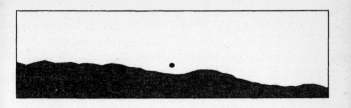

Moon When Chokeberries Are Red

Gustie rose before dawn and performed her morning rituals in the dark. Then, wearing only her shift with a thin shawl over her shoulders, she settled at her table with a cup of dark coffee lightened with a dollop of thick cream. She lit a candle and within its small circle of light considered the journal lying open before her.

This book, begun only days ago, was the first writing for its own sake she had attempted since Clare's death. Her old journal ended with a single entry: "*My dear seems better today.*"

Clare died the next day. Gustie put the book in the bottom of the trunk and had not touched it since. It was full of Clare.

She left this new journal, along with her pens and ink, lying on the table for many days before she began, tentatively, to describe and reflect on the prairie, the weather, the plants and animals, plus incidents from her life here.

Each blank page was an empty frame of hope and possibility, to be filled with something that always fell short of her aspirations. But the process delighted and satisfied her. Gustie liked the physical act of writing: the feel of the pen in her hand and the sound it made against the paper, how the writing filled the page and brought it life, how her large scrawling hand was always less legible at the end of a page than at the beginning. Once she began, the writing became easier and pages filled faster. Gustie wrote for herself only, sometimes indulging in flowery descriptions, sometimes recording fragments of observations and memories. She did not write much about people, with one exception: Dorcas. She had many pages of notes on Dorcas. She felt it was important to record everything about her.

Gustie had tried to write about Jordis, but she couldn't find the words to capture Jordis's spirit, her stature; how the sun rose when she smiled and the clouds roiled when she frowned; the depths of her eyes; how, astride the white horse, she looked like a centauress. Gustie was embarrassed by such thoughts, and found the pen awkward in her hand. On the subject of Jordis, the blank page remained blank.

Gustie looked at her pocket watch lying on the table and noted the time. The circle of candlelight had been swallowed in the ocean of dawn. Outside her window the land was waking up. Colors of sky and earth were distinguishing themselves from the gray wash of twilight. A moth wobbled out from the corner of her window ledge and clumsily spread one wing, then another, to the warming light. Birds opened their throats to announce themselves to the sun. She closed her journal, drank the rest of her coffee, and went to finish dressing.

The skirt and blouse she planned to wear to the Fourth of July celebration were already draped across the bed. As she pinned up her hair she considered herself in the mirror. Her body was wraithlike, wearing thin just like her clothes. She found the notion amusing that she and her wardrobe might disappear together. All that would be left would be her watch, which remained the same but for a softer lustre than when her father had presented it to her ten years ago, her glasses, and a mass of brown hair showing more and more strands of gray.

Before she dressed she must bandage her wounds. Lately she had begun to leave the bandages off at night and to replace them lightly every day. She carefully pulled her shift over her head and studied her naked reflection.

The center of each wound was still a furious red, tender, unhealed. Around the edges the skin was knitting itself together in a pebbly formation, pearly white against the pale pink of her undamaged flesh. There would be no zigzag lightning pattern here, no dance of leaves, just this rough whiteness. She looked long at the forming scars and liked them. They gave her courage. They made her feel free.

Gustie drove up the winding drive to Lena and Will's house, surprised to see another wagon ahead of her. It was not yet six o'clock in the morning.

She maneuvered Biddie under the trees by the well and recognized the short, squarish form of Hank Ackerman standing by his wagon talking to Will, who bent his tall frame slightly toward Hank and cocked his head so that his good ear got all of the conversation. Will did not see Gustie at first. She had driven up on his blind and deaf side. When he straightened up to reply to something Hank said, he saw her and waved her over.

Hank touched the brim of his hat with his left hand and grinned. "Morning, Miss Roemer."

"Morning, Mr. Ackerman. How is Orville?"

"Oh, doing pretty good. I make him do a little reading every night so he doesn't lose the hang of it. You need anything done around your place, Miss Roemer?"

"I may need a fence."

"He could do that. Put up a nice one for you." Hank grinned and his blue eyes, strikingly pale in his ruddy brown face, lit with pride.

"I'll let you know then when I'm ready."

Gustie saw the tips of straw in the back of Hank's wagon shift. She peered over the sides of the wagon. Lying on her side in the straw was a sow with five piglets. Two were sleeping, three were busy with breakfast.

Hank, she could see now, was holding a sixth in the crook of his right arm. He scratched it behind the ears and it smiled a piggy smile, eyes closed in contentment. He put the piglet back down in the straw and it squirmed in among its siblings and began to suckle.

Gustie had never seen such little pigs before. "May I?" she asked.

"Go ahead. She won't mind. She's used to it."

Gustie gently lifted one of the piglets out of the wagon bed and held him in her arms. He folded his tiny hoofed feet under himself and snuggled in, relaxing against the warmth of her body. She was stunned at the babyness of him.

"Hank was just sayin' they're having a big Fourth of July doings over in Wheat Lake, too," Will said.

"*Ja,* I thought about takin' my pigs there instead of here in Charity, till I heard the Indians were going to be there. Giving a big powwow. Then I changed my mind quick. Maybe there is some that finds that heathen squalling and jumpin' around interesting, but not me. I won't mingle with dog eaters. No sir."

A small coldness took possession of Gustie's center. "What?"

"Dog eaters," Hank explained cheerfully. "They eat dog. Turns my stomach just thinking about it."

Will said, "Well, we got plenty doing right here in Charity, and you'll get a good price for your pigs here, as much as you would over there. Don't you worry."

"You're probably right."

Will went on. "Lena's baking pies enough to feed the county. There's a band and going to be some horse racing. Old Tom is too old. In his day, boy, he could keep up with the best of 'em. Don't you worry about that. Then later I guess Ike Thorson's going to play his fiddle and we'll have a little high-stepping."

Gustie was still cuddling the piglet and running her finger along a soft, pink ear that was sparsely layered with long blond hairs. He peeped up at her through pale lashes, then closed his eyes again in drowsy peacefulness. She asked, "Mr. Ackerman, what are you going to do with these pigs?"

"Well, folks always need a porker or two to fatten up. Will's right. I'll get a good price for 'em here as much as Wheat

Lake." He got up into his wagon and picked up the reins. "Want to buy that pig?" He grinned down at Gustie.

"No. Thanks." She returned the baby pig to his mother.

"I'll keep after Orville and his readin'. You send for him when you're ready. He'll build you a real good fence. He is sure good with his hands and building things."

"Thank you, Mr. Ackerman. I will."

As his wagon rumbled down the drive, Hank called over his shoulder, "I'll fatten him up for you, Will."

Will nodded, grinned, and waved back.

Gustie asked Will, "Aren't they too young to sell?"

"He sells 'em but they stay with the sow until they're weaned. People pick the one they want, he tags 'em, and they pick up the pig when it's ready. He was just letting me have first choice. I drilled him a well last year. He paid half but he's been short on cash so he's giving me the rest in pig. Come on in. Lena's just about got breakfast ready."

Lena's house smelled of perking coffee, toast, and frying ham.

"Look who's here, Duchy!" Will hung his hat on the hook in the shanty before he entered the kitchen. Lena bustled around her small domain. The table was already set for three. Gustie washed her hands in the sink. "Just sit down now," Lena commanded. "We'll eat first. Will has to go to the fairgrounds and help stake out the horse race." She was pouring batter into the frying pan. Gustie served the coffee all around and brought the platter of ham to the table, where a stack of toast was already in place. Will was spreading a slice liberally with butter and chokeberry jam that was so deeply purple it was almost black.

When they were all three seated, Lena bowed her head for a silent grace. Will paused in his chewing and Gustie waited to take her share of the pancakes. When Lena finished her prayer and looked up, Will passed Gustie the meat.

"No, thanks."

"I thought you liked ham," Lena said.

"I'm afraid I just lost my taste for it." Gustie raised her eyebrows and offered a self-deprecating half-smile.

Will chuckled. "Oh, *ja,* Hank's pigs. Never seen the little ones before, huh?"

Gustie shook her head.

"They're sure cute little buggers all right. But they grow up ugly. Mean codgers, too. Hang your leg over the rail of a pigpen, they'll chew it off as look atcha." He chuckled some more over the rim of his coffee cup.

Lena sniffed. "Oh, don't talk such foolishness. An animal is as good or bad as you treat it. When I was a little bit of a thing we had a big sow." Lena took a bite of pancake. Some syrup dribbled from the corners of her mouth. She caught the drips with her tongue, dabbed at her chin with her apron, and continued her story. "Named Emma. My pa always warned me to stay away from Emma. But I didn't pay any attention to that. I was always crawling around in the barn with the horses and the cows, so I didn't see any reason not to crawl into the pigpen just the same. And I did—when nobody was looking. One day Pa said he found me—I don't remember this—said he found me sitting on her, straddling her, you know. She was lying on her side, and there I was pouring sand into her ears with a spoon. Didn't seem to bother the pig. Pa lifted me out of there and Emma got up and shook her head. All that sand came flying out all over. But Pa figured after that I was more harm to the pig than she to me, so that was the end of my playing in the pigpen."

"Well." Will was grinning and his mouth was full. "I still say the best thing about a pig's the bacon." Will pushed the plate of pancakes toward her. "Better eat now. The only thing you take with you is what you eat."

Gustie reached for another piece of toast just as Lena jumped out of her seat, responding to a smell so faint only the cook would notice. "Uh-oh. My potatoes boiled dry." She grabbed a pot holder and swung the heavy pot off the stove and over to the sink. She lifted the cover to inspect the damage.

"Burn 'em?" asked Will. "Duchy makes good potato salad," he said to Gustie.

"They're not too bad, I guess. Most of 'em will do for the salad. The rest I'll fry up for breakfast tomorrow." Lena took her place at the table once more. "When the potatoes boil dry it means it's going to storm," she said.

Gustie smiled mischievously. "Doesn't it mean you should have paid closer attention to the potatoes?"

Will laughed, sputtering through a mouthful of coffee, "She's got you there, Duchy!"

"Nobody likes a smarty-pants." Lena made a face at Gustie and they all had to laugh.

"I should be back here about noon. You two women be ready by then?" Will gulped the rest of his coffee and grabbed another piece of toast as he stood up. Gustie was amazed at the quantities of food Will Kaiser could put away in short spans of time.

"I don't see why not!" Lena took the empty platters and her own plates to the sink. She poured hot water over them from the kettle on the stove. "It doesn't take five hours just to bake a few pies. Don't you be late, now. You'll have to clean up before we go back. You can't go looking like that. I've got your white shirt all clean and pressed for you."

"Don't you worry. I won't be late."

Will slapped her lightly on her behind and she chased him with her dishrag, swiping him across the back of his neck. He grabbed his hat, running and grinning on the way out.

"That man!" Lena was smiling as she came back into the kitchen.

Gustie carried her own dishes to the sink and was about to start the washing up, when Lena stopped her. "Oh no you don't. Don't go getting your bandages wet. I'll do this. You peel apples. There's a bucket for the peelings and there's the bowl for the apples." She nodded toward the bucket on the floor and the bowl sitting out on the counter.

Gustie tucked up her skirt, put the bucket between her knees, and began to peel apples, clumsily, aware that her peelings were thick. They fell heavily, thudding into the bucket. A lot of apple going to waste. But it was the best she could do. She had seen Lena peel apples so fast and with such precision that the peelings floated downward in long translucent curls.

Lena read the dismay on Gustie's face. "Don't worry, we'll take the peelings to Hank's pig this afternoon. So we get it back in the end." That did not make Gustie feel better.

When the breakfast dishes were drying on the drain board, Lena began mixing up a bowl of pastry dough. To Gustie's everlasting wonderment, Lena never measured anything. She dumped the flour in by the handful, cut in random spoons of lard with a fork, sprinkled just enough water over it all so the pastry formed pea-sized pellets.

"Have you heard anything more from the sheriff, or the lawyer?" Gustie had not spoken to Pard Batie herself since her return.

"No. Both of them say they are working on it, but I don't know what they mean by 'working.' I don't see either one of 'em doing anything more than they ever did—sitting around drinking coffee, shooting the breeze," Lena replied as she scooped out a palm-sized ball of dough. She shaped it into a smooth, round, and somewhat flattened shape before applying her rolling pin. Lena put her arms and shoulders into rolling out the crust. Short, even strokes in every direction formed a round pastry. Then through her fingers she sifted more flour over it and turned it around 180 degrees and vigorously rolled a perfect, thin circle. "Everybody's talking and seems to think it was some stranger, but I don't know—there's enough hard feelings in that family."

"What kind of hard feelings?"

"Those two sisters, peeking over at one another all these years. And Pa Kaiser going back and forth between them." Lena shook her head and frowned as she powered her rolling pin. "Once he went over to Julia's and stayed there for over a month, but then he went back again to Gertrude's house. I don't know what she did or said to get him to go back. I'm not supposed to know about that, but Nyla told me. Oscar was old enough to remember it." Lena ran a spatula beneath the circle of pastry dough and folded it neatly in half. She brought a pie tin to the board and placed the folded pastry so the fold ran directly down the middle of the pan. She unfolded it, pressed the dough into the shape of the pan, and with quick strokes of a sharp knife cut all the way around the rim, trimming off the excess crust and sliding the pieces over to the corner of her floured board. Then she began again with another scoop of dough from the bowl.

"Pa just walked over to Julia's one day and kept going back there at night after he came home from work. But he went back all right—back to Gertrude's, I mean. He was a weak man. Folks say that in the beginning he'd courted Julia, but old man Gareis talked him into marrying Gertrude. Pa got his first well rig in the deal. So he went along with it. Fool man. Can you imagine marrying a woman to get a well rig? Good night!" She finished the second crust and lined the second pan in her same sure manner, and moved on to a third. "Guess they thought nobody would ever marry Gertrude, and Julia was a pretty little thing in those days so someone else would come along for her. Only nobody ever did. She stayed an old maid all those years—except for that one month."

Gustie still struggled with her apples. At least ten of these apples were needed to fill one of Lena's pies. "How could they live so close together like that?" Gustie was all amazement at what she was hearing. She stopped peeling to flex her fingers, which were beginning to cramp from her tight grip on the knife. "After he had lived with Julia? How could Gertrude take him back? How could Julia stay around after he left her and went back to Gertrude?"

"No place to go. None of 'em. No place else to go. Gertrude sure couldn't go anyplace. She already had two little boys—Oscar and Walter. Where would she have gone? Julia had no place to go either. So they all stayed together. One big miserable family. Then, after Pa went back to Gertrude, along came Will, and then Frederick, and Julia started pitching in and helping a little with the boys. Though to hear Ma tell it, she never did a thing. I don't believe that. I think she did help. Especially with Frederick. Gertrude was getting too tired to cope with a new little one so late in her life. I guess she had no milk left. So Frederick was the only one of her babies to be bottle-fed. Julia could have helped there." The tins were all lined with pastry and three perfectly formed circles lay folded in a row, waiting for the time when she would lay them over the apple-filled pans and close the crusts around the rims. She sat down and absently, without missing a beat in her storytelling, began to slice the apples Gustie had peeled, letting the pieces fall in even layers into a readied pie tin. "Ma probably appreciated Julia's being there. Even though she will never admit it." Lena paused and looked out the window. "You know how I think it worked?" She pointed with her knife, visualizing the scene. "I think that neither of them really loved Pa. They sort of put up with him, you see, and they didn't feel it so much when . . . well, I don't know." Lena shook her head and went back to slicing apples.

When the pie pan was filled to her satisfaction, Lena went to the cupboard and came back with a tin of sugar and small boxes of cinnamon and nutmeg. She sprinkled the sugar and spices liberally over the apples, tossing them lightly with a fork to evenly coat all the pieces. "And it was Gertrude who had children. So she was more or less tied to Pa, you know. What a mess it would have been if Julia'd had any. Whew! But she was lucky, I guess, that way."

"Do you think one of them killed him?"

"I don't really know. If they were going to kill him, they'd have done it, one or the other of them, when they were young. Not now, when they were all three of them old and one foot in the grave. Don't you think? What's the point? They'd stood it this long. Besides, if anybody was going to kill anybody, I always thought it would be Ma killing Julia, or vice versa. Oh, shoot, I'm running out of sugar. Thought I had another whole can, but I don't. Don't know where my mind is lately."

Gustie tilted her head. "You don't?"

"Well, O'Grady's is open till noon. Then everybody shuts down for the Fourth."

"I'll go get some. Anything else you need?"

Lena shook her boxes of spices next to her ear. "Nutmeg? And cinnamon?"

Gustie paused at the door, then turned back to Lena. "Have you told all this to Dennis, or Pard?"

"No. It doesn't seem right to bring it all up. Like gossip." She waved the idea away like a pesky fly. "Phooey! Folks don't go around killing people over things that happened thirty and forty years ago. It must have been like they say—a stranger. More like an accident."

Gustie didn't feel like letting it go. "Who found the body?"

Lena stopped her peeling. "Well, I'm not sure."

"Who saw Will coming out of the barn?"

"Oh, that was Alvinia. She don't miss much." Lena abruptly changed the subject. "It's the strangest thing. You know, Kenny says we have a credit. That he overcharged us on something or other, I don't understand it. Some mistake. But whatever it was, it was in our favor. So you won't need any money. He'll just subtract it from our credit." Lena shrugged.

When Gustie returned with Lena's spices and sugar she was surprised to see Old Tom back under the trees, and yet another wagon in front of the house. *This is a busy place,* she thought. The horses hitched to the visiting wagon looked familiar: dapple-gray Percherons—not as well brushed as they might be, but well fed and healthy-looking otherwise.

Gustie hadn't reached the door before Lena opened the screen and flapped her hands. "What's the matter? Here's your—"

Lena interrupted her with a hiss and more frantic waves of her hand. "Go home, now. Go on now."

Before Gustie could voice her annoyance at being shooed off like a stray cat, there appeared behind Lena an old familiar face, smiling a nasty smile. The man, impeccable, as usual, in an exquisitely tailored gray suit said only, "Well, Augusta."

Lena threw up her hands. "I tried. We didn't tell him anything. Believe me. You might as well come in, then. No sense standing out there in the sun. It's going to get hot."

Gustie nearly lost her nerve, but as her left wrist began to throb, she felt a sudden grounding in her own pain. She said, "I'd rather speak to him in private. Wouldn't you prefer that, Peter?"

"Peter?" Lena eyed the man. "You said your name was Steven."

He ignored Lena and continued to smile at Gustie. His way of smiling without showing any teeth made him look more sinister the more he smiled.

"It's Peter," Gustie said. "Peter Madigan. What's wrong, Peter? So ashamed of your mission you couldn't use your own name?"

From inside the house, the pleasant smell of apples was over-powered by acrid cigar smoke. She heard Walter's gravelly laugh and placed the Percherons. They were his horses, part of Pa Kaiser's big draft team used to pull the well rig around.

Maintaining as much righteous dignity as possible, the stranger said, "I think this *would* be better discussed in private."

The two of them walked away from the house.

Lena spun around and shook her finger at Walter. "You dumb cluck! With the whole town not knowing who or where Gustie is, you have to parade him over here!"

Walter gestured with his cigar. "You being a friend of hers, I thought . . ."

"You thought! You thought, my eye! Oh, sit down and be quiet. You make me tired. And put that cigar out. Who said you could smoke that thing in my house?"

Walter sat as he was told, looking wounded. Will handed him a tin ashtray for his cigar.

Lena watched through her kitchen curtains. She could see that the discussion between Gustie and Steven, or Peter, or whatever the heck his name was, was heated even though she could not hear their voices. When the man made a move as if to strike Gustie, Lena said, "That's it! Will, you better get out there right now! I think he might hit her."

Will was up and out the door, making himself visible very quickly. He ambled casually over to where Gustie and Peter Madigan stood arguing under the chokecherry trees.

"Everything all right out here?" he asked, cleaning his teeth with a toothpick.

Neither Gustie nor Peter Madigan spoke. She glared at the man, her jaw set, her face deeply flushed.

Peter, hoping perhaps to find a kindred male spirit in Will, said stiffly, "I have a right to see my sister's grave, *if* she is dead, like Augusta says."

Will looked down and stirred the gravel with the toe of his boot. "That right? Is his sister dead?"

"Yes, that's right." Gustie answered, her voice low and angry.

"You know where she's buried?" Will tossed the toothpick away.

"Yes, I do, and he has no right to anything." Gustie spoke quietly, but defiantly.

"I am not leaving here till I see the grave," Peter Madigan said.

"Rot here, then." Gustie turned away and Peter grabbed her roughly by the arm. Will stepped in and with a grip that promised even greater strength lifted Madigan's hand off Gustie's arm. At the same time he gently rested his other hand on Gustie's shoulder. She stopped her retreat.

"Maybe you should just take him to his sister's grave, Gus," Will said. "If he is the brother, he has a right to see it."

"It's a long way from here."

"I've got plenty of time." Madigan spoke more civilly, now that his wrist felt Will Kaiser's iron grip.

Gustie felt beaten, trapped. Will let go of Peter Madigan. He kept his other hand resting lightly on Gustie's shoulder and, ignoring Madigan's presence altogether, said, "I'll go with you, Gus. Don't you worry. I won't let you go off alone with this piker. Then we'll be rid of him. Whaddya say?"

Gustie said nothing. She felt she had no choice.

"Just have to go tell Lena. You—" he spoke sternly to Madigan "—get over there and get on that horse." He pointed to Old Tom, saddled and ready to go. As an afterthought Will asked Gustie, "Where we goin'?"

"Crow Kills."

Will paused for a moment, then went into the house to tell Lena.

. . .

In the wagon box, Will took up the reins. Gustie sat beside him. Peter Madigan, still on his own two feet, looked with dismay at the narrow wagon seat. Will said, "You're going to have to ride that big fella over there," he pointed to Old Tom switching at flies under the trees, "unless you want to sit in the back like a sack of spuds." Will chuckled quietly.

Peter Madigan clambered aboard Old Tom, who was a very big horse.

Will made clucking noises and tapped Biddie on her rump with the reins. "Okay. Here we go."

Gustie had never made a longer journey. They could not go too fast, because Madigan was no horseman. She looked over her shoulder from time to time to see him bouncing painfully up and down in the saddle. She suspected that Will was keeping to this pace deliberately, a quick trot, at which he knew Old Tom's gait was the most bone-jarring.

At least Madigan had lost his smile (along with his hat), and he was quiet. All his concentration was required to keep a white-knuckled grip on the saddle horn. Perspiration trickled down his face.

Will was not much for conversation, so Gustie was left to her own reverie. This was the same spring wagon in which she and Clare had journeyed for two weeks, all their belongings tied to the back. When they finally had their things loaded and were driving out of Apple Creek, Wisconsin, Clare had breathed relief: "No more train." Gustie had thought it was the train ride that was making Clare feel so ill. The cars were stuffy, crowded, and Clare hated the confinement. So they had got off in Wisconsin, where the conductor told them they would find decent lodgings. While Clare rested, Gustie bought the horse and wagon. She had not liked spending Clare's money. But Clare insisted: "We're going to need them sooner or later. We're just getting them sooner, that's all."

Several nights spent in a soft bed with fresh sheets, a steamy bath, and good food seemed to restore Clare, and she declared herself ready to travel. They set out for South Dakota. For a while Clare had felt better out in the open air, under an expanse of sky that had lifted their hearts. Out here there was more sky than earth. Gustie sensed that Clare, for the first time in her life, felt real freedom. The nervousness that had kept her scanning the faces of all the passengers on the train was gone. They had mild weather and slept under the stars.

The man Clare had feared now rode behind Gustie. She felt it almost as a grace that Clare was finally beyond his reach.

Gustie's wrists and breast throbbed with pain. She had not counted on being back at Crow Kills so soon. Would Jordis be there? Gustie looked back again, wondering how Peter Madigan would last the hours it would take to get there.

But last he did.

"Let her go. She knows the way," Gustie said to Will, who gave Biddie her head. The mare turned right off the dirt road and pulled them up and over the rise. She stopped in her usual place.

Will and Gustie got down and stretched their legs and arched their backs to get the kinks out. Peter Madigan slid off Old Tom. His legs were wobbly and Gustie wished he would collapse.

Madigan looked around. His pale face was sunburned. His nose glowed red.

"There's nothing out here. This is no graveyard. Where have you brought me? What are you up to now?"

Gustie had slipped into an exhaustion so deep, it was all she could do to reply, "I'm not up to anything. You wanted to see her grave. There it is."

Before anyone else, Will saw the form rising up from the lake: a vision out of the not-so-long-ago-past of a dark woman in butter-soft doeskin that clung to her body agreeably. As she moved up from the lower ground with the stretch of sparkling blue water behind her, it looked to Will, his one eye squinting against a high noon sun, like she rose out of the lake. In the blinding sun, the blue beads glistening across her shoulders and down her sleeves looked like part of Crow Kills come with her. She climbed toward where they stood, the three of them, looking at the subtle rise of earth under the lone-standing cottnwood tree. She came closer. Will Kaiser took off his hat.

When Gustie saw Jordis she felt a jolt in her stomach and a flash of heat rise up her throat. The past dimmed for an instant in the brightness of this moment. "You look beautiful," Gustie said, finally, softly, the words carrying on the wind like the whisper of leaves. Jordis smiled. Peter Madigan was forgotten.

"Happy Fourth of July," said Jordis. There was irony, humor, and welcome in Jordis's voice. Gustie laughed.

Madigan would not allow himself to be out of mind for long. "What's going on here?" he demanded.

"This is Clare's brother," Gustie said. Some of her weariness lifted in Jordis's presence. "He insisted on seeing her grave. I'll get him out of here as soon as I can." With more cordiality, she nodded to Will, "This is Will Kaiser, Lena's husband. Will, this is my friend, Jordis."

"Very pleased to meet you." Will nodded and shifted from one foot to the other, grinning like a pup. Jordis returned a silent greeting, then her eyes went back and forth between Gustie and Peter Madigan, reading the trouble in the air between them.

Madigan stared at the first live Indian he had ever laid eyes on. Gustie observed him assess Jordis, then dismiss her. She was quite sure Jordis saw the same thing.

"There's no grave here," he said to Gustie. The strain of the long ride and the heat had eroded his composure. "Where is she?" His tone was strident.

"She's there." Gustie nodded her head sadly toward the grave.

"This? What's this? This is nothing!" The wild swing of his arm included all the land he saw.

The long fringes on her sleeves danced on the wind as Jordis extended her arm and pointed to the exact place beneath the cottonwood. "It's a grave, White Man. And this is the woman who dug it."

"How would you know?" Peter Madigan sneered. Gustie wanted to kill him.

Jordis dropped her arm. "This is my land. I found her just as she was finished."

"*You* found me?"

Gustie had no time to absorb this information, for Peter Madigan was murmuring the words "*you killed her.*"

Then in full voice, he said, "Why did you have to drag her off to this godforsaken place?" As strongly as she hated him, Gustie pitied him.

"She had been very ill for a long time. I didn't know how ill, and she didn't tell me. She knew I wouldn't have made this journey if I had known."

"What happened to her? Why out here?" Madigan's voice broke. For a moment Gustie understood how alone and small he must feel in this shadowless land that to his eyes looked barren. She saw a little boy and girl playing in a big house, with a sick mother and a distant father. The same childhood that had made Clare sweet, quiet, and strong had made Peter bitter, forever grasping and trying to hold on to things no matter how they would slip through his fingers. She saw a man who had a house with too many rooms, a closet full of perfectly tailored suits, and nothing else. The dearest thing in his life he had hurt and driven away. She understood, yes, but she did not care.

"You couldn't have at least buried her in sanctified ground? Not even a Christian burial? Not a decent headstone?" Tears spilled onto his burned cheeks. He wiped them away quickly with his fingers. Gustie was unmoved. Peter sank to his knees by the grave and wept. Finally, he asked, "How did she die?"

Gustie's mouth remained set in a taut line. She had never spoken of Clare's death and would not now give him Clare's last moments, or her own feelings about it. Peter cried again, "How did she die?"

Gustie was rigid.

Jordis said, "Tell *me*."

Gustie looked at her, uncomprehending.

Jordis said, "Give me your story, Gustie."

"He—" Gustie indicated Madigan.

"He does not matter. Tell *me*."

Gustie trembled all over.

"Tell me." Jordis's voice drew Gustie into a world as private as Crow Kills at night, with the moon shimmering across their bodies and the surface of the water.

Gustie told her story:

"We traveled for such a long time, days and days without seeing a town, a house—nothing. I didn't know where we were anymore. Clare was so tired. In Apple Creek—where we got off the train—I made her see a doctor. She told me he'd said it was nothing serious. All she needed was rest. If she'd told me the truth then, I'd have turned around and taken her back. But she knew that. She didn't want to go back. The night before she died she said she didn't ever want to go back. That she wanted to die out here. I thought—I wanted to think—she was talking about her old age.

"We had to make some kind of permanent camp. She needed rest and I had to get my bearings. I had no idea we were as close to Wheat Lake as we were. We smelled the water and cut over the hill, and here was Crow Kills. The most beautiful lake we had ever seen."

Gustie did not weep. Her voice did not waver. She spoke

only to Jordis. "I made her as comfortable as I could. I took everything out of the wagon and made her a bed in there. She was happy. She loved this prairie. She loved the lake and the sky. Everything. She'd have been very happy out here. I was clumsy with cooking over a fire. It took me a long time to do the simplest things. I was making us some tea. She was propped up on the blankets and bags I used as pillows for her. She was reading. Tennyson. I came back with her cup of tea and she was gone. The book was open to *The Lady of Shalott*. She looked so peaceful and happy. I sat by her, drinking tea, as if I were expecting her to wake up. I knew she was dead, but I sat with her like that for a long time. All night. Then in the morning, I knew I had to bury her here. I couldn't cart her around looking for a strange town and strange people to bury her. It had to be right here. This *is* holy ground. I felt it then. I still feel it.

"I had a shovel and I started to dig. I was very stupid. I didn't think at all. I started digging over there." Gustie pointed down the hill, toward the lake. "I dug down until I was worn out. I had to rest. When I came back to it, the grave was full of water. I screamed at the lake. I threw rocks and mud into it. I threw the shovel and had to wade in after it. So I looked around and saw this little knoll away from the lake. I started to dig again. Then I carried water up from the lake. I washed her body. I dressed her in white. I wrapped her in a blanket and laid her in the grave." Gustie paused. "Then I filled it up. And lay down. I never thought I'd get up again."

Gustie's thoughts traveled back over her long recovery period.

"Yours was the second voice I heard, wasn't it?"

Jordis nodded.

"You looked after Biddie?"

Jordis nodded again.

Gustie looked down toward Crow Kills. "You filled the first grave."

"Dorcas and I were visiting Little Bull and Winnie. When we came back, I saw Biddie down by the lake. Then I found the wagon, and you lying facedown on the grave. I helped Dorcas take care of you until you started to come around. Then I left—to go help Little Bull."

Madigan was on his feet again, picking grass off the knees of his trousers, his face and manner having already re-formed themselves into their usual arrogance, and, stone-cold sober, Will wanted very badly to punch him. Instead, he strode over to Gustie and put his arms around her and held her in a bear hug.

"You're a grand girl, Gus."

"Will, you're a good man. You have to stop drinking so much, you know." Gustie gave his arm a rough but affectionate pat. He let her go.

"I know, Gus. I know."

Peter Madigan intruded himself back into their consciousness like a buzzing insect. "There is still the money. It belongs to me. That's what I came for."

Gustie faced him, stunned for a moment that he could speak of money standing over his sister's grave. Then she remembered more of him. "That money was Clare's. Her rightful inheritance."

"She stole it out of Father's safe and ran off without his blessing. She had no right to inherit anything!"

"I don't think your father looked at it that way, or he would have sent you, or someone, after us right away. But he didn't. Isn't that right? He wouldn't let you come. I assume he is recently dead." Madigan's silence confirmed it. "I imagine his body isn't cold yet."

"It's *my* money!" Peter's voice was rising in pitch.

"The money was Clare's!" Gustie's was getting lower.

"And Clare is dead!" Peter affirmed what he only recently had accepted as true.

"Yes," replied Gustie evenly. "So now it's mine. You know,

Peter, for a long time after she was gone, I considered returning the money to your father. I never touched a penny of it. But when I heard you were looking for her, I knew why, and I remembered why she left home. It wasn't simply to be with me, but to get away from you. It became a matter of principle with me to not let you have it. You can threaten me. Do anything you want. You won't find the money. You will never get it back, nor anything that was hers. Not a scrap of her clothing, not a photograph. Nothing. Clare and I had an understanding. What we had, we had in common, like husband and wife."

Madigan brayed, "Let's hear you talk like that in front of a judge and before a courtroom of decent people!"

Gustie continued, almost casually. "Anyway, the money's gone. I spent it."

He was incredulous. "What could you possibly spend that much money on in a few days out here?"

"Let's see. I bought a rocking chair and two beds for Mrs. Many Roads, Jordis's grandmother." She turned to Jordis. "The beds I had to special-order. Don't tell her. It's a surprise."

Gustie turned back to Madigan. "I got enough supplies to get them through till her next annuities are due. Some clothes——"

Madigan was sputtering. "That's ridiculous. You can't have spent all that money on an old squaw." He made a move toward Gustie.

"You watch yourself, Buster, or I'll knock your block off." Will's hands were twitching. Then he added, "No, she didn't spend it all on Mrs. Many Roads. She spent it on me. Sorry, Gus. Denny told me. He just figured it out. Pard didn't say nothing. So there's no blame there. Didn't know the how or wherefore of it, but we knew it had to be you because it couldn't be anybody else."

"I will get it back. You——" At that moment the malice on Madigan's face caused Will to take a step toward him, when around the southern curve of Crow Kills appeared a lengthening line of trotting ponies, bedecked with feathers and bright cloth. Upon the back of each pony rode a Sioux warrior in full regalia. Heading the procession rode an old man, the feathers of his war bonnet cascading down his back. Beside him was Little Bull bearing a long, feathered lance. Behind him rode a boy wearing the buckskin shirt Gustie had seen in Dorcas's cabin. Will squinted to see them better with his one eye, then climbed onto the wagon to get a better look.

Little Bull trotted out ahead of his father. When he saw Jordis and Gustie and the man in the gray suit, he picked up the pace and the others followed him up the hill. To the amazement of Peter Madigan, the Indians formed a circle around them and sat, silent, looking fierce and bloodthirsty. The only sounds were the ponies, shifting from leg to leg, blowing through their nostrils, and the chittering of birds and insects. Madigan turned white and a line of sweat broke out upon his upper lip; more began to trickle down his temples. He swatted angrily at mosquitoes that did not seem to be attacking anyone else.

"You've found your place, all right," he snarled at Gustie. "Among these filthy savages." But he faltered as Little Bull heeled Swallow in his left flank and the horse stepped forward out of the circle with a prancing step. There seemed to be a lot of pent-up energy in that horse, and it was shared by the Indian on his back. A long knife hung from Little Bull's belt. His hand moved toward it but stopped, resting so lightly upon his thigh it seemed to hover there. Will Kaiser remained seated in the wagon. His hands covered his face.

Little Bull looked at Jordis and made another movement toward his knife. She shook her head slightly. None of these movements were lost on Peter Madigan, who was now as gray as his suit. A dark stain appeared on the inside left leg of his trousers.

"Will, you're a white man. You aren't going to let them . . . my god, man!"

Will took his hands away from his face. He looked very pained. Slowly he climbed down from the wagon and approached Little Bull. He spoke in low tones to the Indian, who sat back up on his horse and said, "Hmph!" with a loud grunt. Will rubbed his face hard and turned toward Peter Madigan.

"Well, Madigan, it seems to me you've got one chance. The chief here looks upon Augusta as a friend. You see, the Indians are funny about their friends. He wouldn't like to see her harmed or threatened, you know. You're on Indian land, so their law is what goes around here. They can do pretty much what they want. Whatever they'd do would take a long time and wouldn't be something I'd want to watch, I'll tell you. I would say you can leave now, while I've got the chief calmed down." Will pulled his watch out of his pocket. "Don't you worry. There's a train leaving in an hour or so from Wheat Lake. You can get back on Old Tom there and ride to the station. Leave him with the station manager—he's a pal of mine—and I'll pick him up later. That's just my idea. You know these Indians. They'd never let you be. But you do what you want." Will looked down at his feet and then not at anyone in particular.

The stain had grown on the inside of Madigan's pants. He lurched stiff-legged over to Will's horse and pulled himself up into the saddle. "How do I get to Wheat Lake?" he choked.

"Just follow that dirt road out, the way we came in, and take a left instead of a right when you come to the fork. You'll go right into town. You better skedaddle if you're going to make the train."

"I won't forget this, Augusta."

Little Bull stirred on his mount and the bay did a little hop step in place. They looked ready to charge. From the direction of Dorcas's cabin came what sounded like a bloodcurdling warwhoop. Madigan kicked the horse's sides and almost lost his balance, but hung onto the saddle horn for dear life as Old

Tom trotted his bone-cracking gait back the way they had come.

Will could stand it no longer. He crumpled onto the ground and began to laugh until tears rolled down his face. The fierce countenances of braves in war paint dissolved in smiles and laughter as well. Even Gustie laughed. Only Jordis was not amused. She reached out and touched Gustie's arm lightly then looked out at the tiny disappearing form of Madigan on Will's horse. "The stupid son of a bitch. He thinks we're still on the war path."

Little Bull dismounted. In a voice that bore no resemblance to the grunt he had uttered a moment ago, he asked "Are you all right, Gustie?"

"Yes. Thank you."

"It might have been fun to scalp him."

"When was the last time you used that knife?" challenged Jordis.

"Actually, I never have." Little Bull made a fierce face in her direction and sheathed the knife.

Gustie surveyed the riders and clasped her hands in delight. "You all look . . . magnificent!!"

Some had their faces painted red, some had red stripes down their bare arms and chests. Some wore bright shirts and leather leggings, with feathers streaming out of braided hair, or headbands holding back shorter, cropped hair.

Little Bull said, "Gustie, I'd like you to meet my father, Chief Good Wolf." He escorted her to the side of the spotted pony and spoke to his father in the Dakotah language. The old man looked down upon her. His face of a thousand lines broke into a cheery smile. He replied in Dakotah.

Gustie said, "I am honored to meet you, Chief Good Wolf." Little Bull translated.

Chief Good Wolf was very old but his eyes were bright. His thinning hair fell down to his shoulders unbraided. Long fringes hung from the V shaped insert at the neck of his heavily beaded buckskin shirt. The loose sleeves of the shirt were beaded and fringed as well. He wore buckskin trousers. The chief kept smiling and said a few words more.

Little Bull chuckled.

"What did he say?" asked Gustie.

"He said you were unusually polite for a *wasichu*."

Gustie smiled again at the chief and then turned her attention to the young man in Dorcas's buckskin shirt. "You must be Leonard." He nodded shyly, and his face lit up when she said, "You will be the prime attraction of the celebration tonight."

Leonard wore a headband of a bright red fabric. His features were unmistakably those of his father, but softened, more rounded. Gustie had yet to meet Winnie.

Little Bull looked the part of the future chief. Two eagle feathers fastened to the back of his braided hair pointed straight to the sky. He too wore a beaded buckskin shirt, though it was not as ornately worked as his father's. Instead of the leather insert, the shirt was left open, and he wore a red bandanna around his neck and a metal medallion imprinted with the face of President Grant on a long cloth ribbon.

"Jordis," Little Bull said, noting the doeskin dress. "I'm glad you decided to join us."

"Dorcas wanted me to wear it. It was a small thing to do to make her happy—to let her see someone in this dress again. That's all. I'm not dancing."

Little Bull smiled. "Winnie sent this along just in case." Leonard handed his father a red shawl with long fringes, which Little Bull in turn gave to Jordis.

"It will be chilly tonight. Come in handy. Thanks." She casually draped the shawl over one shoulder.

Gustie looked over the hill and saw a large wagon drawn by two mules, one of whom no doubt had sounded the war cry that spurred Peter Madigan east.

"We've got to go. We're supposed to mark off the part of the fairgrounds we want to use as a dancing ground. Emil said we should get there early to make sure nobody else sets up a wagon or anything." He asked Jordis, "Are you ready?"

She nodded.

Then, to Gustie and Will, he asked, "Will you come with us?"

Will was still shaking his head and chuckling. "I'll drive with you to Wheat Lake, then I got to pick up Old Tom, and wipe the piss off the saddle."

Gustie rode back to Wheat Lake with Will. He did not say much, but grinned all the way back, occasionally chuckling to himself. Gustie knew he would have a good story to tell for years to come, about the Easterner frightened off by wild Indians.

"Whoa, old girl," crooned Will. He pulled back gently on the reins. Biddie came obligingly to a stop in front of the depot at the north end of town.

Will jumped to the ground whooping, "Yo! Joe! Where are ya? Wake up! You got customers!"

Joe Gruba appeared from around the corner of the small brown building, his mouth wide in a grin that exposed blackened teeth and a gap where two were missing. "Hey there, Will! Whaddya know?"

"Ain't got the time to tell you, Joe."

Joe grinned again as the two men shook hands.

Will said, "This here's Gustie Roemer. Friend of ours. Old Tom around here somewhere?"

"Yeah, he's in the back there. You'll have to saddle him up. I didn't know how long you was going to be, so I took his saddle off and rubbed him down good. The fellow who left him popped off in a hurry. I thought if you didn't show up pretty soon I'd have to sell him to the Indians." More grins.

Gustie tried to keep smiling.

"You lookin' a little peaked, Gus. Maybe you otta take it easy here awhile. That okay with you, Joe? We rode out pretty early this morning."

"Oh, sure. Sure." Joe Gruba hooked his thumbs under his suspenders, the only thing keeping up his baggy trousers. "The missus has fixed up a nice little room in the back. There's a cot in there and she always has some fresh water and a plate of biscuits. Just for folks who need a little lay-me-down between trains. Nobody there right now. You go make yourself at home and I'll take care of your horse."

Gustie dabbed at the perspiration on her forehead with the back of her sleeve. "That would be nice. I do feel tired. Thank you."

As Joe led Biddie away, he said over his shoulder, "Will, why don't you show her the room. Anything you want, miss, you just holler. I'll be out back here."

Will and Gustie passed through the main room of the depot. Next to the ticket counter was a handwritten poster stating ticket prices and the one rule of conduct that governed the place: "No Spitting." The door in the back opened into a tiny room with a neatly made cot, and, as Joe had promised, a pitcher of water and a plate of biscuits set out on a small square table.

"Will, thank you for coming with me today."

"Well, I sure wouldn't let you traipse off with that guy by yourself. That bugger—in his blood there's more spite than red, I'll betcha. No tellin' what . . ." He trailed off and looked around the room. "You stuck by me, Gus, when nobody else did. Not even my own folks. Without Pard talkin' for me I'd be a goner, and I know it. You stuck by Lena. We'll never forget it. Don't you worry. Yup." He shoved his hat back on his head. "I better be gettin' back to Duchy. She was lookin' pretty tough when we left."

Gustie nodded and Will was gone. The exhilaration of seeing Jordis again and relief that Peter Madigan was gone had buoyed her through the last hour, but now Gustie felt drained. She needed a few moments to refresh herself before going to the fairgrounds to look for her friends. She unbuttoned the top three buttons of her blouse and lay down.

When Gustie opened her eyes she saw nothing but bare, white-washed walls. She wiggled her toes. She had lain down without taking off her shoes. Now her feet were free and under a coverlet of some kind. She looked down. She was covered from shoulder to toe with the red shawl. She sat up and took out her watch: eight o'clock. She pulled on her shoes and laced them up as quickly as the tiny hooks would allow, splashed some water on her face, and tidied her hair as best she could.

Outside, Joe Gruba sprawled in a rickety chair, enjoying the evening breeze and a wizened little cigarette. He grinned his blackened, gap-toothed grin. "Hey there, Miss Gustie. You had quite a sleep there."

Gustie referred to the shawl folded over her arm. "Someone was here?"

"Yup, yup. One of the dancers from the powwow over there come lookin' for you. I says you was sleepin' and she says 'good' and just looks in on you a minute. She was sort of nice-lookin' so I thought it was okay."

"Yes." Gustie suddenly felt very warm.

"She says to tell you when you woke up to come over to the dancing grounds. Over that way." He pointed a skinny finger to the east.

"Mr. Gruba . . ."

"Call me Joe. Call me Joe."

"Joe. Thank you for everything. I hadn't expected to sleep all day." Gustie gave an embarrassed little laugh.

"Well, you sure look a little rosier now. That's for sure."

"Do I owe you anything for—"

"No sir. No sir. Will and I go way back. We do favors like for each other. Any friend of Will's . . . Oh, your horse is around back there. I harnessed her up again for you. Fit as a fiddle. Figured you'd be gettin' to go pretty soon."

"Thanks again."

"Any friend of Will's . . ." Joe Gruba grinned and took a long drag of his cigarette.

Curls of smoke rose from the cooking fires of the Dakotah camped in the pasture east of the fairgrounds. The evening was rich with smells bubbling up from stew pots and the smoky aromas of spitted roasting meats.

Gustie had missed all the afternoon's events. The non-Indian people were already packing up their blankets and picnic baskets and loading them into their wagons. A few left the fairgrounds. Most stayed, however, and gathered around the dancing ground. Gustie supposed that most of those who stayed did so out of curiosity. Since the Sioux had been prohibited from dancing for a long time, this was the first opportunity to see an Indian powwow. Today the Indians had been given an open dispensation to dance. But Gustie hoped that some might be there in genuine support of their Dakotah neighbors, knowing the admission fee was to support their school, and remembering, perhaps, how their parents or grandparents only made it through their first winter in the Dakota territory with help from the Indians. Besides, unlike the Teton and the Cheyenne to the west, or the Santee in Minnesota, these people of the Red Sand had never risen up in war against the white settlers. Dorcas had once said they didn't fight, not because they lacked courage, but because they knew a lost cause when it landed on them.

As Gustie threaded her way through the crowd, she could not see Jordis or Dorcas anywhere. The drum began. She stopped where she was.

• • •

The longer Gustie listened, the more she felt the drum engulf the rhythms of her body. It controlled her heartbeat, dictated the throbbing of her pulse. Should the drum fall silent, she felt her heart would stop.

Time passed and Gustie began to feel herself carried on a great river of sound. The shrill singing that had at first sounded so plaintive to her ear now held notes of rejoicing.

As she watched and listened, the boundaries between sight and sound blurred in the flash and crackle of tin bells, painted gourd and turtle-shell rattles.

A silver ring or bracelet glinted here and there, but most adornments were of soft-sheened bone and shell, feathers and fur that glistened and trembled with each movement and every breeze. Shells gleamed in white rows against the dark blue trade cloth of the women's dresses. Glass beads sparkled red, blue, green, and yellow across arms, chests, and foreheads.

The women danced. Their many-colored shawls and blankets swaying above demurely stepping feet evoked a field of butterflies. The men danced and the field became alive with cavorting animals and birds.

Gustie singled out Little Bull at once. He wore a magnificent sheath of eagle feathers that Jordis said had been passed down from his grandfather, to his father, to himself. Every feather was sacred. His movements suggested the great bird. Never far from his father, Leonard danced his own dance. Many children danced by themselves or were carried on the backs or in the arms of a dancing mother or father.

As her mind wandered in and out of the currents of sound, Gustie longed to enter the circle, pound the earth with moccasinned feet, whirl, and give herself to whatever spirit would claim her. But she knew she would only make herself ridiculous, so she tapped her foot, swayed with the beat, and surrendered to the intoxication of sight and sound. Gustie felt a shimmering sense of the glory that was this people, and she understood with a sharp pain why Jordis refused to teach the white man's way.

Gustie was suddenly aware of Jordis standing by her side. As Gustie handed her the shawl, Jordis held her gaze a moment, then she asked, "Do you want me to dance?"

Gustie felt the relentless beating of the drum carry her dizzyingly forward into unfamiliar terrain. She wanted to cry out to the drummers to stop so she could breathe her own breath, feel her own small heart beating by itself, and escape, for a moment, the current of Jordis's eyes. She also felt challenged, a feeling she disliked, and that gave her the strength to stay afloat in the forward-moving turbulence around her. She hung on to that strength as if it were a tree in the midst of a flood. "I want you to be happy, Jordis," she said.

Jordis unfolded the shawl and draped it over her shoulders. Its fringes trailed the ground. She took in the dancers, all men and boys now, a trace of a smile upon her lips. With a slight horsey toss of her head, she said, "I will dance for you."

Jordis moved away from Gustie, out of the ring of spectators into the dancing circle, slowly, easing herself into the song, her knees rising higher and higher, her arms floating up and out. The shawl flared like wings. Gustie watched her go and tumbled headlong into the rapids.

Little Bull saw Jordis enter the dance. A brightness settled upon his face and Gustie thought he danced with more joy.

Jordis dipped to one side, then the other. The beads across her chest flashed blue between the arc of red made by the shawl, and for an instant her eyes met Gustie's over the curve of her arm.

Jordis danced. The red shawl became like fire. Tongues of red flame leapt up as her arms descended, and the flames trailed behind her and flared up all around her as she danced, more and more frenzied, but with some control, as if something was contained still within that circle of fire.

The men and boys in the dancing circle, one by one, stopped where they were to watch her. Soon all were still, their eyes upon Jordis.

Then Jordis stopped dancing; her body continued to pulse with the drum.

The drummers and singers, knowing that the song was an integral part of the unfolding drama, never wavered, but kept the steady, driving beat.

Jordis stood rock-still now and stared at the pale evening sky above Gustie's head. Her eyes wide, her lips parted, she was rapt in a vision that no one else could see, but that everyone there among the native people respected, and the non-Indians, bewildered, but curious, kept quiet and watched to see what would happen next. Whatever it was that Jordis saw caused her to relax a little and drop the shawl. Gustie felt a jolt, like something being pulled rudely out of her grasp. Then, very slowly, Jordis raised her arms straight out from her sides. Little Bull removed his sheath of sacred eagle feathers and brought it to her. He slipped a loop over each of her arms, and the leather thongs in the center he tied gently around her shoulders. She seemed unaware of what he was doing but remained poised with her arms outstretched, just like wings now that she was adorned with the feathers, waiting. Little Bull stepped back. Leonard moved swiftly into the circle, picked up the shawl, and withdrew. The other dancers, as one, moved to the perimeters of the circle to watch and wait. The deafening throb of the drum continued. The very earth and air pulsated around them. Suddenly, Jordis smiled a wide, beautiful smile showing her splendid teeth. Then she threw back her head and laughed. Gustie knew now that Jordis no longer danced for her and she let her go. Gustie's eyes filled with tears.

Jordis looked long into the sky again and closed her eyes. Her head came down, her back arched upward, her shoulders moved forward and her arms folded the wings in close to her sides. She held there for a moment, then her head began jerky birdlike movements from side to side. She began the dance of the Eagle.

The drum and voices intensified and picked up speed. Jordis crouched low, then spread her wings and danced the sacred dance with strength and power. Whatever had been contained was set free. The spirit of Eagle had come down and the woman danced him. The two-spirit woman danced the Eagle Dance.

Jordis was still in the world of spirit, but Little Bull did not want her to face the scrutiny of the crowd alone when her dance came to an end, as it must. He began to dance, beckoning Leonard back into the circle. Then, others, sensitive to the mystery that was about to come to its conclusion, moved back into the circle as well. Men and women and children danced around her, dancing their own dances.

It ended. The final drumbeat. Silence.

The dancers stopped and milled around, greeted one another as if nothing extraordinary had happened, and went off to find refreshments. Little Bull was at Jordis's side, and so was Dorcas. He took the sheath of feathers from her, and Dorcas wrapped her in the shawl, for a cold wind had come down from the north. Little Bull put his arm around her and escorted her off the dancing ground. She seemed not yet quite of this world. He handed her to Gustie, who put her arms around her. Together with Dorcas they made their way through the crowd back to Gustie's wagon, where Biddie stood patiently waiting to go home to her bucket of oats.

With surprising agility, Dorcas stepped up into the wagon

seat and took up the reins. Gustie helped Jordis up and then squeezed in beside her. Biddie pulled them off the fairgrounds out along the winding wagon path that would take them back to Crow Kills.

Happiness played upon Jordis's face. "I saw him," she said.

"Who did you see?" Gustie tucked the shawl securely around Jordis so she would not get a chill, and kept an arm around her. The heat from Jordis's body gave off the scent of sage.

"He came down out of the sky like a bird, but he was a man and his hair was long and stretched far behind him, like a road to the ends of the earth."

"Who?"

"My brother. And he was not a boy. He was a man. The age he would be now, if he'd been allowed to grow. He is a man, and he told me to dance the Eagle Dance. He told me he was happy. He told me not to be afraid to dance the Eagle." Jordis's eyes were bright.

Gustie tenderly pushed the damp hair off Jordis's forehead. "Jordis, you laughed." She spoke softly. "What made you laugh?"

Jordis laughed again, a deep, chesty laugh, and her head came back against Gustie's shoulder. She laughed. "Because he said he didn't give a shit about my hair!"

A cold wind swept across the lake. The trees creaked and branches scraped against each other. Leaves rattled under a rapidly darkening sky.

"Smell the rain," said Dorcas.

As she helped Jordis down from the wagon, Gustie said, "I'll take the tent tonight."

Dorcas nodded.

"I'll see to the horses," said Gustie, giving Jordis over to her grandmother's care.

Gustie unhitched Biddie and brought her and Moon together down to the lake to drink. On the farther shore, a doe stepped gingerly down to the water's edge. She gazed at Gustie and the horses without alarm, then disappeared into the blackness behind her. Gustie's already full heart was moved almost to overflowing by the sight.

She tethered the horses close together in the shelter of the trees behind the cabin and fastened a blanket over each of them—some protection if there was hail. She left them each a bucket of oats.

When Gustie returned, the cabin was cloudy with aromatic steam from some brew Dorcas had made Jordis drink.

Jordis was already under a blanket on the cot usually occupied by Gustie. She looked half asleep.

Gustie leaned over her and put a hand on her forehead. It was cool and dry. Jordis opened her eyes and whispered, "You're going to play at being Indian?"

Gustie smiled and nodded.

"Good luck," Jordis replied softly and drifted to sleep.

"Take this." Dorcas handed Gustie a hammer.

"What's this for?"

"Pound the stakes more. Give 'em an extra whack. Can't hurt. Otherwise, you blow away."

Gustie went out and did as she was told. The wind was now even stronger. Even though Jordis had pitched the tent under the trees, the canvas heaved and strained against the wind. The stakes held.

Inside the tent, Gustie wrapped herself in a blanket and listened as Crow Kills crashed against its boundaries of rock and bank and slapped up against the trees that guarded its shore. She felt quite snug. The thunder rolled and a sheet of rain covered everything, muting every other sound, except the voice she heard in her head just before she fell asleep. It was Lena's voice saying, "When the potatoes boil dry, it means it's going to storm."

• • •

"You're back early," Lena said. She appeared neither glad to see him nor reproachful of his absence. She sat at the kitchen table nibbling a slice of bread.

Will hung up his hat and stamped the dust off his shoes before entering the kitchen. "Yup. Well . . . I rode ole Tom pretty hard. I think it's going to storm. Tried to beat it back."

He washed his hands and Lena poured his coffee and set a plate and knife before him. Will helped himself to bread and butter.

They chewed and sipped quietly. The wind came up and battered the windowpanes. Will said, "It's going to be a real corker."

Lena carefully brushed errant bread crumbs off the table onto her empty plate and pushed it aside. "Iver stopped by after you left. I gave him all my pies to take to the fairgrounds. Told him to leave them with Alvinia where the Circle ladies were serving lunch. Kept one for us."

Lena took her plate to the sink, refilled her coffee cup, and sat back down while Will had a second slice of bread and jam. When he was through he said, "A piece of that pie might go good if there's any more coffee."

Lena rose to accommodate her husband.

Will began casually, "I don't think that piker will be hangin' around here anymore." He chuckled and went on, enjoying the telling of Peter Madigan's fear of the Indians as much as he enjoyed Lena's pie. When he got to the part about the braying mule he laughed out loud. Even Lena had to smile.

After a pause, he said, "Gustie's a great gal. Been a good friend to us, all right. No question about that."

"No one could say any different."

"Those Indian ladies—they're nice women. Met the old chief and his son, too. They seem like nice fellas."

Lena's neck stiffened and she felt her lips getting taut.

"And they sure think the world of Gustie," Will added for good measure.

"Apparently." Lena had listened to Will's story, her hurt feelings equal to her interest in this part of Gustie's life that Gustie had kept hidden from her. "I guess she's spent a lot of time out there with them." She paused. "And never saw fit to mention it."

"Nope. I guess not." Will rubbed his forehead and ran his hand over his hair, ending with a scratch behind his ear. "It was Gustie, you know, put up my bail and hired Pard." Will had saved that for last.

Lena opened her mouth but could say nothing.

"I know you thought Walt and Oscar and maybe Ma had a part in that, but they never done anything like that for me and never would. I knew it wasn't them. Dennis and me figured it out. Had to be Gustie. And when I asked Pard, he said that was confidential information. So I figured Gus had a reason to not tell us. I just figured she'd tell you when she got good and ready. Now, I guess I know why she didn't. But I haven't got it figured out yet. Something about that woman she came out here with who died. That must have been a rough go and she didn't want to talk about it. I don't know. But I'm tellin' you now just so you have it in mind."

Lena's spine became board straight. "We'll pay it back. Every penny." Her fingers traced the rim of her coffee cup.

"Don't think she expects that. No telling how long it would take me to pay back that kind of money." Will peered out the dark kitchen window.

Lena cleared her throat and was about to offer to take in washing to bring in extra money, but Will didn't let her begin.

"You're smarter than me, Duchy. Always was. I always knew it and was proud of you for it. You think about things— religion and all—things that don't mean nothing to me." Will drained his coffee cup and set it down with more delicacy than she was used to seeing in him. "I seen people go to church on Sunday and do nothing but meanness Monday through Saturday."

"Medicine is for the sick, and church is for the sinner," Lena affirmed.

When she was in one of her righteous moods, Will was no match for her. But this time he gave it extra effort. He sighed, pushing his empty plate away from him, "Well, I never seen Gustie do anything but good by the people around here. She's sure been a great pal to me. I know you don't like Indians and now Gustie's got them as her friends. Maybe that's why she didn't tell you. She knew you wouldn't like it. Guess she figured what you didn't know wouldn't hurt you. Come to think of it, it didn't, either. As far as the Indians go, as far as I can see, they have their good ones and their bad ones, like everybody else. I owe her. And I'm not going to see her thrown to the wolves around here."

"You make it sound like she's going to be taken out and tarred and feathered or something. That's foolishness."

"Well, I know how people can get started on something around here and get carried away with it."

Lena's gall was rising. "What would you know about that? You're always drunk and out of your mind someplace while I have to face this town. Don't tell me what people chew over. I've been chewed over enough! You don't care about that, though, do you?"

Will was confused. He had been talking about Gustie, and now Lena was in a fit over his drinking. He hadn't had a drink since the night his pa was killed and he swore he'd never have another. That sip of Walter's whiskey at the open house sure didn't count for much.

"It's going to be all over town that Gustie is laying around with those Indians over on the reservation, and it won't matter that they think the world of her, or that she's your pal, or any other blame thing. Being your pal is no great recommendation anyway." Lena threw her spoon down and it clattered against her saucer. She almost tipped the chair over as she pushed away from the table and ran into the bedroom and slammed the door.

Will rubbed his face hard and went outside to bed down his horse.

Gustie had no idea of the time, but she thought she could not have slept more than two or three hours. The wind still strained the moorings of the tent, but she no longer heard the sound of rain pelting the canvas. She lifted the tent flap. The sky was very dark except for a star here and there twinkling through breaks in the clouds. She slipped outside the tent and felt the wind lift her hair, the earth wet and bristly under her bare feet. By instinct she found her footing up the incline, past the cottonwood tree by the grave, and beyond to where the land rolled in ever steeper undulations. She walked into the wind until she came to the crest of the highest rise.

She stopped, put her hands on her hips, and looked up. As the wind blew, more and more stars began to shine through, until the sky became a patchwork of solid black and starry black. Occasionally there was even a glimpse of moon. Her loose hair blew wildly in a constant swirl around her head. She tucked her skirt beneath her to keep it from flapping and sat, her arms wrapped around her pulled-up knees, and became, happily, a part of the storm-swept prairie.

Under the sound of the wind in her ears she heard her name and she turned her head. "I didn't want to startle you." Jordis stood next to her, not looking at her but at the sky. She was wearing the clothes Gustie had first seen her in, the day she appeared on Moon with the chickens for Dorcas. "Do you want to be alone?" Jordis continued to stare up at the sky.

"No," Gustie said simply.

Jordis descended slowly to her knees and sat back comfortably, her hands resting on her thighs. "What are you doing up here?"

"Watching the wind blow the clouds around."

The wind eased a little. Gustie said, "What are *you* doing here?"

"I saw you . . . when the moon came out for just a moment, I saw you silhouetted here. I . . ." Jordis stopped herself.

Gustie laughed softly. "Thought I might do some more scarifying?"

"No." Gustie thought she heard a smile in Jordis's voice. "I was just curious as to what you were doing out in a windstorm in the middle of the night."

"I was wide awake. I like weather. I like feeling it. Not always being separated from it."

The wind filled their ears once more, then calmed a bit.

"I'm sorry I rode away from you." Jordis looked out over the dark prairie.

Gustie replied, "I pushed. I shouldn't have. It's not my place."

A splash of moonlight tumbled over the edge of a cloud, revealing Jordis's face full of things unspoken, and her eyes, large, luminous, surprised in their sheltering darkness, unclothed—without that hard glint that dared anyone to see anything of her through them. The moonlight lingered and Gustie looked away, out of courtesy, not having been invited to see so much.

"We could not sleep in your house. We made you angry."

"Yes."

Neither could give, or expected, an apology.

The clouds made another effort to unite over the moon. They held for a few minutes before breaking up again, giving way before the insistent wind, and the high round moon shone whole.

Jordis said, "Do you know that I can quote Shakespeare, I can even read French, but I can't speak the Dakotah language with my people?" Not exactly a question. More like an invitation.

Gustie turned toward Jordis, moving herself to a kneeling position so their eyes were on a level with each other. A thick strand of hair blew across Gustie's face.

Jordis moved the hair away with two fingers, then held it back with the side of her hand. Gustie's hair blew about fiercely with a life of its own like the clouds, and Jordis brought up her other hand and softly brushed it aside. She kept her hands there, lightly framing Gustie's face.

Gustie's fingertips wandered over the backs of Jordis's hands. Her left hand lingered, covering Jordis's right hand on her cheek, while her right hand traced the outline of Jordis's lips, her chin, her cheekbones, those heavily lidded eyes. "I didn't know if I'd ever see you again," she said.

"You'll always see me again," said Jordis, so softly that Gustie didn't know if she had heard her or merely read the words on her lips.

The moon, fully liberated now, made silver the edges of the clouds most near to it and sailing away from it like galleons casting off from a lighthouse—its beam flung along the shuddering grass to where Gustie and Jordis knelt and pulled themselves close together in a kiss as inevitable and surprising as a child's first word.

The kiss lasted a long time. Then they rose and walked, hand locked in hand, back to Jordis's tent.

That night, Gustie rode the eagle's wing and cried hot tears on Jordis's breast.

· · ·

The Eagle beats his wing upon the drum and Eagle Children fly among the stars. Their wings hum the night music. And I who had no voice, sing. I who had no music, dance. I who had no place, roam the land where Eagle flies.

She brings the stars down from the skies and puts them in my hands.

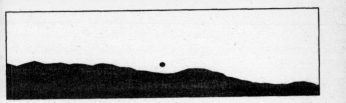

Moon When All
Things Ripen

After just a handful of summer, a cool breeze sifted through the hot winds of August, and every prairie dweller knew that there would be no lingering autumn to enjoy, but a quick freeze, hard ground, and heavy skies to contend with soon.

Chief Good Wolf was dead, proving Dorcas prescient that he would not see another winter. Little Bull was chief. Winnie was nearing her time to bring forth a sibling for Leonard.

Will Kaiser was released by a bored judge after a half-hearted prosecution by John Anderson and a meticulous presentation by Pard Batie on the shallowness of the evidence.

Gustie got her money back, except for Pard's fee, which was modest. She suspected he took less than his usual. She bought herself a saddle and a split skirt and in the remaining days before the start of school rode Biddie every day. She was not good at it. She laughed at herself and frequently apologized to the mare. Yet somehow they got along, and she became more and more secure on horseback.

Gustie had to learn to ride if she was to shorten the distance between Charity and Crow Kills. Even so, the weather would soon be the biggest obstacle between Gustie and Jordis. Neither could leave where they were to live with the other. Gustie had her school; Jordis would not leave Dorcas, especially not during the winter. In the coldest months, Jordis shared Dorcas's cabin; her small army-issue tent was no weatherproof tipi. Even if Gustie could make the trip through cold and snow, Dorcas's cabin could not accommodate three people for long.

While Gustie rode on and off the Red Sand at will, Jordis stole in and out of Gustie's life at night. The only other visitors

Gustie had were Orville Ackerman, who did indeed build her a nice fence, and Will Kaiser, who gave her the lumber from the barn they had torn down—Ma's old big barn. Gertrude had asked for it to be brought down. Apparently she didn't want to look at the place where her husband had met his end. So the boys (even Frederick donned work pants and chipped in) dismantled it board by board. Will took what he knew Gustie needed for her fence; Walter and Oscar claimed the rest for their own purposes.

Will stopped in two or three times a week for a visit and a cup of coffee. He was casual. Always "just passing by," but Gustie knew he took special pains to see her. Lena remained conspicuous by her absence, and Gustie stayed away from her. Gustie knew that word had filtered back to Charity that she had been seen at the Wheat Lake powwow, probably even that she had left the grounds with the same two "squaws" she had befriended in Charity. She knew that there were those in Charity who, if they knew, did not care, and those who cared very much. Gustie had little concern for what people said about her, but she did care what was said about Lena, because Lena cared. So she kept away from her friend for friendship's sake.

Will sat at her table sipping coffee, making the usual small talk. Gustie asked, "How is Lena, Will?"

"Like a long stretch of bad weather." Will scratched the side of his jaw. "She's doing good," he said at length, with a little lopsided shrug of his shoulder. He reached for his coffee. Gustie thought he would end the subject there. In over two years with these stoical people she had learned that that was frequently all anyone would say about anyone else, no matter what difficulties or feelings might lie beneath the surface. Will surprised her by continuing. "She's a stubborn one. She gets things into her head—you don't know what they are half the time, or where they come from—but it takes an act of the Almighty to move them out again. I've tried talking to her but she just . . . You see, about Lena, she's got to understand every-thing. Explain everything. Be right about everything. Always been like that. She comes up against something she don't un-derstand, it's like she comes on a house with a locked door. No, she'll try with all her might to knock that door down, peek in the windows. She'll try everything every which way, but if the door don't open and the windows don't give, she'll never go near that house again. She'll pretend the house isn't there. She'll go a mile out of her way around it so she don't have to look at it. You know?"

"Yes, I know. And what about you? The things you don't understand?"

Will grinned broadly, and chuckled in that silent way that Gustie was used to. "Hell. If I was to get worried and bothered every time I didn't understand something, I'd lock myself up in a johnny and jump down the hole. Oh, here, I brought you a little something." Will fished in his big jacket pocket and came up with a parcel which he laid carefully on the table and unwrapped, revealing two goose eggs.

"I had a bunch of sausages that Hank give us, but I figured you were still off eatin' pig."

Gustie nodded and thanked him for the eggs.

Will tossed back the dregs of his coffee and got up. "Well, I see your screen door is a little loose on that hinge there." He ex-amined it more closely. "Oh, *ja*. Rusting out. I'll bring you a new hinge next time. Fix it lickety-split."

"Will, I appreciate what you do for me, but you don't have to, you know. I don't feel you owe me anything. You and Lena were my first friends when I came to Charity. My only friends. You've already done a lot for me. I'll never forget it."

Will put his hat on and shoved one hand in a pocket, and wiped his nose with the back of his other hand. He really did remind Gustie sometimes of the little boys in her school. "Well, I'll just bring that hinge by next time I'm passing."

Gustie waved as he rode away on Old Tom. She was hungry and went back inside to scramble the goose eggs for her dinner. Outside sounds brought her back to the window. She saw Lester Evenson climbing down from the far side of a buckboard, Sighurd Dahl tying up the reins and hauling his great bulk down. Axel Kranhold, tall and stooped-shouldered, was already approaching her door. They were three of the twelve members of the school board. Twelve: like the apostles; like a jury.

She opened the door in welcome. "Good afternoon, gentlemen. Please come in."

They removed their hats and came in, filling her small house in a way that gave her a moment of discomfort. She offered them all seats and cool drinks. They took the seats, and refused the refreshment.

"I'm glad to see you. I was going to ask if the school couldn't be whitewashed this year. It is looking a bit drab. The children are always more cheerful if—"

Sighurd Dahl interrupted her. "Miss Roemer, the school will be whitewashed." He flushed a deep red. "But that isn't why we're here."

Gustie sensed something was going to happen she was not going to like. She pulled up another chair and sat facing them. Her hands rested in her lap.

Sighurd made the opening sally. "There's a lot of talk around."

"Oh?"

Sighurd Dahl was so visibly uncomfortable that under other circumstances Gustie might have felt sorry for him.

Axel Kranhold took up the sortie. "About you spending time on the reservation."

Sighurd gained in confidence. "Are you teaching out there, Miss Roemer? We understand the new chief is building a school, and we certainly approve of that."

"No. I'm not teaching. And the school has been built. It was completed some time ago."

"Well." Sighurd shifted in his seat and looked to Axel for more support.

Axel obliged him. "What are you doing out there?"

Lester Evenson lowered his head.

Gustie remained silent for some time. Finally she said, "Visiting my friends," offering it up as the most natural thing in the world, to visit one's friends.

"I understand that many of the people on the Red Sand are Christians," Sighurd said hopefully.

Gustie was aware that all three men before her were deacons in the church. She, nevertheless, told them the truth. "Some, far better Christians than I, as I do not profess the faith."

The deacons fell into a fidgety silence.

"We know you're a fine teacher, Miss Roemer," Sighurd Dahl began again. "I can't tell you how pleased we were when we got your letter answering our ad for a teacher . . . what was it now"—he turned to Lester for verification—"about three years ago? You had such a fine education. Such a fine background."

"My education and background have not changed."

"No, of course not." He fumbled, and flushed. "And as I say, you have proven to be a fine teacher. My boy and girl, why, they think the world of you."

Gustie responded, "Then what has changed, gentlemen?" It was painfully clear what they were about and she was losing patience.

Axel Kranhold spoke. From his sharp-featured face she saw beams of serenity that could only emanate from one who inhabits very high moral ground.

"Miss Roemer, we feel that someone who instructs our children should not only teach reading and writing and such, but also set a *Christian* example. We can't allow anything to affect our children that might be harmful or misleading." He pronounced the words "our children" as if he had procreated at least every other child in the county, though to Gustie's knowledge he and his wife were childless.

Axel had apparently come to the end of his say. She looked again at Sighurd, who was still pink, then at Lester Evenson, who returned her gaze without flinching, without the defense of moral rectitude. Lester said, "I came along, Miss Roemer, to tell you myself, that I disagree with their decision. But mine was the only dissenting vote, and I failed to sway them."

Gustie nodded her thanks.

She looked again at each of them. No one said any more. "How soon would you like me to leave this house?"

All three men started. "Oh, we aren't asking you to leave the house!" Sighurd Dahl appeared much relieved to give her this assurance. "You can stay here until a homesteader makes a formal claim. Just as you've been doing. It doesn't belong to anybody. It's still on the books as public land. Nobody's going to throw you off. We'll see to that." The three men nodded enthusiastically.

"That's generous of you," Gustie said. She meant it.

The men became restless and, sighing in three-part harmony, rose and muttered their goodbyes.

She let them pass her and open the door themselves. Lester was the last. He stopped in the doorway and turned. "Miss Roemer, this doesn't change anything as far as the bank is concerned. You are still in good standing . . . just the same. No difference at all."

"Thank you, Lester."

"I don't like what just happened here." He shook his head sadly, and left.

Gustie closed the door and sat by the window watching them drive off. *Well, Lena, you were right.* She remained staring out across the land, a land that neither passed judgment nor afforded any sympathy. She had said nothing in her defense. She could have said she was teaching Indian children, or ministering to the Indians in some way, in the spirit of the missionary or the reformer. They would have accepted that. But she had not lied to them, nor told them the whole truth. Gustie uttered a little laugh and shook her head. She thought, *They fired me for the wrong reasons.*

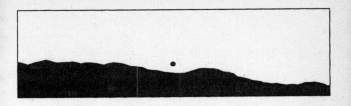

Moon When Wild Rice Is Stored for Winter Use

Biddie cantered easily, Gustie astride her back, across a fallow field scattered over with yellow mustard that filled the air with a warm musky scent. Ahead, a small stand of cottonwoods marked the beginning of wetland. A flock of blackbirds ornamented the trees like dark fruit, the sound of their chirping in harmony with the rustling of leaves. As Gustie passed, the birds, in threes and fours, took flight, leaving the cottonwoods to sing alone.

Gustie reined the mare to the left. After a half-mile they turned right onto a narrow wagon path that continued on raised dry ground to the west, toward Charity. On their right, the marsh smelled wet, reedy, and sweet, like something being born. A snake streaked off the road in front of them. Small yellow butterflies moved in clusters over the tops of brush and grass. With a piercing unearthly buzz, dragonflies lifted themselves out of the vegetation that encroached on the path.

Beneath the robin's-egg-blue sky, the prairie glowed with a porcelain fragility. The greens of early autumn were dark and rich, having steeped in sun, warmth, and moisture all spring and summer. Corn was shoulder high. The binders were already leaving swaths of shiny stubble through the wheat fields. Stacked hay glistened like the gold in a woman's hair. Stone County had been blessed with a near-perfect year.

Lena came home to a musty house. She had been out most of the day visiting, so before she went about opening windows she pulled the pins out of her hat and took it off carefully, placing it on the kitchen table. She poured herself a glass of cold buttermilk from the pitcher in the icebox, sat a moment, and considered the hat. She must change the pink flowers and ribbon to something darker for the fall. Perhaps the gold ribbon with that little batch of brown feathers she had saved from last year.

I thought I left those blame windows open. Lena was irritated by her own forgetfulness. On the first cool day she would scrub the house from top to bottom. In the meantime, she could stand it no longer. Lena demanded a fresh house. She drank the last of the buttermilk, got up, and went through the house checking windows. On her way through the dining room she noticed one of her chairs missing. *What in Sam Hill?* All the downstairs windows were open. As it had not been a sweltering summer, she had not had to open the upstairs window, which she did when it was necessary to lift the air and keep it circulating.

The second story had never been finished. The floor was laid, but nothing else had been done. If she and Will had a child they planned to finish it. Until then, they didn't need the room. Lena seldom climbed the stairs—the emptiness up there only reminded her of her childlessness—but she needed to get that window open.

The stairway was in the front of the house, narrow and steep with a bend near the top. A thin iron rod was bolted to the wall as a handrail. Halfway up the stairs the smell was stronger. Whatever was making the house smell so peculiar was coming from upstairs. Probably a dead squirrel or raccoon. Sometimes they found their way inside a house and then couldn't find their way out again. If that's what it was, Will would have to remove it when he got home. She wouldn't touch anything dead, that's for sure.

A small square landing marked the bend in the stairs. In the wall above it, just enough light filtered through a tiny window to form a dusty glow on the landing. As she stepped into that pool of light Lena knew exactly what she was smelling. Human excrement. *Oh, for heaven sakes! Who's been up here? Someone has been in my house!* She wavered between anger and fear. Then she thought, *It's Will. He didn't go to work today. He got drunk—he's passed out up here and dirtied himself.* She was burning mad now, turned and took the last three steps bounding. An archway of bare boards to her right marked the division of a space that would someday be two rooms and also served as support for the roof, which sloped down toward the sides of the house. The smell was strong but not fresh, and the drone of flies filled the emptiness. *It can't be Will.* She had seen him only this morning and he was sober. He couldn't have gotten so drunk as to pass out up here, make a mess, and then lie in it awhile—there had not been time enough.

She saw the body hanging, its back toward her, the rope strung over a ceiling beam. Only a few inches between the floor and the bottoms of Tori's feet marked the distance between his life and his death. The flies buzzed over a pile of black excrement that had formed on the floor as it had dribbled down his pants leg. The missing dining room chair lay overturned to his right. Lena made a little grunting sound and then said over and over again, "Oh, Jesus, Jesus, Jesus . . ." She ran down the stairs, knocked herself hard against the right wall as she turned the corner, almost fell, and ran out of the house. Halfway down her driveway she stopped: *What if he's not dead? What if he just needs help?* Lena turned and ran back into the house, stumbled up the stairs, and stood again behind the lifeless body of her brother. She touched his back. Then she reached up and lay a finger on the back of his neck. It was cold. But what did that mean? She was too warm. She had been running. Anything would feel cold. She could not bear to look at his face. Flies buzzed there too. His hair stuck out in all directions and she resisted the urge to smooth it down. His hands hung at his sides. She touched the back of his left hand, then felt for a pulse, all the while making inarticulate soft cries. Finally she turned away from the horror that was once her brother and ran again down the stairs and out of her house. She continued running down the driveway, whimpering, "Jesus. Oh, Jesus. Oh, Jesus." She kept running.

Gustie tethered Biddie in the shade of the barn with her water bucket and went into her house. She poured herself a glass of water and put on fresh clothes. She intended to ride into town to pick up some things at O'Grady's. A pounding on her door startled her. Jordis never knocked, and she so seldom had any other visitors that she paused for a moment in surprise before going to the door. She opened it to Fritz Mulkey. From the look of his horse, he had been riding hard.

"Miss Roemer. I come to tell you. I thought because you're a friend of hers, and her sisters aren't here and prob'ly won't be, you might . . ." He rubbed the sweat off his brow with a broad handkerchief.

"Fritz, what's the matter?"

"It's Mrs. Kaiser, ma'am."

"Lena?"

The deputy nodded.

"What's happened to her?"

"Well, we picked her up a while ago. That is, Iver Iverson saw her running down the road and picked her up and put her in the back of his cream wagon. He couldn't get anything sensible out of her, so he took her to the office and Sheriff Sully got it finally that her brother Torvald is hanging in her attic."

"What do you mean, he's hanging in her attic?"

"By his neck, ma'am. Looks like he's killed himself."

"Oh, dear God. Where's Will?"

"He's there. I went and got him—he was drilling up on the Swenson place north of here not too far. He rode back like a house afire on Old Tom. The O'Grady boy's gone to tell Ella and Ragna in Wheat Lake. Didn't think it was right to just break that kind of sorry news in a telegram. And Orville and Hank went out to the Peterson place to tell them poor old folks. Don't know who else to get. So I come and am gettin' you."

"Thank you, Fritz. You go on. I'll be right behind you. My horse is saddled."

Gustie saw Old Tom and the sheriff's quarter horse under the cottonwoods by the well. She tied Biddie next to them and strode toward the house. Even before she opened the screen door, she heard Lena crying. She took a deep breath and went in. She stopped in the dining room. From there she could see Will in the big living room chair cradling Lena in his arms. Her small form shook with sobs. Her fist was knotted around a piece of his shirt, her other arm was around his neck. Will rocked her. Big tears rolled down his face and dripped off his chin, wetting the shoulder of her dress. He looked directly at Gustie, but nothing registered but the woman in his arms. Above her head Gustie heard feet scuffling, then a thud. More noises and voices. She could not distinguish words, but she recognized the tenor of Dennis's voice giving orders. Then she heard a clumping down the narrow stairs. She ran to the front of the house to open the door, making sure the men would not carry the body through the house, past Will and Lena. The body was wrapped in a blanket and she could smell the unmistakable odor of the loosened bowels of a strangled man. The sheriff nodded his appreciation as she held open the door to allow the men laboring under the dead weight to pass through. As the men laid the body in the back of a flatbed wagon, the sheriff turned to Gustie and ran his hand over his head. He made a sound from deep in his throat and said, "It's a shittin' mess up there. Sorry, ma'am. Maybe her sisters will help so she doesn't have to clean it up."

"I'll take care of it, Dennis. Did someone go for Doc Moody?"

"Yup. One of Alvinia's boys is out looking for him." The sheriff ran his hand over his head again and then over his face. "Never seen nothing like this. Never seen a suicide. Seen a lot of things. But never a suicide. It makes me—I got to tell you, ma'am—it makes me kind of sick."

Gustie nodded her understanding.

"We took the chair out. Didn't think she'd want to look at it, it being the one he used and all."

"Yes, that's fine."

Someone was coming in through the back of the house. Gustie excused herself and returned to the living room. Will and Lena had not moved. Doc Moody rested his hand on Will's shoulder. He looked up when he heard Gustie.

"Miss Roemer," he said in greeting. If he felt any animosity from his last encounter with her, he did not show it. He just shook his head and turned back to Will. "I think we should get her to bed, Will. I can give her something to help her rest."

Without even a nod, Will stood up. Lena was so light in his arms he didn't seem to feel her weight at all. He carried her into their bedroom and laid her down on the top of the patch-work quilt. She still clung to his arm and his shirt, so he remained kneeling on the bed. Lena's body was clenched, like her fist.

Gustie knelt on the other side of the bed and gently pried Lena's hand open and away from Will's shirt, then slowly eased her down onto the pillows.

Doc Moody had mixed something up in a glass of water. "Hold her head up just a bit, Miss Roemer." Doc Moody's voice was mellow, a voice practiced in inspiring confidence. "It's all right, Will, just lie down next to her. She'll rest better that way. Come on now, Lena. Try to drink this."

Lena's eyes were wild, her teeth clamped shut and her lips stretched wide apart in the rictus of grief.

Will urged. "Drink it up, Duch. Drink it up good now." Lena obeyed by loosening her jaw and sticking her lips out to receive the rim of the glass. Gustie held it to her lips and tipped it gradually so she wouldn't choke. Lena drank the whole glassful without a breath, then fell back onto the pillow. So far she had seen no one but Will, but now her eyes took in Gustie. In a moment of recognition she held up her hand, and Gustie took it swiftly and strongly in her own.

"Gustie." Lena gripped Gustie's hand so hard it hurt.

"Yes." Gustie gripped back.

"My little Tori. My little brother," Lena wept.

"I know, Lena. I know."

"He's upstairs . . ." Her face took on that wild look again.

"No, he is at rest now, Lena." Gustie forced her best soothing voice, though she felt like crying herself. "He is being taken care of."

"He's dead."

"Yes, he's dead."

Lena relaxed into the quilt and pillows and her grip on Gustie's hand eased. Gustie laid Lena's hand down at her side. Will lay along her other side, protectively. He seemed to be trying with his large form to curl around her and shield her, and absorb her pain.

The doctor indicated that Gustie should follow him. In the kitchen he said, "Can you stay with them for a while, Miss Roemer? I don't think they should be left alone."

"Of course. I'd planned to stay."

"I'll leave you some of this." He set a blue bottle on the drain board of the sink. "A little in a glass of water. If you think she needs it, give it to her. Give it to Will too, if he'll take it. The best thing for them right now is just to sleep. It's a terrible thing. What got into the boy? I can't understand it."

"I can't either."

Gustie heard another wagon pull up in front, stop, and pull away. She was surprised to see Mary Kaiser come through the door, looking pretty, and cool, and fresh as she always did.

"Hello, Doctor. Hello, Gustie." Her voice was soft, breathy.

"Hello, Mrs. Kaiser," Doc Moody greeted her. "How are you?"

"Oh, I'm all right," she said, smiling again as if to say she was always all right and it was of very little consequence if she were not.

"I'll leave Lena in your good hands, then. I'll stop by tomorrow." The doctor nodded at both women and left.

"How is she?" asked Mary.

"Not good. She'll sleep now. Doc Moody just gave her something. Will is with her."

"What can I do to help?"

Gustie did not know Mary Kaiser well. Lena held both her sisters-in-law in disdain. But Mary was here, and she was offering to help.

"There's a mess . . . I'm going to go up and clean it. I don't want Lena to have to see it again. You could perhaps . . ."

"I can help you do that."

Gustie could not imagine this flowerlike woman doing such a job, but she reserved judgment.

"She keeps some old newspapers out here." Mary went to the shanty. "And there's a bucket and brushes under the sink, I believe." Mary's soft, breathy voice belied her rather brisk efficiency as she brought in an armful of folded newspapers and gathered rags and lye soap while Gustie filled the bucket with water. Together they quietly ascended the stairs.

The mound of excrement had been smeared around somewhat. A piece of rope still hung from the beam where the sheriff's men left it after they cut the body down.

Mary put down her papers and cleaning things, looked at the rope and crossed herself. Gustie was surprised. She had not thought Lutherans did that. Then, without a word between them, the two women cleaned and scrubbed the floor. When they finished, Gustie surveyed the room. She frowned and said, "I didn't think Lena used this upstairs for anything."

"She doesn't, that I know of. She doesn't even store things up here. Lena's not a pack rat."

Gustie stepped out of the room and looked at the other half of the upstairs. "Mary, look at this."

"What?" Mary came behind her. The rest of the upstairs space was nothing but wood floors covered with a thin layer of dust.

"I don't see anything," said Mary.

"Look at the floor."

"It's just a floor. A dusty floor."

"That's what I mean."

Mary looked behind her. The floor was clean, and not just where they had scrubbed. They had cleaned only the area that had been soiled.

"Where's the dust?" Mary asked.

"It doesn't seem very likely that Tori would mop the floor before hanging himself," Gustie said dryly.

"No."

"Why is there no dust?"

The roses in Mary's cheeks lost their hue. Her voice was barely a whisper in the empty room. "So there would be no footprints."

Gustie said what they were both thinking. "He wasn't alone up here."

"I wonder if the sheriff noticed."

"Frankly, I don't think Dennis noticed anything . . . he seemed pretty shaken to me. We'll have to tell him. One of us will have to go to his office. Someone has to stay here."

"I can stay till six o'clock. Then I've got to be home. Walter doesn't like it if his supper is late."

"Mary, how did you get here?"

"When Iver delivered my cream he told me what happened. I knew Ragna and Ella couldn't come. So I asked him to drive me."

"What about Nyla?"

"Nyla isn't very good when it comes to troubles of any kind. She won't come."

"All right. I'll go see the sheriff now and come back and stay here this evening. How will you get home?"

"I can ride Old Tom. Will won't mind. I'll bring him back tomorrow morning."

"Can you ride?"

"Oh, yes. I'm a good rider," she said without a hint of boastfulness. Mary looked fragile, and she was indisputably sweet, but she was no shrinking violet.

Before she left, Gustie checked Lena's cupboards and made a mental note of things to get from O'Grady's on her way back. She and Mary worked out a schedule to spell each other for as long as it might be necessary, and Gustie rode off to Sheriff Sully's office.

The first to pay a condolence call, Alvinia Torgerson swept into Lena's kitchen with four children attached by little fists to her skirts.

"How is the poor thing?" she exhaled as Gustie relieved her of a heavy basket covered over with a clean square of flour sacking. As she placed the basket on the table, Gustie glanced up through the kitchen window and saw more children in the wagon outside.

Alvinia continued. "Too many trials for one family to bear. Lordy livin'. I brought some of my brood in because Lena just loves these children. Thought we might be able to cheer her up. I heard she is taking this pretty hard."

"Yes," Gustie said. "Doc Moody gave her something. She's asleep."

Alvinia nodded sympathetically at the same time as she grabbed a small hand reaching for the basket, which was giving off some very pleasant aromas. "Vernon, don't touch that!" She smiled at Gustie. "Eldon, that means you, too! There's just a little something in there. We'll be going now, then. I'm glad she's able to rest then, poor thing."

"I'll tell her you were here. She'll be grateful."

"Nothing to it. Let me know if you need anything. I'll send Kermit over once in a while to check." She nodded toward the wagon outside, indicating a boy of about fourteen holding the reins to the team of horses. "Tell him if you need anything." Alvinia's hand rested upon a small towhead. She absently caressed the cornsilk hair that nearly matched her own. "Lena loves little ones so. Too bad I can't give her some of mine." She laughed heartily and turned to go. "Come on, you chickens." The children still clinging to her skirts displayed no fear of being given away to the neighbors anytime soon. "Just tell her how sorry we are." She sighed deeply and shook her head. "It sure does make you stop and think."

After Alvinia was gone, Gustie pulled back the cloth and saw fresh rolls, a still-warm deep dish of beef, potatoes, and carrots comfortably reposed in a thick gravy, and a rhubarb pie, its crust sparkly with sugar. Gustie sighed. She could live a hundred years, and never learn to cook like any one of these women.

Except Ma Kaiser, she amended her thoughts later, as she lifted the heavy lid off the iron pot Will's mother had just left. A thick layer of grease floated over a lumpish liquid in which were suspended some pasty-looking dumplings and gray vegetables nearly indistinguishable from fragments of bovine tail.

"Will's favorite, oxtail stew," Ma proclaimed, puffing and perspiring as she lifted the heavy pot onto the stove. In spite of the warm day, she was still draped in black taffeta.

Frederick, looking dapper as always in a light brown jacket and crisp white shirt, followed Gertrude into the kitchen. "Hello, Gustie. We heard you were here. Glad to see someone taking care of things."

Gustie tried to be a good hostess. "Lena is asleep, but Will should be back any minute. He went to Molvik's. Please, sit down. Can I offer you some coffee? Some rhubarb pie?"

Gertrude ignored Gustie's efforts to be hospitable and said again, "Will's favorite stew. He's a working man. Got to eat." Her tone suggested that without her pointing out this fact to Gustie, Will would surely starve to death.

Gertrude Kaiser seemed outsized and ill at ease in Lena's small kitchen. Gustie did not know how to make her comfortable. "Can I get you a cool drink, then? Frederick?"

Ma Kaiser said, "No. I got to go. Work to do. We'll come back tomorrow."

Frederick shook his head regretfully. "Maybe some other time. Thanks." He turned back to Gustie after Gertrude was out the door. "Don't mind Ma too much. She means well, you know."

"Oh, I'm certain of that. She's . . . you've all had a hard time of it lately."

"I'll drop by tomorrow. Is there anything I can pick up for you this evening? O'Grady's doesn't close shop till about eight. I could take Ma home and then—"

"No, thank you, Frederick. I stopped there myself this afternoon while Mary was here. And Alvinia brought all this." Gustie indicated the full basket.

"That Alvinia." Frederick smiled again, but this time

Gustie was unsure just how to interpret the smile. Perhaps he was not as fond of all those children—his closest neighbors besides his Aunt Julia—as Lena was.

Gustie remained at Lena's bedside, watching her struggle in and out of sleep. She recalled her own illness and her first memory of Dorcas: a walnutlike face hovering over her, a face out of dreams. She thought it *was* a recurring dream. As she drifted in and out of consciousness, there was always that face, a vision of lightning, falling earth, and voices. Such strange dreams. One day, not only the face, but the rough beams of the ceiling came into focus behind it, as well as the army-issue blanket that covered her. Then the form that went with the face: the long braids, the shirt buttoned up to the neck and down to the wrists, tucked into a dark, shapeless skirt. She remembered her first completely lucid moment, being not afraid, simply bewildered. "You are on the Red Sand." She heard the words but did not see Dorcas's lips move, and thought, *What red sand? What are they talking about? Who are they?* She saw only Dorcas. Then she went back to sleep. The next time she woke up with a clearer head. The ceiling beams, the blanket were just as she remembered them. So she knew she had not dreamed them. So was the woman with the long braids down her back. It came to her also: Red Sand. Yes. She knew that South Dakota was Sioux country. Or at least part of it was. And the big Dakotah Sioux reservation east of the river was called Red Sand. She had wandered onto Indian land. When she realized that, she was terrified—not of them, but for what she had done.

"Did I do anything wrong?"

The old woman turned and squinted at her. (She would get used to that squint!)

"I buried someone." Gustie went cold thinking about that grave and what the old woman's answer might mean.

"No, you done nothing wrong. Drink." Dorcas held a tin cup steady to her lips, supporting her with her other arm. The liquid she gave her was warm and tasted like grass and bark—not unpleasant, though it left a tingling sensation on the back of Gustie's tongue that soon turned to a temporary numbness. (She was soon to get used to that, as well.) "You sit up? Eat something?" With Dorcas's help, Gustie did sit up and ate a few mouthfuls of some kind of meat stew.

Gustie had never awakened to an empty room. Dorcas had been always there, or Jordis. Strange, that now she knew Jordis had been there she was having memories of her—brushing her hair, bathing her. The memories returned in small pictures. One came back from the very early days of her illness, when she was still wrapped in a cocoon of pain and fevers and splitting headaches. The veils lifted only slowly as she came more and more to consciousness for greater lengths of time. She watched the old woman brewing her tea, carefully steeping it, straining it through a piece of cloth. Then she brought the cup over to her and as she always did, held her up while Gustie sipped from the warm cup. On this occasion, Gustie began to weep. She wept bitterly and buried her face in Dorcas's soft shoulder. Dorcas set the cup on the window ledge above Gustie's head, held her, and crooned some melody that sounded utterly strange and soothing at the same time. Finally, Dorcas asked, "Do you cry for the woman?"

"No—no one has ever taken care of me before."

"You had no mother, no father, no grandmother?"

"Yes, but they never touched me. I had nannies."

"What is nannies?"

"People you pay to take care of children."

"Not family?"

"No."

"The *wasichu* do not love their children. Ooohooh." The old woman crooned her strange little song again and Gustie fell asleep.

She had forgotten this incident till now. Gustie wanted to be there for Lena whenever she woke.

The first time Lena woke after her drugged sleep, Gustie gave her some water to drink and Lena said, "Oh, Gustie, I had the most terrible dream. About Tori."

"It wasn't a dream, Lena."

"Oh, my, oh, my," and as Lena cried, Gustie held her hand. "Where is Will?"

"He's at Molvik's."

And Lena cried again. "He was such a beautiful little boy. Pa's favorite of the boys. I was his favorite of the girls, of course. Well, he's with Pa, now. They're both happy." Reassured, she relaxed back into her pillows and drifted back to sleep, muttering, "Pa's been waiting a long time for one of us."

Lena willingly drank the stuff Doc Moody left for her, but Gustie wondered if it was a good thing for her to sleep through days of grief and planning. Will and Mary had gone to the church to talk to Pastor Erickson about the funeral service. Alvinia and Mary had arranged for a reception to be held in the church following the funeral, since it was clear that Lena would not be up to receiving anyone in her own home. Will had still to go to his drill site and finish the well he had started for the Swensons. He had committed to drilling wells for several more farmers and had to get them done before the ground froze. So during the day Gustie sat with Lena, while Mary did most of the housekeeping and entertaining of well-wishers who dropped in with food and curiosity.

Those times she was awake, Lena would sometimes talk. The talking made sense if one knew Lena and got used to the way her mind jumped around under the influence of her medicine: "He was the sweetest little boy. He would suck his finger and smile and smile. And you could give him anything, it didn't matter—a cookie, a pretty stone. He'd giggle and play with it, and save it. Always happy. Ma and Pa didn't have much time for him. He was no trouble, you see. Not like me. I was always getting a whipping for something. Then the twins were born and Ma really had her hands full. Ella and Ragna were older and took care of the house and the cooking. But it was always Tori and me. When the twins died, Ma lost interest in all of us. Pa started drinking. Ragna's too blame old to have another baby. That's why she's so sick. But she just can't keep that Pete off her. He's no better than an old billy goat. Tori had the blondest hair. More white even than yellow. It darkened up when he was about fourteen. My pa was a good man. Even when he drank he was quiet and gentle-like. None better when he was sober, that's for sure. So the Lord came for him Himself. When Pa died, I was in his room and he said to me, 'There He is. He's come for me. It's time to go.' And I looked to the foot of the bed, where Pa was looking, and Jesus was standing there. And Pa was smiling. I looked back at Pa and he was gone, with that smile still on his face, and Jesus was gone then too. I was only sixteen then. The Lord came for my pa Himself. For me, probably just an angel or two. That would be fine. For Tori, I'm sure it was the Lord Himself standing there with open arms for my little brother like He was for Pa. And whoever did this to my brother will go to the other place. I know that, too. The fires will consume him. It won't be the Lord with His sweet smiling face, but fire he'll see."

Gustie was startled. She had assumed that Lena, like everyone else, thought Tori's death was suicide. She had not discussed with Lena her and Mary's conclusions about the cleaned floor. Gently, she asked, "You don't think it was a suicide?"

"Suicide?" Lena threw up a hand and snorted in derision. "My Tori? Never! He wouldn't have thought of it, you see. He was always so happy. Used to irritate me to death when we were younger. Always that smile. That happy way about him. No, someone killed him. And whoever it was will pay for it. If not in this life, then in the next."

"Do you have any notion who?"

"No. He never hurt a soul. He was a little angel of a child, my Tori. He shouldn't have died that way." And then Lena sobbed horrible wracking sobs and Gustie relented and gave her another drink of Doc Moody's medicine to calm her and make her sleep—to escape this convulsing sorrow for a few hours more. Gustie understood grief, that there was nothing more private. She was also beginning to understand that Lena's grief for Tori was much more that of a mother than of a sister.

During one of Lena's deep sleeps, when Mary had gone home early and Gustie was in the kitchen making sure there was something for Will's supper, Julia arrived in Ma Kaiser's carriage, driven by Frederick. He helped her down, said a few words to her, then drove off again. Julia entered the kitchen, her arms laden with peonies in full bloom. Their huge blossoms nodded, heavy with rich magenta color. When Julia saw Gustie a shadow passed across her face, but disappeared quickly, leaving her usual expression of faint surprise. As Gustie took the bouquet from her, she noticed red ants crawling among the pink inner petals. She put the flowers in a jar of water and left them on the drainboard. "These are beautiful," she said, smiling. "I'll put them on the dresser so Lena will see them when she wakes up."

"Oh, is she still sleeping?" Julia asked with the same mild wonderment with which she greeted almost every remark.

"She just went back to sleep. Will said she had a very restless night. I know she had a difficult morning. Would you like some coffee?"

"That would be very nice."

"We've got pie, and rolls, and three kinds of cake . . . people have been very generous."

"Any apple pie? I'm so fond of apple pie. Though I really don't need it." She giggled coquettishly.

"Apple it is." Gustie poured the coffee and dished up a slice of pie.

Julia sat in the chair next to the window. Gustie tried to keep the conversation going on the weather, the visitors, the food. Julia's white, blue-veined hands moved back and forth across the tablecloth like creatures that had lived generations in the dark. As they moved up the curtains, she said, "Lena is such a lovely seamstress. See how everything is finished just so. Never a loose thread."

"Yes," Gustie agreed. "She is very accomplished."

The conversation flagged. Julia ate her pie.

"How is your little cat?" Gustie asked.

"Feather? Oh, he's fine."

"Lena told me of that unfortunate incident at the open house."

"Oh, yes my little Feather is fine. The little rascal." Julia, faintly smiling, rubbed a small circle on the table with her finger, as if she were rubbing out a slightly soiled spot, although the table was perfectly clean. "He is my treasure. Always getting into mischief."

Gustie was relieved when she saw Frederick drive up in the carriage to retrieve his aunt. "I'll tell Lena you came by. I know she will love the flowers."

Gustie waved as they drove away. When they were out of sight, she took the peonies outside and dunked them in a bucket of water till the ants floated. Then she emptied the bucket, leaving the ants to scurry about in their new world of grass, gave the flowers a gentle shake, and returned them to the jar of water. She placed them on Lena's dresser.

• • •

The day after Tori's funeral, Gustie made a decision. She arrived early, before Will left for work. She asked him to bring up the washtub from the basement. Gustie cleaned the kitchen after Will's hasty breakfast, made a fresh pot of coffee, and took her place at Lena's bedside as usual.

When Lena opened her eyes Gustie began to talk. "Lena, Alvinia was here. She left so much food. She brought her children to cheer you up."

"Oh, they are precious. Every one of 'em. Such a nice family." Lena said it with such sadness and longing, Gustie almost cried. But she remained firm. "So many people have been here to wish you well. Lena, I want you to get up. Will brought up the tub. It's a warm day. You can have a nice bath, and I'll change your sheets."

"Oh." Lena looked frightened. "I don't feel like it."

"I know you don't." Gustie left her side for a minute to get her a cup of coffee. "Here, drink this."

Reluctantly, Lena took a sip, sputtered, and made a face. "Oof!"

Gustie laughed. "It's coffee the way *I* make it, and the way you need it right now. So make all the faces you want, but get it down. I'm going to fill the tub in the kitchen. I want you to take a bath and wash your hair. You're a mess."

"I am?"

"Yes."

"Where's Will?"

"He is out on the Swenson place. He said he might be late tonight. He's trying to finish the well . . . so let's get you up and fresh to see him when he comes home."

"How long have I—"

"You've been in and out of sleep for three days."

"Yesterday was the funeral?"

"Yes."

"Was it nice?"

"Yes, Mary said it was a very nice service."

"Were a lot of people there?"

"The church was full, Lena. Mary had a book there for people to sign. You'll be able to see that everyone was there."

"I'm glad. Tori would have liked to know that." Lena began to cry and Gustie left her to her tears while she went into the kitchen and filled the tin washtub with bucket after bucket of water. Then she warmed it with several pots of boiling water, so it was a comfortable temperature when Lena slipped into it.

"Where's Mary?" Lena asked. "She has been here, too, hasn't she?"

Gustie answered from the bedroom where she was changing the bedding. "Yes, Mary has been here every day. We've taken turns looking after things."

"That was nice of her, to think of a book for people to sign."

"Yes. She is a very thoughtful person."

Lena peered through eyes squinted nearly shut to avoid the soap she had just scrubbed over her face, and noticed her dining room set still missing one chair. "Where's my dining room chair?" she called out to Gustie.

"Dennis took it. He thought Tori had used it . . ."

"Well, he *didn't* use it! The idea—that Tori would jump off a chair in my attic to kill himself! No wonder that Dennis is sheriff. He's too dumb to be anything else. Tell him I want my blame chair back! It was my mother's." Lena choked again on tears but continued scrubbing herself. "What happened to my medicine? Did I drink it all up?"

There was a slight pause before Gustie answered. "You drank enough of it. I threw the rest down the toilet."

"Well, what do you know," Lena muttered to herself, and lathered her hair.

• • •

Will came home late, hungry, and covered with mud and grease, but he broke into a wide grin when he saw Lena, dressed, at the door to meet him.

"Hey, Duchy!" he said, and kissed her lightly on the cheek.

Gustie appeared behind her. "Supper is ready when you are. Lena waited to eat with you."

"Okeydokey! I'll just get cleaned up."

He washed himself out by the well and put on a clean shirt and trousers. When he came in he noticed the table was only set for two. Lena sat, rather peevishly, while Gustie served up a hearty supper of various dishes left by neighbors. "Aren't you going to sit down and eat with us, Gustie?"

"No, I am going home and leave you two alone."

"She has been very mean and bossy all day," Lena complained.

Will chuckled.

Gustie said, "Mary will drop by in the morning, and I'll be here for a while in the afternoon. Good night, you two."

Moon When Quilling and Beading Are Done

The sun lets fall its cold glare down upon the town of Charity. Breath crystallizes in the early-morning air. Flies are sluggish and easy to kill. The mosquitoes are already dead. What a mercy! The summer-golden hay now lies dark, blackened from the first night frosts.

A thin figure in black leans into a sharp October wind, making her once-weekly round of Charity: the bank, where she receives a warm welcome from Lester Evenson; O'Grady's, where she does her shopping; Koenig's livery, occasionally, to check her horse's hooves and shoes; then an hour or so in Olna's Kitchen, where she has coffee and sometimes a light dinner, sometimes alone but oftentimes in company with Lena or Mary Kaiser.

People wonder about her. Where did her money come from all of a sudden? She has gone from being poor as a church mouse to at least being able to maintain herself in the necessities of life. Some say it was that strange fellow from the East. Must have brought her some money—maybe an inheritance of some sort. Some worried about her when they heard she'd been dismissed as teacher of the section school. Offers were made: from Kenneth O'Grady, a part-time position as a clerk in his store; from Lester, the same in his bank. She gratefully acknowledged their kindness and graciously refused them both. They wonder, the good people of Charity, why she prefers to spend so much time with Indians over decent white people.

The men treat her no differently than they ever did. Behind her back, perhaps a few of the earthier still crack, "We know what she needs," and another will say, "Maybe she's gettin' it. I've heard some of those big Indian bucks can sure do their homework!" And they snicker knowingly. Some of the women may still raise an eyebrow and exchange an oblique word or two among themselves. They may even show some aloofness in her presence. But she has known much worse—open hostility, downright nastiness. These people are not given to such displays. They keep their feelings, for the most part, to themselves. "Live and let live" is the motto. And, as the cold weather gathers and people pull inward, readying themselves and their households and stock for winter, even the wonderings become as sluggish as the flies, and eventually subside. Gustie finds it easy to live here.

She walks, leaning into the sharp wind, a gentle smile on her lips and a warm place in her heart. She is happy. She has no way to describe the source of her happiness, nor any language to make known to the people of this town who she is. Gustie remains invisible for want of the words to describe her. Meanwhile, she walks and thinks, but mostly remains in her house, waiting for time to ripen, for the next chapter of her life to unfold, a chapter she never thought to have. When Clare died, she had thought the book was ended.

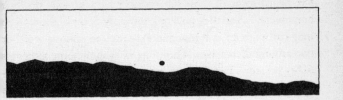

Moon When Horns Are Broken Off

· ❧ · ❧ · ❧ · ❧ ·

"You drunken fool! I'm not cleaning up after you this time. You straighten yourself up and get away from me! Don't you touch me, you dirty thing!" Lena's voice was jagged with anger.

Next, Gustie heard a bellow of rage, followed by words so slurred and guttural she could barely make them out: "Go on, get out of here. Go on. And don't come back."

"Oh, I'll be back." Lena spat out the words. "And if you're not cleaned up or out of here, and this place clean, I'll call the sheriff on you and don't you think I won't!" Her voice was getting louder, more strident.

So was Will's. "You call the sheriff all right. That's right. All right. You call him. You cow."

"He can lock you up this time and throw away—"

"That's fine. That's fine. I'll be out of this shithouse."

"If it is, who made it one? You tell me that?" They were both yelling now, at the same time.

"You bitch! You'll call him all right. He'd like that. Don't think I don't know . . . Come back here."

"You filthy pig!" Lena screamed. There was a thud, then a little squeak from Lena as she scuttled out of the bedroom with a carpetbag slung over one arm, her purse over the other. She grabbed her hat and coat, which were draped over a chair, her muff, and ran past Gustie. Crying "Let's go! Let's get out of here," she was out the door.

Gustie was about to turn and follow her, when Will staggered out of the bedroom. He stopped when he saw her, swayed, and tried to focus his good eye upon her. His jaw hung slack. Spittle oozed from the corners of his mouth. His long underwear, which was all he had on, was wet halfway down the open front and soiled at the crotch. He smelled like a whiskey-soaked outhouse. Gustie's stomach lurched. His lips formed a weird little smile as he recognized her. "Gustie." It was as much a belch as a spoken word. He continued in a little singsong, "My pal. You're my gal and my pal. Don't you worry." He leaned forward and caught himself on the door frame. "We'll always be pals, you and me. You and me."

Gustie ran out the door after Lena. Once seated in the wagon, she snapped the reins over Biddie and the horse jumped forward. She kept the pace brisk as they headed out of town. A wretched silence hung about Lena, and Gustie let it be. She was shaken herself. She had heard about Will's drunken episodes, but this was the first she had witnessed. She was filled with fury and pity, a mixture that made her stomach hurt.

They were well outside Charity on the straight road to Crow Kills before Lena spoke. "I don't know what I'm going to do, Gustie."

Gustie didn't either, so she kept quiet.

"He's killed it. Any love I had for him. He's killed it."

Gustie took a sidelong glance at her friend. Lena looked like a woman who's love wasn't dead, but wounded and in terrible pain.

Lena became quiet again. Gustie searched the sky. The thin white haze above them could either melt away in the unpredictable November sun, or thicken and drop the first snow of the season. She hoped it wouldn't be the latter and wished they had gotten an earlier start. Both because of the weather and because then she might have missed that scene between Will and Lena.

Long stretches of road passed beneath them with no sound but the clopping of Biddie's hooves and the rattle of the wagon.

"He hadn't had a drink since Pa's funeral," Lena said.

They passed between two cornfields, stubble now. A couple of hopeful blackbirds pecked about for any kernels that might have been overlooked by man or beast. By the time the wagon passed the corner of the field, the birds were above them, flying south in search of better forage.

Lena continued her train of thought as if there were not long minutes between each sentence. "I thought Pa getting killed would straighten him out. He was scared enough, I'll tell you. I didn't think he'd ever touch another drop."

Suddenly Gustie felt her own happiness wash over her like the summer wind. She looked across the long back of the black mare and was grateful for this faithful, affectionate animal, for her little house where peace reigned, for her inexplicable friendship with Dorcas, and, most of all, for Jordis's love, which never ceased to amaze her. Gustie did not doubt Jordis's love, for she felt it as surely as she felt the sun and the rain and the wind against her skin. But she did not understand it. She felt herself so ordinary, so plain, and Jordis was everything vibrant and lovely and surprising. "What can I possibly be to you?" Gustie had asked her one morning on their way down to the shore of Crow Kills to fish for their dinner. Jordis stopped and shot Gustie one of her inscrutable looks. She laid her pole and bucket down, sat Gustie down under a tree, and seated herself next to her. Then, looking out across the lake, Jordis told a story.

"Back in Pennsylvania they introduced me to a lot of people. I was a good moneymaker for the school—a book-smart Indian. Once they took me to the governor's mansion. I walked into a great hall. I had never been inside a building so large. Vaulted ceilings. Winding staircase. Red carpeting. Large paintings on the walls. I had never seen such things."

Gustie knew what Jordis was describing. She had been in the same foyer several times with her father.

"I had never even imagined such a place. But the most wonderful thing of all was the chandelier. It was made of hundreds, maybe thousands of pieces of glass. I couldn't stop staring at it. The governor skipped the formalities, and for my pleasure, asked his staff to cover all the windows. The hall became dark. Then they lit the chandelier. It was like a star captured from the sky and suspended there in that hall. It glowed there in the dark with crystals hanging all over it, like icicles, or long crystal tears. I will never forget it."

Gustie was fascinated by the story but wondered what it had to do with herself.

Jordis continued. "You are like one of those crystal tears inside me. I can feel you running from my throat down to my toes, and when I look at you, sometimes, I feel it—the crystal—vibrate. It shimmers and tingles and sounds a note as if it has been struck by a silver spoon. Someday, I think it will vibrate so hard it will shatter and I'll be full of tiny shards of glass, all reflecting light and cutting me to pieces and I shall die an exquisite death."

Gustie's throat felt swollen shut.

Jordis kept speaking, looking at Crow Kills. "You are life to me. When you die, I shall die. If you go away, I shall disappear."

Such words from anyone else could have been dismissed as hyperbole. But Jordis's words, Gustie knew, precisely described Jordis's experience. Gustie had never encountered words that held such verity, like a sapphire its star.

Gustie could not match Jordis's eloquence and she did not try. She said with a slow smile, "Well, I'm not going anywhere without you, and I don't think I'm going to die. I feel quite well."

Jordis took Gustie's left hand and held it palm up in her own two larger hands. She brought it to her lips and kissed the center of the palm, then held it to her cheek, then to her forehead.

When she let it go, she rose and brushed the twigs and grass off her skirt. Gustie rose also, surrounded by a rosy glow, and followed her down to the lake.

Reliving this lovely moment now, Gustie felt a small twinge of guilt, seated next to her troubled friend. Was there no end to the burdens this tiny woman had to bear?

It was a useless gesture, but Gustie made it anyway. "My house is always open to you."

Lena nodded and answered in a quivering voice, "I will not be driven out of my own home."

Lena wiped her eyes with the handkerchief she had been clutching inside her muff, and for several miles continued to dab at her eyes and try to cover her sniffles. They passed some rolling ground in which rocks were embedded in a scattered formation. Gustie tried to make conversation. "Look . . . how interesting those rocks are."

"Look like dead sheep. They should haul them out of there and plant something. Rocks aren't any good to anybody."

Gustie chuckled.

"I'll bet you we get snow," Lena said, pointing to the sky.

The miles rolled on. The hills began to grow as they got closer to Wheat Lake and Crow Kills. A sharp wind rose. Gustie handed Lena the reins and buttoned up her coat. She put her cap on and tied a scarf over it to cover her ears.

"He was a handsome man when I first met him," Lena affirmed, with a little satisfied nod of her head.

"He still is." Gustie took back the reins.

"When he's cleaned up," Lena qualified. "Will's mother, you know, didn't want us to marry. She didn't care when Oscar and Walter got married. She thought she'd just have two more people to boss around in Nyla and Mary, and she thought right. Anything she says is okay by them. But not me.

"Now, Nyla and Oscar are *still* in that house with her and Frederick—who'll *never* move out. Good night—he's thirty years old! They should all be at their own places by now: but no, I can just see it. Every time Nyla and Oscar make a move to go home she'll be whining, 'Ooooh, don't leave me yet.' " Lena imitated Ma Kaiser's high wheezy tone and put on a face to match. "She'll get the whines and the vapors and they'll stay another month. She did that on me and Will, by heck, on our wedding day! We were married in the morning because Pa and Oscar and Walter—they were all still working together at that time—they had to go to Argus to get pipe or something. They were going to have to stay there overnight and come back the next day. Oh, did she carry on! And after the little reception we had, and they left, she cried and cried." Lena screwed up her face again and whined in such a wicked imitation of her mother-in-law that Gustie started giggling. Lena was a superb mimic: " 'Oh, don't leave me alone in this big house.' I don't just remember where Frederick was at the time. 'All my boys are leaving me. All my boys,' and she whined and carried on. She wanted Will and me to stay there until Pa and them got back the next day. Well, I'll be jinxed if I was going to spend my wedding night sleeping with my mother-in-law! No sir, and I said so, too! Will was inclined to stay. Now he's always been good to his mother. There is no wrong in that, but this was too much, I thought. We had rented that little apartment over the bank and I had spent two months painting it and fixing it up and it was all ready for us. Our clothes and everything we'd moved in the day before. So I said to him, 'Will,' I said, 'I'm a married woman now, and I'm going to spend the night in my own home. You can do as you please. You know where I am.' And I up and walked out of that house and walked home to our apartment. I fixed a little supper and ate it by myself and went to bed early. Then about eleven o'clock I hear him coming up the stairs lickety-split!" Lena was smiling. She paused briefly, then added, "We were busy that night, I'll tell you!"

Gustie stared at Lena, then they both threw their heads back laughing. Biddie slowed down and looked over her shoulder. "Mind your own business!" Lena reprimanded the horse, and their laughter rang out again against the dull sky. Curious cows looked up, then went back to pulling on the cold grass.

"My! The first time Will brought me home to the Kaisers' for dinner, I didn't know what kind of nest of something I'd stepped into. It was Pa and Ma at the table, one at each end. Will was at his mother's right, then me, then Oscar and Mary, I think. Across from me was Nyla, who never looked up. Not once. What a sourpuss! 'Course, married to Oscar, I can't blame her. Frederick was across from Will, at his mother's left, then next to Pa at the end was Walter. What a bunch! Only Walter and Will talking, and me, when I would think of something to say . . . and there was Ma spooning potatoes onto Will's plate and ladling gravy over them. Oh, that gravy! Mostly flour and potato water and salt and pepper. Ishta! For heaven sakes, I thought. Is she going to cut his meat for him too? But Will didn't pay much attention. He doesn't seem to notice her doting on him something sickening. I almost didn't go with him again, after that, but . . ."

"But you did . . . in spite of his family." Gustie reminded her.

"Yes, in spite of them, it was. Pa was good to me, though. Quiet-like. 'Course, I didn't know why at the time. Why he was quiet, I mean."

"Why was he?"

"He was drunk all the time. Drunk as a hoot owl! Ma told me that. Just after the funeral. He was not a drunk like Will is. Pa was always well dressed, and thought well of himself in his younger days. A ladies' man. Carried over into his middle years, as I told you. Oh, well. He was a man. They're not like us."

"No," Gustie agreed, smiling slightly.

"No, not by a long shot!" Lena slapped her thigh and they both began to laugh again.

When they came to the road that led to Crow Kills, Gustie had to rein Biddie in hard, in the opposite direction toward Wheat Lake. It was about four o'clock in the afternoon. The sky had thickened steadily and snow carried by a bitter north wind was already beginning to smart against their faces. *Perfect timing,* thought Gustie in relief. One could never be sure what was going to be a light snowfall and what would turn out to be a killer blizzard. Gustie had heard enough stories about the blizzard of 1860, and every other year for that matter, not to want to be caught out in a heavy snow. On the prairie, away from shelter, snow and freezing weather meant death.

She decided to drop Lena off at Ragna's without staying for conversation and head directly out to Crow Kills before things got any worse.

The desolate row of wood buildings that was Wheat Lake's main street looked poor and spare compared to Charity.

Gustie happened to glance to the right down the side street. What she saw there made her pull Biddie to a halt.

All up and down the street were gathered many Dakotah, sitting, standing, wrapped in their blankets, trying to keep warm. Some were seated in their wagons, some hunched over on ponies that drooped and shuddered in the wind.

"What's the matter?" asked Lena.

Gustie nodded in the direction of the people hunkered against the cold.

Lena sniffed, "Oh, it's just those dirty Indians waiting for their handouts." She added under her breath, "Nobody ever gave me a handout." Uncharacteristically, Lena bit her tongue and said no more.

So it was the day the people on the Red Sand got their annuities, thought Gustie. But why were they just standing there? She spotted Dorcas sitting in the back of a wagon that was filled with older women huddled close to each other. Her feet were dangling over the edge and her knees were covered with a blanket. A younger woman held on to another blanket that sheltered them both.

Gustie turned Biddie down the street in their direction. She didn't answer Lena's "What are we doing?" but handed her the reins and jumped out of the wagon almost before it came to a halt. She stepped gingerly through the people sitting on the ground, old men and women, young women with babies and children, sullen young men. All looked nearly frozen.

She stopped in front of Dorcas, who had seen her coming but made no move or any sign of greeting. Her head was covered by a wool scarf tied under her chin. Gustie said, "Dorcas? What are you all doing here?" The younger woman with whom Dorcas shared a blanket looked familiar.

"Waiting for annuities." Dorcas did not focus her eyes on her. She could have been answering anyone, or voicing a thought in her head.

"Why are you out here? Why don't you go inside? What's happening?"

Gustie looked around at the people again. From their weary, cold faces they clearly had been waiting for some time. The agency doors were shut. There seemed to be no activity inside the building.

"What's wrong? Why aren't you getting your rations?"

Dorcas shrugged. "Frye is sleeping. We wait till he wakes up."

"You mean he is in there drunk!" Gustie knew Jack Frye's reputation. "He's passed out and you have to wait out here till he comes to?"

Dorcas nodded once at each statement.

Even in the cold wind, Gustie felt hot with anger. "Why don't you just go in and take what's yours? Why are you all out here freezing?"

No one responded. She did not know if anyone besides Dorcas even understood her words. She asked Dorcas, "How long have you been here?"

"Since this morning. Maybe six o'clock. Maybe."

Again, directly to Dorcas, Gustie demanded to know, "Why don't you go in?"

"We can't take stuff. Has to be written in the book, or they say we steal it and we don't get nothing next time."

Gustie took a deep, heavy breath and let it out with a noisy sigh of frustration. "Where's Little Bull? Where's Jordis?"

"Jordis never comes here. Little Bull is busy. He comes later. Maybe. Winnie is here for their stuff." Now Gustie knew why the younger woman next to Dorcas looked familiar. She had seen the shadow of her face on Leonard's.

Gustie stomped over to the agency door, ready to pound it down with her fists if she had to. It was not locked. She pushed it open and went in. Lena was right behind her. "Gustie, what in Sam Hill are you doing?" Then she wrinkled her nose. "Phew! It stinks in here!"

Gustie went forward to a door just opposite the one they'd entered through. She assumed it opened into the agent's living quarters. It did. Jack Frye lay on a dirty cot in filthy long johns, snoring noisily. The room smelled of whiskey, sweat, and urine. Lena peeked under Gustie's arm as she held open the door. "Good night, not another one!" she said. Gustie shut the door, then turned and faced the room.

"I'm going to give these people what's theirs. You can take Biddie and go to your sister's. I'll come along later."

"Well, I sure won't leave you alone here."

"I'll be fine. If you're going to stay, would you please move Biddie around to the side of the building out of the wind and put her blanket over her? I'm going to look for that book."

Gustie found it immediately. It was not hard to find—a big leather-bound affair with the names of the people along one column and a number by each name, then more columns. A check in each column under dates indicated each time they had shown up to collect their annuities. Gustie saw another door to the right and guessed it led to the storehouse. She opened it and again was proven correct. Filling the room from floor to ceiling were bags of flour, coffee, salt, sugar, boxes of bacon, canned goods and other foodstuffs, bundles of blankets, clothing, even boots and shoes.

Lena was back adding kindling to the stove and stoking up a blazing fire. She heaved in a large chunk of wood and shut the stove door with a clank. Gustie went outside and addressed everyone.

"Will you come in now—as many as can fit in here—and get yourselves warm? Then, a few at a time, give me your tickets and I'll check you off in the book."

Nobody moved.

A few men had gathered at the end of the street. Apparently they had just come out of the saloon around the corner, attracted perhaps by Gustie's raised voice. They looked warm from the heat of the saloon, the wool in their shirts and coats, and the whiskey in their blood. Gustie noticed them but had no time or thought for their amused faces or their remarks. She knew that most people thought her odd, if not a little crazy. But Lena saw them and her blood boiled. She stepped down off the agency porch and headed straight for them. A few feet away from them, she stopped. "What are you looking at?"

They were good-natured in their reply. "Oh, nothing missus. We're just passing by."

"Well, just keep passing. You should have better things to do than stand here looking your looks at Augusta Roemer. She's a better Christian than all of you put together. You all, this whole blame town, just squatted here all day while these people here have been out in the cold. Did one of you offer to open a door for any of them to come in and get warm? Not so much as a hot cup of coffee. Not even for the children, for goodness' sakes. You could have taken in the children. 'Suffer the little children to come unto me, and forbid them not,' " Lena quoted in righteous wrath. "He might also have said, looking at the bunch of you, 'and ignore them not!' It is enough to make the Savior weep. You all make me sick and tired. Go home!"

The men dispersed, some with the smile shamed off their faces, others with Lena's name added to their list of crazy women. Lena returned to the agency building to check on her fire.

The Dakotah had listened to Gustie, but had not stirred. Finally, Dorcas said a few words to the women in the wagon. They nodded and word went softly through the people.

They began to bring their children, and then the old ones into the agency building for warmth.

Dorcas was the first to come to the counter where Gustie stood ready to mark the book. She presented her ticket and Gustie matched the number to the number in the book, and read what she was supposed to get, so many pounds of this and that. It was all listed on the back of her ticket.

"Go back there, Dorcas, and Lena will show you what you get."

A large man with a hooked nose and pockmarked face stepped forward. Gustie recognized him. "Red Standing Horse. Hello. How are you?"

He nodded. "I will help," he said. A few other men joined him and the procession of people began to the counter, where Gustie marked the book; back to Lena, who pointed out what they were to get; and then, laden with bundles and bags and boxes, outside to their wagons and travois. Dorcas was also the first, but not the last, to point out that she was taking more than she usually got. "That's what it says here you're supposed to get, so take it." Gustie realized with a growing rage that the agent had been cheating them all along. They couldn't read and did not know what they were supposed to get. He could short them in small ways and they would not notice. No doubt he sold the excess and pocketed the money. Gustie found herself getting angry with Jordis and Little Bull. They could read. Where were they?

An hour passed smoothly, with several families packed up and already on their way back to their homes. There were stirrings from the back room. Lena heard them and came out of the storeroom. She scanned the wall next to the door. A key hung there. She took it, slipped it into the lock, and turned it. A loud click signaled that Mr. Frye was securely locked away. She put the key in her pocket with satisfaction and went back to the storeroom. After some minutes they heard Jack Frye fiddling with the door. At length, he realized in his half-drunken, wholly hungover state, that he was locked in. He began to yell and bang on the door: "Hey! Open this door! Who's out there? Let me out of here." His yelling turned to howling and his language became more obscene as his frustration grew.

After fifteen minutes of listening to him, Lena muttered, "He is making me tired. I'll put a stop to this." On her way to the back door she grabbed a cast-iron skillet that hung from a hook above the stove. She opened the door. Jack Frye was standing there in his long johns. Lena hit him over the head with the frying pan. He crumpled. Outrage-turned-to-surprise melted fast to unconsciousness before he even hit the floor. "There. He'll be quiet for a while. Can't stand that hollering."

Lena hung up the skillet, and went back to work. Gustie was openmouthed. "You might have killed him!"

"Well, what if I did," Lena snapped. "He's a thief and a drunk and they can throw me in the pokey for it. I don't care. Things can't get any worse."

Red Standing Horse looked down on Lena. Her nose came to just above his belt buckle. "We don't see nothin'."

Three hours later most of the people were gone, except for

the families of the men who had helped all the others load up. Gustie looked at the bottom of the first page in the book. There was noted a certain number of head of cattle.

She asked Red Standing Horse, "Are you supposed to get cattle, too?"

"Yup."

"Where are they?"

"Back down the hill over there." He pointed with his head to somewhere vaguely south of Wheat Lake. "There's some corrals down there. They put 'em there when they come off the train."

"Can you men go get them? I'll mark it off here. I'll sign it. It will be my responsibility. Just go get them and divide them among yourselves?"

"Yup."

"Good. Take the rest then, whatever is in there, for yourselves, and we're finished."

When they were gone, Gustie looked at Lena with approval. Lena had done more than her share, her dislike of hypocrites at last overcoming her distaste for Indians, and her love for children overcoming all as she asked to hold the babies while mothers loaded their things.

Except for Lena's sermon on the corner and the ruckus with Frye, the whole operation had been carried out more or less in silence. Lena had been eager to get the job over with, Gustie had been choking on her rage, and the people seemed anxious to collect their annuities and get going before the agent woke up again—if he woke up at all.

Gustie wrote in the book, "I, this day of 1899, have distributed annuities to all who were present, as marked in this book." She signed it boldly *Augusta McKenna Roemer,* so there would be no doubt who was responsible. Then she sat down and put her head in her hands. "He's been cheating them. He treats them like dirt. He is supposed to help these people." She raised her head. "Look at this place." The agency was supposed to be a place where the people of the Red Sand could come for their annuities, to trade, and to buy things. The shelves were poorly stocked and what was there looked too old to be of use anymore. In fact, many things that had looked usable Gustie had moved into the storeroom and added to the rations given away that day.

Gustie sighed. Lena sat down, too, and knew better than to say anything.

Gustie put her hands on her knees and looked up and around. "It's not going to continue."

"What are you going to do?" Lena was alarmed.

"I don't know. Something. Let's get out of here."

They were putting on their coats when they heard a sliding, scratching sound in the back room. Jack Frye was not dead after all. He was pulling himself up and over to the door. "Don't hit me," he whined. "Just open the door. I gotta have some water, bad. I gotta pee. Real bad, ma'ams."

Lena jumped up and grabbed the skillet again. "I'll teach him a lesson. I'll break his head open, the little shyster," she said vehemently as she opened the door.

Jack Frye cringed. "Don't hit me. Just some water. I'll sit right here." He backed up with his hands in front of him to ward off any blow and sat on the edge of his filthy cot. Spindly legs and arms, four days' growth of whiskers, a pot belly peeking through his long johns where buttons had popped off—he was not a pleasant sight. His greasy brown hair stuck to his head. He had the temerity to point a grubby finger at Gustie. "But you, ma'am, I'm going to report you to the gov'ment."

Gustie was buttoning the last button on her coat. "I hope you do. Indeed, sir, I hope you do." Frye looked surprised and unhappy.

"Let's go. Your sisters will be wondering what has happened to you."

Lena picked up her muff and threw the key at Jack Frye. "Get your own water, you pig."

That night, by candlelight at Dorcas's table, Gustie drew out her writing papers and pen and ink from the case she always carried with her now, and wrote letters—detailed, scathing letters—to the Department of the Interior, the President of the United States, and, finally, to a man widely known for his devotion to justice and his connections to people in high places, no less so than the United States Senate. She wrote:

Dear Father,

I know I have disappointed you. I write to you now, not as a daughter who has never ceased to think of you often and with love and respect, but as a citizen writing to a man who is passionate about correcting wrongs. For a terrible wrong has come to my attention which I cannot ignore. . . .

She wrote far into the night. When she finished, she addressed the envelope: *The Honorable Magnus August Roemer.* Then she added a postscript to her letter:

My dear Father, as you know, when I left, I didn't take any part of my inheritance or any of the money you offered me. I felt that since I had disgraced the family and hurt you so deeply, I had no right to it. I have changed my opinion. If you have a mind to send it, I could use some money.

Always, your loving Augusta.

She addressed and sealed the other envelopes. When she finished, Dorcas, who she believed had been asleep for hours, said from beneath new blankets on her new bed, "Won't do no good."

• • •

Gustie seldom woke before Dorcas. This morning had been one of the exceptions. When she returned to the cabin with two buckets of icy lake water, Dorcas was awake, dressed and sitting on the edge of her bed.

"Stay right there," commanded Gustie. "I'm going to wait on you."

"Wait on me? I'm right here." Dorcas sounded cross.

"No, I don't mean I'm waiting for you. 'Waiting on you' means that I will serve you."

"You treat me like a baby," Dorcas grumbled. "Or a man."

"No, I treat you with honor."

"Oh." Dorcas's pouty face brightened. "That's pretty good, then. When do I get my coffee? I'm thirsty."

"Soon." Gustie cooked with near efficiency now at Dorcas's awkward stove. She kneaded the bread dough and hoped that Jordis would return in time to join them. Dorcas had finally explained last night that Jordis and Little Bull had been kept from the agency by the stove at the school, which belched smoke and sparks, driving everybody out and setting fire to some crates the children were using as benches to sit on. They had put out the blaze and spent the day taking the stove apart and putting it together again. Without it, the school they had labored so long over would be useless till spring.

Gustie had the impression that Little Bull was everywhere, on and off the reservation. He showed up to mend stoves or arbitrate disputes. Already, since becoming chief, he had been to Pierre to speak to the state legislature on behalf of the Red Sand. He still found time to visit Dorcas once in a while, and Jordis helped him where she could but still adamantly refused to teach. Since the weather had looked threatening, Jordis would have spent the night with Winnie and Little Bull. But the morning skies were clear; she would come back soon. Gustie brimmed with anticipation.

The coffee was just poured and the bread fished out of the

popping grease when Gustie heard Biddie whicker, the muted gallop of Moon's unshod hooves stopping in front of the cabin, bounding feet on the porch steps. Jordis burst through the door. The blue beads on her high winter moccasins flashed from beneath the hems of her split skirt. She wore several heavy flannel shirts that looked big enough for Little Bull, and a poncho cut from an army blanket. She dropped the sack she was carrying and took Dorcas's hands in greeting. "Hello, Grandmother." Then she reached for Gustie.

"Where you been?" Dorcas demanded through a mouthful of fry bread. "We sittin' here waitin' for you."

Jordis took Gustie's hands and brought them to her lips. "You didn't tell me you were coming."

"Your hands are so cold!" exclaimed Gustie. "Don't you have any gloves?"

"I've got some rabbit-fur mittens somewhere that Winnie made for me last year. It's not cold enough yet."

"Not cold enough! You're so tough," Gustie teased as she rubbed Jordis's hands briskly between her own. "I didn't know I was coming till last night, when Lena asked me to drive with her. Her sister is about ready to have that baby." Then she gave Jordis a warm cup of coffee to hold.

When they finished the plate of bread, Jordis announced, "I brought you something."

"What?" Gustie gathered the plates and put them in the bucket of water she had been heating on the stove.

Jordis held up her forefinger in a "Just be patient" gesture and pulled open the sack she had brought in with her. She took out a pair of moccasins similar to her own, but with more elaborate beading. Gustie admired them and waited for the next thing, the small thing that might be for her, to come out of the bag.

Jordis leaned back in her chair and folded her arms across her chest. "Well, try them on, Augusta." When Jordis used her full name, she pronounced it with a degree of dry pomposity that always made Gustie smile.

Gustie took one of the moccasins. She traced her finger over the many tiny beads sewn across top and sides and examined the fringes that ran along the side seam. "These are for me?" she asked softly.

"Red Standing Horse's wife Carrie made them. She was saving for a special giveaway. She wanted this to be it."

Gustie sat on the edge of the bed, untied and pulled off her shoes, and eagerly slipped her feet into the moccasins. The leather was supple, the fur lining soft and warm. She had never worn anything so comfortable in all her life.

"That's not all." Jordis took out a beaded leather sash.

Gustie stood up and tied it around her thin waist. Then she turned like a prima donna, letting Jordis and Dorcas admire her.

Jordis commented, "The moccasins aren't as soft as buckskin, but they are pretty good. We can't get buckskin anymore."

"Why not?" Gustie sat down on the bed and stuck her feet out, admiring them some more.

"No deer," said Dorcas.

Gustie laughed. "What do you mean?"

"No deer around here anymore," explained Dorcas. "They went with the buffalo. All dead. All gone. Saw the last one many winters ago."

Gustie thought she was being teased, but Dorcas went on grimly. "That's why we eat the white man's cattle. Spotted buffalo, we used to call them. They smelled bad, all penned up together. We did not understand how the *wasichu* could eat such bad-smelling things. Tasted funny too. But we get used to it."

"But I've seen deer," Gustie ventured.

Dorcas's eyes glittered. "Where?"

"Here at the lake. And I saw one behind my house once."

"Where they come from?"

"I don't know. They were just there, and then they were gone." Gustie shrugged.

"Mm." Dorcas squinted hard at Gustie. Then she muttered, "She comes to you, then." The old woman nodded her head in satisfaction.

"Who comes to me?" Gustie was confused.

Dorcas spoke sharply. "You two get out. I want to drink my coffee and think without all this talk."

Gustie grabbed her coat and Jordis her poncho. They filled Dorcas's cup with the last of the coffee and left the old woman to her thoughts.

Gustie and Jordis walked hand in hand. The hills, thinly dusted with snow, sparkled like sugar candy under a bright blue sky. The air snapped with cold.

"What was that all about?" asked Gustie finally.

"I don't know."

They walked along in silence. Finally Gustie asked, "Why don't you and Little Bull put a stop to it? You know Jack Frye has been cheating you."

"Little Bull has tried. He's been to Pierre. He's written letters to Washington. He has confronted Frye. But he wants to get rid of him legally. I think Little Bull is wrong. The white man's law has never worked to our benefit. I just wanted to kill Frye. That's why I don't go for annuities anymore. Little Bull won't let me kill him."

Gustie was not sure if Jordis was serious or not. She was afraid to ask.

But now she was finding it hard to say what was on her mind, what she had come to Crow Kills for. "It's going to be a long winter."

Jordis nodded.

"There is nothing to keep me in Charity anymore."

"You have friends there."

Gustie felt annoyed. "You're not there."

"I visit."

"I don't want visits!"

The long pause that followed made Gustie's stomach tighten and confirmed her fear that she had spoken too soon and in the wrong way. She wished she could take the words back. They could go on like this—visits back and forth, endless days of waiting between—for all eternity if that was what Jordis wanted. She didn't want to lose her. She was willing to be with Jordis on any terms. Gustie looked at the ground, then out across the sugar-candy hills. "I'm sorry. You think I'm crazy."

"Yes. I think you are completely crazy. We will have to build a house. I thought—right over there." Jordis pointed to a spot in a clearing of cottonwoods about a quarter mile east of Dorcas's cabin. "Close to Grandmother. The snows are coming. The house will have to wait till spring. But you could move to Wheat Lake. There's an old place on the outskirts of town to the south. It's not as nice as what you have now, but I'll help you clean it up. We could make it winter-tight. Little Bull and I are now stove experts."

"How long have you been thinking about this?" inquired Gustie through slitted eyes.

"Since the Fifth of July."

"I see."

"I found the empty house in Wheat Lake about a month ago. I didn't think you would be ready to move before now, though."

"I guess you had it all figured out."

"I guess."

"You're very clever."

"Sometimes."

Gustie looked down and saw a dip in the earth filled with snow. She quickly scooped up a handful and threw it at Jordis, who squealed in surprise. There was hardly enough snow for a good fight, but they managed. Finally, Jordis, out of breath from laughing and throwing snow and dodging Gustie, stood wiping her face with the tail of her poncho, and said matter-of-factly, "I told you you would live by a lake, didn't I?"

Gustie shook the snow out of her skirts and hair, and remembered the night in the lake when she'd poured water over Jordis's back for the first time. "Yes, you did."

"Grandmother says I'm a pretty smart Indian."

"Too smart." Gustie kissed her.

They walked slowly, happily, back to the cabin. Dorcas, co-cooned in her blanket, stood on the porch watching them. She looked like a statue hewn from an old tree. They stopped at the foot of the stairs and looked up at her.

"Augusta Roemer. We will talk." Gustie and Jordis started up the stairs. "Not you." Jordis stopped. "Go play with your horse," Dorcas commanded. Gustie's expression clearly asked *Now what?* and Jordis's answered *I have no idea—you're on your own, Augusta.*

In contrast to the cold, bright outdoors, inside the cabin was hot and dim. Gustie shed her coat and removed her glasses to wipe off the condensed moisture. She sat across from Dorcas. On the table between them rested a wooden box that Gustie had not seen before. "I want to give you something." Gustie was about to protest that she'd been gifted well enough for her role at the agency. Dorcas raised her hand, and Gustie held her tongue.

Dorcas considered her through squinty eyes, produced one slow back-and-forth motion of her head, and said, "No deer."

Gustie, afraid that Dorcas would think she was mocking them, claiming to see deer when the Indians could not find them, replied gently, "I did see them."

"There's no deer. But Deer Spirit comes to you. Very sacred thing. The spirit of deer is your helper."

"How can these things have anything to do with me? I am

not Dakotah. I don't even know about these things."

"The deer people are gentle. You have the deer spirit. You walk softly, Augusta Roemer. You can be quiet, so you can hear. You can see. The deer are gone, but Deer Spirit is still here. That is good."

Gustie did not doubt the earnestness of Dorcas's beliefs. She felt, though, that the old woman was influenced by wishful thinking, a longing for the past. No matter how flattering it might be for Gustie to believe, she did not. She had seen real animals, not spirits—stragglers, perhaps, passing through on their way to somewhere else. But she did not feel like arguing with Dorcas.

"Now we call you Woman Who Sees the Deer," Dorcas said. "Woman Who Sees the Deer," she enounced again with satisfaction. "I give this to you now. It is your medicine." Dorcas opened the box and took out a small piece of bone on a leather string. When Gustie held it in her hand she saw it was the tip of an antler, hollowed out for the leather to be run through, and smoothed at the edges. Nothing could have been plainer; nothing could have filled her with more tenderness, even awe. She put it around her neck and looked around at the tiny cabin, so poor in every way but warmth. "Why have you been so good to me?"

"Old Indian legend," Dorcas said. "You rescue somebody, you stuck with them for life. Can't help it." She continued seriously, cocking her chin toward the outside, where Jordis murmured to the horses. "My Little Wounded Bird—you took the arrow out of her heart." A warming quiet filled the cabin as Gustie, used to Dorcas's silences, waited for her next words. The old woman's head was down, almost as if she had dozed off, but Gustie knew better. She waited patiently.

When Dorcas lifted her head her eyes were open, but, in the way of some of the very old, she seemed to see the past more clearly than her present surroundings. She began as someone who has been waiting a long time to tell a story. "I want to tell you about my people. Our old ways. How it was before the Black Robes and the missionaries. And the soldiers.

"There was a woman among my people. When I was a child, she was very old. She lived alone in her own tipi. She was no man's wife. Never was. She was a two-spirit-person. One sent to us with two spirits, the spirit of the man and the spirit of the woman in one person. The two-spirit ones are blessed, since the Great Mystery gives them two, not just one spirit. They were respected among the people and were always invited to the naming ceremonies to give the secret names to our children." She paused, and continued with more animation. "But the stories told about her were not told because she was a two-spirit woman. The stories were told about how she got her name. I heard this story from my mother and my grandmothers, and from all the old people who were there and saw it. Once, I heard it from her. In her own tipi.

"There was a terrible battle with our enemies, the Rhee. Our warriors were outnumbered and all had got away but Walking Crow. His horse was dead and he was on the ground surrounded by the enemy. His sister—the two-spirit woman—watched the battle with the women on the hills. At that time her name was Blue Stone. Blue Stone and Walking Crow, brother and sister. Blue Stone looked down and saw the warriors running for their lives. She looked down and saw Walking Crow, her brother, on the ground. She jumped on her pony and galloped in among all the enemy warriors. She did not make the tremolo in the way of women, but the warrior's yell. Blue Stone came riding through all the enemy warriors making the warrior's yell. Her brother swung himself up behind her and she rode out with him. No arrows touched her. The warriors on both sides cheered her. The Rhee and the Dakotah cheered her, and the women on the hills made the tremolo. There was a great feast that night. We lost the battle. But Blue Stone's courage lifted the hearts of the people and made our enemy respect us. Blue Stone was given a new name:

Warrior Heart Woman. Two more times she went into battle, at the side of her brother. Two more times, no arrows touched her. She lived in honor her whole life. She wore the eagle feather because of her victory in battle. She took a wife. When I was a child she had already lived many winters. Many many winters."

Gustie's heart was racing.

"Some winters after Warrior Heart Woman passed on, there was a young man among us who liked to wear the women's clothing. A *winkda,* too, he was—a two-spirit person. My people were glad because they had someone among them again touched by Wahkon Tonkah, someone to give the secret names to the children. It was a good thing to have another *winkda.* He had a brave heart. He could ride and hunt and do all things properly. He danced to the sun, sacrificing for his people three times. But now the missionaries started coming to our villages. They shamed him and made him wear male clothes like the other men. And he sickened in his heart and died. After that we had no one blessed by Wahkon Tonkah with the two spirits, the spirit of the man and the woman in one person. The *wasichu* consider this a very bad thing. I do not know why." Dorcas shrugged her shoulders sadly. "I saw what happened to that *winkda* boy, and I was afraid for Jordis. For I knew she had two spirits, and my heart fell down because her life would not be one of honor, but one of sadness and loneliness. My Little Wounded Bird rode these hills like a ghost until you came.

"In your sickness, you talked of the woman who died. I was sorry for you. But I believe you were brought here by Wahkon Tonkah. It does not matter if you believe this. You are here. That is plenty. I knew that you, too, were a *winkda,* a two-spirit person, and that you had been guided here for my wounded child. I was glad. I could join my mothers and grandmothers with a good heart, knowing my Little Wounded Bird would fly. Even our own people—some have forgotten that the *winkda* is a gifted one from Wahkon Tonkah and should be treated with respect. Now you two must take care of each other. It will be very hard, I think. But you are strong, and she"—Dorcas treated Gustie to one of her rare and brilliant smiles—"is stubborn."

Gustie's heart was singing with the knowledge that there had been others, like her, and that they had had a name—the *winkda,* the two-spirit people. They had been respected and honored. She felt like she could do anything, be anything, soar as high as a skylark.

Maybe Dorcas was right after all. How *had* she come here? She had begun with an empty and fearful heart and a soul that sat darkly like a lamp without oil, in a big house with thick carpets, chandeliers, staircases, and many fine things she could no longer even remember . . . she had turned her back on them all for her strange love. And then her heart, after being utterly broken, was mended and whole once more. She had discovered a new way of being that had nothing to do with doing or having. Gustie was not a religious person, but she felt touched by a mystery that quickened her pulse like the dancers' drum, that gleamed in the old woman's eyes and throbbed in the air of the tiny cabin.

"Why didn't you leave me on that cold pile of earth to die? You couldn't have known then—"

Dorcas interrupted her. "I wanted lots of new stuff. New chair, I got. New bed—I got. See? Pretty good deal. Now I can throw you to the fish. I am tired, Granddaughter. I want to have a little sleep. Go away now. You—" she nodded again toward the outside where Jordis waited, "—have many plans to make."

"Yes, Grandmother." The words came easily out of her mouth. She took her coat, kissed Dorcas on the cheek, and left the cabin.

• • •

Gustie's heart was full. Dorcas had called her "Granddaughter." Gustie stood in silence. When Jordis appeared from behind the cabin she asked, "Who were the Black Robes?"

"Catholic priests. Why?"

Gustie told Jordis all the things Dorcas had said.

"She is not my real grandmother, you know. We are not blood relations. I call her Grandmother as an endearment, and out of respect because she has been a grandmother to me. I never knew her before she came to the mission school to take care of me. You have been adopted by her as much as I have."

Moon and Biddie were standing ready, Biddie saddled and Moon in her winter blanket. "Let's ride," suggested Jordis. They mounted their horses and strolled them up away from the cabin. They could see the road winding from Crow Kills toward Wheat Lake. A horse galloped toward them, stirring up the dry snow.

Gustie recognized the rider. "It's Lena!"

Lena was going so fast she rode past them and had to rein her horse in and turn around. "Gustie! I've got to go back to Charity! Now!"

"What for?"

"I've got to see the icehouse!"

"What's in the icehouse?"

"I don't know. But I've got to see for myself."

"Why?"

"Ella said that Tori was here to visit them. He . . ."

Lena started to cry. Jordis and Gustie dismounted and helped her down.

"It's all my fault. I should have . . ."

Lena was crying hard, unable to get out full sentences. Gustie kept an arm around her until the spasm of grief passed.

"I'm sorry," Lena said, reaching into her coat pocket for a handkerchief. She blew her nose loudly. Over the top of her hankie, she cast a watery look at Jordis.

Gustie had forgotten that the two had never met. "This is my friend Jordis. Jordis, this is Lena Kaiser."

Jordis only nodded. Her eyes narrowed.

"How do you do?" said Lena, as polite as she could be with her streaming eyes and runny nose.

"Well, I was talking to Ella this morning . . ." Lena blew her nose again. "And she said when Tori was here he was saying—" Lena wailed. "I didn't even know Tori had been here. After Pa's funeral I just got so wrapped up in things, with Will and all, I didn't even think about Tori. I didn't think about him not being to see us or anything. But he came all the way here, and he told Ella and Ragna that as soon as Will's trial was over he was going to get it all fixed up. And they asked him what it was he needed to fix up, and he said he couldn't say now while I had so much on my mind, because he'd made a promise, but when it was all over, then he could come and talk to me and put it straight. They tried to get him to tell what it was, but he said he'd made a promise. He was such a child that way. He wouldn't say anything more. But when they asked him to go to the icehouse he started to cry, and he said he couldn't go to the icehouse again. Not till he talked to me. They didn't understand it at all. He was just a dummy to them, you see. They let it drop because they just thought it was some dumb thing. And when he died they didn't think of it then, either. They never paid any attention to him. But I always knew that he had a kind of . . . oh, I don't know, things made their own kind of sense to Tori. You just had to try to see it his way. If you could see a thing the way he saw it—simple—things he said would make sense. I could do that, you see, and that's why he came to me with everything. I never laughed at him. He told me everything that was bothering him. So that's why I knew that when he said he couldn't go into the icehouse, he didn't mean their icehouse—well he did, but he got it mixed up in his head. He was thinking of them as the same icehouse."

Gustie shook her head. "Lena, I don't understand you. What was in your sister's icehouse?"

"Nothing! Nothing was in *her* icehouse. It was in Pa's icehouse. When he came out of Pa's icehouse the day of the funeral he was sick. Something must have happened to him in there. I don't know. But I never paid attention. I never asked him." Lena started to cry again. "But I've got to go back and look in there. Right now. Can you go with me, Gustie? I don't have anyone else. Will is a mess. Please?"

Gustie and Jordis exchanged a long look. Then Gustie nodded. "We will go with you."

The cold snapped. No cloud broke the way of ascension from earth to sky-high infinity. No breeze disturbed the powdery ground cover of snow on this bright day as three women rode out from Crow Kills. They rode the straight road, abreast, sun on their faces. Only hooves disturbed the snow beneath them as their horses took the distance between Crow Kills and Charity in a ground-eating lope. An unlikely trio, these three, with little in common but the rhythm of their horses, moving in sync, and the sudden, unexpected tendrils of love and friendship.

Gustie had never seen Lena on a horse before, but she was obviously at home there. "Oh, Pa put me on a horse before I could walk," Lena said. Gustie surprised herself as well, by her ease on Biddie's back. Her months of practice had been well spent. Jordis rode, as always, like she was part of the horse.

We ride—my love and I—and my love's friend who is now my friend—who, were it not for Gustie, would not allow herself at my side, but now her red-brown mare moves abreast of Moon and the black—the magnificent black of my love's riding. We are like the moon, the night, and the red earth flying.

It is a fine thing to ride a straight road with friends.

• • •

"Now, why in Sam Hill would anybody lock an icehouse?" Lena rattled the icehouse door in frustration. "Where there's a lock there's a key," she asserted, and stalked through the back door of Ma's house. On the walls of the shanty were several tiny nails, all bare. Then Gustie followed Lena next door into the back of Julia's house while Jordis stood, rather uncomfortably where she had dismounted from Moon. To her right were the two Kaiser houses, Gertrude's and Julia's; to her left, a barren spot where the big barn had recently been torn down, the icehouse, and beyond that, and directly behind the house that was Julia's, a small barn. A light dusting of snow covered everything. Since last night, at least, no one had been back here to disturb it, except for clear tracks to Julia's barn, where a team of horses had been taken out that morning. Gustie and Lena came out of Julia's back door. Lena had a key in her hand.

When Lena slid the key into the padlock on the icehouse door, it snapped open. "Hmph," she grunted in satisfaction.

Jordis wondered what the point was of locking a door if the key was so easily found.

"Where is everybody?" Gustie asked.

"It's Sunday," was all Lena said, and Gustie remembered that, except for Will, the Kaisers were a churchgoing family.

The door to the icehouse was proportioned large, like a barn door, so that when it was open two people could pass through with a block of ice carried between them and the inside would be illuminated; there were no windows.

Lena, Gustie, and Jordis stood together in the doorway, then they moved to the side to let in more light. "Good grief, what's all this?" Lena asked. She went inside.

In the middle of the icehouse was a rocking chair. Piles of straw had been pitched all over, covering the ice blocks, and packed into the empty places, and everywhere candle drippings spattered the ice and straw.

"This is sure peculiar." Lena fingered a small hard mound

of wax on the nearest straw pile. "But I don't see anything in here that would make Tori sick. I was looking for blood or something, you know."

Gustie and Jordis stepped inside. Both women were taller than Lena and had to stoop slightly to keep from bumping their heads on the roof. Jordis asked, "Is there always so much straw in here?"

"Well, I suppose as they take the ice out, they bring in more straw to insulate what's left. I don't know. It's a good place to store it, now they tore Ma's barn down. Julia's barn is small."

Gustie felt, rather than heard, a low humming, like distant earthbound thunder. She was overcome with dread, cold, and felt herself suffocating. *Oh NO! Please, no!* The avalanche of earth was pouring down upon her again, crushing her. It had never come upon her wide awake. She was not dreaming now. *What is this?* Her sight dimmed. She thought she was going down, though she did not feel the impact of the ground. *I'm dying. Now.* She almost gave in to it. Then . . . *Clare . . . JORDIS! Help me!* She did not know if she said it or thought it.

Jordis had moved farther into the icehouse and begun to examine the piles of straw. She stirred the straw with her hands, but in places it was packed too hard. She was looking around for a pitchfork when she heard her name and an eerie little cry for help. She whirled and saw that Gustie had collapsed and was choking for air.

Gustie felt strong hands lift her up off her knees and help her outside. Once out of the icehouse she could stand again; she could see and breathe, but she could not speak to answer Lena's and Jordis's worried faces, for she was overcome by a wrenching sorrow. She began to weep uncontrollably and did not know why. This weeping was not for Clare; Gustie knew *that* sorrow. It was clean. Its edges were gone. This was a sharp, murky, fearful thing.

"What's the matter with her?" The unsympathetic voice fell

on them like a chill. Lena and Jordis both started. Oscar Kaiser was watching them. His left armless sleeve was tucked into his coat pocket, his right arm hung at his side. More sounds at the front of the house told them that the family was home from church. Julia and Frederick appeared around the corner and stopped short when they saw Lena and Jordis, their arms around a weeping Gustie, the icehouse door agape.

Frederick echoed his brother, but with more concern. "What happened?"

"I don't know. She got in there and went all to pieces," Lena answered.

Oscar asked, "What were you doing in there?"

"We were just looking," said Lena.

"What for?" Oscar seemed annoyed, but Lena couldn't tell if it was because they had been in the icehouse or because of their commotion, he was going to be delayed sitting down to his dinner.

"You tell me." Lena could get just as annoyed. "Come here," she commanded. Oscar followed her back to the icehouse. "Look at this. What's Ma's rocker doing out here? What's all this wax?"

When Lena went in, Oscar remained in the doorway, killing the light. He was not as tall a man as Will, but he was broader and heavier. "You make a better door than a window," Lena commented.

Oscar shifted to the side. "Ma probably wanted that chair out of her way. Nyla's brought in some things of her own, so the house is crowded. No place to put things since we took Ma's barn down. I told her we shouldn't have done that," Oscar growled. "Julia's barn is just big enough for the team. You keeping company with squaws now, Lena?" He produced a leering kind of grin.

"What do you care who I keep company with?" Lena snapped like a terrier. She asked again, "What's all this wax?"

"Don't know."

Lena threw a hand up in frustration and, pushing past Oscar, went back outside. "It's freezing." Gustie still sobbed and Jordis stood with one arm around her protectively. Julia had apparently gone into her house, and Frederick stood eyeing Gustie and Jordis, then Lena and Oscar. His ears were red with cold, but he made no move to go inside or warm himself.

Lena returned to Gustie's side. "Let's get her indoors."

"Bring her into Julia's," Frederick said. "It's warmer than Gertrude's."

Jordis shook her head. "This is a bad place. I'm taking her out of here."

Just then Julia came flying out of her house, shrieking, "Where's Feather? Where's Feather?"

Jordis looked astonished.

"That's her cat," explained Lena.

"I saw a cat slip out when she went in. It went for the icehouse," Jordis said.

"Funny I didn't see it," Lena said.

"You were talking to him." Jordis nodded toward Oscar.

Julia was crying and wringing her hands. "Oh, no. He'll freeze. He's so little. He'll freeze to death!"

Frederick patted Julia's arm, murmuring some assuring words. He was about to go bring the cat back to her, when Ma Kaiser came through her back door. Frederick saw her and stopped. Lena thought he seemed suspended between his mother and his aunt, but now there were two people crying and no one doing anything. "Will somebody get that blame cat? Honest to Pete, I don't know . . ." To Jordis she said, "Take her out of here, you're right." Then, in exasperation, Lena went back into the icehouse to get the cat herself. She found Feather down in a hole between two blocks of ice. He had burrowed his way into the straw. *Probably a mouse nest down there or something,* thought Lena. She bent over the ice block and called the cat's name. When Feather raised his head, she scruffed him and hauled him up neatly, just as Frederick came in.

"Oh, you've got him."

"Yup, I've got him." Lena held the little animal securely in her arms and ran her hand soothingly over his head.

"Is he all right?"

"Well of course he's all right. Why shouldn't he be? For heaven sakes, such a fuss! Her blame cat is fine."

Frederick let Lena pass him, then he closed the icehouse door securely. Julia had gone back inside her house, but her wailing could still be heard. Lena was so disgusted with her that she handed the cat to Frederick. "Tell her to keep him in the house if she's so worried about him. I'm going to go with Gustie and come back later without all this fracas."

Jordis had just helped Gustie up on Biddie. Both Oscar and Ma had disappeared as though they had never been there. No one had offered to help Lena or Gustie, or even Julia, for that matter. And, except for Oscar's nasty crack, Jordis had apparently been invisible to the others. *What a bunch!* thought Lena. Gustie, slumped in the saddle on Biddie, was no longer sobbing, but her face was gray, wracked with grief.

Lena looked her over. She had never seen her friend so distraught. "Maybe we should take her over to Doc Moody's."

"No. I don't need a doctor," Gustie said weakly, and to herself, *I need Dorcas.*

"I'm fine. No, I am perfectly fine," Gustie protested Jordis's insistence that they keep riding on out of town to Gustie's house. "I feel like nothing ever happened. I remember it happening, but I don't feel it anymore—not a trace of it."

"What did you feel?"

"The dream again. Inside the icehouse it was that dream. But of course I was wide awake, and this time it was not anything to do with Clare. This time it was . . . I was not the grave digger, I was the one being buried. But when I got outside it changed again."

"What did you feel then?"

Gustie took a deep breath and brushed her fingertips across her lips in an effort to find the right words. "It's difficult . . . I felt . . . like my heart was breaking. But I didn't know why. I don't know why." Gustie stopped talking for a moment, than asked, "Where's Lena?"

Jordis answered, "The last I saw, she was going into Julia's house."

Gustie sat, her hands braced on the saddle horn, her face deeply troubled and her eyes seeming to look inward, not out at the world. Jordis respected her silence and waited. At length, she said, "Lena will not be allowed back into the icehouse. They won't let her."

"Who's 'they'?"

"I don't know."

"You can't go in. The same thing will happen to you again."

"Yes, probably."

"I can go in."

"I don't like to ask you."

"You didn't. I volunteered."

"As you said to me once, this has nothing to do with you."

"I was wrong then."

Gustie considered. "How will we manage it? The key isn't going to be so easy to find this time."

"Could Will help us?"

"Perhaps. One can't be sure of Will, though."

"I thought you liked him."

"I do. But he has a problem with whiskey."

"Oh."

They left Moon and Biddie at Koenig's livery stable and went to Olna's Kitchen for dinner. The main Sunday dinner crowd who came directly from church were mostly gone. They chose a table in the back by a window.

Betty Torgerson approached their table. "Hi, Miss Roemer." She smiled at Jordis with the curiosity of the young. Then she asked politely, "How is your friend?"

Jordis remembered the girl from the afternoon that she and Dorcas had asked her about Red Standing Horse. "He's fine. Thank you."

"We had roast beef and roast chicken today," Betty said. "But the beef is all gone."

"Chicken then." Gustie smiled. "With everything."

"Be right back." Betty disappeared into the kitchen. She returned with plates piled high with Olna's home cooking.

They ate more or less in silence. A few people whom Gustie knew came in and exchanged brief greetings with her and nodded to Jordis. The tables immediately next to them remained empty. Gustie didn't mind a bit. "They'll get used to us," she said, biting into a hot biscuit. "Give them time."

Mary Kaiser came in and looked around the room uncertainly. She saw Gustie and lifted her hand in a shy wave. Gustie motioned for her to join them.

"Hello, Gustie."

Gustie made introductions.

Jordis nodded to Mary in a friendly way.

"Sit down, Mary . . . if you like."

"Thank you. I'm just waiting for Walter. He's up the street talking well business with some men. I'd rather be comfortable in here. He can take a long time when he gets to talking."

Betty came back and Mary said, "A cup of coffee please, Betty."

Gustie asked, "Mary, what do you know about the icehouse out back of the Kaiser place?"

Mary was thoughtful. "Not much. After Pa died, Tori was the first one that I know of to go out there. Do you think there is something in there?"

"I think so," replied Gustie. "Or, if not, then something . . . happened in there."

"Pa was killed in the barn, not the icehouse. That's what Dennis said." Mary looked back and forth between Gustie and Jordis.

Betty returned with Mary's coffee. When she had gone again, Gustie continued. "I know. But something happened in there before that. A long time before that."

"How do you know?" Mary fixed her luminous eyes upon Gustie.

"I don't *know*." Gustie described for Mary her episode in the icehouse earlier that day.

Mary wore a very serious expression. "Only Pa ever went in there. Walter and Oscar and Will helped him cut ice and haul it back, and after Pa got older, they'd carry it in. But he was in there telling them just where to put it. It was his little domain, the only thing he kept his hand in, really, after he sold off his business to the boys."

Gustie wondered, "Why would he be so possessive of a little shed full of ice?"

Jordis said, "Maybe he had some documents or money hidden in there. Something worth killing him for."

Mary was almost breathless at the thought. "Oh, my! Pa made a nice living, but you can see we are not rich people. Nobody has money out here. Nobody kills anybody for money, do they?"

Neither Gustie nor Jordis said anything to that. But Gustie did agree with Mary that there was not much money to be had out here. At most, people might have a little savings which they kept in Lester's bank. With Clare's inheritance, Gustie herself was probably the richest woman in Stone County, if not far beyond.

"We've got to get back in there, but I don't know how. The door's kept padlocked with a key that's hanging in either Ma's or Julia's back porch. I gather it moves back and forth. After our poking around in there this morning, it may be in somebody's pocket. We won't find it."

Mary took a sip of coffee, swallowed, and said, "There's a second key."

"There is?"

"Oh, yes. It's in a broken china cup in the big hutch in Ma's dining room. It's always been there."

Gustie and Jordis looked at each other, then at Mary.

"I can get it for you," she said, taking another sip of her coffee. "Walter is going to pick me up, and then we'll visit Ma and Julia before we go back out to our place. We always do on Sundays. I'll get the key and leave it for you behind the outhouse. There's a big rock back there. I'll leave it under there."

"Won't they notice?"

"No one ever notices what I do."

"There's somebody in there," Gustie whispered. They had waited till after midnight to go back to the Kaiser place, approaching it from the pasture that backed the property. From where they crouched behind Julia's barn, they could see light flickering within the icehouse.

"Let's wait and see who comes out."

They waited all night, under a cold sliver of moon, afraid even to whisper, for sound carried so far in the cold. All the small creatures and insects that throughout the summer and fall provided night music were already in their winter stasis. There was nothing to cover a sound that might give them away to the person inside the icehouse. They sat, tightly clasping each other's hands, and watched. Gustie had become almost numb by now and was dozing off, when Jordis jostled her arm and pointed.

A small form was leaving the now-darkened icehouse. "It's

Julia!" whispered Gustie. Julia was the last person she had expected to see. Julia quietly entered her own house. No light came on in there.

"Either she's the one who's been camping out in there by candlelight, or she was in there looking, just like we wanted to."

"Do you suppose she found something?" Jordis wondered.

"Who knows?" A light came on in Gertrude's house. "Someone's up over there. We can't risk going in now."

"Let's wait. We didn't sit here all night just to leave now. Just wait." Jordis settled back on her haunches to watch the activity in the two houses.

The back door of Gertrude's house opened and the matriarch herself came out, carrying a chamber pot. She went into the toilet. Gustie and Jordis pushed themselves close to the back of the barn so they would not be seen.

Gertrude returned to the house. A few minutes later Nyla came out. They waited huddled behind Julia's barn for forty-five minutes until the entire Kaiser family—Ma, Oscar, Nyla, Frederick, and finally Julia—had been to the outhouse.

After another half hour, Gertrude came out the back again and emptied her slop pail into the frozen weeds.

The door opened again. This time it was Frederick, dressed in a long coat, as if he were going out, but he went only to Julia's.

Oscar emerged and came directly toward Gustie and Jordis. They held their breaths. He went into the barn. He led the horses out, harnessed them to the buggy, and went back inside the house. They heard his loud, angry voice. Nyla was apparently too slow for his pleasure. Fifteen minutes passed before she came out with Oscar and they climbed into the buggy and pulled away.

Jordis and Gustie waited another half hour. Frederick still had not come out again from Julia's.

Jordis said, "I'm going in."

"Shouldn't you wait till Frederick leaves—or at least goes back to Gertrude's?"

"He may have already gone out Julia's front door. I want to get in and out of here before Oscar comes back. He's the one we have to worry about, I think."

Jordis lit one of the candles that were set randomly about the place. The morning had lightened so that no one would now be able to see a candle flickering inside the small shed. Yesterday, there had been only candle drippings. Julia had apparently left the candles behind her. Maybe that meant she had been here only last night, searching. Or maybe it meant she was becoming more careless.

Jordis stood for a moment and looked around at everything carefully. Some ice blocks were pushed up against the back wall, and another row was in front of them, but not flush against them. Yesterday, the straw had been tightly packed into that space between the two rows. Now the straw appeared loose, as if it had been dug out and tossed back in without being tamped down. That is the place she went to. She shoved the candle into a chink in the wall and pulled out the hay. Then she slid ice blocks aside so she had room to get on her knees between them. She pushed aside the straw on the earthen floor, only to find that the floor was not earth, but wood. By feeling along the floor carefully, she realized it was not all wood, but that the wood had a rectangular shape and fitted into the earth. She pulled on it. It came up easily. Someone must have recently worked it out of the frozen ground. It surely could not have been Julia. The little old lady would not have had the strength to do it, nor could she have moved even one block of ice. In the dim light Jordis thought she saw colors: yellow, blue, pink . . . She rose, removed the candle, and brought it low over the cavity she had just opened.

A little sound of pity and sorrow escaped her. She thought *Ah, these wasichu.* She knew why Gustie had wept.

"Did you find anything?"

Jordis suddenly felt the cold of the long night as she had not before. "Yes," was all she could say.

"Worth killing for?" Gustie's eyes were large and fearful.

"Oh, yes." Jordis felt very tired.

"Tell me."

She could say nothing at first. Gustie urged again, "Tell me!"

"I can only tell it once. We must get to Lena's."

"What if they see us?"

"It doesn't matter now." Jordis grabbed Gustie's hand and pulled her into a long stride that turned into a sprint. She dropped Gustie's hand and ran like a horse. Gustie was bewildered and could not keep up with her. Jordis slowed to keep a pace Gustie could match.

I am filled with fear.
The Eagle is far away.

Lena rode home on Millie, enjoying the fine, cold day. She had been out early to do her shopping. Her few purchases from O'-Grady's were tucked in the saddlebags. It was exhilarating to be on a horse again. She hadn't ridden much since she was a girl. Old Tom was so tall and cantankerous, she didn't feel secure on his back, and they could not afford another horse for Lena just now. She would be sorry when she had to return the sweet mare to Ragna and Pete. She doubted that Pete was as good to his horses as he should be.

When she left O'Grady's she rode out to check on Gustie. Lena was deeply worried about her. But she wasn't there. It was a funny thing, but it looked to Lena like she and Jordis hadn't been there. Did they go straight back to Crow Kills? That was not likely. They would have given their horses a rest first. Gustie was sure good to Biddie. Jordis looked like she would know how to take care of a horse, too. Now *there* was a strange one, that Indian, and what Gustie wanted to hang around those people for, she didn't know. But Jordis seemed clean enough, and she was educated. That made a difference, no doubt—a decent, Christian education. Jordis might even be a pretty girl if she would do something with her hair. Maybe she had lice and had to shave her head. Lena had heard that Indians had lice. She shuddered.

Lena wanted to tell Gustie that she would be going back to Wheat Lake this afternoon to take her place with Ragna and relieve Ella, whose patience, and that of her husband and children, was wearing thin. She had come back all this way and not discovered anything at all. An icehouse full of candle drippings. What in the world did that mean? Yesterday, when she'd asked Ma about it, the old thing had got all huffy-puffy and said the icehouse should be torn down along with the barn. Julia's reaction was pure fright, especially when Lena confided in her that Tori's death was not suicide, but murder. Dennis hadn't let it get out that it was murder. He thought it would help him in his inquiries if everybody still thought Tori's death was a suicide. So much for his inquiries. That sheriff didn't know beans about anything. Lena could understand Julia's fear. To think that there might be strangers lurking around the place . . . camping out in the icehouse, for heaven sakes! What if it was the same as had killed Pa? Maybe Ma was right. The icehouse should come down. Electricity was all anybody talked about now. When the lines were strung, people would start getting those electrical iceboxes and nobody would need icehouses anymore.

In appreciation of Will's meeting her at their kitchen door yesterday, clean and sober, Lena planned to fix him a good dinner before she left, with lots of extras that he could nibble on for a few days before he had to start eating at Olna's. Or he could eat at his mother's. *That'll make her happy. She'll probably want him to move back in with her!* Lena snorted. Well, he could do as he pleased. Mary might fix him a meal or two as well . . . now *that* was a surprise, Mary turning out to be a brick.

Will and Lena's barn was big enough for a couple of horses and feed storage. Will also kept some equipment and tools in there. The door was ajar. That meant Will was home.

Lena slid down off Millie and led her to the barn. She opened the door wider so they could get through. Old Tom wasn't there. Will must have come home and left again.

Lena left the barn door halfway open so she could see what she was doing without lighting the lanterns. "Okay, old girl," she crooned, "I'll fill your water bucket in a minute. Let's just get you comfortable here."

Lena untied her head scarf and draped it over the side of the stall. As she did so, her eyes took in a shape, straight ahead, denser in its darkness than the surrounding shadows. She stopped to focus on it and as her eyes adjusted to the dim light, and the barn door creaked open another few inches moved by a gust of wind, she saw a pale smiling face materialize out of the gloom. She sucked in a breath and uttered a cry of alarm, then she brought her hand to her heart. "Oh, for goodness' sakes, you scared the life out of me! What are you doing out here? We looked for you yesterday. Where'd you disappear to? What are you doing out here? Why didn't you go inside? Will'll be back pretty quick, I expect."

The smile grew. "No, he won't," said Frederick, who was seated on an upside-down cream can.

Lena felt queasy. "Has something happened to Will?"

"Nothing out of the ordinary." Frederick beamed. "I left him about a half an hour ago at Leroy's."

Her stomach settled when she remembered what they still

owed Leroy's Tavern. He wouldn't extend any more credit to Will Kaiser. "All he's going to get there is water to drink."

"Oh, no," Frederick disagreed pleasantly. "I gave him some money. He'll be there for a while." Her brother-in-law chuckled.

Lena felt a certain dread creep over her. And a dead calm. "Why would you do that, Frederick?"

"So I could have some time with you." Frederick's voice sounded flat. So far he hadn't moved, or even shifted his position. His hands were shoved deep into the pockets of Pa Kaiser's old greatcoat. Lena had never seen Frederick wear that coat before. He seemed small inside it.

"Why don't we go into the house then, where it's warmer," suggested Lena, although the barn suddenly felt plenty warm to her.

"No. I'm comfortable."

Lena licked her lips. "What do you want to talk to me about?"

"Mother. She says I have to go away."

Well, it's about time. Lena thought Ma Kaiser never would have the gumption to throw him out. *Good for her.* "Frederick, you're thirty years old. You should be out on your own. Don't you want to be out making your own way?"

"No." He was sullen now, withdrawn. He rubbed the knuckles of his right hand, hard. "Where am I supposed to go? What am I supposed to do?" He looked Lena squarely in the eye. "You really balled things up."

As much as Lena had always thought that Frederick should be shown the door of Ma Kaiser's house, she had never discussed it with anyone. "Why is it my fault? I haven't even talked to Ma about you. How could I have anything to do with her throwing you out?"

Frederick shook his head and pursed his lips together tightly, and continued to massage his knuckles. "You come snooping around, my snoopy nosy bitch sister-in-law. Just like your stoopy snupi—snoopy stupid whiney-boy brother." In his agitation he was mispronouncing words. Lena was ready to laugh until she heard "brother."

"Tori?"

"Toritoritori?" He mimicked her in a high falsetto voice, then added in his own, "Whiney-boy sissy-pants Tori."

The dead calm deepened in Lena. She was beginning to see the picture, though she didn't understand it. She could figure it out later. Right now she wanted to get out of the barn. She had to maneuver around or under the horse just to get out of the stall before she could make a run for it. Frederick saw her eyes flit to the door and read her mind as she calculated time and distance.

He reached into the deep pocket of the coat. "You know Pa's gun he always kept in the cabinet in the dining room?"

Lena nodded.

"It still works." Frederick produced the gun. "I tried it out yesterday. It's fun to kill gophers. I think I'll take it up. It settled my nerves. We can't have a garden out back because they tear everything up. Now I'll kill them."

"You killed Tori."

Frederick shrugged and smiled crookedly.

"Why?" she asked him very gently. Lena saw madness before her and she did not want to provoke it.

"I made him promise not to tell you until Will's trial was over and you didn't have so much on your mind. I thought that by then he'd forget about it. But he didn't." He was the Frederick she knew speaking now, almost, pleasant, reasonable, a serious, concerned expression replacing the crooked smile. "He came in to tell you. And, because he was such a good boy, he told me first." The eerie smile returned.

"What was he going to tell me?" Lena kept her voice steady, reasonable. "What he saw in the icehouse?"

Frederick lapsed into a mimicking voice again that gave Lena a chill. " 'OOOOH . . . I saw something soooo bad in the icehouse. It made my widdle tummy sickums.' The drooling little shit. I said I'd come home with him so he wouldn't have to tell you alone. We went upstairs. The stupid dummy waited for me while I came down to the barn to get the rope! He watched me make a noose and throw it over the beam. He thought it was a game, I guess. I put it over his head and yanked. He wasn't heavy at all. Just flopped around a little bit." Frederick made a waggling motion with his fingers in the air. "I added the chair later," he added, almost modestly.

Lena felt the barn turning around. She grabbed the top of the stall and hung on.

"What did he see in the icehouse?" Lena's own voice sounded strange to her, speaking in an even tone while inside her head she was screaming.

Frederick's eyes rolled. "What did *you* see?"

"A rocking chair. A mess of candle wax."

"What did Gustie see?"

"The same thing I did."

His singsong falsetto began again. "Toritoritori lifted out a hunk of ice . . . and what he saw, it wasn't nice, and it made him sick to his tummins."

Lena slid her foot a short distance to her right and eased her body after it, hoping Frederick would see her as just shifting her weight, and not moving closer to the edge of the stall.

"Actually, it was that fucking cat. Once we stirred things up in there, that cat couldn't leave it alone. The smell I suppose. Tori tried to get the cat out of the icehouse when it followed him in there. That's when he found them. I wanted to get rid of the cat. She threw a fit. I wanted to get rid of *them*—she threw another fit. Said now she had them again, she would keep them close to her."

"Who?" Lena edged to the right again.

"Mother thought the little shit killed himself, like everybody else. Then you had to come snooping around and tell her he was murdered, and she got ideas and now she wants me to leave. I can't leave."

Lena took another small step. "You don't have to go anywhere, Frederick. If you can't stay with Ma, you can stay here with Will and me till you get a place. You're welcome here for as long as you like."

"Yes, come out of that stall," Frederick said, pointing the gun at her. "Come over here." He beckoned toward himself with his free hand.

"Did you kill Pa?"

"Come here," he beckoned again, "and I'll tell you all about it."

Lena didn't want to get any closer to him, but she came out from behind the stall. She considered bolting for the door. If he shot her, maybe he would miss, maybe it would not be a mortal wound. He stood between her and the side door, which she noticed now was also ajar, so that exit was not an option. Her curiosity was at work too. She wanted to know why he had killed his father. She was horrified and fascinated.

"I didn't kill Pa. Mother did. When I killed that whiney-boy brother of yours I did it for her." His voice broke in a sob, but he recovered himself immediately. "And now she just wants me to leave. She's afraid everybody will find out. But nobody will find out if you're not here to stir it up."

"Don't you think that killing me will just lead to more people stirring things up?"

"Won't matter. This time they'll find the right thing."

"What's that?"

"My big brother. He'll come home drunk. I'll pour some more whiskey down his throat and it will look like he did it, and then they will know he did everything—killed Pa, and Tori, and you. There won't be any getting around it this time. I'll make sure. And then she'll want me back."

"You can't kill Gustie."

"Why not?" The eerie smile took possession of his features once more.

"You can't kill everybody!"

"Why not? I'm a chip off the old block."

Lena made up her mind to run for it too late. She was slammed against the barn wall. Frederick's right forearm pressed against her throat and the gun in his hand was cold against the side of her face. His body pressed hard against hers. She was pinned to the wall and choking.

Lena stopped resisting, hoping Frederick would ease his pressure on her windpipe. He did not. Her acceptance came quickly, simply . . . *I didn't think it would be like this* . . . , and she began to pray, *Our Father, which art in heaven* moving her lips lightly, although all sound and breath was choked out of her.

The gun stayed against the side of her head, and with his left hand Frederick brought a knife out of his pocket.

Hallowed be Thy name. Oh Lord Jesus, he's going to cut me! Why the knife should horrify her more than the gun she did not know. *Thy Kingdom come. Thy will be done* . . .

She felt the knife working at her breast, cutting through her thick wool coat. *On earth as it is in heaven.* He was making sawing motions, like he was not going to stab her, but cut off her breasts. *Oh dear Jesus what madness is this? Give us this day* . . . She could hear nothing but Frederick's heavy breathing, strangled by dry sobs. *Our daily bread, and forgive us our trespasses* . . . And then a clear voice sailed through the dusty air of the barn like an angel. "Stand away from her, Frederick." *As we forgive those who trespass against us.*

Frederick stopped sawing at her coat and turned his head slightly toward the voice, which sailed again, cool and author-

itative, filling the barn with sweetness. "Stand away from her."
And lead us not into temptation . . .

"I'm going to hurt her," he said breathlessly.
But deliver us from evil . . .

A different voice now, deeper. A musky voice that Lena
could not place, though she was sure she had heard it before. In
her dreams: these were angels; she was dead, floating in a place
just off the earth where she had heard that spirits linger before
flying to the arms of Jesus. *For thine is the kingdom* . . . The
other, darker, voice said, "You won't leave this barn alive. Let
her go." *And the power* . . .

Frederick pushed himself away from the wall, bruising
Lena further as he did so. The knife in his hand clattered to the
floor. *And the glory* . . . He was in a tantrum of rage and frustration, sobbing without tears, sputtering in an infantile madness without words. Lena fought for air and brought her hands
to her throat and breast. *Forever* . . . She did not know if he had
gotten through the coat, if she had been cut. She did not know
if she was bleeding. She did not know if she could still live.

The first angel came closer. "Lena, are you all right?" *And
ever* . . . Lena tried to turn her head to see. At the same time
Frederick raised his gun. The musky-voiced angel snarled.
Lena felt her knees give way beneath her as the gun went off.
Amen. She was looking toward the voices now and saw Jordis
thrown back into Gustie's arms. The two of them sank to the
floor while Frederick ran crying out the side door.

Lena willed her legs to hold her and her head to clear. She
pulled herself up and went to where Gustie was holding Jordis.
Gustie's face was white. She held her hand on Jordis's head.
Blood seeped through her fingers.

Lena took off her coat and put it over Jordis, ran to the wall
and took down two of Tom's blankets, and laid them gently
over her as well. "I'm going for the doctor!" She backed Millie
out of her stall. "I'll be right back!"

Gustie nodded mutely and kept her hand over the wound in Jordis's head.

As Millie stretched into a full gallop, it occurred to Lena that she did not know if Jordis was alive or dead.

It is light here. And cold.

It is winter here.

I am cold

I am cold.

I am cold having walked far in the snow.

There is a tipi ahead with a closed flap. Smoke rises from the top. It is a plain tipi of thick hides.

I open the flap and go in.

Strange in here but I am not afraid. The floor is covered with many furs. There are furs and blankets all around and old women huddle to the right laughing. They nod at me and go back to their jokes. They are eating heart berries and the tips of their fingers are stained red.

At the center of the tipi a fire burns. A pot steams over the fire. A good smell comes from the pot, carried on the steam. A woman kneels at the fire. Her back is to me. She tends the fire. She tends the pot.

She is round. With wide hips. A thick glossy braid hangs down her back all the way to the ground. She turns to me. She is dark and beautiful. She is beautiful where I am not. How I have missed her. My mother smiles at me.

She beckons me to come sit beside her at the fire.

I sit wrapped in a blanket of many colors and a bowl of soup rests in my hand. I am happy.

I will stay in the tipi of my mother.

Hank Ackerman was in town trading pig meat for credit at O'Grady's. He was just coming out of the locker where O'Grady rented his freezer box when he saw Will Kaiser's wife galloping like a bat out of hell up the street. He stopped in at Leroy's Tavern and voiced his amazement at the sight of Lena Kaiser flying up main street at a full gallop.

Leroy said he'd just made someone go and get Dennis Sully a while ago to haul Will out of the tavern before he got tight. The idea of that young brother springing for drinks for Will, knowing what they knew about Will and his recent troubles and all, didn't sit right with Leroy. He said maybe Hank ought to go to the sheriff's office and see if Will was still there and tell him about Lena. Hank thought it was a good idea.

Will was visiting with Fritz, a cup of Dennis's black brew in his hand. He didn't look drunk. Leroy had got him out in time. Hank said, "I think you better go and look out for your wife, Will." He told him how he'd seen Lena galloping like a steeplechaser with nothing on in this cold but a thin dress that was riding up so you could see the tops of her stockings.

Will grabbed his hat and coat and was heading up the street on Old Tom in time to see the doc in his buggy snapping the whip over the back of his chestnut and Lena out ahead, high-tailing it back home. Will spun his horse around and followed.

"Keep her head steady there," Doc Moody said. Gustie held Jordis's head while Will slipped his arms beneath her limp body, and together they carried her into the house, where Lena had their bed ready for her. Doc Moody arranged his instruments. Gustie refused to leave the bedroom.

Lena and Will waited in the kitchen. After an hour or so Doc came in with a bullet rolling around in the basin in his hand. "Got it," he said. A little blood spattered his arms and white shirt. He rinsed his arms off under the pump at the sink. "She's alive but she's still unconscious."

Lena handed him a fresh towel.

"We just have to wait and see. I'll be back tomorrow. If there's a change during the night, come and get me."

While they were waiting, Lena had told Will what happened in the barn. Now he got up. "Well, I got to go report all this to Dennis. He can pick Frederick up. Don't think he's gotten far if he ran out on foot. Or, if I get my hands on him first, by God, I'll kill the bugger."

"Let Dennis handle it, Will."

"Yeah, Duchy, I'm just talking." Will's eyes fell on her coat draped over the back of the chair, its front slashed away to the lining, and he grabbed Lena and lifted her to him and cried into her neck, unashamedly.

"There now, Will, I'm just fine now. Not a scratch on me. It's that girl in there we have to pray for."

Will put her down and wiped his nose with the back of his hand. "After I see Dennis I'll stop at the telegraph office."

"What for?" Lena wondered out loud.

"I better telegraph Joe Gruba to go out and get Mrs. Many Roads. She ought to be brought back here. She's the girl's grandmother."

"Well . . . where are we going to put her?"

"I just thought . . ."

"Will, the girl won't even know she's here. I just think . . ."

"Okay, Duchy, okay. I'll just have a talk with Dennis, that's all."

When Will was gone Doc Moody took a sideways glance at Lena, but said nothing as he finished cleaning up at the sink.

Lena made up a bed on the floor in the living room for herself and Will. Gustie lay down on the bed next to Jordis but was afraid to move for fear of disturbing her, so she went back to sitting in her chair and remained wide awake all night long.

The next day the *Stone County Gazette* added a page to its weekly fare of church events, births and deaths, weather reports, and the menu from Olna's Kitchen:

A terrible tragedy was visited upon Charity and the Kaiser family late last night when Julia Gareis, sister of Gertrude Kaiser and sister-in-law of the late Frederick William Kaiser, along with Frederick Kaiser, her nephew, son of Gertrude and Frederick Kaiser, burned to death in the icehouse behind the Kaiser home.

Neighbors, alerted late last night by smoke and flames rising from the Kaiser family property in the northeastern part of Charity, gathered in front of the icehouse and observed Julia Gareis in what Alvinia Torgerson described as "a long white nightgown, her hair undone and flying all about, and smiling sweetly," standing in the door of the icehouse holding a bundle to her breast. In the words of Mrs. Torgerson, who was first on the scene and first to alert the sleeping Kaiser family, "She could have walked right out. The icehouse was afire, but she stood just inside the door and could have stepped out. That's why nobody ran in to get her. We assumed she'd just come out." Several neighbors said that by the time they realized that Miss Gareis was not going to come out, Frederick Kaiser appeared in the crowd and ran into the icehouse. All there believed he would pull his aunt out of the flames to safety. As the onlookers watched, horrified, Miss Gareis moved back away from the door, farther into the burning building and sat down in what appeared to be a rocking chair. Mr. Kaiser knelt before her and lay his head in her lap before the view of them was obstructed by smoke and flames. Again, by the time the shocked neighbors realized that the two were not coming out, it was too late, for the door frame collapsed and the entire structure exploded into a roaring inferno. Some neighbors reported hearing the strains of high singing just before the final crash of the front of the building.

The mystery of why Miss Gareis did not, when she so

easily could have, save herself, and why Frederick Kaiser did not save them both, when he, too, could have done so, is deepened by the reports that neighbors had ofttimes late at night, for the past several months, thought they saw a pale light flickering through the chinks of the ice-house and occasional high singing, as of a lullaby. No one reported these observances before since "No harm was being done" and "people mind their own business when they can," said two neighbors who wished to remain unnamed.

What was contained in the bundle that Miss Gareis was seen holding in the doorway also remains a mystery. Sheriff Dennis Sully and Deputy Fritz Mulky are investigating. None of the Kaiser family has been able to offer any explanation of these strange and terrible events.

The fire went out in the potbellied stove and the cabin quickly became very cold. A gust of wind found a chink in the wall, lifted a corner of the dry cowhide, and withdrew, leaving the hide to fall back against the wood planks with a slap. The old woman did not notice. She sat at the table, knowledge that something terrible had happened running in her veins, her bundle of memories laid out before her. She had arranged each precious object on the open blanket to her liking, with the turtle shell closest to her.

She used to have some power of Turtle. She felt it most after her moon times stopped, but there had been seasons before when the Turtle medicine had flourished. To glean what power she could from those times, she closed her eyes and called back memories.

Under the buffalo robe for the first time with the young warrior Many Roads so many winters ago she had lost count.

The children who made them proud: Willow—a quiet little beauty who showed signs early of inheriting some power from her mother; Little Shield—a strutting warrior-child who made his father's eyes bright; and Pretty Hand—who couldn't get enough of horses and was always missing, only to be found running and giggling among the grazing herds who tolerated her tugging their tails and disturbing their peace.

The winter that Turtle had no power against the white man's sickness. When more than half of her village died, among them Many Roads, Willow, Little Shield, and Pretty Hand.

Turtle medicine's return when she lived alone with her herbs and roots until Louis Butler, a white trapper who brought her meat and furs and taught her English. She cooked his meat, kept him in winter moccasins, and warmed his bed at night. She was content with Louis Butler. He was kind and did not drink too much. Louis Butler fell out of a tree and broke his neck. She never found out what he was doing up that tree. She missed Louis Butler, but she did not grieve for him as she had for Many Roads, Willow, Little Shield, and Pretty Hand.

Many winters and summers when her people came to her for help. She could cure almost anything but the white man's diseases: against those terrible sicknesses she could only comfort, and ease a little, the dying.

The night they came for her, two white women, shaking with fear—of her, of the night, and for the child they told her about. Dorcas went with them to the mission school. She followed them, creeping, up a narrow black stairway to the child with the bloody back—her back oozing blood and foul green and white matter that smelled of death. But Dorcas saw the power in her, prayed to the Great Mystery, and called to Turtle to add to the child's own power. That night and every night for three moons, she anointed the little one's back with ointments and made her drink cup after cup of the soups and brews she spent her days concocting. The child healed and called her Grandmother and made her heart rise again.

Now the old woman had to summon Turtle once more. She had to ride Turtle's back. It would not matter if she could not return. She only needed the strength to get there.

Without flinching, Gustie had watched Doc Moody remove the bullet. When the bandage lay white across Jordis's dark forehead, he answered the question that lay in Gustie's eyes. "I don't know. The bullet was deep, but not so deep as to . . . you know, I've seen people die from this kind of a wound, and I've seen them get up and walk away from it too." He raised an open palm in a gesture of helplessness. "We have to wait and see. If she makes it through the night, she's got a chance." Doc Moody left the room.

If she makes it through the night.

Had Gustie been alone in the house she would have flung her head back and howled in rage. Had she been in her own house she would have smashed every dish, every cup, ripped her papers, broken her pens, and torn apart her books. But she was not alone and she was in someone else's house. What Lena saw when she came in later to check on Gustie was so disturbing that Lena ran back into the kitchen to sit alone with the dying light of the cold November afternoon, waiting for Will's return.

In the last six months Lena had seen many things she would rather not have seen and would never be able to forget: her husband behind bars, Tori's body hanging from a rope, the pale moon of Frederick's face as he appeared in the barn only this morning, and Gustie holding Jordis, bleeding and still, in her arms. Now, here was another picture for Lena to hang in her gallery of sorrows: Gustie, her mouth open, teeth bared in a voiceless scream, her hands clenched into fists, pounding— beating upon her thighs, as she sat, silent and upright in her chair.

I am not dreaming but I recognize this place as the place where dreams are born. This place is as real as any other. The landscape is different, that's all, and different rules apply.

I see the face of Turtle in the rainbow that curves over this winter land. She beckons me with ancient eyes. I cannot get too comfortable here.

I do not know how to get back.

"You did not know how to get here, but here you are." There is a smile in those ancient eyes.

I want to go back into the tipi of my mother and my grandmothers, eat soup and heart berries, and swap stories. I turn, but the tipi is gone. I turn again. The rainbow is gone and the face of Turtle, her ancient eyes smiling, is gone. I am alone and the snow is deep.

I know that even in the birthing place of dreams I will freeze to death if I do not move. So I begin. One direction is as good as any other in the trackless snow.

Thursday morning Lena woke before Will and started the coffee. She hoped that when she peeked into the bedroom, she would find Gustie asleep.

In three days Gustie had neither eaten nor slept. Her face was mere skin stretched over bone, the normal ruddy tones of her complexion were gone. She was now dead white, with bluish gashes under her eyes and in the hollows of her cheeks. Lena brought Gustie a cup of coffee that was half milk. It was the only nourishment she could get her to take.

Doc Moody came morning and evening to look at Jordis. Each time he said, "We just have to wait and see."

Dennis had come on Tuesday to question Lena. He tried to speak to Gustie as well, but she did not seem to hear him and would not respond to his questions, so he left her alone.

Lena felt nothing when she heard Frederick was dead. She was sad about Julia and blamed Ma for everything. Frederick had said right out that she killed Pa. Gertrude had wished her sister dead, and Lena told Dennis so. She didn't understand why the sheriff didn't arrest the old thing.

The Kaisers were as nothing to her anymore, except for Will, of course, and Mary, who stopped in once a day and quietly made herself useful. She brought cooked food, did some of the washing up, and tidied the kitchen. She chatted a little with Lena, and even sat for a while each day with Gustie and Jordis. Mary was not bothered, the way Lena was, that Gustie would not speak.

Once Lena went to Gustie's house to get her a change of clothing and a pair of shoes. Gustie thanked her for the clothes. When Lena offered the shoes, Gustie looked down at her moccasins and said, "These are my shoes."

Jordis's breathing was so shallow and her pulse so weak, they were barely perceptible. Gustie put her mouth close to Jordis and breathed into her nostrils and tried to discern her breath coming back. She kissed Jordis lightly on the lips and left the room.

Will and Lena sitting at the kitchen table were surprised to see her out of the bedroom. "I'm going out to the barn," she said. "Just to see how the horses are getting along."

"I took care of 'em this morning," Will assured her. "Don't you worry."

Gustie went out as if she hadn't heard. She did not take her oat from where it hung in the shanty. She wore Jordis's red shawl around her shoulders over her dress.

Will rose from the table to go after her, but settled back into his chair when Lena said, "Just let her go, Will. It's good to see her out of that bedroom. Let her go to the barn. She has no place else to go."

The cotton sky was turning to gray at the northern horizon. Wind blew from the north as Gustie slid the barn door open and closed it behind her.

The barn was snug and fragrant, with fresh hay in the mangers and clean straw on the floor. Each horse had a bucket of water and another of oats. Gustie lit the lamp that hung on a large nail from the center post. Its yellow light reflected softly off the shining coats of the three horses, brown, black and white. Gustie petted each horse wordlessly and sat on the edge of the manger between Moon and Biddie. Over the rim of the stall she could see the place where Frederick had pushed Lena against the wall. She saw the place where Jordis had slipped in front of her, growling like a mad cat at the first sight of the gun, taking the bullet that had been aimed at Gustie. Over the last three days Gustie had lived that moment over and over again. Why hadn't she stepped forward herself? Why hadn't she pushed Jordis aside? Why hadn't she . . . Each time she relived it she tried to keep it from happening. But each time, the shot cracked and Jordis fell heavily into her arms.

Clare had not been so heavy. Clare was a small woman, and wasted by her illness. She weighed practically nothing at all. It seemed to Gustie now that Clare had come all this way just to die. There were no good places to die back east. Here there were many.

After two years of only nightmares, Jordis had enabled Gustie to dream. After two years of making no plans, Jordis had given Gustie a future.

Gustie's dream had been simple: a happiness she could take

for granted, like the comfort of her moccasins—the feeling of her feet not being cold; the feeling of a shoe not pinching too tight.

Gustie had endured a life of loneliness, mitigated briefly by Clare, then by Jordis. Both small flarings of joy had been swiftly, brutally extinguished. She did not think there would be any more.

She knew what she would do. One bitter cold night, she would walk far out onto the prairie and fall asleep. This time, she would go somewhere where no one, not Dorcas, not anyone, could rescue her.

This land sucked feeling out of people. She knew now why these people were stoical. She had not understood before how amid such beauty, people could go crazy. How all faith and hope could be siphoned out of you by this vast, shadowless land until you were a husk floating along the surface, blown by the winds, then merely dust. She no longer cared about the land. Only the sky, and her stars. She could still walk among them. The stars were hidden now, but they were there waiting for her. When Jordis was gone, she would pick her starry night.

Gustie, calm in her decision, petted the horses once more on her way out to return to the bedroom, where Jordis lay, not alive, not yet released into death.

When Gustie slid open the barn door she faced a wall of white, through which she could see nothing. The house was only a few yards away, a little to the right. She pulled the barn door closed behind her, adjusted her angle toward the house, and headed into the snow.

The wind blew from all directions, first batting her in the face, then pushing her from behind. A swift buffet to the side knocked her down. When she got to her feet she no longer knew in which direction she faced. Everything was solid white—blinding white. *I fell to the side,* she thought. *I was facing* that *way. I got up, still facing that way . . . I think . . . well . . .* She pushed ahead.

She walked, knocked about by the wind, seeing nothing but her hands in front of her trying to shelter her face from the biting snow.

When Gustie realized that she was lost and that she must still be only a few yards from either house, or barn, or outhouse, she smiled to herself. Not exactly how she had planned it, but nearly so. Therefore, it did not matter whether she found her way back or not, if she kept walking or sat down. Oddly, she was not tired now, nor did she feel the cold. Caked with snow, her glasses were useless. She took them off and slipped them into her pocket. Feeling certain now that Jordis was gone, she experienced no surge of sorrow, only the thought: *Everything has been death since I came to this country.*

As Gustie plodded on, she felt as if she were pushing through whirlpool after whirlpool in a sea of snow. She could not tell how much snow was actually falling because the wind did not let it rest. She did not have drifts to wade through yet. At most, the snow was ankle to midcalf deep.

Gustie was numb. She no longer felt the sting of the snow, nor the push and pull of the wind. She felt, in fact, as if she had no body at all. She was merely an impulse to keep going. Then, ahead of her, the whiteness, in places, congealed to gray. The grayness seemed to have form and substance. "Who is there?" The wind howled in her ears so she could not even hear her own voice. A trick of the snow in her eyes and her poor vision without her glasses—the gray form was no longer there. Beneath the howling she heard a blowing sound behind her, like the sound a horse makes to clear its nostrils; but it wasn't a horse. She did not know what it was. She turned, then turned again, for she thought she saw another gray-brown shadow in the snow. Something brushed against her side. She had been beaten by the wind so much she was not certain if it was wind she felt, or something more solid. She turned and saw something black. She found herself turning in circles to grasp the fragmented visions of this thing that moved around and around her like a phantom. Then, peering out of the white flurry was a large warm brown eye that blinked once and disappeared. She looked up and saw a curve of bone. *What is this thing?* A black nose breathing silver steam. A squared-off rump materialized in the maelstrom and disappeared again. *How many are there?* She could only see one, but there seemed to be many . . . Then she saw the complete form of one as the snow cleared a moment. A stag, with flaring antlers, stood before her. He stamped the snowy ground once, twice, three times in measured, quick succession, then the snow swirled about him again and all she saw was a patch of brown hide to her right. She blinked her eyes hard and wiped her frozen hands over her face. The shapes were in a circle around her . . . or was there only one? Oh! She couldn't be sure. Deer!

Of course. They have come close to people because there are barns here. They must smell the hay. They are hungry. Gustie could not speak. Her mouth was frozen but she thought, *If I knew how to get back I would give you some hay.* A circle of warmth closed in around her. She was surrounded by hides and outlines of gracile limbs as they picked their way deliberately, delicately through the lashing snow. Gustie had no choice but to go with them. *They can smell the barn.* She heard a cry, faint on the raging wind. She kept walking, forced to keep pace with them, as they surrounded her, even bumping her if she slowed. The cry on the wind grew more distinct.

"Gustie!"

Then, "Will! Will! She's here! Oh, Gustie! We thought we'd lost you. Will! WILL!" Lena tugged hard on a taut rope that was fastened to an iron ring just inside the shanty door and extended out disappearing into the blizzard.

Will appeared, pulling himself back to the house, hand over hand on the rope. "Oh, Will!" cried Gustie. "Can we give some hay to the deer? They are hungry."

Gustie found herself pulled and shoved into the shanty. Two pairs of hands brushed snow off her roughly and rubbed her icy hands.

Gustie thought she was speaking clearly, but the looks on her friends' faces were clearly uncomprehending. Maybe she was babbling. Her mouth and jaw still felt frozen stiff. She tried to force each word out slowly. "The deer. They are hungry. We must give them some hay. Can't we give them a little hay?"

"What? What are you talking about?" Lena kept rubbing and slapping her all over. To Will, Lena said, "She's off her head with cold."

"No. I must go to the barn. I promised them some hay."

Will, half pushing her, half lifting her off the floor, maneuvered her into the kitchen where a blast of hot air hurt her face. How could one live in such heat?

Lena was already busy at the stove and Will was back in the shanty stomping the snow off his legs and feet and hanging up his coat and hat.

"The deer," Gustie pleaded again.

"I told you. She's delirious," Lena said over her shoulder.

Lena filled a saucepan with milk and waited for it to warm up. She suddenly turned on Gustie. "You foolish woman! What do you mean going out into this weather like that? You knew we would come and get you. We waited because we thought you needed some time to yourself, and then Will went out to the barn and you were gone! Haven't I told you time and time again . . ." Lena, close to tears, grabbed Gustie and hugged her hard and then pushed her away and went back to the stove. "Oh, my milk is going to scald."

Gustie sat down. "I'm sorry, Lena. I didn't think."

"Oh, I know. I know. You just scared ten years off the both of us." Lena filled a cup with hot milk and sprinkled ginger into it.

"I wish you would see to the deer now, Will. They were with me. They've come back for the hay."

Lena put the cup in Gustie's cold hands. It burned. "Gustie, there is nothing out there. You came right up to the door by yourself."

Jordis opened her eyes that evening. She had been unconscious for nearly four days. "I'm thirsty," she said. Her voice was low and scratchy. "Why are you crying?"

Gustie just shook her head. She could not say a word.

Lena appeared at the door and saw Jordis's eyes open and Gustie's full of tears. She clasped her hands together, crying, "Oh, my! Oh, my. Thank you, dear Lord," and ran to tell Will.

Dennis found the letter, sealed and addressed to Lena, placed carefully in the center of Julia's kitchen table and weighted down by a vase of dried flowers. Next to it was an opal ring.

Before he could deliver it, the storm broke and raged for several days. When the sky cleared and a cold sun bounced off a landscape of endless white snow, the sheriff put on snowshoes and trudged to Will and Lena's house with the letter in his pocket.

"For heaven sakes!" was all Lena could say when she saw him at her door. Dennis grinned sheepishly and stamped the snow from his feet in the shanty before entering her kitchen, where he was made to sit down and drink several cups of hot coffee.

Lena took the letter into the living room, and Gustie and Dennis stayed in the kitchen so she could read it in private. Will was outside shoveling. Jordis was asleep. Gustie and the sheriff rushed into the living room when they heard Lena wail.

"I can't read it!" she cried. "You read it. Take it. I don't want it." Her hands were shaking as she held the sheets of paper away from herself as if they were on fire. Then she dropped them.

Gustie gathered them up. She knew what they must contain because Jordis had told her what she had seen in the icehouse. Since Frederick and Julia were both dead, they thought it was not necessary to tell Lena. There had been enough dreadful revelations. But now it was to come out anyway. The letter was dated the day Lena, Gustie, and Jordis had come back to Charity and looked into the icehouse. She must have written it that night.

Gustie glanced at Dennis. He nodded and she began to read out loud:

Pa Kaiser killed my babies. All my babies. Gertrude told me they were stillborn, all but Frederick, the first, which they let live but didn't let me keep. They said it was best that we say he was hers. As if anything so fine could ever come from her. Anybody with eyes can see that he's no more hers than— He is mine! He has always known it. I wasn't supposed to, but I told him and it has been our secret all these long years.

They told me they were stillborn. I knew they lied so they could take my babies away from me. For Frederick's sake, I pretended to believe them, knowing I'd given birth to living children. I gave birth to all my babies and they took them from me and put them in the icehouse to freeze to death. Then, he buried them there.

All these years I thought they had been taken to Argus. It makes me laugh to think of it—how but for needing a bit of ice for my cream jug and these skinny old hands, I would never have found out. Iver delivered my cream early in the morning, you see, and I had run out of ice the day before. I went out to get a piece of ice to keep my cream until Pa got back to get me a good big chunk. I looked for a corner of a block of ice that I could knock off and carry myself. I chipped off pieces and put them in my bucket. My hands were cold. My ring slipped off. It fell down behind some ice. So, later on I got Frederick to help me. When he moved the blocks of ice, we felt around for the ring in the straw and we found wood . . . like a trap-door in the earth, and I made him dig around it and pry it open. I thought it was something Gertrude was hoarding down there. Something of Mother's. There were so many of Mother's lovely things missing that should have been mine. That would have been just like her, to hide them away like that where nobody could use them rather than let me have them. We opened it. I saw what he'd done. My babies, wrapped in the little quilts I'd made for each of them. Frederick wanted to go straight to Dennis and I said wait till I talked to Pa, myself. I waited for him to come home—it was very late. I stopped him before he went into the house. I said I wanted to talk to him. Not in his house where Gertrude would hear, and not in my house, because Frederick was there. We went into the barn and I told him I knew what he'd done.

He stood right there and told me to forget it, it was all so many years ago. That it wasn't important anymore. My babies weren't important anymore! He said they didn't suffer. Then he told me not to tell Gertrude! Not to tell Gertrude! She thought he had given them away to the foundling home in Argus or to immigrants passing through. I said, "Why didn't you?" And he said it seemed easier this way. Easier! The pulley for the hayrack was hanging there between us. I pulled it back and swung it hard toward him. He could have moved but he didn't. I believe he didn't think I would do anything, or that I wouldn't be able to swing it hard enough, or that I'd miss. He probably felt that nothing could hurt him. Most men do, you know. But the pulley hit him square in the temple—because he turned his head. He'd heard a sound, you see. It was Will in the stall behind him. So in a funny way, Will did kill him. If Will hadn't been there to make that sound, Pa would have kept looking at me and seen the pulley coming so close and he would have ducked it.

Of course, I let the blame fall on Will. He was her favorite. I wanted her to know how it felt to lose a baby. I didn't mean to hurt you, Lena. I've always been fond of you. I knew you could do better than a Kaiser. They are a bad bunch. I would have done you a favor, freeing you from them. You'd have found a decent husband.

But everything has changed now that I know what Frederick has done. He did it for me. He is such a good boy, but this is not right and I blame myself. It is not his fault. He did it for me. He has always thought of his mama. But it is more than I can bear. I have told Frederick to go away where no one will find him and I have given him all my money—all the money Pa left me. No one will find him. I am going to my other children.

At the bottom of the page, Gustie saw a scrawl, as if added in haste as an afterthought. She read: "*Lena, please take Feather. Otherwise Oscar will kill him.*"

Lena had listened to the letter with her head down, her face buried in her hands. When Gustie was finished reading, Lena jumped out of her chair and ran outside and vomited. She rubbed her face clean with snow and came back in.

Dennis said, "Well, that lets old Mrs. Kaiser off the hook. I've got to tell her about this, I reckon."

"Take the letter," urged Lena. "I don't want it in this house."

Will came in from the cold, grinning in anticipation of a cup of coffee and piece of pie, until he saw the faces on everybody.

"Will, I think you better come with me to see your mother," Dennis said.

"You okay, Duchy?" Will asked. Lena's face was ashen.

"Yes, Will. Go along. Ma will need you."

Will looked confused. He'd never heard Lena solicitous of his mother before.

The sight of Gustie spending her grief and rage quietly upon herself in the bedroom had marked the beginning of Lena's discomfort, which only increased as she watched Gustie care for Jordis: with what tenderness and familiarity she touched her, with what intimacy. It didn't matter that Jordis had been unconscious for much of that time.

Lena could not understand her own perturbation. She could not put an outline to the vague shape-shifting thing that troubled her the way a dream that you can't quite remember might haunt you after you were awake. But she was sure of one thing that filled her with a very describable fear. Lena simply didn't know what to do.

Gustie found Lena with the Bible open on her lap, the tip of her finger in her mouth, staring out the living-room window at the ice blue sky and the stretch of white beneath it.

Gustie moved a chair so she could sit in front of her. Lena smiled a sad smile.

"Lena, Jordis and I will be leaving here soon."

Lena's eyes grew big and round. "How?"

"I asked Arnold just now when he brought the mail. Apparently not everybody is reduced to getting around by snowshoes. He told me that Iver has a team of oxen that's pulling through most anything. He's been using them for his cream deliveries and clearing some of the streets with them. Arnold's going to find him and ask him to take us home."

Lena was relieved and disconcerted at the same time. "Are you sure it's all right to move her?"

"If she's bundled up warmly, the short trip to my house won't hurt."

"Well, then, I suppose . . ."

"We'll see. Iver might come for us this afternoon. After he's made all his town deliveries."

"That soon?"

"It's possible."

Lena lowered her head.

Gustie recognized Lena's discomfort. She knew its cause, even if Lena did not. She had just done what she could to bring it to an end. She observed her friend with a detached compassion.

When Lena looked up, she said, "Gustie, I'm not an educated person like you. I don't know much. I've never been anywhere farther away than Argus. I only know what I've been taught and what's in here." She rested her palm gently on the open Bible. "You've always been good to me in every way. Better than my own family. Sure better than Will's. You and Jordis saved my life. I'll never forget it. And I'll never forget what you . . . both of you had to suffer because of it." Lena stopped speaking. Her chin and lips began to tremble and her eyes filled with tears.

"No one blames you for anything," Gustie reassured her quietly. "I don't. Jordis doesn't."

Lena nodded gratefully and wiped the tears spilling onto her cheeks. "I'm pregnant."

Lena's face showed no happiness at this long-awaited news. Gustie withheld her congratulations.

"I had a dream about the baby last night. It's a girl. I've waited so long, but now I'm scared. I'm scared to bring a child into this family. The sins of the fathers are visited upon the children to the seventh generation. It says that right here." She patted the open pages of the Bible again. "I know it's true. Will carries that rotten old man's curse. Frederick carried it, and killed for it and died of it. Oscar and Walter . . . they're both . . . well . . . you've seen them."

"Break away from them." Gustie leaned forward. "Found your own family. Be the first generation."

"You think we can?"

"I think you must."

Lena smiled weakly. "You're a brick, Gustie."

Gustie left her sitting at the window, staring at her open Bible. She didn't envy her.

Jordis was propped up on pillows sipping hot broth and looking so well that were it not for the bandage still swathing her head, there would seem to be nothing wrong with her at all. She was getting stronger every day. The little gray cat was curled up by her side.

Gustie sat on the edge of the bed and grasped her hand, something she did unconsciously now whenever she was near enough. "I asked Emil . . . the postmaster . . . if he could scare us up some transportation out of here. You feel up to moving?"

Jordis replied thoughtfully, "This isn't a bad bed. But I like yours better." Her dark eyes shone.

Gustie chuckled. "You'll give Lena apoplexy. She's pregnant, by the way."

"I know."

"How did you know? She just told me a few minutes ago."

"She has a look about her. Winnie had it, too."

Gustie, bundled up in coat, mittens, and wool scarf around her head, stepped outside to welcome Iver Iverson.

Through the crystal lens of winter air, the prairie, stretched beneath an ice blue sky, dazzled. Everything that was not snow stood in sharp relief against the infinite white. Voices rang sharper, clearer, and carried farther in the cold. Sights and sounds were magnified and crackled in this bright, frigid, cleansed, and otherwise quiet, world. The sight that greeted Gustie was something out of mythology. Four of the largest animals she had ever seen stood placidly, filling up the drive.

"Sally, Joe, Kate, and Daisy—the best team in the Dakotas!"

Iver proudly announced, patting their buff-colored rumps as he moved around them. "Yup, they can get you through almost anything if you got the time. They go anywhere, but they don't go fast."

Behind the oxen was a contraption that Gustie would be hard pressed to describe in her journal: an enormous bargelike affair on runners, poles rising from its surface like masts on a ship. A railing ran along one side. Behind the driver's seat, a wall formed an enclosed wagon bed at that end, while the rest was open. Gustie laughed and brought her hands up to her face. "Iver, you're only taking two people and some blankets. We could fit everything in Lena's whole house on there!"

"It's the only thing I got with runners on it. I thought while we're at it, we'd load up your horses. Take 'em along and they don't have to wade through this snow. That's hard on a horse, you know."

"Iver, you're a . . . brick! Come in for some coffee and we'll be ready in a few minutes."

"You think Lena's got some pie in there?"

"I wouldn't be surprised."

Lena jumped into action when she saw Iver out the window. She was already packing up a box for Gustie and Jordis to take with them when Gustie passed through the kitchen.

"What are you doing?"

"You'll need a few things to tide you over till you can get to O'Grady's," Lena said.

Will filled the back of the barge—for that was what Gustie called the thing in her mind—with straw and hay, then covered the corner with blankets, while Gustie dressed and wrapped Jordis up in several blankets till she complained. Gustie paid no attention.

Will came in and over Jordis's further protests picked her up and carried her out to the wagon and laid her gently on the blankets. He brought Biddie and Moon out of the barn, led them up the ramp and onto the barge floor, and tied their reins to the poles.

Lena came outside and went to the side of the barge. From inside her coat she withdrew Feather and handed him to Jordis. "Here. He likes you, and he just reminds me of . . . things. You know." Jordis smiled and tucked the cat under her blankets.

Gustie said, "Lena, thank you for everything. I'll return these blankets and things to you as soon as I can."

"Phooey," Lena sniffed. "Don't worry about it." Then she said brusquely, "Now you take care of yourself. If you need anything, you let us know." She threatened Gustie with her finger. "We'll be checking up on you." Lena walked Gustie around the wagon and in a low voice confided something to Gustie that made her laugh and hug Lena before she took her place in the corner of the barge, Jordis's head in her lap.

Iver, back in the driver's seat, clucked loudly and commanded, "Go on now . . . *whup whup!* To the right a little, Sally. Pull on, girls! Come on, Joe, show 'em how!" The runners squeaked against the crisp snow, then with a mere whisper slid down the drive.

Will stood waving and grinning, and Lena, tucked into the curve of his arm, waved slightly, a worried, hopeful look on her face. Gustie smiled in deep satisfaction remembering what Lena had said, cocking her head slightly toward Jordis: "She has nice features. She should curl her hair a little and she'd be a pretty girl." There were some things one could count on: that the sky would forever change; that, but for the passing of the seasons, the earth and Lena Kaiser would ever remain the same.

Moon to Plant

In early May, Gustie received a letter postmarked Philadelphia, addressed in a familiar hand.

Dearest Augusta,

    I have missed you, Daughter, and am relieved to know you are well and still stubborn. I feel quite sorry for Mr. Frye, coming up against you, but not so sorry as to flag in my duty as a father and a citizen.

    I have put in a word here and there that may, I trust, be of value to you and your concerns. Mr. Frye will, no doubt, be seeking new employment come spring.

    You are right to ask me for what is yours and I have set up an arrangement with Fitzimmons at the bank to forward your monthly stipend until my death, upon which occasion you shall inherit all. In the meantime, enclosed is a check to tide you over till the arrangements are in motion. We were not kind to you.

    Your loving father.

Gustie burst into tears.

EPILOGUE

I Corinthians 13

Though I speak with the tongues of men and of angels, and have not charity, I am become as sounding brass, or a tinkling cymbal.

2 And though I have the gift of prophecy, and understand all mysteries, and all knowledge; and though I have all faith, so that I could remove mountains, and have not charity, I am nothing.

3 And though I bestow all my goods to feed the poor, and though I give my body to be burned, and have not charity, it profiteth me nothing.

4 Charity suffereth long, and is kind; charity envieth not; charity vaunteth not itself, is not puffed up,

5 Doth not behave itself unseemly, seeketh not her own, is not easily provoked, thinketh no evil;

6 Rejoiceth not in iniquity, but rejoiceth in the truth;

7 Beareth all things, believeth all things, hopeth all things, endureth all things.

8 Charity never faileth: but whether there be prophecies, they shall fail; whether there be tongues, they shall cease; whether there be knowledge, it shall vanish away.

9 For we know in part, and we prophesy in part.

10 But when that which is perfect is come, then that which is in part shall be done away.

11 When I was a child, I spake as a child, I understood as a child, I thought as a child: but when I became a man, I put away childish things.

12 For now we see through a glass, darkly; but then face to face: now I know in part; but then shall I know even as also I am known.

13 And now abideth faith, hope, charity, these three; but the greatest of these is charity.

The Bible, *King James Version*

About the Author

Paulette Callen grew up on the South Dakota prairie. She still misses the weather. In the early seventies she moved to New York City and decided to stay because she liked the coffee. She makes her home on the Upper West Side with Miss Ellie, an indomitable rescued Shih Tzu.